Airships &
Alchemy

Kit Marlowe

ISBN: 0692516212
ISBN-13: 978-0692516218

DEDICATION

For Alessandra, my jester

CONTENTS

ACKNOWLEDGMENTS

My gracious thanks are due to so many people: first to my dear friend and jester, the poet Alessandra Bava, who is the reason the alchemist is Italian (and named Alessandro). I advise anyone visiting the Eternal City to have a Roman guide as wonderful as she is. It is the only way to see its glories for many hide away from the well-trod tourist routes. Thanks, too, to my knight whose name I stole for the Venetian lion, even if I did spell it wrong. Now why couldn't I get Ghibli in there too? Any mistakes in Italian (as in French and Latin) are my own errors. Poetry rules!

Special thanks to the Queen of Everything, Stephanie Johnson for the beautifully evocative cover art that brilliantly captures the whimsical adventurous spirit of the novel. Flint & steel always, my friend!

Thanks to Charlotte Brontë for writing the timeless novel that gave birth to my heroine. I apologise for stealing Mr Rochester but he was longing for a little adventure (and we know Jane is never *really* separated from him, but she could use some time alone as well). Surely she would have named her daughter for the first dear friend that she lost.

Thanks to the folks who read this novel as it was in progress on the blog, on Textnovel and on Wattpad. Thanks to the Tuesday Serial blog for helping all us serialists get the word out each week. It is always better to write with an audience. In particular, David Schmidt, you were a cheerleader on many a gloomy day along the protracted path of this novel, even as it got continually thrust aside for more pressing matters. Thanks to Mr B for proving to me there is nothing wrong with laughing at your own jokes.

Big grateful thanks to my Dundee family who surround me with love and who lay in a yet misty future when I began writing this novel back in 2010. How much can change in five years! I am happy to have a life so full of love, surrounded by people who cheer on my writing. I feel so very lucky. Like Helen Rochester I follow the advice of Anaïs Nin, "Throw your dreams into space like a kite, and you do not know what it will bring back, a new life, a new friend, a new love, a new country." Do not be stingy with love; it has such rewards when you share it freely.

Kit Marlowe

Dundee, Scotland

August 2015

1 THE AIRSHIP

Helen Rochester ripped the goggles from her eyes and gaped at the controls. "Signor Romano, why are we losing altitude?"

The Italian whirred the wheel around with haste, grabbing for a lever above it. "I am not certain, *signorina*. Everything appears to be in order, I cannot explain—"

"Well, do something!" Helen leaned over the side of the gondola. The moors were yet a comfortable distance away, but this would not remain so if they continued to drop as they were. It was as if some kind of weight had landed upon them. "We're going to be upon Cringle in no time."

Pietro Romano continued to frantically check the dials and wiggle the levers, but the airship dropped inevitably lower. Helen did her best to quash the fury that began to rise in her breast and instead listened carefully to the engines. They were chugging along as usual.

Helen's scrutiny was interrupted by a flurry of black feathers as a large raven perched on the side of the gondola and began croaking at her as if issuing orders from Odin himself. "Tuppence!" Helen cried, her irritation plain, "If you can't do anything useful, do get out of my way."

The raven continued to croak at her, flapping its wings to keep its balance on the edge of the frame. Helen looked more carefully at the bird. "Did you see anything up there? Can you see anything?"

Romano looked up from the flight controls, a look of alarm on his face. "The raven—she is a bad omen!"

"Stuff and nonsense," Helen said, watching the great black bird rose aloft to fly over the craft. "I've had Tuppence since I was a child. My father claims the ravens have always favoured our family. He had a pair of them when he was a boy, too." She looked over at her engineer, who did not seem comforted by this family history. "They are connected with royalty in this land, *signore*. We are proud of our ravens."

Romano did not seem immediately convinced, but that may have been because he had caught sight of Cringle Moor and Round Hill looming ahead of them as they continued to sink ever lower. "*Signorina!* You must make yourself safe. We cannot possibly ascend quickly enough to avoid the hills. Please!"

Helen pursed her lips, but had to admit he was correct. She grabbed the goggled that hung around her neck and put them back over her eyes. With staggering steps, for the airship's downward trajectory had begun to pick up speed, she fought her way back to the seat at the back of the gondola and used the rope to tie herself into it.

Romano strapped a metallic hat on and wrapped goggles around his head as well. In the distance, Helen could hear the raven croaking yet, but its message—whatever it might be—was no use to them now as the ground rose to meet their ship. They braced as well as they could for the impact with the harsh limestone of the moor, but there was no way to really prepare.

The gondola made a horrible bounce upon contact and Helen gritted her teeth as the ship continued to make its ragged progress forward until banging against a cliff, the forward motion stopped and they floated downward to finally come to rest.

But where was Romano?!

Helen tore at the ropes with fumbling fingers. How could they have gotten so tight so quickly! With effort she finally pried her finger into the midst of the knot and loosened the bonds. *Must remember to invent a knot for quick release*, she thought, *or some kind of device to keep passengers safe in rough landings.*

"*Signore!*" Helen heard no responding call. Making her way between the detritus that now filled the gondola, Helen looked around her quickly at the rough face of the moor. Romano was nowhere to be seen.

She gazed with dismay at the smashed bow of the gondola. The impact had been enough to splinter some of the wood. The control panel, however, seemed sound, though the shrieks of the motors were still indicating some difficulty. That would be easy enough to repair given Romano's facility with gears—assuming he had survived the crash, she added grimly.

The envelope seemed to be continuing to lose loft. The guide ropes were slack. That was a much bigger problem. *One problem at a time*, she scolded herself. "Romano?"

A groan came off to her left. Helen crossed over the edge of the gondola, sat on the wooden frame, grabbed her voluminous skirts with one hand and maneuvered her feet over it to drop to the ground. Curse, these hideous fashions for women! Madame Sand had the right idea. If it weren't for her mother, Helen might don breeches as well. Surely they were much more practical for this kind of endeavour.

"Romano!" she cried again, this time answered by another groan that seemed to come from beyond an outcropping of limestone. She bustled over. Her pilot and engineer lay on the ground, holding the helmet, which now had a large dent in it.

"You're alive," Helen said, stooping to take a closer look at the Italian. "Any broken bones?"

"No, no," he said at last, "but this helmet! I can't get it off. *Prego, signorina.*"

Helen gripped the edge of the helmet and gave it a pull, but the thing wouldn't immediately budge. "Did you hit the rock?"

"Yes, I think so. It all happened so quickly." A trickle of blood ran down his forehead and he tried to blink it away.

Helen felt alarm at the sight, but redoubled her determination. Taking a better hold of the helmet, she leaned back and tugged as hard as she could and suddenly it popped off.

Blood, as she would be reminded later, proved to be a good lubricant.

There was a deep cut in his forehead, doubtless caused by the impact of the helmet with the rock. Its edge had a dent that must have bit into Romano's skin. There was a good deal of blood now that the metal hat had come off.

Fortunately Helen was untroubled by the sight of it, unlike most women or so she was told. Her mother had once bandaged up her father from a nasty wound caused by an eccentric family member, and thus thought it wise to prepare her children for such emergency duties. Attempts to get either of her parents to elaborate on that adventure had proved fruitless, though she often thought it might have been the mysterious cousin Rivers who had died in India.

Helen shook out her good handkerchief and applied it to the wound with some pressure. "Do you feel disoriented or faint?" She examined his eyes to see if his gaze wandered, but while they were slightly bloodshot, they did not seem dazed.

Romano said, "No, *signorina*, but it is rather painful. Here, let me hold that in place." He moved his hand up to the handkerchief and Helen leaned back to look at him more critically.

"Any other pains? Do you think you might have injured yourself elsewhere?"

Romano laughed gently, wincing a little. "No, my head softened the fall for me."

Helen smiled. While Romano might laugh in the face of danger, she was certain he could not be badly hurt. "Do you think you're ready to stand?"

He took her offered hand and staggered to his feet, the reddening handkerchief still sopping up most of the blood. "Look!" he cried, pointing at the dirigible.

Helen turned to see Tuppence perched on the rudder at the rear of the ship. The raven croaked now that it had an audience. Squinting, Helen looked closer. There was a rupture in the frame. "Looks like my bird found something." She looked at her pilot. "Perhaps that hole has something to do with our losing altitude."

Romano peered where she was indicating. "How strange! I shall have to investigate, at least now I know where to start looking." He groaned a little, rubbing his head.

"You should sit down," Helen said in a voice that brooked no opposition. "I'll go get help."

The Italian shrugged. "It's not so bad. I can walk."

"Nonsense," Helen barked. "You will have to move too slowly. I can get back to the house and get some of the men together to carry the ship back and a horse for you. We need to have Doctor Ponsonby look at that cut on your head."

"*Per favore*, it's nothing. A little alcohol to clean it and *voilà*."

Helen chuckled at his mosaic of languages. "Nonetheless, we should have your head examined, as we say. My pilot must be in tip top shape."

Romano sighed. "And your airship, too. We must put off the voyage until we are certain it is safe."

Helen blinked. "What? Nonsense! I intend to keep to

our timetable."

"But *signorina*—"

"I intend to keep to our timetable, Signor Romano." Helen's voice was not loud but there was little doubt of her resolve.

Romano sighed then looked startled. "Who's that?" he cried pointing at a rider on an immense black horse who was rapidly approaching.

The stallion's legs pounded along like pistons, its nostrils wide from the exertion. The magnificence of the animal was echoed by the black rider who looked as if he had ridden from the flames of hell to this desolate place. The powerful beast rapidly closed the distance between them.

Helen looked down at Italian pilot who seemed to have become rather nervous. "It's only Papa," she said, patting his shoulder.

"This is your father?" Romano shook his head in wonder.

"Yes," Helen murmured, standing up once more. "I hope he hasn't come to interfere."

The hooves beat a staccato across the expanse of the moor. Helen noticed that her father was hatless. Whether he had left the manor that way or not was uncertain. It was not unknown for him to ignore such niceties. At least that beast Cerberus was not with him. The black wolfhound recognized no master but he. Helen decided she ought not mention the dog to Signor Romano.

Helen took a few steps forward and waved wildly. Her father raised a hand in greeting, corrected his trajectory slightly, and seemed to increase his pace. The great black horse was upon them and her father swung down from his back as the horse snorted and danced.

"Darling Papa, how kind of you to come all this way." Helen stepped up to kiss her father on the cheek.

"Your mother demanded I find out whether you were dead," her father said, his voice gruff though his expression revealed kindness. The scars on his face suggested a past tragedy and his left eye showed a milky blindness. "Is he dead then?" he continued, pointing at Romano, one eyebrow raised.

Romano coughed and tried to stand. "No, *signore*, I am just a little bruised, but I shall be on my feet in a moment." However, he staggered immediately and sat back down on the hard ground, holding his head and wincing.

"Don't be a fool, *signore*!" Helen cried. "Papa, we must take him back to the house to wait on Doctor Ponsonby. I shouldn't like to find he's had a concussion."

"Sit down, you Italian nincompoop." Helen's father leaned in to take a closer look at Romano's wound. "It doesn't look that bad," he said at last. "Best to be certain."

"He shall take Belial and be back in no time," Helen said, giving a quick nod of her head.

Her father laughed. "I'd like to see that."

"Papa! You must see it is the best thing."

"*Signore*, how are your riding skills?" Helen's father narrowed his good eye at Romano. "This horse is a veritable devil. You'll have to be a better one to stay on him."

The Italian looked alarmed. "I don't know—"

"You must," Helen said. "You'll be perfectly fine."

Her father laughed.

"Well, come on then!" Helen's father shouted at the poor Italian. "Mount up!"

"Papa," she hushed him. "Give him a minute. He's been injured."

Romano rose on unsteady legs, giving a baleful look at Belial, who stamped his feet as if to emphasize that he was no horse to be trifled with—as if his size and fierceness had not already conveyed that information to the injured pilot.

"Let me lend you a hand," Rochester said, his voice genial and a look of amusement on his craggy face. "Up you go."

Romano lifted a foot tentatively and Helen's father grabbed it and tossed him aboard the stallion. Belial immediately shied to one side, as if testing the rider for soundness. Romano clapped his legs tighter and grabbed for the black tendrils of his mane for security.

"Right as rain!" Helen said to encourage the Italian, though she couldn't help looking askance at the horse's dancing.

"The reins, curse you," her father rumbled, his always short patience already gone. "Damme, man. Have you not been on a horse before?"

"Ah, *signore*, not since I was a little boy." He fumbled with the reins, unable to let go of the hair that seemed to feel more secure in his hands. "I always take carriages."

Helen frowned. "Perhaps I should ride with him, help hold him on the horse."

Her father guffawed. "I'd like to see your mother's face if she saw the two of you riding in on Belial. You want her to skin me alive? No, this will do."

"Perhaps the *signorina* has the right idea, I think I would feel more secure if—"

"Nonsense!" Rochester stepped back and slapped the stallion's hind end. "Home, Belial!"

The horse was off like a cannonball, hurtling away down the moors—thankfully, Helen noticed, in the general direction of the house. She glanced at her father who still laughed raucously at the flying black shape.

"Father, stop laughing," Helen scolded. "You are most unkind to my friend."

"Friend!" He threw back the tousled hair that struck her as far too similar to the demonic horse he rode. "The man was actually going to allow you to ride with him on that horse. Most indecorous. Even *I* know that. Your mother would have my guts for garters."

"Oh father, you've been reading novels again."

"Braddon is quite bracing and I've got the next Dickens waiting in my library for a pipe and some leisure.

8

Will you read to me tonight? I must know what happens."

"Where's Edmund?"

All the laughter disappeared from his expression. "That jackanapes! If he knows what's good for him he'll stay out of my sight, such as it is," he added with a bitterness that was more habit than feeling.

"It's true then? He's been sent down?" Helen frowned, too, unconscious how much it made her look like her father.

"Sent down indeed! A waste of money as I knew it would be from the start."

"Father, you must be patient. Edmund has yet to find his feet—"

"Well, he will find mine applied to his posterior if he does not figure out something useful to do with all his talents and energies. Something other than gambling and carousing."

"Papa, it's not as bad as that. A few youthful indiscretions—I wager you were not without a few of them yourself." Helen looked at her father out of the corner of her eye to gauge his reaction to that.

"Your mother has been telling tales, eh?" Rochester smiled grimly. "I paid for my mistakes. Your brother should avoid having to do the same. We're not a family with a great deal of luck."

"Mother would disagree."

"Your mother is a singular person and makes her own luck. We can't all do the same." Nonetheless, his looks softened. "There's no person on this earth like your mother."

"Let me anchor the ship and we'll race down to the house," Helen offered. She took her father's bark of laughter for assent and cast about for a likely anchor for the ropes.

"It doesn't look likely to go anywhere," her father remarked, frowning at the damaged gondola.

Helen grimaced as she pulled on the rope leading from

the port side of the ship. "It's losing air through a rift near the rudder, but there's an awfully good chance of it floating off if the winds pick up."

He grumbled something unintelligible, but picked up the other rope. "What do we tie this infernal machine to?"

"We're going to have to see if we can fasten it to this rock. It's the only thing remotely useful in that way." Helen looped the rope around the stone and tied a couple of half hitches to tighten it. Her father tossed his rope around the stone in like manner, tying his knots as well as he could.

"Doesn't look very secure." He tugged at the knots, which held nonetheless.

"We haven't much in the way of choice up here. I'm going to have to work on some kind of mobile anchor, something that could help lock rope into place on unusual surfaces." She looked at her father. "Why are you grinning like a monkey?"

"You will make a good little tyrant. I like seeing you so self-sufficient, makes me hopeful I won't have to house all of my children when I am decrepit."

"Papa," Helen scolded. "You won't have to worry about taking care of me. I can take care of myself. Come, Tuppence!" The raven flew down from the rudder and croaked as it lighted on her shoulder.

"How are you, you murderous old bird?" Rochester greeted the raven with jolly laugh. "When are you going to settle down and find a mate?"

"Shall we race back to the house?" Helen said.

"Don't be ridiculous. You could already run faster than I when you were twelve. Even with all those skirts, you'll have the advantage."

They hadn't gone more than half a mile when they spotted riders heading their way. "I take it your Italian friend made it back in once piece."

"That's encouraging," Helen said, waving at the group. She could see that the lead horseman was Thompson, her father's head groom. As pleased as she was that they were coming to retrieve the airship, she found herself even more pleased that Thompson was leading two more horses for them to ride home. It was no hardship to walk the rest of the way, but she was eager to get back and discuss the failures of the flight and possible fixes.

The men pulled up, all of them approximating some level of bowing from horseback which led to an awkward and stilted performance that made her father glower. "Thank you, Thompson," Helen said, taking the reins of her dapple grey mare. "Is Signor Romano all right?"

"He were bleeding a good bit, miss," Thompson said, "But he seemed to be right enough. I don't think you have to worry about him."

"Thanks, Thompson. That sets my mind at ease. Ready to ride, Papa?"

They parted from the crew and galloped homeward. At the last stile, the dark mass of Cerberus waited, barking loudly once before he leapt up to greet his master. "Down, you devil," Rochester growled, but Helen saw that he was smiling. At the house, the young stableboy waited, his cap too big for his head, his hands shaking as he tried to take the reins.

"Don't shilly-shally, boy," Rochester cried as the timid lad once again missed the reins.

"Papa, don't frighten him. It's all right, you're doing fine," Helen reassured him. Turning back to her father she gave him a severe look, which he pretended to ignore. Trotting inside the house, Helen found a harried looking housekeeper wringing her hands. "Mrs. Hitchcock, what's the matter?"

"Oh, Miss Helen! I had hoped the horse I heard was the doctor. I am so afraid for your Italian friend. He is in a most alarming state."

"Nonsense," her father said as he barreled past the housekeeper. "He's just got an excitable nature. Where have you put him?"

"In the library sir."

"Good god, you haven't got him bleeding all over my surveying maps, have you?" Rochester stalked off toward the library.

"I'm sure he'll be fine," Helen reassured the harried looking woman, but then she noticed the bloody shirt in the housekeeper's hands. "Who went for the doctor?"

"Your brother. He didn't want to go, but all the men had to set out for your balloon thingee and there was no one else to go."

"I hope he doesn't stop to talk politics," Helen said, annoyance sharpening her tone. Curse that Fairfax. He did nothing in haste. Her father joked that he would even fall off a cliff slowly.

Helen stifled her irritation at her brother and his penchant for wasting inordinate amounts of time rehashing the endless bickering that was politics and hurried toward the library, her father stumping along in her wake. She feared to see her pilot looking even more peaky than he had looked upon the moors.

"How are you, *signore*?" Helen said, her voice gentling as she took in the pale figure on the sofa. "Are you feeling better?" It was worth asking. Romano didn't actually look much worse than he had just after the crash. Besides, the library fireplace was crackling merrily and Mrs. Hitchcock had tucked a nice tartan rug around the Italian, which looked very snug.

"I-I am trying to hold on, *signorina*," Romano said, his words sounding more persuasive than his voice did. "I am feeling rather faint, I think."

"Well, at least you're already lying down," Helen said, hoping the comment seemed helpful. The bandage around his head had a large red stain on it that appeared to be slowly growing. "The doctor will be here soon. I think you may have a concussion."

"Concussion!"

"It's serious, *signore*, but it's not life threatening. We'll know more when the doctor arrives."

"Perhaps I should rest," Romano said, closing his eyes with evident weariness.

In the back of her mind, Helen remembered something about head injuries and keeping the patient from drifting off. "Not just yet, *signore*. I think we should keep you awake until Doctor Ponsonby gets here. Besides, I want to go over the last part of the flight."

"*Signorina*, I am not certain that can be fruitful at this juncture," Romano muttered. "And if I close my eyes for just a moment, I know I will feel much more vibrant."

Helen pulled up a chair and took the pilot's hand in hers. Then she began to slap it with her other hand. "Come now, Signor Romano, stay awake!"

"*Signorina!*" He stared at her with surprise in his eyes. "This cannot be proper."

Helen heard a bark of laughter as her father entered the library. "Proper! The day my daughter recognizes propriety—"

"What?" At the sound of this new voice both Helen and her father started. "What will happen on that momentous day, Rochester?"

"Mother!" Helen leapt up and rushed over to her. "Have you seen Signor Romano? Do you think he will survive all right?" she asked, lowering her voice precipitously for the second question.

"Signor Romano has an extraordinary constitution," Helen's mother announced. Patting her daughter's hand, she added in a more confidential tone, "Although he would benefit from a head as hard as your father's."

"Don't pretend you didn't mean for me to hear that," her father grumbled as he poked the fire. Looking over her shoulder, Helen saw that a small grin lit his face, making his rugged face nearly handsome.

While her mother's face could not be called handsome in any sense, it was so full of lively intelligence that one could not help liking it. Helen had admired her since she could remember, eagerly shadowing her about the house. Her mother's will had such firmness that Helen could not imagine ever getting the better of her in a disagreement, even though she towered several inches over her.

"Mother, do you think Fairfax will get the doctor here soon?"

"Don't worry, he knows this is important. I'm sure he'll be back directly." She took the seat Helen had brought over and took up Romano's hand. "We'll have you up and about in no time, *signore*, but you need to stay awake. If you cannot keep your eyes open lying down, I'm afraid we're going to have to make you sit up, painful though it may be."

Leaving the pilot in her mother's capable care, Helen turned back to her father. "I'm going to need some more funds for repair, Papa. I don't know if Fairfax will give me enough. He was rather meanly inclined the last time around."

"Your ship requires a lot of funds."

"But I desperately needed those upgrades to the motor and vent system. And the payoff will be enormous when I show how beneficial cross continental travel can be."

Rochester turned to regard her with a raised eyebrow. "Beneficial? To crash into the sides of mountains, to drown your passengers in the Channel? I supposed you could round up superfluous relatives and have them disposed of quietly." He laughed at his own wit.

Helen did not allow that to discourage her. "I am going to fly to France."

"Someday my dear, surely." Her father smiled indulgently as he poked the fire.

"I am going to fly to France next week!"

Helen's father stared at her. "Don't be ridiculous. Look what happened today."

"That's exactly my point. Look what this kind of penny-wise pound-foolish economizing has led to." Helen warmed to her topic, pacing in front of the fire. "If I weren't trying to make do with less than optimum equipment, we wouldn't have had this accident today."

"What do you propose to do?" her mother asked.

"I will beg, borrow or steal enough money to patch the tear near rudder and make the renovations to the engine assembly that we have been discussing for some time. I shall see the ironmonger in the morning."

Rochester made as if to wave her words away. "None of this is relevant. You are certainly not going to fly to France in that contraption."

"You needn't worry, Papa," Helen said with a smile at her father's frown. "We shall be safe as houses."

"Houses! If an infernal house took a notion to fly, it would end up just as disastrously. I will not countenance such a journey." He threw himself into the large armchair and glowered from its depths.

"Father," Helen said, her voice taking on a tone distinctively similar to his and a look of determined stubbornness, "I will be flying to France next week as soon as I can get the ship repaired. *Signore,* you will doubtless be able to pilot again by then, too, I expect."

Romano nodded, but groaned a little as he did so.

"Helen, perhaps you should take a little more time to assess the damage," her mother said, her tone as placating as the words. Her eyes were on her husband who still mumbled from the depths of his chair. "Surely a short delay will lend you the opportunity to go over all the mechanicals thoroughly."

Helen shook her head. "We don't know how much longer the good weather will last. We cannot wait more than a week or we risk that being a factor."

"Fine, then you can put off the journey until spring and use the winter to tinker away at that contraption," her father announced with satisfaction. "Or find other interests," he added in a low voice.

Helen folded her arms and regarded him. "This is not a whim, father, this is my passion and I will not retreat one iota from this goal. Air travel is the future! I plan to be one of the trailblazers."

There was a commotion in the hall and Mrs. Hitchcock's voice could be heard distantly.

"I expect that's the doctor at last," Helen's mother said, patting Romano on the shoulder gently.

However, when the housekeeper appeared at the door to the library, she appeared alone. "Miss Helen, I have a letter for you."

Helen walked over to take the letter and tore it open to devour the contents. Her parents exchanged a puzzled glance. When she finished reading, Helen let out a cheer and said to Romano, "He is in Paris and will be glad to work with us!"

"Wonderful news, *signorina*!" Romano said, wincing a little with the pain of exertion.

"He is attending the *Exposition Universelle*, he says," Helen continued, rereading the missive. "I wonder if he is exhibiting? He does not say."

"Who are you talking about, my dear?" Helen's mother prompted her gently.

"Alessandro Maggiormente," Helen said grandly, a broad smile across her face.

"Of course," her father grumbled. "Him."

Helen looked at him with amusement. "The premiere alchemist in Europe, Papa. Signor Maggiormente has been responsible for some of the most exciting developments in alchemy for this century."

"What the devil do you need an alchemist for?"

"Edward," his wife tutted. "Do be more temperate in your language indoors. You are not addressing your dog."

"Alchemists are little more than hucksters and mountebanks," Rochester insisted. "There's not one whose work holds up under scrutiny."

"You confuse the sensational trials with the quiet accomplishments. Maggiormente has been responsible for some exciting developments in fuel sources."

"And what is it you propose to do with this charlatan?"

"I will be consulting with him in the hopes of securing his assistance with a new undertaking that will revolutionise the flying experience!"

"You don't mean to say—"

"Yes," Helen said with satisfaction as she took in her father's dismay. "I will be flying to France to collaborate with Signore Maggiormente."

"I forbid it," Rochester announced with finality.

"You cannot forbid it," his daughter said with equal fervor.

"I am your father!"

"And I am an adult. Don't be ridiculous, Papa."

"Adult? Who's being ridiculous now? Why, you can't be more than—than—" Rochester turned to his wife. "How old is she anyway? Fifteen?"

His wife smiled gently at him. "She is nineteen. I was on my own at a younger age."

Rochester looked at his wife with disbelief. "Surely not." She nodded. "Well, those were…extraordinary times. I am not about to let my only daughter go gallivanting about in the sky with an Italian on the way to France to meet another Italian whom none of us know."

"Father," Helen said, "You can't be serious. This is the modern world! You have to move with the times."

"I realise I may seem utterly ancient to you, daughter, but I assure you I have not lost all my faculties."

It was that moment Tuppence chose to appear outside the window, resting on the rhododendrons and making her hoarse croaking that sounded very much like laughter. Rochester scowled. His wife, however, hid a smile.

Helen regarded him with folded arms. "I am flying to France next week, Papa. There is no use arguing. I have a career to build and a new technology to demonstrate. I can make this scheme a successful one if I can collaborate with Signor Maggiormente. You can't stand in the way of progress!"

Rochester got up to stalk before the fire, hands clasped behind his back, muttering words that his wife knew she did not wish to hear aloud. At last he stopped to address his recalcitrant offspring once more. "I am not standing in the way of progress: I am merely voicing the necessary concerns of propriety. It's not as if he were English, after all," he added, gesturing toward the injured Italian.

"*Signore*," Romano said. "I am an honorable man." He winced with the effort but went on. "Your daughter is safe with me. Further, I am engaged to a beautiful woman in my hometown. I have no designs upon your daughter."

"Not good enough for you?" Rochester barked at the young man.

"Papa, leave him alone. First you think he's going to compromise me, then you're afraid he won't. It's irrelevant. I am quite capable of handling myself. You taught me to shoot, you should know. I'm a better shot than you."

"I don't think your father is only worried about fisticuffs," her mother said, walking over to lay a gentle hand on his arm. "It's only natural that we should be concerned for your safety. I realise you have ambitions and we do wish to support them, but we must be have certain safeguards in place to be sure that you will come home to us in one piece."

"But mother—!"

Mrs. Rochester continued, "Which is why I have suggestion that will suit both your scheme to travel and your father's concerns about your safety. Quite simply: your father shall accompany you."

All three stared at her. Tuppence croaked again from the window, flapping her wings against the window panes to punctuate the silence.

"Madness!" Rochester sputtered.

"You can't mean it!" Helen said, but she was already recalculating the fuel resources that would require.

"Darling, listen: you want to watch over our daughter? Do it yourself. You've been kept too close to home for too long. You haven't been as far as York in months. When's the last time you were in London?"

"Well, I haven't had much to do, what with Fairfax handling all the business dealings…"

"Exactly. You're beginning to wear on my nerves somewhat, so I can only imagine that you are feeling fractious as well." She tapped her husband's arm. "Admit it."

"Well…"

She looked up at her daughter. "And wouldn't your father make an excellent addition to your crew?"

"What's he going to do? Shout at poor Signor Romano? Curse at my airship?" Helen smiled as she said this and her mother knew that she had won. "Well, as long as he is part of my crew."

"Meaning?" her father demanded.

"You must obey me."

"I'll do no such thing." His wife elbowed him gently. "What? You don't really mean I should obey this chit?"

"My ship, my rules, Papa."

"Infernal nonsense!" He stomped over to poke the fire.

"That means he agrees," Helen's mother translated for her.

"I know." Helen threw her arms around her mother. "Thank you!"

2 THE ALCHEMIST

Alessandro Maggiormente frowned. There was something wrong with the formula but he could not locate where he had gone astray. He looked up at the array of beakers and frowned more.

"You've missed an important ingredient," Eduardo said, the languor of his voice conveying a sense of unutterable boredom.

"That is apparent," Maggiormente muttered without looking over his shoulder at his familiar. "If you could actually pinpoint the missing element, that would actually prove useful."

"I suppose," Eduardo said, raising his face to the warming rays of the sun, "but I have not been able to pay attention today. This is the first sun we've had since we came to this wretched land."

Maggiormente looked up. "Is that so? I had not noticed."

"You never do."

The alchemist ran his finger down the page, mentally ticking off each herb and tincture. Perhaps it was something in the order of elements—oh, if he had to start over again! How tiresome. He rubbed his eyes. Perhaps he

20

had been at this for too long today.

"Yesterday," Eduardo said, stretching.

Maggiormente looked up at that. "What?"

"You've been at this particular round since yesterday. You're too tired to think straight. I bet you're hungry, too. I know I am." His big green eyes blinked. "Very."

"You're always hungry," Maggiormente said absently, but rubbing his eyes he realised he was famished. "Do we have something left to eat?"

"No, we need to go out." Eduardo became mobile instantly, shrugging off the sunlight-induced indolence with shocking ease. "Let's go out!"

Maggiormente looked down at him. "Remember what happened last time we went out."

"That was not my fault."

"You frightened that woman very badly."

"Some people frighten easily."

"She had every reason to be alarmed. You roared at her most inexcusably!"

Eduardo snorted. "You'd think the woman had never seen a lion before."

Maggiormente put his hands on his hips and glowered at the cat. "You are the last of your kind, Eduardo. No one has seen a Venetian lion if they have not seen you."

"I'm sure there must be some others around," Eduardo said, flexing his wings a little with a shake. "They just have better things to do."

The alchemist sighed. "I hope your presence does not overshadow my own experiments at the Exposition."

"I can't help it if I am beautiful," Eduardo said.

"Not to mention insufferable," Maggiormente muttered.

The cat pretended not to hear him. "I smell duck. Wouldn't duck be just the thing? And maybe some chicken afterward. And a cow."

"Maybe you should wait here while I go get some victuals."

"I promise to be on my best behaviour," Eduardo said, raising a paw as if to swear.

"Why don't I believe that?" the alchemist said with a snort.

"I will, you'll see. I shall be genteel and nod politely and say 'please'."

"Perhaps you ought not to speak at all."

Eduardo looked affronted by that. "Next you'll make me wear a hat."

"Not a bad idea."

"I am not a monkey."

Maggiormente sighed. "You would be easier to manage if you were."

"Monkeys are no help at all when it comes to alchemical workings. And they smell."

"True enough. But they look very smart in hats."

Eduardo narrowed his eyes at the alchemist. "If you absolutely insist, I will wear the fez. But I will not be pleased."

"Done."

The alchemist his Venetian lion squeezed down the narrow corridor together. They had rented the top floor of this Montmartre rooming house because it had good light and seemed relatively inexpensive (for Paris anyway). The workspace helped them overlook the other drawbacks, like this narrow passage, which was not really suited to a six-foot tall alchemist and a full-grown predator of Eduardo's size.

Another drawback appeared when they had descended to the ground floor.

"Monsieur Maggiormente!" The ebullient voice of their concierge, Mme. Gabor, struck the alchemist between his shoulders like a sharp knife. He stifled the impulse to sigh.

"Get rid of her," Eduardo whispered, "for I shall be very tempted to bite her."

"Don't be impossible," Maggiormente hissed back. "We need this flat." In a louder voice, he answered,

"Signora Gabor, how delightful to see you."

"Oh, *charmant*!" The woman clasped her hands together while grinning at the lion. Eduardo did not return her look, but a low rumble echoed in his chest. "The little hat! So charming, monsieur!"

"Ah, *merci, signora*. I'm afraid we're in a bit of a hurry—"

"Now now, what have I told you about Parisian life, Monsieur Maggiormente?" She batted her eyes at him coquettishly, the heavily kohled rims emphasizing the bloodshot red spiderwebbing the white around her brown irises. Paired with the heavy rouge on her cheeks, it gave her a seedy look at odds with her well-maintained figure and chic clothes.

She was a mystery, but one that the alchemist experienced very little curiosity to investigate. "Ah, yes, that was, erm—"

Her laughter was like a peal of bells—large bells, like those in a sturdy cathedral. The sound could frighten a less well-prepared man, but having heard her laughter before, Maggiormente had already braced himself.

"Oh monsieur! There is always time, always time. Enjoy every step, embrace every moment." She leaned close to the alchemist, bringing to him a whiff of tobacco and cherries that always seemed to linger near her. Mme. Gabor squeezed his large arm with a familiarity he did not share. "You must savour life in Paris!"

"Indeed, *signora*, indeed." Maggiormente edged away from her toward the freedom of the door where Eduardo waited, tail lashing. "Well, *au revoir*!" He pried her fingers from his arm. He could not help thinking that the glossy varnish of her nails looked as if she had drawn blood.

Safely out in the bustling streets, Eduardo grumbled, "This would not have happened if you had not made me wear this ridiculous hat."

"Don't be foolish. She would have found some other reason to speak to us."

"To you." Eduardo sniffed. "Why does she smell like cherries?"

"It is probably some kind of liqueur," Maggiormente said, stroking his beard absently, wondering the same thing. "What kind of liqueur does one make from cherries?"

"Something horrid," Eduardo said, spitting his contempt at the pavement and inadvertently frightening a young woman who leapt backwards, knocking down a grocer with a box full of turnips, which rolled into the street frightening a pair of carriage horses who reared up, whinnying loudly, then charged away down the street, loosing the barrels of wine that had been their cargo, which then rolled away down the street in the direction of the Seine as people leapt out of the way, shouting in alarm.

Eduardo watched the scene unfold with a look of pleasure, but turning to his master, he found the alchemist continued lost in thought. "You missed it," Eduardo said, pacing along beside him.

"Hmmm, yes," Maggiormente said, nodding and ruffling his beard.

Eduardo rolled his eyes. There was no talking to him at times like this, so he amused himself glowering at passersby who, unlike Mme. Gabor, were not charmed into complacency by the fez. *I am a wild beast after all,* Eduardo thought with admirable satisfaction. *People should fear me and respect me. I am the king of the beasts!*

"Can we get cakes?" he asked Maggiormente, who muttered to himself indistinctly.

"What?"

"Cakes. I want cakes."

"Where are we going to get cakes?" The alchemist frowned.

Eduardo sighed. "The bistro, remember? We are going to the bistro." He lifted a paw to point and flapped his wings for emphasis.

"Ah." Maggiormente recalled their errand as he looked

up at the familiar façade of the Cossack Bistro. "Shall we stop for some food?"

Eduardo blinked. "Yes, why not. Let us savour Paris cakes." He laughed.

"Monsieur, a delight to see you again!" The restaurateur greeted the alchemist like an old friend, which he seemed to have become in the short length of their stay in the City of Lights. The Cossack Bistro had first been a convenient place to eat due to its location, but they had not wandered far abroad for food because the atmosphere within was so welcoming.

When you are traveling with a Viennese lion, welcomes can be a challenge to locate.

"And Eduardo, *mon cher*! How is your appetite today?"

"Excellent, of course," the lion said, perching himself on a stool near the small table in the back. Experience demonstrated that the two were less likely to draw unwonted attention when they were seated there. The day the tall bearded alchemist and his familiar had taken advantage of the sunshine to sit on the sidewalk like most Parisians had been an inadvertently eventful one.

"I must say, Eduardo, that hat suits you right down to the ground."

Maggiormente laughed, but the lion raised himself proudly. "Thank you, monsieur. What have you in the way of cakes today?"

The restaurateur rubbed his hands together with enthusiasm. "Better today than cake mince pie! An imported tradition, but one I am certain you will enjoy."

"There aren't any leeks in them, are there? I can't abide leeks."

"No leeks at all."

"I'll have three." Eduardo stretched his wings with pleasure, knocking a painting askew on the wall but otherwise harming nothing.

"And *monsieur le alchimiste*?"

Maggiormente pulled his beard in thought. "Potato and

leek soup, I think."

"In a trice," the restaurateur said, bowing and spinning away to fetch the viands.

"Must you do that?" Eduardo said, his voice taking on a cold wind of annoyance.

"Do what?"

"Eat leeks. You know I hate leeks."

"I'm not making you eat them," Maggiormente said, absently drawing on the menu, sketching out a new plan for the procedure. *Surely it was in the order and not the ingredients that I have erred.*

"Yes, but your breath will smell like leeks and I will be miserable all day," Eduardo said, raising a paw for emphasis. "It's quite uncharitable of you."

"I think we should connect the siphon directly to the beaker here," he said, ignoring the lion's complaint. "Look, this is what's throwing the process off, don't you think?"

Eduardo looked at the sketch. "Hmmm, possibly. But if you add it there, won't there be a greater chance of explosion?"

Maggiormente frowned. "What else can I be missing? Should we aspirate the coelestino more?"

"Where is my pie?" Eduardo looked in the direction of the kitchen as his stomach rumbled loudly.

"Can you never think of anything but your stomach?" The alchemist scowled. "Our booth at the Exposition becomes available in a matter of days. It would be helpful if we actually had something to show for it."

"I'm sure everything will come out fine…eventually." The lion rubbed his face with his paw to distract his thoughts from hunger. The couple at the table next to them paid hastily and left even more so. Eduardo watched them go.

"You don't care about this project!" Maggiormente said, crashing a fist down onto the table and rattling the cutlery. Other people in the café were beginning to eat faster.

"I think you just worry too much about insignificant details," Eduardo said, concealing a smile. He could smell the pies now. It would not be long.

"My reputation and a good deal of money are at stake. You do not want us to have to return to live with my mother, do you?"

Eduardo shuddered. "No. I shan't have my choice of hats then."

"Well, either you help me get this process to work or we will have to resort to you telling fortunes and juggling in the kiosk."

For a moment, Eduardo forgot his pies and stared at his alchemist between narrowed eyes. "You wouldn't."

"It is a very expensive undertaking to have a booth at the *Exposition Universelle*," Maggiormente said, staring back at the lion. Neither made a sound for some time.

"Mince pies for Eduardo!" The restaurateur beamed with happiness as he placed the pies in front of the Venetian lion, who bared his teeth happily as a greeting. This proved too alarming a sight for another table of people, who hastily left their money on the table and skittered off into the street.

"*Ma cherie* Sophie has your soup, Monsieur Maggiormente. She won't be a moment." He bowed and backed away. Even as he turned, his young daughter came out of the kitchen balancing the tray with the soup and brioche on it, her expression very serious as she stalked across the dining room, endeavouring not to spill a drop.

"*Merci, merci, mademoiselle* Sophie," the alchemist said, patting the young girl lightly on the shoulder. "Well done, *brava*."

The child looked up shyly then grinned broadly. "May I pat Eduardo?"

The lion had been about to begin gobbling up his pies, something he did without much daintiness at all. He grumbled slightly, but it turned to a whine as

Maggiormente lowered his eyebrows at him and frowned. "Yes, of course you may."

Eduardo dutifully bent his head toward the child's outstretched hand. Her small fingers tapped his forehead with tentativeness, then with greater force. The big cat ground his teeth impatiently, but under the glowering gaze of his alchemist he did not make any other sound.

"Pretty," the girl said at last and skipped away.

"May I eat now?" Eduardo's sour question made Maggiormente grin.

"Yes, of course. *Buon appetito*!"

Eduardo bit into the first pie and growled his delight as his tongue worked busily. "*Apri il vino*."

"I knew I forgot something. Monsieur!" The alchemist turned to find the restaurateur already bringing a bottle of his good red, a glass, and a bowl for the lion in the other hand. "You are a wonder, *monsieur*!" He clapped the man on the shoulder.

"Only the finest for our friends!"

While the more timid folks had been frightened off by the hungry lion's growls, the Cossack Bistro was filling quickly with a midday crowd. More than a few of them cast not so surreptitious glances at the winged lion in the fez, the hat now askew as he bent over the mince pies, chewing with vigour.

Maggiormente dipped a piece of the brioche in his soup and popped it in his mouth. The leeks were pungent and the broth rich and buttery. *Not like Mama makes*, the alchemist thought, *but it will do*. He tried to ignore the stares. They were merely curious. It's not every day they saw a Viennese lion.

Of course he did, but some of the wonder never went away completely.

Noticing that Eduardo was now licking the pie plates clean, he decided to broach the other subject that had been on his mind. "So, what shall we do about the English lady?"

Eduardo licked all the way around his mouth, as if fearful he might have missed a tiny crumb somewhere. "You told her to come to the Exposition, yes?"

Maggiormente nodded. "Yes, but English women— who knows? She may never come. Like the one in that story, you know."

"What story?" Eduardo began to lap wine from his bowl.

"Oh, you know the story, the one where the English woman is traveling but never arrives at her destination…"

Eduardo looked at him, one eyebrow raised. "English woman traveling?"

"Oh, you know the story I mean!"

"I do not." Eduardo lapped some more wine.

"Well, I just don't know whether she is some crackpot or a real inventor. It is so difficult to tell with women."

"Why is that? She was quite specific about the fuel, was she not?"

Maggiormente shrugged. "Ah, but women…what can I say?"

"Something definite would be a nice change." Eduardo narrowed his eyes. "Are you nervous about meeting a woman?"

The alchemist flushed. "What a ridiculous thing to suggest! I will not countenance such foolishness."

"Ha! You are." The lion leaned back his head and roared with laughter. "Oh, she's probably just some crackpot old biddy with more money than sense. Which could be very useful," he added.

"Idiot," Maggiormente muttered. "I don't want to talk about it."

"But the English lady—she could be our salvation," Eduardo insisted, licking the last of the wine from his bowl.

"I don't think we should count on that. We need to focus on the work." The alchemist frowned. "Perhaps we should go to the Exposition today."

The lion had a full belly now, so he was reluctant to consider something quite so strenuous as a meandering journey through the pullulating crowds at the exhibit. "Oh, I don't know about that, *mago*. Focus on the work, indeed. But in our aerie, yes? Perhaps we need to revisit the structure of the process."

Maggiormente emptied the last of his glass of wine and wiped his mouth. "*Non so.* Perhaps I have miscalculated. Perhaps my ego has got the better of me." He put his head in his hands and groaned expansively.

"*Non ti preoccupare*," Eduardo said, his tone reassuringly low. "You are certainly brilliant, *piccolo mago*. You have been too close to the process. We need to look at the apparatus with fresh eyes." The lion belched, raising a paw hastily but too late to cover the eruption.

The alchemist, however, remained too distracted to notice this rude behaviour. "Perhaps you are right. I quite think that we have overlooked something quite simple in the assembly…" His voice trailed off as he tugged on his beard.

Eduardo stretched elaborately, elongating his body to seemingly impossible lengths. A few people at nearby table shifted their chairs uncomfortably, but did not actually move. The lion had already begun thinking about the way the afternoon sun came in through the large windows at the top of the house and how pleasant it would be to doze in that warmth while the magician dismantled the entire apparatus.

He could always wake up long enough to offer an opinion.

"Let's go," he urged Maggiormente, leaping down from the stool where he had sat and stretching even further. "No time like the present."

The alchemist waved over the restaurateur and paid him handsomely with as many compliments as francs. "We are delighted that you welcome us here, monsieur."

"The Cossack Bistro shares your delight. Let us be your

kitchen, *signore*." He clasped the alchemist's hands in his own with a wide grin.

Eduardo stood in the doorway, his nose in the air. His nostrils widened. There was something unexpected in the wind. He couldn't quite distinguish what it was and yet there was something familiar about it. "Maggiormente, I think we need to go."

"*Sì, sì*, I am ready." The alchemist indulged in an elaborate stretch himself and patted his happy stomach afterward. "*A presto!*" he called to the chef, saluting as he walked out of the bistro. "There is something supremely satisfying about a well-cooked meal," he confided to his familiar.

Eduardo snorted. "Particularly so when one does not have to cook the meal."

"Indeed." The alchemist smiled. "You are pleased not to have my spaghetti Bolognese today, are you not?"

Eduardo grimaced. "I did not enjoy living with your mother, but at least her food was edible. Do you smell that?"

"Smell what?" Maggiormente looked about him as if the eyes might aid the search.

Eduardo looked suddenly to the north. It came from that direction. "Fire."

"What?"

Before the lion could respond, a huge crowd of people came rushing along the street, down the narrow road, which they rent with screams and shouts of alarm. Behind them, in the distance, it was possible to see a huge cloud of black smoke.

"What on earth?" The alchemist stepped back as the crowd of people surged by, hands in the air, mouths open in non-stop exclamations of alarm.

"I think there's a fire," the lion said, sitting on his haunches on the pavement.

"Of course there's a fire," the alchemist huffed. "Where is there a fire? Why is there a fire? And what is to be done about it?"

"Shall we investigate?" Eduardo stretched elaborately once more, but curiosity had got the better of him for the moment. His afternoon nap would have to wait. He had a moment's worry about his fez, but that was the sort of risk one had to take if one were to indulge in adventure.

"Yes, do let's. Perhaps we will discover something useful."

The two of them began to swim against the tide of fleeing pedestrians, fighting their way upstream with deliberation. The crowd began to thin but not before they encountered a thin white figure.

"Run! Save yourselves! It is a disaster!"

"How can you be sure?" Maggiormente said, waving him aside.

"Because I caused the conflagration!"

"And who is it you are?" Maggiormente inquired, examining the queer pale figure with some curiosity.

"Manet." The man shook his hand absently, his thoughts elsewhere. "What am I going to do? Berthe will be so angry!"

"Can we help in some way?" Maggiormente asked while Eduardo sniffed discreetly at the man's trousers, which seemed to be spattered with a variety of colors. "Is the fire uncontrollable?"

"Oh, everything is quite quite gone," Manet said, a sigh of unutterable sadness escaping him as he looked back down the street. "All that work, wasted!"

"Perhaps we should investigate. You never know. Things may not be as bad as they seemed at first." The alchemist smiled, trying to convey a sense of hopefulness.

"It smells like a big oil fire," Eduardo said, having finished his examination of the other gentleman.

"Linseed oil," Manet muttered. "There was a case of it. We had thought, 'Such a bargain!' but that turned out to be a false economizing, eh?"

"He's a painter," Eduardo said to Maggiormente whose

brow had been wrinkling with incomprehension. Outside of his own field, the alchemist seldom had much interest in or knowledge about other people's pursuits.

"Houses?"

Eduardo smirked. "I suspect not."

The painter stared at the lion. "Your pet: he talks!"

Eduardo drew himself up proudly. "Pet! I am no pet. I am a familiar." He closed his eyes and looked away.

"Ah, Edo, don't be insulted." Maggiormente sighed. "He can be very touchy about that, monsieur. But how many people have seen a Venetian lion before, eh? Especially in Paris."

Manet looked impressed. "I have certainly never seen such a remarkable creature. Perhaps I should paint him sometime."

"Oh, but I like the color he is," Maggiormente said with a frown.

"*Non fare lo scemo*," Eduardo snapped. "*Idiota*! He wants to paint my portrait, is it not so?"

"Indeed," the painter agreed, giving a small bow.

"Ah, painter. Yes, the other kind." The alchemist tugged on his beard, lost in thought.

"Well, now that we have that straightened out, perhaps we should go see about the fire," Eduardo said at last since no one seemed inclined to move at present. The two men stopped stroking their beards at once and they all hurried back along the road where the painter had come from.

Most of the crowds had disappeared, but as they approached the small house, they could see the neighbours on either side up on ladders, throwing buckets of water on their roofs. Each had a small assembly of assistants: in one case, it looked like the man's family, from a young woman to a tiny little girl, in the other it looked to be a grim-faced group of bakers, clad in white and using mixing bowls to carry the water to and fro.

While smoke continued to hang in the air around the place, there did not appear to be any open flames. A stack of paintings lay on the ground before the house. Gingerly, the three approached the house.

"Do you suppose it will explode?" Eduardo asked.

The alchemist shot him a glance. "Don't say things like that. It's unnerving."

"I'm only asking. I don't want to be exploded."

"I only hope the paintings are all right," Manet said as he approached the haphazard stack.

"They look fine," the alchemist said, peering over the painter's shoulder.

"I meant the ones inside." Manet looked up at the blackened house.

"Let's go see," Eduardo urged.

"Perhaps we should wait until the fire goes out completely," Maggiormente said.

"Surely it must be out now."

"It exploded at first," the painter said. "But now it seems quiet. Shall we?"

"Adventure!" Eduardo said, adjusting his fez. "Excellent."

The alchemist seemed less than enthusiastic, but he fell in behind the lion and the painter as they made their way gingerly toward the smouldering house. They paused at the blackened door.

"Do we knock?" Maggiormente said, trying to be helpful.

Eduardo gave him a withering glance. "I don't think Monsieur Manet needs to knock to enter his own house."

"I only meant," the alchemist said, ruffling his beard with agitation, "it might be a way to determine the structural soundness before entering."

The lion and the painter paused and turned to look at him. Maggiormente cocked an eyebrow at them and they exchanged a look with one another. He had a point.

"Does the door feel warm?"

Manet leaned toward the door and put his palm up against it tentatively. "It is warm, but not hot."

"It's probably not on fire then, Eduardo concluded, nodding.

"Probably," the alchemist repeated. The lion grimaced.

The painter looked worried. "Perhaps you could take a look, first," he said to Eduardo.

"What?" The lion tipped his head back, balancing the fez precariously.

"Couldn't you fly up and take a look through the windows?" The painter gestured toward the lion's wings then toward the first floor above them.

Eduardo frowned and sat down, closing his eyes with a deep sigh. "No."

"But it would only take a moment! And we could be more certain—"

"No."

The alchemist sidled around his familiar to approach Manet. He leaned toward the man and said in a low voice, "His wings are not strong enough to bear his weight. They are merely vestigial appendages in the lions of Venice. They were perhaps airworthy once, but now—well, you see."

Manet's eye widened. "I am so sorry!"

"It is nothing," Eduardo said with a sniff.

"I should not have been presumptive, monsieur." The agitated painter bowed awkwardly then turned back to the charred door. "Shall we simply try our luck?"

"Do let's." The cold tone of the lion carried a final air of censure, but surely it is not to be imagined that he wished ill upon the painter by encouraging a risky action.

Having made up his mind, Manet threw open the door. For a moment, there was only an inky blackness. Then all at once, heavy cottony puffs of smoke rolled out onto the pavement causing the adventurers to take hasty steps back from the onslaught.

The house belched oily clouds for some time, as if a crowd had gathered behind the door like guests eager to leave a party all at once. As if to mirror them, a small crowd gathered behind the threesome, eager to see what they might do in the smoking house. Their chatter made a susurration of sound like leaves falling.

"Can you see anything?" Maggiormente squinted into the depths of the darkness.

Manet peered into the black, unaware that his face had a light coating of schmutz from the passing clouds of smoke. "I do not see any flames." He turned back to his friends. "Shall we go in?"

Maggiormente and Eduardo exchanged a look. The alchemist shrugged. *"Tutto fumo e niente arrosto!"* The lion laughed and the two of them joined the painter at the door. Eduardo stuck his head through the doorway and inhaled deeply.

"There are no flames anyway."

"Don't go in!" A woman's voice carried from the street crowd.

The adventurers turned to regard her. The others around her craned their necks to see how the three would react.

The attempt to dissuade them seemed to stiffen their resolve. The three gave a curt nod to their would-be cautioner and turned back to the charcoaled-door. They had hardly drawn a breath before they ducked into the shadows and disappeared from view.

"We should have brought a torch," Eduardo grumbled.

"Shhh," the alchemist said, blinking in the dark.

"Oh no!" the painter cried. "I cannot believe it!"

"Édouard!" A voice coughed the word into the gloom, but for the moment the three could only see a vague outline of a form.

"Berthe! Is that you?" The painter cried, his alarm plain in the tone of his voice.

More coughs and then a woman emerged from the shadows. She was clad all in black—perhaps her clothes had not been black before the fire, but they certainly were now. In her hands she clutched a small bouquet of violets.

"I hid in the pantry while the fire raged on. What on earth caused it?"

"Berthe! You are all right!" Manet grabbed the woman and embraced her. The lion and the alchemist looked on nonplussed.

"Yes, yes, of course."

Manet leaned back and glared at his friend. "But what were you doing in the house?!"

Berthe laughed. "You did invite me here, Édouard."

"But you were supposed to be out! You might have been killed." Manet reached up to wipe away some of the soot from her cheek.

"I had a wonderful idea for the portrait," she said, holding up the violets. "Just the right touch of colour, a fine counterpoint to the black."

"Good idea!" Manet nodded.

"I don't mean to interrupt," the lion said at last, "But shall we go see how the rest of the house has withstood the damage? There were some paintings, I believe."

"What a lovely lion."

"My apologies!" the painter replied, looking flustered. "I forgot in the excitement of seeing my friend. We should look upstairs—"

"Why look upstairs?" Berthe asked.

"Well, I'm afraid that's where the explosion happened," Manet said shrugging.

"Hold on a moment, *mon ami*. *You* caused this conflagration?!" Berthe's expression looked considerably less happy.

"Well, I'm not certain about it," Manet said, his face suddenly sheepish. "It may have been my attempt to make a new colour…"

"A new colour?!" Berthe slapped her forehead. "Again?!"

Eduardo laughed. If you have not seen a Venetian lion really laugh, you cannot image the extraordinary mirth it conveys. In the midst of a smoke shrouded house, the laughter had a most peculiar quality like a crocus poking through the snow. "Burnt sienna?" the lion asked once he had stopped laughing.

Manet drew himself up. "Burnt amber. It would have a richness that mere amber could not hold a candle to!"

"Perhaps you could call it 'burnt house' instead!" The lion threw his head back and laughed all the more.

"Well, heavens," Berthe said trying not to show her amusement, "Do let us go see if any our paintings remain."

"Some I carried outside," Manet said, an edge of irritation creeping into his voice. "I did not forget duty."

"My grain field?!" Berthe said, clutching his arm.

"Yes, yes, it's all right."

"Let's go look upstairs," Maggiormente urged. "I am accustomed to explosions. I will be happy to go first." The truth was that the alchemist had become bored by all this talk of painting. He had a notoriously short attention span when it came to subjects that were not alchemy. Indeed he was already thinking about how the burning of amber might provide a useful reagent for some distilling work that was in the back of his mind as something to pursue once he had knocked this fuel experiment on the head.

He turned and headed toward the narrow stairs visible across the room. After a moment, Eduardo padded after him, muttering darkly but making no definite arguments against the venture.

"Careful, monsieur!" Manet cried, but the two were already climbing the stairs gingerly.

The two painters exchanged a look. Berthe shrugged. "Why not?"

In a moment all four launched themselves up the stairs with careful steps as the blackened wood creaked.

The air on the next floor remained filled with smoke. "Is there a window we can open?" Maggiormente asked the painters.

Berthe nodded and stepped across the floor. In a moment she had thrown up the sash and the smoke began to escape, clearing the air somewhat.

"Oh dear!" Manet cried. "Look! How horrible!" They all turned where he pointed.

The explosion had piled debris from the attic above in a smoking heap on the next set of stairs. They would not be able to climb higher without removing some of it, but the smoke suggested that the materials were going to be hot yet.

"What do you suggest?" Eduardo murmured to the alchemist.

Maggiormente frowned and answered his lion, "We must find something to shift the debris. At the very least, we need to be certain the fire is out completely. To be safe." The two exchanged a look. It wouldn't do to find themselves in the midst of a re-energized conflagration.

"Have you any tools or implements?" Eduardo asked the painters.

Manet shrugged. "Brushes?"

"Don't be ridiculous," Berthe scolded. "Something sizable." She tapped her chin for a moment. "The fire irons!" The woman strode across the room, shoving furniture from her path until she reached the fireplace. Grabbing the poker, Berthe grimaced and let out a sudden exhalation of breath and dropped the object.

"Hot?" the alchemist inquired.

She nodded. "I should have thought first."

"It's not every day you sift through the aftermath of a fire," Eduardo said with unusual kindness. The alchemist lifted an eyebrow at him, but the lion ignored it.

The painter gingerly picked up the poker again, shifting it in her hand, seeking to find a comfortable grip. She brought it over to the alchemist and handed it over. Behind her Manet had grabbed the ash shovel and joined the others at the stair to the attic.

"I had feared the attic gone," Manet said as he prodded at a black chunk of rubbish from the steps.

Maggiormente poked away at the rubble while Eduardo

pawed at the wreckage standing on the stair. Were it not for his tail whipping back and forth, it would have been impossible to guess that he remained ready to spring away from danger at a moment's notice. His wings flapped gently back and forth as they always did when he was concentrating intently. The movement did help to dispel some more of the smoke, too.

The four continued digging away a the wreckage for some moments in silence, clearing a path up the stairs and beginning to loosen some of the larger pieces to move them aside.

All of the sudden there was a groaning noise from above them. Maggiormente stopped poking the black debris and looked up with a frown.

"Move," Eduardo barked, his wings suddenly folding tight as he reached forward to bite the trouser leg of his alchemist and wrench him backward. All four turned and leapt from the steps and the groaning turned into a hideous screech. An avalanche of soot-covered lumber and plaster fell with a tremendous sound.

The air filled once more with a thick cloud of smoke and they all began choking as they backed away from the corner of the room that led to the roof. Squeezing together the four pressed their faces out the remaining window, gulping down fresh air by the lungfuls.

"That was close," Manet said at last, his voice half-choked with smoke.

"You were very brave, Monsieur Lion," Berthe said with evident admiration.

Maggiormente threw his arms around the lion's neck. "*Grazie, amico mio!*"

"It was nothing," Eduardo said with stiff dignity, trying to ignore the alchemist's embrace. "Only my duty."

Maggiormente kissed the lion's head. "I am grateful, nonetheless."

The lion shook him off and flapped his wings a little as if to shake away the display. He looked over his shoulder.

"Well, I suppose that tells us all we need know about the attic."

The others turned and Berthe gasped. "It's—it's gone!"

Indeed there was only blue sky visible through the hole at the top of the stairs.

"Do you suppose there could be anything left up there?" Manet asked, the sorrow plain in his tone.

"We should at least look," Maggiormente said with a shrug. "Perhaps it is not as bad as it looks."

"Careful," Eduardo said with a little growl in his tone. "Mind that little saying about the frying pan and the fire."

Maggiormente waved away the lion's words. "The worst of it is over. There was no fire in the debris, eh? It was merely unstable. I'm sure we'll be fine. Let's explore."

The lion looked unconvinced, but the two painters were eager to see what remained of their belongings. Carefully the little group negotiated the stairs, stepping over the largest chunks of blackened wood as they crept to the top. Once there they looked around with surprise at the sight before them.

"It's gone!"

Manet sounded so woebegone, even the alchemist felt a twinge of pity for him. He struggled to find comforting words. "Well, the sky is certainly very blue here above your house, monsieur."

The firmament merited that observation. Manet could be forgiven for finding its overarching presence a bit dejecting, as the top of the house was completely gone and with it everything that had been in the top storey.

"Well, what's gone is gone," Berthe said with a shrug. "It is fate!"

"Fate," Manet muttered. "How Germanic. It is an evil conjunction of stars. The work of envious enemies. A cruel act by a cruel deity. But not *fate*."

"It looks like carelessness to me," Eduardo said with a yawn. The sunlight added to his full belly and the exertion of the afternoon made him feel decidedly sleepy. "If you had not used the linseed oil in a precarious location, perhaps this would not have happened."

"I was experimenting—" the painter said, pulling himself up to his full height. "Without experimenting, art will not move forward."

"He has a point you know," Maggiormente muttered as he began wandering around the blackened remnants of the attic space. "Experimentation must be the key to advancement."

Berthe snorted. "The fact remains that he was careless. You have to use a little common sense when you're working with fire." She frowned at the blackened walls looking for something worth saving.

The alchemist nodded, rubbing his beard as he took a closer look at the burnt remnant of frame, poking at the charcoaled remains as if to determine their chemical makeup. "Fire must have your respect. The salamander must be watched."

Berthe raised an eyebrow at the bearded gentleman. "Salamander?"

Maggiormente rubbed his face absently, unaware that he was covering it in black soot. "Yes, the salamander who quells the fire before it can run amok. But he must be invoked, so one must be vigilant for fire's excesses."

The two painters exchanged a look.

"You've never met an alchemist, have you?" Eduardo said, sitting down on his haunches and licking his paw thoughtfully. "He's not so unusual as alchemists go."

"Unusual?" Maggiormente frowned. "What is unusual?"

"Well, we must get busy determining the extent of the damage," Berthe said, rubbing her hand together as if she were cleaning them.

"Oh my yes," Manet said, avoiding the alchemist's puzzled gaze and turning to the debris in the corner. "So very much to do."

"Don't let us keep you," Eduardo said with purr that

could easily have been mistaken for a growl. "Ever so much to do." He rose, stretched and slowly ambled toward the precarious stairs. "Coming?" he called to Maggiormente over his shoulder.

"Oh, yes, I suppose so," the alchemist straightened up and brushed off his sleeves where he noticed some ash had landed. "Best of luck to you," he added doffing a non-existent hat, realizing mid-gesture that he had no hat, and opening his hand in a vague wave. "Do let me know any further developments you have with the explosive qualities of linseed oil."

He caught up with the lion on the stair. "We must get some. I'm sure it may prove useful if it can cause this kind of damage."

Eduardo busied himself looking in the rubble at the bottom of the steps. "Ah ha!" He pounced and pushed aside a broken bit of furniture. There lay his fez. "Oh dear!"

Maggiormente joined him. "I think it's just a bit of soot. We'll put it right." He picked up the hat and gently flicked away the worst of the black schmutz. "Not bad, not bad at all." He set the hat gently upon Eduardo's head. The fez was not in perfect condition, but the damage had been minimal.

"Is it all right?" the lion looked around for any kind of reflective surface but found none.

"Perfectly so."

He frowned. "It cannot be completely clean."

The alchemist thought for a moment. "Well, perhaps not, but there's only the faintest smudge of soot on it. If someone were to notice it, you would simply have to regale them with the tale of how it got there."

The lion mused. "It would make a good story."

"Full of explosions, painters and heroism," the alchemist agreed.

Eduardo grinned. "Let's go home. I need a nap and I have the feeling you need to write all this down."

"I have a new idea for our fuel experiment," the alchemist muttered, stroking his beard as they headed down to the front door.

3 COMPETITION

"Damnation!"

Helen looked at her father with consternation. "There is no need for that kind of language, Papa."

"Hang it, I don't intend to go flying ass over teacup into the great beyond." He clutched the ropes and grimaced. "Can't your pilot do something about this?"

Helen laughed. "It's only a bit of wind, Papa. You'll soon get used to it."

So far her father's first airship journey had not impressed him favourably. The man who was accustomed to riding a horse that had terrorized grooms for the better part of his life and commanded a dog that kept even well-intentioned guests from their door with its ferocity was having a very difficult time of it keeping from looking terrified.

Another gust of wind set the gondola swinging again. Helen swayed with the movement, but her father tried to will it into submission. "Move with the gondola, Papa. Like on a ship. Get your air legs!"

"Air legs!' Her father shouted, making a desperate grab for the side of the gondola. "Utter nonsense!"

Helen sighed. "I told you we could give you a chair."

She held onto the sides of her seat as another gust lifted the ship up and then dropped it just as suddenly. "But no, you insisted you needed no such thing."

Rochester grimaced again and his knuckles whitened as he gripped the ship's hull. "I could have miscalculated there," he muttered at last.

"I'll say!"

"When is this damn thing going to dock again?"

"Signor Romano," Helen called out. "How far shall we travel today?"

"*Signorina*," the pilot called back, "We ought to go at least as far as the sea, eh? I thought we would go up to Whitby and circle back around."

"We bloody well will *not*!"

"Father!" Helen said, truly scandalised this time. "Such language!"

Rochester looked apoplectic. "There's no one to hear us up here," he shouted across the ship. "No one but Tuppence, I suppose. And the bird's heard me say much worse."

As if to agree, the raven croaked loudly, floating in the air beside where Helen sat. Despite her shock, she couldn't help smiling. Her father's insistence on accompanying them on the first flight of the repaired airship struck her as odd at first and then suspicious. Once they were in the air, however, she had been too busy checking their progress and the workings of the motor to worry too much about it.

"We're nearly there any way, Papa," she soothed. "Look—isn't that the sea now?" Helen pointed off ahead of them where the horizon deepened to the dark gray of the North Sea.

If her father had been pale before, he had now turned white as parchment. "We're not going out over the ocean in this clattering, poxy growler!" His tone indicated the utter impossibility of such a thing occurring.

"You know we will have to cross an ocean to get to France, Papa!"

His stricken look suggested that the thought had not crossed his mind. "Not today!"

"No, Papa. Not today. We just need to see the ship handling in variable winds to test the rudder assembly and the new pulley system."

"Could we do so a little closer to the ground?" Her father started as Tuppence began squawking behind his head, as if trying to strike up a conversation. "Get that infernal bird away from me!"

"Tuppence!" Helen called, beckoning to the bird. "*Signore,* can you bring us a little lower? My father is alarmed."

"I said no such thing," Rochester muttered, his expression darkening. "I just don't think it's necessary to soar with the eagles."

Tuppence flew into the gondola and landed in the middle of the deck. She hopped toward Helen's father, croaking animatedly.

"What the devil is that bird screeching about?"

Helen smiled. "I think she's just entertained by your being up here."

He aimed a kick at the bird, who had no trouble dodging his foot. "That bird should have something better to do than to mock me."

Without warning, the ship lurched, seeming to drop in the sky a good measure.

"Heavens! Look!" Helen cried.

"What the devil is that!" Helen's father blurted.

Helen stared, mouth open. "I don't believe it!"

Passing far too closely on the starboard side came another airship, rather larger than hers, but also far more ungainly. Its striped ballooning seemed garish in the early daylight and the engine assembly ungainly and without elegance. Two young men gawped from the gondola.

"The Linton twins," she growled with unaccustomed vehemence.

"Better watch where you're going!" One of the young

men shouted toward their ship, grinning like a monkey.

"You two are a menace!" Helen hollered back.

"What shall I do, *signorina?*" Romano called from the wheel, glancing back over his shoulder with look of agitation.

"You don't own the sky!" the other twin bellowed at Helen.

"Damnation, what are these impudent puppies doing?" her father demanded. Despite his peremptory tone, his face continued to look alarmingly pale as he clutched the ropes of the gondola.

"Hush, Papa!" Helen admonished, before turning back to her rivals. "Simple common sense rules of logic should suggest the utter stupidity of bringing your ship so close to ours."

"We were here first," the twins sung out in unison.

"They are idiot children," Helen's father growled between clenched teeth. "Ought to have been drowned at birth.

Helen ignored his comments. "Take us up, Signor Romano. Get us away from these amateurs."

"Amateurs!" the older twin shrieked. "Our ship is vastly superior to your pathetic little balloon."

Helen Rochester could bear many things with equanimity, but having her ship thus accosted was not one of those things. "Balloon?" she said, her voice cool but her cheeks pink with irritation. "My airship embodies the very finest qualities of a the very cutting edge of heavier than air technology. Your pathetic and inelegant vehicle looks like a whale beside a dolphin."

She had perhaps hit a vulnerable point with her nautical mammal comparison, or—it is just as likely—the brothers were already committed to challenging the intrepid aviatrix. They just wished to nettle her first. "You don't know what you're talking about, Rochester. Why don't you go back to your bonnets and baubles and let men worry about airships."

Helen smiled. It was not a pleasant sight, although her smiles were quite capable of pleasantness. No, this was a smile that made her look very much like her father, although he at that moment found himself startled at the eerie familiarity of that look without being able to trace its cause. Something in the expression kindled a similar temper in his breast.

"You don't mean to accept the insults of that cur without reprisal, do you my girl?" Rochester called across the gondola with a grim smile.

"Certainly not," Helen said, her clear voice ringing across the open air, punctuated by the rasping croak of Tuppence, who flitted up beside her. "I think we need to show you what this ship can be capable of."

"You're on!" the twins shouted in unison.

"Race to Whitby," Helen said. "To the abbey."

"It's a challenge," cried the elder twin.

"Shall we make a wager?" Helen inquired.

"It's only sporting," crowed the younger twin, rubbing his hands together in glee.

"Five hundred pounds!" Helen said, her smile smug.

"Five hundred pounds?!" her father repeated.

The twins exchanged a look. They were arrogant about their ship's chances, but the addition of a considerable purse seemed to make them pause.

"Well, gentlemen. Do you have any confidence in your ship or not?" Helen folded her arms and glared across the expanse between them. "Five hundred pounds."

"You're on!" the younger twin shouted, his tone extra belligerent now that he was so full of doubt.

"May the best ship win," Helen called out as Tuppence perched on her shoulder. "*Signore*, take us up and out toward the sea!"

"As you wish, *signorina*," Romano agreed, looking askance at the courageous woman, then stealing a glance at her father.

"Saints preserve us," the latter murmured, but his

words were snatched by the wind.

Romano's face grew stony as he maneuvered the ship higher. Helen glanced at her father, whose white-knuckled hands gripped the ropes, bracing himself for further shifting winds, then she unstrapped herself from the seat and made her way to the rear of the ship to listen attentively to the engine.

"What are you doing," her father shouted, tightening his hold on the gondola's ropes as the craft shuddered up at an angle. "Sit down!"

Helen ignored him and listened carefully to the chugging gears. Then she smiled. The motor seemed to be running without complications and they were buoyed up by its power at an increasing rate.

Glancing over her shoulder, Helen saw that the Lintons' ship had picked up its pace as well, though not flying as high as hers at present. She hoped they could increase the distance between them.

She could use that £500!

"Take it up to top gear, *signor*," Helen called out to her pilot.

Romano looked at her, his face full of misgiving. "Perhaps we should not risk it, *signorina*."

"Yes, we must try it out."

"But it may not be necessary; I think we can beat them without it." The pilot gestured at the craft below them. There could be no doubting that the gap between the two ships had begun to increase.

Helen smiled as she looked over the edge of the gondola, but when her gaze returned to meet the pilot's, it was lit with enthusiasm.

"I want to try it out."

Helens father fought his way to a standing position. "What the devil are you two talking about?"

The pilot looked apologetic, trying to keep a watch on the dials and levers before him as he tried to remonstrate with his patroness. "We repaired the previous damage—"

"From the failed flight, last week—you remember, Papa."

"I'm not an idiot," Rochester grumbled. "Of course I remember."

Helen smiled indulgently. "I know you don't enjoy the technical discussions."

Her father grimaced. "You're delaying. Your mother will be so proud to hear that you have taken up her extremely irritating habit."

"Sorry, Papa. I took the opportunity we had with taking apart the engine assembly to initiate a few improvements that I think will offer some surprising innovations."

"I don't like the sound of that." Her father suddenly appeared a trifle more pale.

Helen laughed. "It's only a mild increase in speed capability and—you will be glad to hear—an improvement in motor efficiency at those higher speeds."

"Provided the assembly does not overheat," Romano cautioned.

Helen waved away his words. "I worked it all out in the sketches. The bearings and the oil should withstand the friction without trouble."

"But rotation at that velocity!" the pilot said, wrestling with the wheel before him which seemed to be fighting back. "I think we have underestimated the heat generation index for the entire assembly."

Helen shrugged. "How else will we discover whether the calculations hit the mark?"

"You're speaking gibberish," Rochester shouted, feeling courageous enough to let go of the ropes with one hand as he waved the other at the Lintons' ship. "And anyway, it seems unnecessary. We're clearly in the lead. Just maintain that—"

All three of them watched as suddenly the other craft lurched in the air and then began closing the gap between them at an alarming rate. Tuppence croaked from her perch on the ropes as if to warn them of its approach.

"You see?" Helen said, triumph filling her voice. "We've got to test it now!"

"They may not catch up," her father muttered, but she noticed that he took a firmer hold of the gondola's cables. All her life the towering temper of the man who gave her that distinctive profile had demonstrated his fearlessness.

She found it quite enjoyable to be the cause of making him a bit unsettled. For try as he might, Helen could see behind the bluster that he was afraid.

I am being rather cruel, she tutted herself. But the smile spread across her lips anyway. "Top gear," she shouted to Romano. "Let's show these amateurs what a real ship can do!"

Romano turned back to the controls and slammed the ship into top gear. The gleaming instruments reflected his harried face but the ship responded with a smooth acceleration that belied his frantic motions. The pilot's glance tracked the dials but he could tell the ship was ascending as well as speeding up. He smiled.

Helen could feel the flush on her face as she listened to the motor's hum. While the speed increased she had held her breath, anticipating some kind of grinding noise or any sign at all that there could be a problem.

"How fast are we going?"

Helen looked over at her father who appeared alarmingly pale. "Papa, are you quite all right?"

He nodded tersely.

"Are you sure?" If she did not know better, Helen could have sworn her father was about to be violently ill. Even from her station by the rear of the gondola the sheen of sweat on his brow glistened like the surface of the sea at sunset.

That would be a good detail to tell mother, Helen thought at once.

"How fast are we going?" Her father repeated, his brows ruffling with the temper she knew so well. "Just as a matter of record, of course."

Helen smothered a smile. "Are you keeping a record, Papa?"

"Yes, I'm keeping a bloody record," he sputtered as he swayed with the movement of the ship. "I'm recording my last will and testament, too."

"Papa, there's nothing to worry about."

"She's right," Romano chimed in, smiling encouragingly at Rochester in what he hoped would be perceived as a friendly way. He had not quite accustomed himself to the man's barking voice and abrupt manner, though the latter had become slightly more amiable as he got to know the Italian.

Romano kept far away from his dog, however, and released a big sigh of thanksgiving when the *signorina* managed to dissuade him from bringing Cerberus on board for the flight.

"I am enquiring for the scientific record," Rochester said very slowly and deliberately. "I am the observer here, so it is my duty to keep track of things."

Helen shrugged. "All right, Papa. We'll try to calculate it."

His eyebrows shot up again. "What about those dials?" He gestured toward Romano who raised his hands to indicate his blamelessness.

"*Signore*, we don't have one to measure the speed."

"Why not! Seems like the most natural thing in the world." Rochester glared at the pilot as if he were personally responsible for the lack.

"Papa," Helen soothed. "I hadn't thought it necessary." She looked over at the Linton's craft, which continued to lose ground to their steady progress. "I had no intention of racing the ship. We were more concerned with keeping it in the air and keeping an even keel."

"Foolishness! Very short sighted, I must say."

Helen smiled. "I'll be sure to add it in the next upgrade."

"I should think so." He swallowed and looked away.

"Papa, you look a trifle green."

"Nonsense," he said, but his tone seemed less gruff now and more strangled. "So how are you going to determine the speed?"

Helen blinked at him, then decided it would be best to act as if everything were fine. "Well, first we try to gauge the relative speed against a static visual."

"What the devil does that mean?"

Helen laughed. "We look down at the ground and try to get an estimate of our relative speed."

"Look down?" If he had appeared vaguely green before, he had become positively emerald now.

"It may help, Papa," Helen said, making her way over to his side. "Come now, take a look down." Helen gazed down and immediately drew a quick breath. *We must be going 40 knots or more! That will show those Lintons!*

She turned to share her triumph with her father, but saw that his eyes were closed. "Papa?"

Without warning, he spun around, leaned over the side of the gondola and was violently ill. It did not help that Tuppence croaked loudly at him.

Helen tried to smother a smile. "Oh, Papa! Are you all right?"

He stood up, looking alarmingly blanched and wiping at his mouth with his handkerchief. "Why the devil should I not be?"

"I just thought—"

"Well, never mind that." He waved away Tuppence who seemed to want to land on his shoulder. "How are we doing?"

Helen turned back to look over the side of the gondola. "We're doing at least forty knots, I reckon." She smiled over at her father. "And we're putting distance between us and those Lintons."

His bark of laughter sounded harshly, though he continued to mop his brow with the handkerchief. "I knew you had it in you, my girl."

"Papa, you know that I try—"

"Well, trying is one thing," her father said standing more erect. "Succeeding quite another." He took a step away from the edge of the gondola and coughed loudly.

Helen could see the colour gradually returning to his face. It was quite remarkable really. She had begun to think that he would not last the voyage and now that he had been sick over the side of the airship, her father seemed to have recovered himself almost completely.

Tuppence squawked loudly, flapping her wings as if trying to draw their attention. Helen's brows knit as she looked at the raven. Perhaps it was simply upset by her father's passing bout of illness.

"How are things holding, Signor Romano?" She shouted toward the pilot. The wind seemed to be picking up force as their speed increased.

"It's al looking very good, *signorina*," the pilot called back, throwing up a thumbs up gesture. Though a tradition dating from medieval times the pilot assured her, Helen had found it odd at first until learning that some of the local Yorkshiremen used the same gesture

The things you learn when you leave the ancestral home, Helen mused.

She glanced back over her shoulder. The Lintons' ship was falling even further behind. Helen grinned. Things were looking good. Not only would they win the race but she would have enough funds to assure the last of the alterations that would make the ship ready for its debut at the Exposition.

"We are going to make a real splash!" she crowed. Tuppence croaked a response that she took to be congratulatory.

"Splash?" The paleness returned to her father's visage and he lunged for the ropes again. "Are we over the ocean?"

Helen looked over the edge. They might well be doing forty-five knots now. She wished there were a more accurate way to measure the progress of the ship. It was one thing to try to be as accurate as possible, but she didn't want to consider that she might underestimate the speed in the interest of fairness and not *over*estimating the speed.

"We're just coming up to the coast, Papa. Look there!" She pointed down to where the North Sea's grey waters joined the land.

Her father did his best to struggle over to the side of the ship and, Helen found herself impressed to observe, steeled himself to look down below. His grimace showed that it was an effort, but by and by, he relaxed his grip on the edge of the gondola.

"It all looks so far away." Her father's voice had a tone she had seldom heard before. It was wonder.

Helen smiled to herself. This was proving to be a most diverting trip. "It is relatively far. you know." She crossed the gondola carefully balancing herself as had become second nature now. "From the barns to the top of the fields. A good gallop even on Belial."

Her father looked at her with an expression Helen found hard to read. There was a certain puzzlement in it, but something else too. It might have been a kind of astonishment.

Something changed. Helen looked up. The sun had gone. Well, not gone, but it had disappeared behind a bank of storm clouds that were looming before them.

"*Signore*, I think you might want to take us down a bit lower," she called across to Romano.

"*Si, si, signorina*," the pilot shouted back. "I see the clouds. Very bad. I think there is lightning."

"What's so bad about that?" Her father crooked an eyebrow up, looking quite strong now that he had got his stomach back. "I can take a little hullabaloo now."

Helen laughed but the sound came out a little harsh. "We're not concerned about the bumps, Papa."

"What is it then?"

"The lightning!"

"I don't understand," Helen's father repeated. "Surely this thing is weather ready." He looked up to the ceiling of the gondola.

"That's not the issue, Papa," Helen said, peering into the clouds as if she might be able to divine the path of the storm and its ferocity.

"Well, there can't be much rain getting in here." He patted the railing as if to reassure himself of the strength of the conveyance.

"But *signore*, the lightning," Romano repeated. "Very bad."

Rochester began to pace around though his steps remained tentative. "I don't see how, it can't really get in here, surely. It's not going to be attracted to a big balloon."

"Dirigible," Helen corrected automatically, then stopped short to look at her father. "You do realise all the machinery is metal, of course."

He stared at her, blinking, and then turned to gaze at the engine assembly.

Helen tried to remember any other time that she had rendered her father speechless, but was unable to recall a single instance. This day would have to be filed away for special mention in her journal.

If they survived the day, that is.

Tuppence croaked and finally succeeded in lighting on Rochester's shoulder. The bird's presence was enough to irritate him back to normalcy and he waved the bird away with a few explosions of cursing.

Helen threw a look back; the Lintons were no closer and she smiled with satisfaction. Come what may with the storm, there was a great deal of satisfaction in proving the superiority of her ship.

"Can you take us lower?" she called to the pilot.

"Not until we're over the last rise," Romano shouted back.

The moors offered an impassive and forbidding face. Helen knew they would be heartless if the ship came too near their rough surface. There was nothing to do but hold steady at this level and hope the winds did not shift them too much.

"Aren't we a bit too near the ground?"

It seemed a bit odd to have to be reassuring her father so often. Helen experienced another surge of confidence and wished her mother were here, too. "We are trying to keep below the storm, Papa."

"The winds are bringing the storm in from the sea," Romano called out. "They're slowing us down some."

Helen looked back at the Lintons' ship. They would feel the winds no less than they and should be accordingly slowed. But they seemed higher in the sky now.

"I think they fear coming too low," Helen muttered. Glancing down, she saw that the rough surface of the moors lay like strange animal below them, the rough verbiage clinging tightly as if fearing to lose purchase on the rocks.

"Are we too low?" Her father seemed galvanized once more by the nearness of the harsh land below them.

"We'll be fine as long as we keep a good distance between us," Helen said trying to throw some cheery confidence into her tone. "The winds may buffet us a little as they pick up, but we have plenty of room between us and the rocks."

At least she hoped it was still enough. As they approached the summit of Beacon Hill, Helen realised her body had become rigid, braced for disaster. Leaning over the edge of the gondola, she estimated that they had not slowed much though the ground had become much closer.

"Easily fifty yards," she called over to her father who had been making his own survey of the situation.

"Is that enough?" He did not look up.

"It will have to be," Helen said simply. Tuppence landed beside her and made some clicking sounds. She reached out to the bird and stroked the smooth feathers of her neck.

A sudden gust of wind lifted the ship and then dropped it precipitously. Helen grabbed the edge of the gondola and Tuppence lifted off into the air again. The raven circled around the ship, calling loudly.

"See there," Helen said as the ship's path smoothed once again. "Plenty of room yet, we're in no danger."

The words had no more than left her mouth when a loud clap of thunder erupted near to them and shot out a bolt of lightning. For a moment Helen found herself blinded by the glare and felt her fingers dig into the railing.

"That was close!" she squeaked in alarm.

"Perhaps we should land," Helen's father said, the words tripping out a little too quickly. His voice sounded odd, as if slightly strangled in his throat. He gripped the railing of the gondola with both hands and his knuckles were white.

The rushing of the wind and the murk of the clouds conspired to make the scene a trifle nightmarish. They were no longer a good fifty yards above the perilous rocks; more like thirty.

Helen bit her lip. *There was plenty of room yet, surely.* "Signor Romano, what do you think would be best?"

Romano shook his head as he fiddled with the controls. "Too risky!"

"Because of the wind?" Helen's father shouted, his tense voice signaling the need to argue.

"No, *signore*," Romano said. "We are moving much too quickly and landing on this uneven surface could be quite dangerous."

"We just got the ship repaired from the last disastrous landing," Helen shouted across to her father as the wind tried to steal the words away.

"What the devil—?" He shouted back. "Do you reckon our lives less than this bloody machine?"

"Papa, don't swear."

"If there is a time for swearing it's when your daughter is trying to kill you by means of a damned airship,"

Rochester muttered, though he knew his daughter would not be able to hear the words.

Before he could formulate a more genteel inquiry, another bolt of lightning struck, blinding them all momentarily.

Helen fluttered her eyelids to remove the afterimage, then shook her head. A quick glance around the gondola did not reveal any damage.

"All right then?" she called to Romano.

"Nothing's on fire," he said which was something of a reassurance.

"Papa," Helen called, turning back to her father, "Are you—" She stopped and gazed dumbstruck.

"What?" her father barked, trying to decipher the look on Helen's face.

"The lightning hit very near."

"Doubtless, all the more reason we ought to—why are you smiling?"

Helen tried to smother the laughter that threatened to pour forth from her throat. "Nothing, Papa, I—"

"Out with it!"

Signor Romano turned and at once cried out with laughter, doubling over and slapping his knee.

At that outburst, Helen found it impossible not to laugh as well, though she tried to muffle it somewhat with her hand.

"What are you two idiots laughing at?" her father demanded, shifting his gaze back and forth between the two of them.

The hair, always unruly and rather long, had apparently picked up a charge from the lighting strike. It stood out from his head like the prickles of a thistle. To add insult to injury, Tuppence reappeared and added her voice to the general cacophony as if she too were laughing at the sight as she circled the airship.

Rochester raised a tentative hand to his head and felt the effects of the static energy. He glowered at his daughter and somewhat more effectively at the Italian.

"The devil take you all," he muttered as he tried to flatten the unruly hair into some kind of obedience.

"Papa, never mind," Helen said, "It's really a much greater concern than your hair." She had to swallow a smile once more. "Our best bet is to keep low, otherwise we stand an even greater risk of lighting, which could be destructive in all kinds of ways."

"I understand that, but if we were to land—"

"We'd be in even more danger."

"You're not just saying that to try to win the wager?" Her father seemed to have regained some of his humour now that he was calming his hair once more.

"No, although I want to teach the Lintons a good lesson," Helen replied, throwing a glance back to her competitors, "There's no need to—oh my heavens!"

"What?" said her father as he turned to look behind them.

Helen gasped. Her hands flew to her face in a helpless gesture of alarm. Even the pilot turned to gaze at the spectacle behind them.

The last lightning strike had apparently hit the Lintons' ship. Smoke rose from the gondola. The twins waved their arms about and while Helen could not hear the words of their shouts, she could doubtless guess at the nature of their sentiments.

"Good heavens!" she said to her father, who had stalked over to her side of the gondola to get a better look. His hair had calmed somewhat, but Helen smothered another impulse to grin because a wild lick of hair at the crown of his head stood up like a hayrick despite the wind.

"What the devil are they going to do?" her father demanded. "Shouldn't they land?"

"That might be best, but they're in the same position as we are."

"More dangerous to land," Romano agreed, taking a quick glance at the controls over his shoulder then turning his attention back to the Linton's airship. "There could be an explosion. Poof!"

"Shouldn't you have your hands on the controls?" Rochester barked at him.

Romano glared at him. "I can manage the ship just fine."

"We're awfully near the ground."

"Papa, let Signor Romano do his own driving."

"Thank you, *signorina*," Romano muttered with a curt nod.

Helen smiled back but noted that they were rather precipitously close to the ground and began edging toward the controls as she kept her eyes on the Lintons. Tuppence landed beside her on the gondola's edge and began to croak at her.

"Hush," she said, but the bird continued to chatter away at her as if it had something to say. "Go make yourself useful," Helen said at last. "See what's happening over there."

Tuppence took wing and headed toward the Linton's ship.

"Witchcraft," Rochester muttered under his breath, although loud enough for his daughter to hear clearly. "Just like your mother."

"Tuppence is an intelligent and well-trained companion," Helen said, still keeping an eye on the distance to the ground below. "It's no more witchcraft than your ability to communicate with Belial."

Her father murmured something she couldn't quite catch. His gaze returned to the Lintons' airship.

The black smoke billowed around the balloon's semi-rigid frame and flowed up into the sky leaving a perceptible trail in its wake. Helen leaned forward trying to see through the increasing blackness and the rain.

There was no doubt: flames licked the edges of the gondola in the rear. They were small yet, but doubtless they would spread.

"Shouldn't they land now?" Helen's father asked again. "They don't seem to be slowing at all. What the devil are they doing?" he squinted over the distance. His sight wasn't very good at the best of times and in the murk of the day and over the space between them he seemed to find it difficult to make anything out.

Helen took a quick glance down. Much too close! "*Signor...*"

The pilot looked over his should and smiled. "*Signorina?*"

Helen nodded down. Romano looked over the edge of the gondola and his eyebrows shot up. He rushed back to the controls and started the ship on a more accelerated climb. Helen gave her father a quick look but his face was still screwed up trying to see what the Lintons were doing.

She moved closer to him. "They seem to be trying to put the fire out."

"Naturally," her father said dryly. "Imagine that."

Helen smirked. "They don't seem to have anything at hand to do so, however."

"Damned foolishness!"

"Well, they obviously didn't think about the possibilities."

He looked at her with a frown. "Are you prepared for such an occurrence?"

Helen pointed to the buckets of sand lining the back of the gondola. "Just in case."

Her father gave her one of his rare smiles. "Clever girl." He looked up at Romano. "Are we going back up?"

Helen nodded. "The risk of lightning seems past—" An explosion halted her words.

"Heavens!" Helen said. Black clouds billowed up from the gondola of the other airship and the flames quickly became so sufficiently large that even her father could see them clearly across the murky distance.

"What the devil are they going to do now?" Her father's look grew dark. "Have they perished in that conflagration?"

Helen craned her neck. "No, I see them waving the smoke away. I can't tell if they're all right, but they're still standing at least."

"What's that now?" Her father pointed toward the Lintons' ship.

"Ah, a rope. They're going to try to land or else slide down away from the flames. Wisest thing to do."

Her father snorted. "I suppose I should be grateful that you've at least thought about the likelihood of having a fiery end. Not that it hasn't been tried before," he added, a grim smile on his face.

"Oh, Papa!" Helen felt a stab of pain. "I'm sorry, it never even crossed my mind—"

"No matter," he said gruffly, keeping his gaze focused on the black clouds of smoke.

"It's extremely unlikely," Helen added with obvious haste. "They're using a highly volatile assembly: a combustion engine and whale oil."

Her father gestured toward the motor at the back of the airship. "What sort of contraption runs this one then?"

Helen grinned. "I thought you'd never ask about it, Papa! It's a modified version of Jedlik's dynamo, with electromagnetic self-rotators. Quite ingenious really, if I do say so myself."

He raised his eyebrows in mock surprise. "And what does that all mean in the Queen's English?"

"It means we use magnetism rather than a burning fuel. We're far less likely to have any kind of fire, although with heat, friction and a wooden frame one must be prepared."

Rochester folded his arms. "Were you always this clever?"

"Yes, Papa." Helen laughed. "Have you never noticed?"

"I suppose I may have suspected it now and then. After all your parents are both very clever people. But I'm not ruling out the possibility of witchcraft being involved."

"Papa," Helen said, shaking her head. The Lintons were descending now by means of the rope, two blackened figures swinging in the air.

"Well, isn't that why you want to go see that charlatan?"

Helen looked at her father, genuinely puzzled. "Charlatan?"

"Oh, magician, charlatan, mountebank, whatever the devil he is."

"I have no idea what you're referring to, Papa."

Tuppence landed on the rail of the gondola and croaked, flapping her wings. Helen walked over to her. "The engine overheated, didn't it?" The bird nodded and flapped its wings again.

"Will it explode again?" The bird turned her head at an angle and emitted a number of clicking sounds.

"For god's sake, what does all that mean?" Her father made an indistinct clicking sound of his own.

"She's not sure." Helen found the sight of her perturbed father scowling at the raven highly amusing. He would likely not appreciate her telling him that they looked like a drawing from an alchemical text. The thought triggered a smile but also brought her a realisation. "Papa, did you mean Signor Maggiormente?"

"That's the one. Some French magician isn't he?"

"Papa, you know he's Italian."

"A friend of this one?" He jerked a thumb toward Romano at the controls.

"No, but he is a very respected alchemist."

"But why do you need an alchemist?" Her father waved toward the motor. "Magnets you said. No chemicals, eh?"

"The motor is very heavy. Think how much faster we could go if we had a chemical powered motor. And little risk of explosion, too."

"I suppose that might help. What about goblins? Don't you get goblins with alchemy?"

"Oh, Papa!"

This intellectual disagreement evaporated when a shout from Signor Romano interrupted. "*Signorina!*"

"What is it, *signor*?" Helen called turning away from her frowning father to face the front of the ship. The dirigible had returned to a safer height now that the storm seemed to have moved out to sea, so she did not expect they were in any kind of danger.

"Goblins," her father muttered, but Helen ignored him.

"Are we getting to Whitby?"

"*Si, si, signorina*, but look." Romano nodded off the starboard side.

Helen leaned over the railing to look down as Tuppence landed on her shoulder once more. "Heavens!"

Down below there was a crowd gathering, some on foot, some on horseback. They could have been drawn together for any reason, Helen supposed, if it weren't for the fact that many were pointing up at the airship.

"What do you suppose they want?" Romano asked.

Helen thought she heard a tone of worry in his voice. "I'm sure they're just curious to see the airship. There aren't that many around here."

"Everyone's seen your airship," her father said, squinting uselessly down at the crowd below. "Even in Whitby."

"I don't know about that, Papa."

"Well, if they haven't seen it, they've heard about it from other people. How many are there?" he asked, gesturing toward the general direction of the town.

"Not so many, maybe twenty or thirty people."

"Do they look agitated?"

"Agitated?" Romano said, his face taking on a look of agitation itself. "Why should they be agitated?"

"Indeed, Papa. Why do you say that?"

"No reason," but he frowned. "They're not carrying torches, are they? Or pitchforks?"

"Good heavens, Papa. What are you on about?" Helen looked down at the crowd more carefully. They seemed peaceable enough, although they were indeed pointing at their ship.

"Goblins get people riled up."

Helen shot a glance at him but he had that distracted look that meant his thoughts were somewhere else altogether. "There's no such thing as goblins, Papa."

He gave a harsh bark of laughter. "You weren't raised in Thornfield Hall, or you would know better. More things in heaven and earth, my girl."

"*Signor*," Romano broke in, "I suspect they only want to help the other ship. Perhaps they are gathering to rescue the men *singéd* by the fire."

Helen spirits brightened. "I'm sure that must be it! They're only trying to assist the Lintons. They saw the smoke and came to offer aid. How kindly people can be."

Tuppence croaked and flapped her wings. Her father snorted. "Kindly! Do they look like a group of rescuers?" The ship drew closer to the knot of people and Helen had to admit that they didn't look all that cheery.

"Perhaps not." Helen bit her lip. "Shall we go up higher?"

Romano turned back the to controls. Without noticing, the ship had begun to sink lower as if anticipating a meeting with the crowd. "If they are not keen to see us—"

"Well, I don't really know." Helen leaned further over the railing. *Did they think we had something to do with the fire*, she mused. *We're known to be competitors, but surely no one would assume that of me?* Aloud she said, "Perhaps we'll just sail over them and wave as if everything were all right."

"Everything is all right," her father said, although the rumble in his tone suggested that were not entirely true. "But you can't get the mobs to believe that sort of thing."

Indeed even from this distance, they could hear shouts and murmurs from the crowd. Helen raised her arm and sent Tuppence out on reconnaissance. The mood of the mob appeared to be darkening as she watched. "What on earth could that be about?"

Her father shook his head. "You won't like what I will say."

She looked at him, an eyebrow raised. "Why? What are you going to say?"

He laughed. "Goblins."

Helen looked down. There might be less peculiar reasons, but she couldn't think of one that fit.

4 POETRY

"Well, that was a surprise," Signor Maggiormente said, nonplussed.

Eduardo removed his paws from his ears. "Did you say something?"

"Indeed. I said 'that was a surprise.' *Uffa!*"

The lion sat up. "*Ti sta bene!* You go too far. You know the explosive properties of linseed oil. We saw it all too clearly with those painters."

The alchemist threw up his hands. "Where will progress come from if not through risk? We must press on." He poked in a desultory way at the charred spot on the table. "I need new beakers."

"You need a lot more than that," the lion added, raising itself once more to a dignified position.

"Oh yes, my evaporating dish is completely obliterated." Maggiormente shook his head with disappointment, as if the dish had somehow proved substandard. His rumblings about the failings of French alchemists were about to be doubled.

"No, no—I meant that you need to change your tactics!" The lion glared. If you have not seen a Venetian lion glare, you have not felt the full weight of scorn it casts upon the unsuspecting individual. Something about the amber lights in the eyes—which often seem to shoot out from the softer brown behind them—lend an extra weight of censure to just such a look.

The alchemist, however, accustomed to receiving such looks at a greater frequency than most human beings, did not quail. In fact, he did not actually notice it, as he was preoccupied with reliving the steps of the experiment in hopes that he could discover the flaw in sequence that had led to this latest explosion.

"Hmmm?" was all he managed to utter, turning to look at the big cat as it ruffled its wings in annoyance.

"I said you need to change your tactics. I think this linseed oil avenue is simply a diversion. You've been exploding or burning things for days now with no discoveries of any useful nature."

Maggiormente narrowed his eyes to look over at the lion. "In the process of discovery, one must hope for benefits that reveal themselves later. This is not the simple mechanics of mathematics!"

Eduardo yawned. "Mathematics have far greater subtlety than mucking around with oils and unguents."

"You are simply prejudiced."

"Math tends to be less lethal as well," Eduardo added, raising a censorious eyebrow toward the charred table.

"The price of research—" The alchemist's comments were cut short by a peremptory knock on the door. The two exchanged glances. An observer might have commented on the guilty look in those glances, but there was none to see it save the nightingale asleep in its nest on the ledge outside the window.

At last Maggiormente sighed and walked over to the door to throw it open. Doing so revealed the grim figure of their concierge, Mme. Gabor. "*Signora!*" he cried, doing his best to sound pleased to see her.

"*Monsieur*, things cannot go on like this!" She fluttered into the room in a cloud of tobacco and cherry scent, her surprisingly trim figure as always a mismatch to her rather seedy appearance: overly kohled around her bloodshot eyes, too much rouge. "My other tenants, how they complain!"

"Pardon, *signora*. It is the nature of science…"

"But the noise, the smell! I cannot turn my other tenants away! What will I do? Enter the poor house? Surely a wise man like you can understand." She batted her ringed eyes at him.

"Ah…" Maggiormente found himself without further words as the concierge once again squeezed his arm with undue familiarity. The fascination she found with that part of his anatomy stumped him.

"They are all threatening to go. What am I to do, monsieur? If my house is empty, I will be bereft. You can understand." She leaned her rouged cheek upon on his arm, still held captive.

"Ah, *oui…madame*. But science—she has demands, too."

"Oh, perhaps, perhaps. She is a cruel mistress, is she not? How you suffer!" Actual tears appeared to well up in her eyes.

"I suppose," the alchemist responded, stuck for an answer.

"Well, perhaps you can persuade me to let you stay. I can be so easily persuaded by one like you," she added in a whisper.

Eduardo growled. The sound was not loud, but Maggiormente knew what it meant. "*Signora*, I think I had better clear up this mess." He struggled to extricate himself from her surprisingly powerful grasp.

"Oh, *monsieur*! You must persuade me," Mme. Gabor purred. "Do try. I am certain we could come to some kind of, ah, arrangement…"

"Good heavens, look at that smoldering wood!" The alchemist pointed somewhat nervously at the table as he tugged away from vise of her fingers.

71

"Forget the experiment, *monsieur!*" Mme. Gabor batted her not inconsiderable lashes at him.

"Eh, I—what?" Maggiormente looked to Eduardo for help, but the lion merely continued to glare and growl under his breath while flexing his wings.

"Forget the experiment! Come down to my flat and we can talk over some very good cheese from Normandy and a fine bottle of Bordeaux that my *cousine* gave me."

"Oh, erm, I—that's, ah…" The alchemist stumbled over his thoughts as she tightened her grip on his arm.

"*Monsieur,*" the concierge murmured, laying her rouged cheek once more upon his arm. "You are a man."

"Indeed." Maggiormente's eyebrows furrowed as he pondered this seemingly obvious statement.

"And I am a woman."

"Also true." He heard Eduardo's growl deepen slightly.

Mme. Gabor looked up at him and smiled. "Must I draw a diagram for you, monsieur?"

"That might be helpful indeed," Maggiormente said, his gratefulness evident in the explosion of breath behind it. "I find diagrams most helpful when I am sorting out a problem."

She blinked at him and then burst out laughing. The alchemist blinked at her in return with a vague and uncertain smile on his lips. He found himself relieved that she let go of his arm to cover her own face as she guffawed helplessly.

"Oh *monsieur*, you are like a babe in the woods!"

"Erm, yes, I suppose so," Maggiormente said uncertainly. "But I really must clean up this mess now, madame, or we might be in for a fire." It certainly seemed the safest route to pursue, he sensed. A danger to the house might outweigh her other mad obsession.

Mme. Gabor frowned at the table which indeed still smoldered. "I suppose you could be right, *monsieur.*"

"Of course he is," Eduardo said with a snap of his jaws at the end for emphasis. Then he turned sulkily toward the window, considering whether to wake up the nightingale. *No one should have to suffer this alone.*

"Well, yes, it would be for the best…"

"I must go retrieve more sand," the alchemist blurted, grabbing for his hat and scarf and tromping toward the open door.

"Of course, *monsieur*," Mme. Gabor called after him, "But I expect once you have completed these various safety measures to come to my flat. We have so much to discuss."

Only inches from a clean escape, Maggiormente reflected as he paused in the doorway. "*D'accord, madame.*" He squashed the hat down on his head and wrapped the scarf around his neck as if a condemned man. "*Au revoir.*"

Mme. Gabor watched him go with a very catlike grin upon her face. Eduardo regarded her with suspicion from his perch by the window. Things were not at all going according to his liking.

"I don't suppose you have any cakes," Eduardo said morosely.

"I don't normally allow pets, you know," she said apropos of nothing.

"*Buon giorno, signora*," the lion said with all the coldness he could muster.

She turned to regard him, still smiling but there was a return of his coldness. "*Tout à l'heure, Monsieur* Lion." Mme. Gabor laughed again and walked out the door, closing it behind her.

Eduardo lay down with his chin on his paws. There must be many other flats to let in Paris, even for an alchemist and his Venetian lion. They rented to painters after all; surely alchemists were tame in comparison.

"This will not end well," Eduardo said to no one in particular, though perhaps the nightingale had awakened. "He cannot dodge her forever. Of course we could simply blow the building up before that happens." He decided to reflect happily on that thought.

Maggiormente hastened down the stairs and out into the street before drawing breath, as if the sound of his aspiration might be enough to call the *signora* to follow him. Determining that she had not in fact followed, the alchemist slowed his steps as he considered what to do.

Anything but return for her desired *tête-à-tête*!

He was not entirely certain how interested she truly was in his person, but it was beginning to look like *very*. Maggiormente frowned. He did not return her interest. And Eduardo would not much like it if she continued to express her insinuations.

There's so much work to be done! The alchemist shook his head. He did not need interference from anyone at present, particularly from his concierge. How awful to have to consider moving! But if her importuning did not end, it might have to be considered.

Maggiormente had stopped as the horror of the thought occurred to him. Although his original plan had been to get some sand from the river, and indeed his footsteps had taken him down the gentle slope in that direction, his intruding worries had pushed all thought of sand from his mind and he could not immediately remember where he had been bound.

"*Monsieur alchemiste!*" a voice called from nearby.

Hearing himself hailed, Maggiormente turned although the thoughts in his head continued to buzz like bees in a hive. "*Sì?*"

A young man in Bohemian garb waved a desultory hand at him, beckoning the alchemist to join him at the café where he sat. "Come, share a glass with me!"

"Gustave!" Maggiormente's face lit up and the buzzing thoughts subsided like the banked embers of a fire. He walked across the way with eager steps and clasped the offered hand in his two palms. "You have returned to Paris!"

The young man in the rumpled suit nodded, a broad grin brightening his unremarkable face with its uneven growth of beard. Only his twinkling eyes suggested there might be something more to the figure than one of another in the horde of young Bohemians still crowding the Paris cafés.

"I could not last long in the countryside, *monsieur* Maggiormente. I am not suited to the genteel life of the farm."

The alchemist threw himself down in the seat opposite his friend. "Ah, but the country is free of distractions. You must have got much writing done."

Gustave sighed. "Alas, no."

"But surely there was much to inspire you?"

The poet sighed even more dramatically. "Inspiration? Cows? Hayricks? Trees? Wheatfields? Bah! No one could find much in that."

The alchemist laughed. "I think there are many painters who might disagree with you. Pastoral novelists, too. I think there may be a poet or two who found much to immortalize in the countryside."

Gustave rubbed a hand over his face as if to erase the memory of the green. "Bloody Romantics! Don't give me your western winds and burbling streams. I want people, noise, shops, *tavernas,* galleries and fights. City life, monsieur. It is the only true inspiration. And no city is like Paris."

"Ah, but have you been to Rome or Venice? You must see Rome before you die," Maggiormente scolded.

"Gladly, gladly," Gustave said with a vague wave. "If this life does not kill me before I have the chance. Philippe! A glass for my friend." The waiter brought the glass and the poet filled it to the brim before handing it over.

"Oh, no, just a little," Maggiormente said, frowning at the glass. "I still have much work to do——" He broke off, wondering if he would be able to get any work done while his concierge lay in wait for him.

"Nonsense! Drink up! *Santé!*"

"Well, perhaps a little respite…"

The alchemist sipped the wine, grimacing a little to find it overly sweet. All French wine seemed a trifle sweet to him. He missed the bold Tuscan flavours that his local café in Rome favoured, and as soon as he thought of that, Maggiormente could almost taste roasted artichoke and felt a stab of homesickness flick his heart. To distract himself as much as anything else, he asked his friend, "And now that you're back in Paris, have you been writing much?"

Gustave smacked his forehead with an open palm. "Not one wretched word! None! My ink has dried up. My pages mock me. My quills have flown away."

"But you are in the city you love, full of noise and cafés and arguments."

"There's just one problem."

"What's that?"

"I'm in love!"

Maggiormente laughed and clapped the young poet on the shoulder. "In love? Why, that's wonderful. It should lend wings to your inspiration."

Gustave sighed noisily, eyes closed. "No, no, it is terrible!"

"Terrible! But why?"

The poet downed the rest of his wine and filled his glass again. "Because it has rendered me mute!"

"I don't understand," the alchemist said. "Love is a wonderful thing, surely?"

"Not when it's unrequited!" Gustave raised his hands skyward as if to summon an angelic witness. "Then it is purgatory."

"Ah, my poor friend," Maggiormente said, a hand over his own heart protectively. "Tell me everything!"

"Where   to   begin?"

The alchemist smiled. "The beginning usually serves best. Where did you meet her?"

Gustave sighed, slugged down more wine and then sighed again. "I met her at Nancy in the Place Stanislas."

"Where is that?"

"East of here, in Lorraine. I passed through on my return from the family estate."

Maggiormente raised an eyebrow. "So this just happened, eh?"

"Just happened!" Gustave shook his head. "I have spent an eternity in agony."

"But since when?"

"Thursday," the poet admitted.

Maggiormente threw back his head and laughed.

"A lifetime! I burn in hell every hour."

The alchemist tried to smother his mirth. "Tell me how you met her."

The poet closed his eyes, presumably the better to visualize the moment. "I was walking along the square in the dazzling midday sun—not a propitious time, you understand."

"Of course not." Maggiormente had no idea why not, but thought better of asking for an explanation at this early point in the narrative.

"But there she was! Sketching the statue in that glaring light. Her every line bespoke genius. The world did its best to live up to her skills. The morning's rain had left puddles on the stones that shone like crazy diamonds."

"Poetry," Maggiormente muttered.

"Love," the poet corrected him.

"I meant your description."

Gustave waved his hand, dismissing him. "Her hair was abundant and a golden fiery red, warm as a winter fire, bright as persimmons. Her eyes large and green— emeralds! And her lips—"

"Her lips as rich as plums!" Maggiormente suggested.

Gustave glared at him. "Plums?! Don't be ridiculous. Barberries!"

"What is a barberry?"

"Crimson berries that grow on thorny bushes, difficult to harvest but sublime in flavour."

The alchemist sipped his wine. "I'm getting hungry now."

"Forget your stomach!" the poet admonished. "I'm trying to tell you about love!"

"Well, what did you say to her?"

"Say to her?"

"When you met, what did you say to her?"

The poet cried aloud, standing on his feet and gesturing once more skyward. "Are you insane, monsieur? A vision like that? I could not decide if she were woman or goddess. I was speechless before her beauty and grateful I had been granted such a glance at perfection."

"So, you didn't speak to her?"

"No." The poet collapsed in his chair once more and poured out the last of the wine. The alchemist sighed.

"I think the first thing you must do, my friend, is speak to her," the alchemist said at last while the poet continued to mutter quietly to himself.

Gustave looked up, eyes wide. "But I have!"

Maggiormente gaped. "You did? Then what—?"

"Oh, it was a disaster, *mon ami*." Gustave buried his head in his hands again.

The alchemist swallowed a smile. "I'm sure you're simply exaggerating, or rather," he added hastily, "considering it to be worse than it was. Surely!"

The poet sighed. "You won't say that when I tell you what happened."

"Go on, then. Tell me—it can't be *that* bad now, can it?"

Gustave took a deep breath. "Well, I wandered distraught for some hours, lost in my thoughts. Rapturous! She was a vision. At last I realised I must return to the same place and see if I could glimpse her beauty again. I stayed in Nancy that night, sleeping in the park because I knew no one. I had to see if she were real, if her beauty were as compelling on the second sight."

"And was it?"

Gustave struck his heart with his closed fist. "Of course! She was exquisite, an angel, a vision, a goddess." He closed his eyes, a rapturous look on his visage.

"And?"

"And what?"

"Did you speak to her this time?"

The poet sighed again and shook his head while he waved toward the waiter. "Philippe! More wine!"

"Is that a good idea," the alchemist asked, eyeing his friend's flushed features.

The poet waved his concerns away. "There ain't no cure for love, as the poet says. We must only endure it."

"But how much simpler it would be if you simply *spoke* to her just then!"

"Ah, I don't know about that, considering what happened."

Maggiormente raised his eyebrows. "What did happen?"

Gustave covered his face with his hands again. "I awoke at dawn. If the daylight had not roused me the gendarme would have certainly done so. My entire body felt stiff, my fingers and toes cracked in agony. A chill had settled in my bones."

"Not propitious for love."

Gustave snorted. "Nonetheless, I set out for the square, certain that she had to return, my vision, to complete her picture. No artist could abandon a work with so much promise."

"And she did not disappoint?"

"Of course not! She was there by eight o'clock. Her work had delicious life, her hand worked unerringly to capture the shadow and light. One might only wish for a model that more adequately suited her skills."

"Indeed," Maggiormente agreed, pouring more wine from the bottle that Philippe had brought. Both his and

Gustave's glasses were full again, though he suspected that the poet's would not long remain so. Indeed, his friend tipped his head back and swallowed half the glass. "What did you say?"

Gustave's expression fell again. "I knew I had to reveal to her who I was, what I was, so she would understand the depths of my love for her."

"That seems reasonable," the alchemist said, although he was beginning to have his doubts about what the poet might mean.

"She was so incredibly beautiful with the morning sun on her red-gold hair, her green dress and the soft sides of the artist's portfolio she carried. Even her brushes seemed to be in perfect form, the hairs abundant and soft."

"But—"

Gustave shrugged. "I could not be a liar, after all."

"A liar?"

"I could not pretend all was well if it was not."

"So?"

"So I offered a careful critique of her work. Who would not feel impelled to assure her that while in the main her sketch was terrific, there were some points that needed work? What?" Gustave looked at his friend with surprise. "What? Why do you look at me like that?"

The alchemist shook his head, chuckling. "You introduced yourself to the woman you love, this goddess, this angel—"

"I didn't say angel, did I?" Gustave frowned. "I don't want her to be *too* angelic."

"This woman you fell in love with, eh?" Maggiormente frowned, although he found it hard to hide a smile. "Your first words to her are finding fault with her sketch?"

"The perspective was a bit off." The poet shrugged. "What? Criticism helps improve your art."

The alchemist laughed. "Is that why you were so happy with the critic in *Le Figaro*?"

"The fool! He knew nothing of rhyme!"

"And what do you know of sketching?"

Gustave stared at him. "What are you saying?"

Maggiormente shrugged. "I'm guessing your goddess did not respond well to your words of criticism."

The poet covered his face again. "She was livid! She called me names a beautiful woman should not know."

The alchemist pondered for a moment what sort of words those might be, but then turned his attention back to his friend. "As a first impression, criticism may not have been the best avenue to pursue. You should establish a friendly interaction before provoking a hostile one."

"Do you think so?" The poet pulled at his moustache and stared morosely off into space, then reached for his glass and downed the rest of his wine.

"Of course, of course."

Gustave buried his head in his hands. "I'm ruined! She hates me! I will die of a broken heart!"

His muffled words made plain his distress, but Maggiormente had to bite his lip not to laugh at his friend. "There, there." He patted the man gingerly on the shoulder. "Perhaps you can ameliorate the situation."

The poet sniffed and raised his head. "How?"

The alchemist spread his hands. "What are your strengths?"

"What?" Gustave blinked at him.

"What are your strengths?" He repeated. "What do you do well?"

"I can recite the alphabet backwards while standing on one leg…"

Maggiormente guffawed. "Poetry, you fool!"

The young man gaped at him, than laughed and clapped him on the shoulder. "Why of course, of course! I shall write an epic poem detailing how my love has gone awry, I will make people weep and beat their chests—"

"Ah, *mio amico*! That's not what I meant at all." Maggiormente shook his head in disbelief. "You need to change her mind and show her that you are more than just

81

a critic."

"But I was right about the perspective—"

"Would you rather be right or in the arms of your goddess of the red-gold hair?" The alchemist raised his eyebrow at the poet.

Gustave beat his own chest. "My goddess! I must have her!"

"Then write to her! Beg her forgiveness, praise her beauty and her skill."

"But—"

"Do you want to be in her favours again?"

"Yes, of course, a thousand times, yes!"

"Then pour your heart out in a letter, a poem and get it to her."

The poet's face looked sunny again. "Do you think it will work?"

Maggiormente shrugged and sipped his wine. "'Love comforteth like sunshine after rain.'"

It was the poet's turn to raise an eyebrow. "You have surprises, Maggiormente, that I do not expect."

"That is the nature of surprise." The alchemist grinned and drank his wine.

Gustave reached into his satchel and pulled out a much-stained notebook. He took another swallow of wine, then opened the notebook to a blank page. The poet began to rummage through his pockets while the alchemist looked on.

"I have a pencil here somewhere," he said as he continued to pat his clothing. At last he located the object in his breast pocket and looked at it with something akin to surprise.

Maggiormente pushed away his nearly empty glass. "I should leave you to your labours and get back to my own."

Gustave looked stricken. "No, *mon ami*! I need you here!"

The alchemist frowned. "Whatever for? I don't have a poetic bone in my body." He threw his arms wide as if to demonstrate the fact, nearly striking the passing waiter in so doing.

The poet threw up his hands. "Look how far you have taken me already. I would still be in the depths of despondency if it were not for you."

"But love," Maggiormente shrugged. "I know nothing of that art."

A desperate look lit his face. "But that is what I need! Your clear-eyed wisdom. Love as alchemy, a volatile compound."

The alchemist laughed. "I don't know any thing about love, my friend. If I can help somehow, I suppose I shall." He sat down once more and reached for the wine. If he had to assist the poet, surely more wine was a necessity. For a moment, Maggiormente thought with guilt of the Venetian lion back at the work room. Eduardo would be displeased to be longer neglected.

On the other hand, Eduardo tended to do as he pleased, so there was little to worry about. He would doubtless amuse himself.

"I suspect you will be very helpful as I try to compose. It's wonderful to have someone to bounce the ideas off, as it were." The poet ran his fingers through his hair as if to stir up some thoughts.

"Well, how do you usually start?"

"I have a theme—"

"Well, you do."

"Yes, but," the poet paused. "It's not a visual theme."

"You need to see groveling?"

"I'm not groveling."

"You need to grovel." Maggiormente nodded sagely. "You need to grovel a lot."

"I need to show her why she is so important to me, why I had to ask her to seek perfection in her work."

"I think you ought to steer away from any attempt at corrective observations until you have actually convinced her to listen to you."

"Good plan." Gustave put the pencil to the page, then paused again. "So…what should I write about?"

"How about her…eyes?" The alchemist frowned in thought. "They burn like the sun."

"No, no," the poet also frowned. "Her eyes are nothing like the sun…"

"Well, what colour are they?"

Gustave sighed. "Green like the moss deep in the forest, like a wet glen at the bottom of a wild waterfall."

Maggiormente nodded. "Yes, yes. That's good."

"Do you think so?" Gustave but the pencil, screwing his mouth up into a bow.

"Yes, of course, of course. Write it down!"

The poet stared. "But—"

"You can always change it afterward, but it's important to get the first impressions down."

"Do you think so?" The poet repeated.

Maggiormente made an explosive sound of annoyance. "If you don't get down these raw thoughts at the start, you lose the magic. It's important to capture the rich pearls of inspiration—even if you rub most of them away."

Gustave stared at him open-mouthed. "Is this alchemy?"

The alchemist shrugged. "Doesn't poetry work the same way?"

The poet sighed. "When it does."

Maggiormente laughed. "Now, now—you mustn't give in to despair. You've only just begun."

Gustave grinned weakly.

"Have you written down the eyes yet?"

Dutifully the poet scribbled away. "I added limpid, too. That's a good word."

The alchemist found his grasp of French struggling against its limits. "What does that mean?"

"Pellucid," the poet said, a far away look in his eyes.

Maggiormente raised one eyebrow. "I am no closer to understanding. It must be something different in Italian."

"Clear, undimmed, without obstruction. Her eyes were green and limpid."

The alchemist coughed. "Well, I suppose ocular health is important."

The poet winced. "It's not about her health, it's about the clarity of her eye colour. Its perfection."

"Ah." Maggiormente considered this for a moment. "At least you consider something of hers to be without imperfections."

"I am doing my best to remain on a flattering path. But what more about her eyes?"

"Perhaps you should move on from eyes. What's next?"

"Off the top of my head, I'd guess perhaps lips."

Maggiormente frowned. "Haven't you written love poems before?"

"Well—" Gustave looked sheepish. "I have…for other people."

"But not for yourself."

"No."

Maggiormente grinned at his friend, who looked suddenly pink. "That makes this so much more important, *amico mio*. You must go with the truth. From here," he added, thumping his chest with a fist.

The poet rubbed his chin. "Hmmmm."

"So what did you notice first?"

Gustave closed his eyes. Maggiormente supposed he was remembering every detail of the encounter. At least the poet's face showed a flickering montage of expressions as his eyes moved under their lids. At last they flicked open and he stared at his friend.

"Her hair!"

"Perfect. Her hair was red, yes?"

"Fiery." He wrote the word down in his notebook, then frowned at it. "Perhaps that's too strong." Gustave looked up at the alchemist. "She could take that the wrong way."

85

Maggiormente considered the issue. "Is there another word that conveys the excitement of the flame yet sounds less...combative?"

The poet mused, tapping the pencil against his teeth. "Incendiary?"

The alchemist nodded encouragement. "A word for the colour? Red? It seems too mundane. Is there something more, ah, poetic?"

"Crimson? No, inaccurate." The poet looked skyward as if he might pluck a word from above. "Not red, not brown, in between. There's a word for that..."

"Burnt sienna?" Maggiormente suggested, remembering his encounter with the painters.

"No, auburn, that's it!" He wrote the word down hastily as if it might escape before he did so. "What's this 'burnt sienna'?"

"I just learned it recently, in fact I was thinking of making my own range of burnt colours but it took so long to find someone who knew what the sienna was that could be burnt, so I got distracted because there was this linseed business that I was hoping would prove a useful fuel source but so far it has not provided more than explosions, which I'm afraid have not been easy to control."

Gustave blinked at him. "Perhaps I should go with auburn."

The alchemist frowned. "But she is an artist. Perhaps she would appreciate the knowledgeable reference to her expertise. That would be a good thought, surely."

The poet grimaced and ran a hand through his hair again. The wild tumble suggested confusion. "This love is a perishingly difficult business, my friend."

"Agreed."

"Perhaps you should talk about something other than the colour," Maggiormente suggested as his friend stared forlornly at the page on which he had scribbled with animation only moments before.

"Its texture?" The poet squinted at his friend while he sipped some more wine.

"Did you actually feel its texture?"

"No."

Maggiormente stifled an eruption of irritation. "How about shape? That offers a chance to employ some, ah—sensual detail."

The poet's face brightened. "*Oui!* Curves, curls, tumbling down…" He bent over the page again, scribbling furiously.

The alchemist downed the last of the wine in his glass and poured more of the bottle into Gustave's glass. The poet seemed to be operating under his own steam now. "I shall leave you to your task," Maggiormente said as he rose to his feet.

"Hmm? Yes, yes," the poet muttered as he continued to scratch away in the notebook. "Bountiful, yes, that's good, yes."

The alchemist smiled and turned away. It seemed his friend would not notice his absence now. While Maggiormente pitied his friend's struggle, he knew that the poet would be up to the task for certain. Now that his muse burned brightly, there would be no stopping him.

The alchemist started to walk away from the restaurant, raising a hand to wave farewell to Philippe and then wondered what direction he ought to head. He had been wandering in the general direction of the river in hopes of retrieving some sand, but now he wondered.

What was he doing?

It was an important question that had a lot more to it than geography. What was he going to do? What if they had to move?! Oh, that was a thought too horrible to countenance. The problem of the concierge was a complicated one. However, he had every confidence that ignoring the problem was likely to make it go away.

Surely problems always went that way?

The alchemist walked toward the river. Even if he

didn't really care about the sand anymore, it would offer him a good excuse. He pondered the options before him. Either he gave in to the concierge's interest or he struck off in a new direction.

Sadly, a new direction might mean a new location—just when he had arranged his workshop so neatly. The alchemist sighed. Surely it wasn't possible; his concierge wouldn't make him move just for—

Just for what?

Maggiormente pondered. Did she really have the kind of madness that the poet exhibited? No, he was sure not. But then again, what did he really know—about her, about the situation, about any of it?

Not much!

The alchemist frowned. It wasn't so much that he dismissed the attentions of an interesting older woman. In fact, he couldn't think of much that would be more gratifying. However, his concierge's interest didn't seem to be so much in him as in the uses he could provide.

Which rather made him feel like a prize chicken and not a human at all. *I should go back to the house and rescue Eduardo.*

After a moment, the alchemist retraced his steps and bent them toward the familiar steps of the little hotel. Initially he had been pleased to find it as accommodating as he had imagined from Rome, where tales of the Paris bohemians traveled.

Who knew the concierge would offer an interesting twist of her own?

When they had come from Rome it seemed to be everything he had wanted: spacious, slightly remote, with a non-residential feel to it that promised plenty of elbow room for experimentation. They had had a few breakthroughs that gave him hope.

And Eduardo liked the number of pigeons. He was sadly consistent in that.

It needn't be like this, Maggiormente told himself. But

then he pondered the concierge again. She might disagree with that.

"I do need sand," he said aloud, but then bent his trails back to a more classical approach. *Perhaps I ought to be checking on Eduardo. We can explore the sands together.*

The alchemist reversed his path. Concierge or no concierge, he was going to be brave about this. He returned to the flat to discover unexpected quiet.

"She's gone out." Eduardo sat with his paws neatly together, drawn up to his tallest seated position. He even had his fez on.

Maggiormente looked around the room. It seemed entirely empty of occupants apart from his familiar. "I see."

The Venetian lion sighed. "No, she's gone out of the house."

"Ah." Even better that. Maggiormente sat down and contemplated his table of beakers, cylinders and unguents. It would be a lot to have to pack up and move, he realised. They had gotten rid of the crates in which they had brought everything from Rome. Then there would be a cart to arrange as well.

Suddenly he felt very very tired.

"We don't have to move," the lion said, looking a little too pleased with himself. He stretched his wings out to their full size and then folded them back down again.

The alchemist looked at him with an eyebrow raised. "What?"

"I said, we don't have to move anymore."

"We did before?"

"You were thinking it."

"True enough. So why don't we have to do so now?"

Eduardo grinned, showing his big teeth. While the alchemist was very accustomed to this display, many were understandably intimidated by the gleaming choppers, a fact Eduardo chose to be aware of only some of the time. "I solved our problems with the concierge."

The alchemist had a momentary image of the lion eating the poor woman, but doubtless he would be lying down to digest a meal of that size and he was looking far too alert and pleased with himself for that—which was a relief to say the least.

He was not pleased with Mme. Gabor, but he would not wish her to become Eduardo's supper.

"How did you solve our problems?"

"I reasoned with her." The lion looked even more smug now, shaking his mane to emphasize his pronouncement.

"How exactly did you do that? You worry me, Eduardo."

His familiar barked with laughter, which seemed an entirely unsuitable sound for a lion to make. "What can I say? I made her an offer that she could not reasonably refuse."

Maggiormente did not like the sound of that. "What sort of offer? Did this involve pigeons?"

"Only as an example," Eduardo said with a small growl.

"Eduardo!"

"What? She was trouble—and it was only likely to get worse. You need to work. I need to eat. It's a fairly simple equation." The lion coughed and a couple of pigeon feathers wafted out of his mouth onto the floor.

Maggiormente considered the situation. "Well, I suppose anything is worth not having to move again."

"And the pigeons are really fat here." Eduardo licked his paw as if a taste of his feathery meal remained there. "We need to get back to work before the Exposition, *piccolo mago*. It's just around the corner after all."

"And I have nothing to show for it!" The alchemist threw up his hands. "The linseed oil has gone nowhere. I need sand. What if I should be working with magnetism after all?!"

"I think steam more likely to be effective for air travel.

The locomotive is the model to follow after all. More certain."

Maggiormente shook his head. "No, the answer lies in alchemy. A chemical reaction that will take the place of inefficient coal. If not linseed, some other fuel from which I can release its explosive powers."

Eduardo huffed. "More smelly fluids."

The alchemist waved his hand, a faraway look evident in his eyes now. "The secrets to efficient air travel lie hidden in the smallest elements. I must delve deeper and explore the unseen world." He stroked his beard, lost in thought now.

The lion burped. Another feather floated down to the wooden floor, but the alchemist failed to notice its fall.

"I must review my Hitchcock, and perhaps Madame Atwood, too," Maggiormente muttered.

Eduardo laid down and rested his head on his paws and almost immediately slept.

5 MURMURATION

"I told you it was goblins," Helen's father said with smug satisfaction as he threw himself into his favourite chair.

Her mother raised her eyebrows. "Goblins? Really?"

Helen rolled her eyes. "Of course not. But the folks in Whitby have complained about the proliferation of airships over their fair town and claim it is impeding the tourist trade."

"A fair assessment?"

Helen warmed her hands in the fire. "Unfortunately, I'd have to agree, especially after the Lintons' extraordinary conflagration."

"What the devil did they expect?" Her father growled from the depths of his chair, waking Cerberus who had been sprawled at his feet. The great black beast whined and tried to nose his master's hand onto his skull for a patting. Rochester looked down and gave the dog a rough tousle. "Do they think people are going to come just for the ruins of the abbey or to walk up all those infernal stairs?"

"Papa," Helen scolded gently. "People have long been drawn by the beauties of that fishing town. It's romantic."

Her mother laughed. "You know your father has no sense of romance."

"The devil you say!" Her father said with an aggrieved air. "I'm far more romantic than your mother. She bewitched me. I was helplessly besotted."

The witch in question only smiled at her husband. "Am I to be accused of witchcraft anytime I do something you don't anticipate?"

"Yes." Cerberus whimpered and Rochester returned to scratching the dog's ear.

Helen felt a spasm of irritated impatience even as she smiled at her parents' wrangling. "So I think I will fly down to Dover and then over to Paris."

This had the desired effect of startling her listeners.

"Is that wise?" her mother said.

"The devil you will!" her father said.

"It's quite safe. If anything, today's flight demonstrated just how much so. Despite the problems Signor Romano and I were well-prepared for the encounters and we succeeded in the face of all opposition," *and possible interference*, she thought to herself.

"I won't hear of it!" her father protested.

"Papa, you can't forbid me. It's my ship."

"You brother might have something to say about that."

Helen frowned. "I owe him the funds, not the ship. He will never realise his investment until I prove the worth of the vessel."

"Why do you have to go to that infernal land of frogs?"

"Weren't you once partial to that glittering city?" Helen's mother asked her husband who merely muttered something unintelligible.

Helen sighed. "Papa, I've explained. I need to work with Signor Maggiormente. The alchemical-powered engine could revolutionise the entire history of flying machines. But we have to work together. We need each other's expertise."

"Well, why can't he come here? We could find room

for yet another Italiano."

"He's in Paris for the Exhibition. I can't ask him to leave. Papa, I mean to go. This is the goal all my work has been leading toward. I can't wait any longer."

"We understand, darling," her mother soothed. "We're just concerned for your safety."

"And to have you gallivanting around with Italians! Can't be trusted, that much I know. Worse than Frenchmen." Her father scowled from the depths of his chair.

"Isn't that why we agreed you would accompany me?" Helen could not keep a smug smile from her lips as she delivered that *piece de resistance*. "I will be properly looked after and you will get out of Yorkshire for a while."

"I must have been drunk. Surely I never agreed to such an infernal plan. You're a witch like your mother."

A light in his eye suggested that he was not quite as averse to the idea as he made it seem. Helen decided to press the issue. "Papa, you know I won't feel entirely safe in a new country without you there to protect me."

Her mother laughed. "Now, you're overdoing it. Pretend to be put out a little while longer and he'll come around." She sat on the arm of her husband's chair and put her own arm around his shoulder. "Isn't that true, dear?"

"Witches," he muttered. "A fine pair of witches. Doubtless there will be all manner of goblinry, too. It's bound to be a fiasco of a journey."

"Madame?"

Helen's mother looked up from her husband's face, still smiling. "What is it, Mrs. Hitchcock?"

"Mr. Fairfax has arrived."

"Oh dear," Helen said.

"Now, Helen," her mother scolded gently. "I'm sure if you start out irritated you will only get more so very quickly. Think soothing thoughts."

Helen laughed. "I will not ruffle his almighty

equilibrium."

Her father snorted. "Why the one child of mine who has become a success should be the cause of such consternation, I don't understand. Fairfax is a fine young man."

"He's an insufferable prig."

"Nonsense: he's a respected capitalist," his father huffed proudly.

"Exactly." Helen began to gather up the sketches and notes she had spread across the library table.

"Mother, father," Fairfax said as he entered the room, a portfolio under his arm. "Helen."

It would not be entirely accurate to say that the siblings were cool too one another. They were simply too much alike to get on well. Both had their mother's open, intelligent face and no-nonsense movements. They differed only in their zeal for opposing goals.

Fairfax had taken command of the family fortune with a zeal that approached the missionary. He had taken his degree from Cambridge and immediately embarked upon an aggressive plan for expanding their funds with the empire.

Helen, denied a similar opportunity, focused on educating herself with the extensive library her father had gathered and her mother had expanded. Suspicious of the same hierarchies that barred her from formal learning, Helen's character had developed with a scorn for all the conventional attitudes that fueled her brother's work and connections.

Consequently, they did not much understand one another.

At times like this, the clash between the siblings caused a good deal of friction. When one concentrated on holding onto existing benefits and the other on exploring the unknown, breaking new barriers and plunging into new horizons, there were going to be sparks.

And so they began.

"I've just been looking at our latest figures on the Leeds investments…" Fairfax began, talking directly to his father and bypassing the two women in the room. "They're not as strong as I would like them to be but I assume we can make some alterations to the schema that will keep the margins within reason."

"And hello to you, too," Helen snapped at her brother.

Fairfax looked at her mildly. "I'm sure we will have time to chat after Father and I have finished dealing with these matters."

"Oh yes, the matters far too complex for female heads to deal with!"

"I never said that." Fairfax frowned. "But you have never showed much interest—"

"And you have never bothered to include Mother or I in your calculations that manipulate the family finances without regard to proprietary or ethics."

"That's not at all true," Fairfax countered. "You will recall that my training in ethics at Cambridge—"

Unfortunately, any mention of that august institution inevitably resulted in further animosity from his sister. One might think the young man would have learned by now to avoid that controversial topic, but the truth was that he seemed to bring it up with tedious regularity. It would seem the young man remained short of skills when it came to understanding people.

"Yes, we're all well aware of the stellar education you received in the ways of the Empire, the ruthlessness of the capitalist, the slippery 'ethics' of the speculator…" His sister grew pink with irritation.

"I am not a speculator!" Fairfax seemed startled by the suggestion.

"Your schemes are legion." Helen's fixed expression seemed to suggest that his crimes were public knowledge.

"The only 'scheme' I could be said to be engaged in of a dubious nature," Fairfax said, eyes glaring with intense light, "would be funding your hideous machine."

"A marvel of engineering!" Helen said, her voice constricted.

"Now, children, please let's not argue." Their mother shook her head at them.

"I shan't say another word!" Helen said and prepared to depart.

"Now, Helen," her mother soothed.

"Hideous machine," Helen repeated. "He called my beautiful ship a 'hideous machine'!"

"I apologise," Fairfax said, "But you also accused me of speculating. I cannot allow my own sister to accuse me of speculation."

"All right, I'm sorry as well." Helen paused at the door, her hand on the knob. "You're just so infuriating all of the time with your highhanded ways."

"I don't know what you mean." Fairfax looked at her, wide-eyed.

"That's why it's so irritating!"

"What the devil does any of this matter?" Their father glowered at the two of them from the depths of his chair. "I don't need to hear this kind of wrangling from my children. I'd like a little peace in my own home!"

"Things will be quieter in France, Papa."

"France!" Fairfax said. "You're going, too?"

"Against my will," his father muttered. "We can't have your sister running around the land of frogs with strange Italian men on her own."

"You're secretly pleased I think, Papa." Helen laughed.

"I think perhaps Fairfax ought to go with you instead," her father said.

"What!" The two siblings spoke in unison with equal levels of horror. Their expressions gave no doubt about the unsuitability of this idea to both of them. It was only when they noticed their father's barely suppressed mirth that they breathed a sigh of relief.

"You're a very devil, Papa," Helen said, shaking her head in disbelief.

"I wouldn't be at liberty to go anyway," Fairfax added, his voice sounding somewhat nervous yet. He rifled through the papers in his portfolio. "This land matter alone will require a great deal of attention in the next few weeks."

"Not from me, I hope," his father said, apparently somewhat daunted by the thought. While he liked to think of himself as a cagey manager of his estates, he actually much preferred to leave things in the capable hands of his son. Most of their conversations consisted of his nodding in agreement.

It was a suitable charade as far as he was concerned.

"Well, if I must go, I suppose I shall have to reconcile myself to my fate," he grumbled.

Helen was delighted with the speed in which they had moved past the impossibility of the trip to planning its details. "We shall have to find a suitable place to stay in Dover and in Calais, where we can keep the ship nearby."

"I'm sure we can arrange something comfortable," her mother said, "though perhaps not as quickly as you might like."

"Can I bring Cerberus along as well?"

"No, Papa, there won't be room." Helen gathered up her drawings and plans, ready to head to her room for some thoughtful planning.

"We really need to discuss this Leeds plan—" Fairfax began, holding out a very daunting piece of paper toward his father.

His father ignored the paper. "Are you bringing Tuppence?"

"Of course!"

"Well, then I want to bring my dog." Her father folded his arms decidedly. The animal in question raised his head, as if aware of the debate. "It's only fair."

"Papa," Helen said, swallowing her irritation, "Tuppence is a bird and can fly beside the ship. Cerberus is an enormous dog and will take up too much room as well as being an unruly beast with no discipline."

"Unruly! He's a well-trained and magnificent beast."

"Papa, he doesn't even sit on command."

"He's sitting now."

As if he understood—and Helen reflected, it might be entirely possible that he did—Cerberus immediately stood up, wagging his tail gently as he looked at his master.

"Good dog." He patted his pet affectionately. "Well, what the devil am I going to do while you're pottering around with mountebanks and machinery?"

"You could look at some possible investments," Fairfax broke in.

"Hang me if I'll be working on my holiday!"

The laughter that filled the room came unexpectedly from Helen's mother. "Holiday? Well, there you are. Problem sorted."

Her father frowned. "What the devil do you mean?"

"It's a holiday. So that means you will enjoy yourself, you will not have to do any work, and you will leave Helen to manage her own work."

Fairfax looked disappointed. "Can we at least finalise the details on the Leeds project before you go off gallivanting across the channel?"

"Yes, yes, all right. But while I'm gone your mother will have to be consulted. And yes," he added with a smile that was perhaps a little too pleased, "You will probably have to explain some of the finer points to her."

"As I know nothing about the project," the mother in question added dryly.

"But she's got a great head for figures and far more sense than I have." As usual when he was complimenting his wife, Rochester's voice got gruffer as he went on.

Someone unfamiliar with him could easily assume that his tone indicated anger. His fire-ravaged visage recoiled with something that appeared to mimic pain, yet signaled something far different.

A fact his wife had long been aware of, naturally. She

crossed over to his side and sat on the arm of his chair. "You need to get away. It's been far too long since you've wandered further than York."

"I don't need to wander," he said, putting a rough hand on top of her smaller one.

"Perhaps not, but I think you will find that you do need to get out into the world a little and stretch those long legs of yours somewhere other than this library."

"It will be a terrific adventure, Papa." Helen added. "You will find many things to amuse you and cause all manner of trouble."

He made a rumbling sound that was not easy to interpret. "But I can't bring the dog."

"Papa—"

"Oh, all right." Though he frowned theatrically, both his wife and daughter knew he was pleased.

In the morning, preparations began. The days whirled past, chockfull of activity. Letter sent here and there, provisions planned and bought, weighed and stowed. Until at last the day awaited arrived. Helen hopped out of bed at an early hour, waving away her maid Edith's well-intentioned attempts to help her dress. "I will have to dress myself on this trip, Edith. Only simple clothes, things I can easily slip in and out of."

The maid tutted. "You make it sound positively indecent."

Helen laughed. "There will be no possibility of anything indelicate with Papa along."

"Oh, Miss Helen, he's going to be no end of trouble to you, I expect."

"Nonsense," Helen said as she rubbed a smudge off her favourite goggles. "Papa will lend a sense of gravity to the adventure."

"And to the gondola," Edith added.

Helen threw back her head and laughed. "The ship has plenty of lift. It won't be a problem."

She shared the comments with her mother and took an

excited farewell of her. Her mind was on the amusement and she was still chuckling when she headed out to the stables, never noticing her mother's unshed tears. Her father's voice rose in the distance, remonstrating with Thompson about some doubtless meaningful detail of Belial's maintenance in his absence.

"Not the common oats," he warned with severity. "The pressed oats with honey. Don't forget!"

"Of course not, sir," Thompson said. After many years he had become inured to the imperious demands of his employer and remained as phlegmatic as the elderly bay gelding he generally rode on errands. "The oats with honey."

"Mind you, don't *over* feed him. He can be a greedy beggar." Rochester thumped the huge stallion's neck affectionately and the horse nosed him just as roughly, forcing him to take a step back.

"Right, sir, not overfed," Thompson repeated.

"Papa, we really must get going." Helen pulled at his sleeve. "Signor Romano has the ship ready to fly."

"Yes, I suppose." He swung up on the horse as Helen climbed aboard her fat grey mare. "Did you say farewell to your mother?"

"Yes, of course. Did you?" Helen enjoyed seeing her father blush.

"Don't be impertinent. Let's go." Belial wheeled around and the two of them clattered off through the courtyard in the early morning light.

They rode up the slope toward the spot where the dirigible was tethered. It offered a peculiar image in the early light, floating like a low-hanging cloud above the heather and the rocks.

"My god," Helen's father said with feeling. "I can't believe I am trusting my soul to that infernal machine."

Helen dismounted and handed her reins to young groom who had been drafted to help with the send off. He looked rather nervous which may have had as much to do with her father's reputation as with his horse's.

"Mind you keep a close eye on this beast," her father said as he turned the reins over to the timid young man. "Don't let him rip your arm off."

If the lad had looked frightened before, now he grew quite white. "Yes, sir," he managed to squeak as he stared at the snorting black beast, who—sensing an advantage— pawed the ground with a theatrical sense of menace.

"Don't worry," Helen said with a chuckle. "He seldom eats meat."

The young groom did his best to smile and looked a little relieved. Helen turned to regard the ship. "All ship shape, *signore?*"

"All is well, captain," the Italian said, waving his bandaged arm at her. "Everything ship shape. We are ready to sail into the winds."

Helen checked the assortment of luggage stowed around the gondola. "What's that?" she asked pointing to a rather large case that had not passed her inspection.

Her father leaned over the side of the ship to follow her pointing finger. "That? That's my town wear. I had Dennison pack my best."

"Oh, Papa!" Helen snorted. "There's no need for that. Signor Romano, chuck that over the side, would you?"

"You wouldn't dare!"

"Papa, you are not going to have to dress to impress anyone in Paris. We are not hobnobbing with the *ton.*"

"I will have some business to engage with while I am there," her father said stiffly as he frowned at Romano as he struggled with the case. The young groom tried to lend him a hand after hastily tying the horses' reins to the nearby paddock's fence.

"Papa, do you wear these clothes when you conduct business here?"

"Sometimes…"

"Papa!" Helen scowled.

"Oh, all right. But don't blame me if I get snubbed in

Paris and we lose a fortune. I hear they can be pernickety when it comes to sartorial effects."

"If it comes to that, Papa," Helen said with a sharp look, softened somewhat by a smile, "We can buy you some new clothes in the City of Lights."

"Needless expense," he muttered.

"They would be somewhat more fashionable than your current wardrobe."

Her father stood up straight and stared at her. "I thought I brought you up to flatter your Papa."

Helen laughed. "I'm afraid we've failed then. Papa, you know it's unnecessary."

"Very well." He crossed his arms. "I know I'll feel the absence of that silk cravat."

His daughter ceased to pay any attention to him. "*Signore*, have we got the rest of the cargo distributed sufficiently well?"

The pilot stood upright once more examining the gondola. "We should be all right, *signorina*. If not, we should be able to shift things during flight." He looked over at Rochester with a dubious expression. "As long as we are cautious."

Helen ignored her father's snort of derision. "How do the seats seem?"

The pilot patted the nearest one with pride. "I think we will find them quite comfortable for the longer journey."

Helen's father leaned over the gondola. "Am I sitting on that?"

"Yes, Papa. We all are. At least when we're not busy with other duties."

"Duties! I thought this was a leisure trip."

"Maybe for you. I have work to do." Helen climbed over into the gondola. "Are you ready to come aboard, Papa?"

"Aye, aye, captain."

"*Buon giorno, signorina*," Romano said cheerfully as Helen and her father climbed aboard.

"How's your arm?" Helen asked, frowning at the sling on her pilot's arm.

"This? This is nothing." Romano waved away her concern. "The physician, he wanted me to take precautions. It is well wrapped. I have little pain."

"And your head?"

The Italian raised his cap to show her the bandage wrapped around his head. "Nearly healed completely, *signorina*. No real damage." He grinned as he dropped the cap down once more. "My head is quite hard, like most of my country men."

Helen laughed. "I am relieved to hear it."

"Shall I tie myself in?" Helen's father interrupted their exchange as he lounged in the chair Helen had indicated.

Helen raised an eyebrow at him. "It's not strictly necessary. If we hit some turbulent weather, you may be more inclined to make use of it."

"Shall we ascend?" the pilot asked, seating himself at the controls.

Helen looked around the gondola and nodded. "Yes, we're ready."

With a little bit of a shudder, the engine powered up and the flaps lifted, until the ship began to rise. Helen waved to the young groom, whose face bore a look of fear yet as Belial snorted in his face. Nonetheless the young man dutifully raised his hand in a farewell gesture.

A flurry of black feathers ruffled into the gondola. Helen's father cried out and waved his arms at the interloper.

"It's only Tuppence," Helen soothed.

"I wasn't scared," Rochester said gruffly.

"Of course not, Papa."

Helen inclined her head toward the raven. "Any news?"

The black bird croaked and ruffled her wings, then stepped a few paces along the length of the trunk on which she had perched.

"Well, I suppose it's just as well that we're getting an

early start," Helen said, nodding.

Her father exhaled noisily. "You can't claim that damn bird has anything intelligent to say." The two adversaries glared at one another.

"Papa, I rely completely on Tuppence's weather reports." Helen looked off to the west. "If she says there are storms coming in from the west, I know well enough to trust her advice."

Her father craned his head around as they rose higher into the grey sky. "I don't see anything."

The raven croaked again, but it sounded suspiciously like laughter. Helen smiled. "Of course not, it's a good way off yet."

Her father stared at the bird, who took his look as a challenge and hopped toward him, flexing her wings. "I don't like the way that bird looks at me."

"Look, Papa! There's mother waving. Do see." Helen leaned over the side of the gondola, waving vigorously at her mother and Mrs. Hitchcock who both stood in the garden looking up.

Her father gave over glaring at Tuppence to glance down at his home. "They look so very small." His voice sounded somewhat less sure than normal.

Helen looked over at his ravaged face and saw a hint of sadness there. He had not left Thornfield for some time. Despite his constant grousing, she couldn't help wondering if it were a bit difficult for him. "Look, Mother's smiling up at you. She's going to miss you so much."

Her words had the desired effect. His face transformed into its usual grumpiness. "Women, always trying to keep you tied to the hearth. About time I had some adventure." His eyes however betrayed a gentleness that belied his harsh words.

"We shall have wonderful adventures, Papa. And quite possibly make history."

"History?" Her father cocked an eyebrow at her.

"History! You didn't say anything about making history. I'm not sure I want to be written down in some dusty old books."

Helen laughed. "Whether you wish it or no, Papa, you may find yourself in its midst, if our alchemist comes through with his discoveries."

"That mountebank?" Her father shook his head. "Damned unlikely I think."

"We shall see, Papa." Helen waved one final farewell and then turned to her pilot. "Let's get on to that horizon, *signore!*"

The clear fresh air in the ascent invigorated Helen. She found a special thrill in lifting into the clouds. As the world fell away beneath them and the clouds drew closer, her heart swelled with an immense feeling of freedom.

"When do we eat?"

Her father's words jarred her from the pleasant reverie. "Papa, we've barely begun to ascend."

"My hunger is not dependent upon height."

Helen raised her eyebrow at him. "I merely meant that we have barely begun our journey, so if we eat now we will be eating food meant for later."

Her father huffed. "You have a conveniently ordered anatomy. I did not breakfast yet, so I want some food."

Tuppence croaked and flapped her wings. "Look, even your bird agrees with me."

Helen looked back and forth between the two of them. "I begin to suspect a conspiracy."

"A little nibble of something would not go amiss, *signorina,*" Romano called back from the controls.

Helen sighed. "Well, we have a variety of edibles in the hamper." She crossed over and flipped open the top of the wicker basket. "Cheese and bread all right with everyone?"

They enjoyed a simple meal as they passed over the moors toward the coast and the weather continued fair.

"We're lucky we don't have to sail over Whitby again," her father remarked as he threw a little bit of crust toward

Tuppence who caught it in her beak and settled down on top of a crate to devour it.

"I'm sure it would be fine, Papa," Helen said.

"Are we stopping in Grimsby?" Her father pointed at her with a finger that had a little butter anointing its tip. "I have never gone to Grimsby but once and I found it full of Liverpudlians for some reason. I am not certain that is always the case."

"Papa, we need to get down to Dover tonight if at all possible."

"What about Hull?"

"*Signorina*," the pilot called from the front of the gondola. "What is that?"

Romano pointed toward the morning's skyline. Helen narrowed her eyes to look into the rising sun. A large cloud drifted in a rather strange manner ahead of them. Its movements puzzled her.

"I thought your bird said the day was clear," her father said with a clear note of triumph in his voice before he popped another bit of cheese into his mouth.

"It is clear," Helen muttered, her eyes fixed on the growing dark shape. There was something familiar about it.

Her father had finally turned his attention to the mystery before them. "Are we near one of the industrial centers? Are there mills here?"

"No, Papa."

The cloud grew darker and began to twist and revolve in the air. The shapes of it became almost mesmerizing, Helen thought, as they mutated against the pale blue of the early morning sky.

"*Signorina*, shall we descend?" The pilot's voice carried a note of alarm.

Helen considered for a moment. "No, let's stay on course. Perhaps the cloud will go around us or we will simply pass through without harm. Surely it's—"

She cocked her head. An audible sound began to make

its way toward them, melding with the hum of the airship's motor.

"I don't much like the look of this," her father said. He glared off into the distance as if he could will the cloud away.

The cloud suddenly spiraled into a funnel shape then swirled again to form an oblong. The feeling of familiarity grew in the back of Helen's mind but she couldn't quite put her finger on it. It was the growing sound that pricked her memory. The racket had begun to drown out the motor's murmur.

That was it! "It's a mumuration," Helen exalted.

"A what?" Her father and Signor Romano spoke in unison.

Helen laughed and opened her mouth to explain, but suddenly the cloud was upon them. The black shape exploded before them and they were engulfed by the dark masses of loudly chattering little beings.

"What the devil!" her father shouted as they were immersed in the murmuration.

It was a cloud of starlings that engulfed the airship. There were hundreds, perhaps thousands in the murmuration—darting through space, swooping and diving through the air—but they had not expected to meet such a large object in their path.

The three humans instinctively ducked and wrapped their arms around their heads. A cacophony filled their ears.

The wings were disturbing somehow as they brushed their hair and limbs. The eerie feeling of feathers whispered against them, sometimes augmented by the thump of small bodies as the birds misjudged the path.

The worst had to be the beaks. The tiny little beaks were pointy and hard. One seldom gave thought to the fate of the caterpillars and moths who met their grisly end between the starling's mandibles, but it must indeed be gruesome, Helen couldn't help thinking.

She attempted to make her way toward where she thought her father had been sitting. Her progress remained slow. It proved difficult to know for certain what direction she was heading.

"Papa!" she cried.

No sound came but the cacophony of the starlings. Helen continued with determination, one arm over her eyes to protect them, the other outstretched, feeling for something solid.

The horrible racket! Helen recalled watching the black pools of starlings pulsing overhead as she stared up from the moors as a child. They were rare inland, usually only seen in the warmest months. Helen had never imagined being in the centre of that maelstrom.

She took another step and thought she had just heard a promising sound through the unceasing din. Moving carefully she thrust her hand into the storm.

From everywhere, tiny beaks and feet scratched her skin and feathers ruffled against her clothes. There was something unsettling about it. Unintentionally Helen began to dredge up from her memory some lines about a starling.

Who had written the lines? A German composer, she seemed to recall. Was it Mozart perhaps?

Hier ruht ein lieber Narr,
Ein Vogel Staar…

As she staggered through the cloudy cacophony, Helen tried to remember how the rest of the lines went. Snatches of words bubbled up as she fought her way across the gondola, rhyming pairs but not their context. *Todes bitter Schmerz,* which she was quite certain rhymed with *Herz* but there was not much more welling up from the memory banks now.

Her distracting ruminations gave way when she caught a shouted and incoherent phrase that had to be her father's voice. "Papa!" she cried once more, struggling forward further.

All at once a hand gripped hers and pulled her toward

him. Father and daughter embraced with relief.

"These devil birds will put us all in our graves!" He shouted even though their heads were very close together.

"They don't mean to do it, Papa. We're the interlopers here in the sky."

"Damnation! You didn't warn me there'd be such perilous effects."

Helen winced from a particularly sharp beak blow to her head. "Honestly, Papa, I had not anticipated this sort of quandary."

"You should have planned better," his voice rasped in her ear as he flailed one arm helpless against the horde.

"Papa, the odds of this kind of happening were miniscule—"

"So you did calculate the risks?"

Helen sighed and tried to ascertain whether it was just hope or if the sound of the murmuration were beginning to lessen. "At least now we have a new problem to solve based on actual experience."

"The problem could be solved by staying out of the sky!" her father barked.

She ignored him. "Listen! I think the worst of the flock has begun to pass."

The racket assaulting their ears continued, but it did seem to be growing somewhat less. Helen lifted her head from her father's chest and made a quick reconnoiter of the gondola. The swift black shapes continued to flit through, but it had become possible to see individual birds rather than just the black mass of bodies. A few unfortunates lay on the floor of the gondola. She hoped some of them were merely stunned from having run into the sides and the equipment.

Helen cocked her head anxiously, but the engine continued to hum on with blissful regularity. She sighed. That was a relief. But another though occurred that had her glancing quickly around the ship.

"Tuppence!"

Helen's frantic gaze swept around the gondola but she could see no sign of her raven. A pain stabbed her heart. She had had the bird since childhood, ever since she had found the fledging had tumbled beneath the towers of the old house.

With Thompson, the head groom, they had been able to return the small heap of feathers to the nest high in the blackened ruins, but the bird had remembered the girl's kindness and often flew down near her as she gamboled among the fallen stones and timbers.

Over time, the friendship grew apace and Tuppence began to follow her around and finally all the way home. While she would often fly away for days at a time in her younger years, the raven always returned. Eventually, she would not part from Helen for more than an few hours. The two formed an unusual bond. The raven appeared to regard Helen as her own particular pet.

Helen's father had named the creature whose croaking often seemed aimed at his grumbles. He didn't see why the bird should offer its tuppence-worth to every conversation, but after the outburst, the name stuck and Helen became more curious about the bird's language.

The mood of her speech she found simple enough to parse. The raven's animated body language also contributed to her understanding. Helen learned to appreciate the different croaks and clicks, whistles and whatnot. Amusingly the bird had learned to make a noise uncannily like her father clearing his throat, which irked him more than anything else.

Gradually she had discovered that Tuppence understood her better than she imagined, responding to questions and performing small tasks like finding her horse in the meadow or a good shelter for them both when they were caught out on the moors in a sudden gale. After many years the communication they took for granted still mystified others.

"A hundred years ago," Helen's father found it

amusing to claim, "They would have hanged you for a witch."

There were some in the town who regarded the pair of them with something approaching suspicion. It irked Helen who knew the close friendship between the two of them relied on careful observation and the repetition of patterns. Really, it was all about paying attention.

All very scientific!

But this ought to have been an indication of the further paths she followed. There were those who continued to think flying machines were somehow unnatural, who considered the very idea of human flight to be some horrifying kind of hubris.

Encountering these reactions, Helen had often been inclined—uncharacteristically—to agree with her father that the world had more than its required share of ignorant and small-minded people.

Unlike her father, however, she generally thought that they could be won over. Helen's hope was that pioneers of flight like herself (and, grudgingly she thought, also the Lintons) would make the idea not only acceptable but popular and one day flying in a dirigible would be no more unusual than riding a horse.

In fact, it would be far superior as ships could carry a much greater number of passengers than any horse-drawn vehicle. The whole of the future could open up before them with new opportunities for travel around the world!

Of course they would have to sort out little things like flocks of birds sharing the airways, too. Surely that was the nature of exploration.

But where was Tuppence?

Signor Romano occupied himself with brushing the little bodies and feathers away from the console. "Everything seems to be in perfect working order, *signorina*."

"Excellent, excellent," Helen said teetering across the gondola as a gust of colder air jostled the ship. "Have you seen Tuppence?"

"No, *signorina*."

"Papa, I don't suppose—"

"One of the damn things is in my pocket!" Her father threw the offending creature out of his hand. They were all surprised to see the little black shape unfurl its wings and swoop out from under the curves of the ship and disappear in the wake of its colleagues.

"I hope to never see another starling." Her father harrumphed as if to put an end to the issue. He looked a bit shaken however, and Helen thought something bracing might help.

"There's some brandy in the medicine kit," she said and her father flung the cover back immediately and grabbed the bottle by the neck. "Papa!"

He ignored her protest and drank a swig from the bottle's neck. "Best thing."

"Papa, that's enough."

"You want some?"

"No, Papa. *Signore?*" Romano shook his head and continued to clean feathers from the dials. "Well, I can't imagine what has happened—"

A familiar croak reached the gondola and Helen turned with a smile. "Tuppence!" The raven sailed in and perched on Helen's chair, shaking itself and clicking loudly.

"I bet the damn bird wants some brandy," Helen's father said with something approaching friendliness in his voice.

Helen rubbed the raven's chest feathers to reassure it, but Tuppence remained agitated. Her clicks and croaks demonstrated her displeasure as she ruffled her feathers repeatedly.

"What the devil is the matter with the bird?" Her father's words sounded more harsh than his voice. The brandy had certainly mellowed his mood.

"Papa, that's medicinal. I think you should save some of the brandy for an emergency."

He gaped at her. "If being consumed by a cloud of starlings isn't an emergency, I'd like to know what does qualify."

"Certainly fire or an explosion," Helen retorted.

"As long as we're clear on the issue." Her father harrumphed. "Here, give some brandy to that damned bird and calm her down."

"She doesn't need or want spirits, Papa. She's distressed about the starlings."

"As am I." He took another swig and stared down Helen's disapproval. "Wait, she's distressed in what way? She's not pitying those little blighters, is she?"

"No, Papa. She was in even more danger than we were."

"How so?"

Helen smoothed the shiny black feathers on Tuppence's head. "Have you never seen a flock of starlings go after a crow? They like ravens no better and they might well have turned on her, had they not been flummoxed by the unexpected meeting with the ship."

"So she pulled up sticks and legged it—or should I say, took wing—for her own safety. Pity she couldn't have warned us sooner."

"She tried, Papa." The raven croaked more quietly now.

"Well, what disaster shall we face next?" Helen's father at last put the brandy away, but he seemed to have retained its cheery effects well enough.

"It depends upon the weather along the coast," Helen admitted. "However, I suspect that the rest of our journey may prove free of disasters and even drama.

"I see nothing but blue skies ahead," Romano added from his seat at the controls.

"I don't know that I would trust such an assessment," Helen's father said, but he lounged idly in his chair, seemingly unconcerned for the moment.

As predicted however, the remainder of the flight

proved to be without incident. The day continued fine, clouding over once or twice but there was never so much as a drop of rain discernable. Even the winds were gentle, mostly helping to ease the ship's passage rather than fighting against it.

"I think I'd rather have a disaster," Rochester grumbled after awaking from an unexpected nap.

"Papa, don't say that." Helen scribbled in her log book, trying to recall the important details of the murmuration, searching vainly for clues to its formation in hopes that they could avoid such an experience next time.

This is what it meant to be a pioneer, Helen reflected, *paving the way and recording history as it unfolded.* A sense of awe filled her. It was an awesome responsibility.

Her father interrupted her thoughts. "I am finding air travel to be rather tedious."

"Papa, can't you enjoy the landscape?"

He folded his arms. "When I look over the side of the gondola I start to feel dizzy."

"Well, don't look directly down, as that will happen. Look out across the way."

"There ought to be some kind of entertainment to while away the hours."

"We could try fitting a quartet into the gondola next time," Helen said, closing her log with a sigh. "But I suspect we would find things a trifle crowded if we did so."

"I have a better plan."

His smile had a devious turn to it, so Helen assumed the worst. "Dare I ask?"

"I think sheep's or pig's bladders, filled with something noxious—"

"Aren't the original items already noxious enough?"

"You've never had haggis, have you my dear? Then we wait until we're passing over a small village and go low enough that we can bung them at the people passing below."

"Papa, I am doing my best to make air travel respectable."

"You're no fun anymore," he said, laughing heartily.

6 GENIUS

Alessandro Maggiormente examined the hole in the ceiling with some surprise.

"Did you expect that to happen?" Eduardo said, shaking plaster dust out of his mane. He gave a good flap of his wings, too. A little white cloud surrounded him.

"I did not. This is a very good sign." The alchemist rubbed his beard with satisfaction. There was somewhat less of his beard than there had been a few moments before and the remainder had a singed edge to it, but he did not appear to notice.

"I am not sure Mme. Gabor will agree." Eduardo curled his tail around his feet.

Maggiormente frowned. They both turned toward the door expecting to hear the sound of their concierge's feet tapping their way up the stair, but there was only silence.

"She must be away," Maggiormente said, waving away any concern with her opinion. "We need to test this in a proper way before the Exposition."

Eduardo raised one eyebrow. "How much more of a test is required?"

The alchemist laughed. "I know it has great power, but can it be contained? I shall have to see if it will make a useful fuel."

"Perhaps you should try that outside."

Maggiormente nodded. "I suspect so. I need some kind of engine as well."

"What sort of engine?" Eduardo stretched. He hoped it meant a trip outside away from the unpleasant smells of alchemy.

"Oh, any sort will do," the alchemist said. "Where do you suppose one obtains an engine?"

"Market?"

"Is there an engine market?"

"Perhaps there is an engine area of the local market."

Maggiormente considered this. "Perhaps there are shops that sell them. They must come from somewhere."

Eduardo got his fez. "Let's go looking."

"Ah, yes. We are sure to find some shop or market. Perhaps a cart or vendor in the streets." The alchemist patted his pockets, frowning again.

"What are you looking for?" Eduardo's tail lashed around him, his usual sign of impatience.

"Money. I am always mislaying this abominable French money."

"Let's go. I'm sure we can make some sort of arrangement with a shopkeeper." Eduardo headed toward the door.

"There'll be no cakes if I do not find some money."

Eduardo paused. "Have you checked the wardrobe?"

"Oh, here is my wallet!" Maggiormente retrieved the leather case from the depths of his coat.

"Cakes!" Eduardo bounced. It was an unusual sight. It is easy to forget that however large they may be, lions are yet cats as much as the familiar moggies we know to play with lengths of string or a ball of yarn.

The two of them bounded down the stair and into the street. It was another lovely day in Paris, a fact that had eluded the alchemist until now. He blinked in the sunlight. "This sun almost reminds me of home."

Eduardo sniffed the air. "But it doesn't smell like home."

A passer by stared at the Venetian lion and at the alchemist, too, then crossed hastily to the other side of the street. Most of the people in the neighbourhood had become accustomed to the sight of the large winged lion and no longer shrieked in alarm or ran away.

There were few, however, who welcomed the two of them. Most left a wide berth around Eduardo. Perhaps it was his very large teeth or maybe his rather long claws. Doubtless the growls he emitted when irritated did little to calm nerves.

Not everyone was unnerved by the large creature, however, and the piercing scream that filled the air now did not indicate alarm.

"Eddie! *Mon cher!*"

A small girl shot out of a doorway and wrapped her arms tightly around the lion's neck while vociferously cooing at him. Eduardo took this acclaim with surprisingly dignity and did not bite the head off the child.

"*Bon jour*, Brigitte." Eduardo had to gasp the words as the child continued to squeeze his neck a little too tightly. "Where's your papa?"

"*Charmant!*" Brigitte hugged the lion even more tightly. Eduardo's tongue hung out now as he panted.

"*Ma cherie,*" a stern voice called. "Let him go, you are squeezing him too tightly."

"Alain!" Maggiormente clapped his friend on the back as the two embraced. Eduardo shook his mane and used a paw to rub at the location of his tender assault while Brigitte cooed nearby.

"A glorious day in the city of lights, eh, Alessandro? Where are you two bound?"

"Ah, now that is a good question. You can assist us, I am certain, my friend." The alchemist clapped his hands together in anticipation. "Is there a motor market nearby?"

Alain Fabien raised his eyebrows. "*Mon dieu!* A what?"

"We are in need of a motor. Where does one buy a motor?" Maggiormente frowned. "I have not had to buy a motor before."

"What sort of motor?" The Frenchman rubbed his chin. "A big one, a little one?"

The alchemist considered this. "Any kind of motor would do, I suppose."

"Perhaps a small one," Eduardo intervened.

Fabien pondered. "Perhaps we can borrow one?"

"From where?"

"Can we return it safely?" Eduardo growled, chafing a bit at Brigitte's attempts to plait his mane into little pigtails.

"We just need to test our fuel," Maggiormente said with a shrug.

Fabien nodded. "Surely that won't be a problem."

"The hole in the ceiling says otherwise," Eduardo said quietly.

Fabien regarded him with one eyebrow raised. "That is another matter. Perhaps we should find somewhere for you to purchase a motor."

"Do you have an idea of where?"

"Yes, come. Brigitte, leave Eduardo's mane alone."

"Papa! May I ride on Eduardo's back?"

Fabien and Maggiormente looked at the lion, who flapped his wings gently. There was no telling with the creature. At times he saw everything as a slight to his dignity. But other days he was quite mild and accommodating. The possibility of cakes was often persuasive. He doubtless had in mind that Alain Fabien was a baker of some considerable talent.

"It will be all right, I suppose," Eduardo said at last. Brigitte shrieked and grabbed handfuls of his mane and struggled aboard his broad back between the wings.

"Can we fly?"

"Flying is undignified," the Venetian lion growled.

"I know a man who has repaired motors for the glass factory near here," Fabien explained. "If he does not have a motor to sell you, perhaps he will know where you can get one."

"That would be ideal. I need to test my new elixir." The alchemist stroked his beard with pleasure. Things seemed to be going well.

"Elixir? I thought you were working on a fuel." His friend frowned, puzzled.

"Oh yes, but it is so much more than that!" The alchemist swelled with pride. "This could be an incredible advance in the world, an explosive concoction—"

"Emphasis on the word 'explosive'," Eduardo interjected.

"You are too pedantic," Maggiormente huffed.

"Mme. Gabor will not be so pedantic when she sees the hole in her ceiling."

The alchemist waved his hand at this trivial detail. "Nothing revolutionary has ever been accomplished without a little collateral damage. It is infinitesimal in the grand scheme of things."

"You're not going to start a fire?" Alain Fabien looked rather nonplussed at the emerging details of the experiment. Most people were inclined to look askance at explosive endeavours.

"No, no, nothing like that," Maggiormente reassured him.

"Only the occasional explosion," Eduardo agreed while Brigitte cried, "Wheee!" on his back.

"Well, if it's only the occasional explosion—" Fabien grimaced.

"Oh, it's hardly to be noticed!" Maggiormente explained. "In a motor, such an explosion will be contained. It will only be part of the thrust of the engine. I am nearly certain."

"Nearly?"

The day sparkled. Some days in Paris have that special quality. It brought the painters out of their studios and into the streets and parks, it coaxed writers from their garrets.

As the friends walked along the boulevard, the alchemist, too, blinked at the unaccustomed light.

"It's a lovely day today," he said with some surprise to his friend Fabien.

The Parisian had known the Italian long enough to realise the significance of this utterance. He laughed. "How many days has it been since you set foot outside?"

Maggiormente shrugged. "Not so long, I don't think."

Eduardo snorted. "Three days."

The alchemist pondered this. "Are you certain? Surely it has not been that long."

"It has." Eduardo shook his head. Brigitte had begun plaiting his mane again. "I tried to get you to come out with me yesterday, but you wouldn't."

"I don't remember that."

Fabien laughed again. "I wonder that you remember to eat."

"Oh, I don't forget to eat. I am Italian after all." Maggiormente slapped his belly. "As my dear friend the poet Alessandra says, while you eat, you do not age."

"Very wise."

"Of course when he does decide to eat," Eduardo added with an air of smugness, "It's usually the middle of the night."

"That's when pasta tastes the best," Maggiormente said, but joined in his friend's laughter. "When I'm working on a new process, I cannot pay attention to anything else."

"That is the danger of alchemy." Fabien nodded as if to confirm the sagacity of this observation. Anything that interfered with regular meals surely had to be dangerous.

"The danger of alchemy," Eduardo said as Brigitte bounced up and down on his back, "is that sooner or later something will explode."

"*Sciocco*! You will make Alain think alchemy is something dangerous."

Eduardo looked up at the alchemist. "Are you trying to

say it's not?"

Maggiormente waved his words away. "Every employment has some kind of risk."

"I've never heard of bank clerks exploding their desks."

"Oh, it must happen sometimes—"

"Here we are," Fabien interrupted. They stood before a garage with a small sign that said only *Mécanicien Delon* in a small precise script. "Maurice! *Es-tu là?*"

A shout of '*oui*' resounded from within but the speaker could not be seen. The small group approached closer but could not see the man. "Where are you, Maurice?"

"Up here!" In the rafters of the garage Maurice tinkered with a pulley. "This infernal pulley seems to have developed a most irritating squeak and it annoyed me so much I had to fix it while I should have been working on something else."

"No hurry," Maggiormente said. Now that he had come out into the sunshine he found himself in no hurry to return to the smoky workshop that was his flat.

"I'll just be a moment, *monsieur*," Maurice said, wiggling the wheel of the pulley. "I think this bacon fat has done the trick.

"Mmmmm, bacon," said Eduardo, lashing his tail. Brigitte squealed with delight as the tip of the tail brushed her leg, tickling her delightfully.

"Bacon fat," the alchemist scolded. "Don't beg for treats."

"I never beg," Eduardo said with a sniff.

"No, you wheedle."

"What is *wheedle*?" Brigitte asked.

"Begging under another name," Fabien said with a laugh.

Eduardo narrowed his eyes and showed his teeth. "Wheedling is a dignified way of acquiring what one wishes to have."

"Sounds like begging to me." Fabien chortled.

"So what have you come to wheedle from me?"

Maurice said, swinging down from the rafters. "I assume you need something, eh?" He stuck out his hand to the alchemist.

"*Buon giorno*, I am Maggiormente."

"Delon. I have heard of you and your lion. What can I do for you?"

"I need a motor, *monsieur*."

"What sort of motor, *monsieur*?" Delon asked, hands open as if to suggest the wide world of possibilities that the word 'motor' conjured.

"A small one," Fabien and Eduardo said in unison. The baker slapped the lion on his back in a matey sort of way, which surprised the alchemist's familiar enough that he jumped a little. The child on his back shrieked with delight.

"More, more!" Brigitte cried.

Eduardo ignored this plea. "A motor resistant to explosion would be a plus."

Delon raised an eyebrow and looked from the alchemist to his lion. "May one ask what the motor will be used for?"

"Experimentation," Maggiormente said with evident enthusiasm.

Delon looked at Fabien. "Experimentation? He's not an anarchist, is he?"

The alchemist looked confused. "Anarchist? No, no, monsieur. I am an alchemist."

Delon frowned. "Is that some kind of a political struggle?"

"Magical," Fabien said.

"No, no, no," Maggiormente corrected. "Experimentation, science—I am working on a new fuel compound from alchemical reactions that will provide motors with greater propulsion than coal."

Delon looked impressed. "Such a thing would be welcomed by many."

"You would think," Maggiormente said. "Nevertheless, people seem reluctant to experiment with alchemical combinations."

"It must be the explosions," Fabien said, elbowing the alchemist, who did not appear to be amused.

"Explosions are rare," he said, frowning with disapproval.

"Only one this week," Eduardo agreed.

"Only one," Delon said. He exchanged a glance with Fabien.

"It was a very small explosion," Eduardo admitted.

"With a motor, we will be able to refine the process to avoid any further explosions," Maggiormente said. "The process has been theoretical up to this point. I desire to have this fuel perfected in time for the Exposition."

"It comes upon us," Delon said, looking thoughtful.

"Indeed. Thus my haste."

"What do you hope to power? Trains?"

Maggioremente smiled seraphically. "Ah, no—even better: airships! That is the secret you see."

"Secret?" Delon and Fabien exchanged another look. "Is it secret?"

"Oh, pardon my French," Maggiormente said, slapping his forehead. "I am not expressing myself quite right. The genius—is that what I mean?—the genius is to distill a fuel powerful enough and yet also very light, so it can fuel airships for long journeys."

Delon nodded his head, considering the idea. "That would change the machines for sure. Genius, yes, perhaps that is the word."

"Flying, bah!" Fabien laughed. "You couldn't get me up in one of those things. We were not mean to be like birds—your Leonardo not withstanding." The baker clapped the alchemist's back companionably. "What is it you always say, Eduardo? Flying, it's for the birds!"

Eduardo growled. "I have never said that."

"But it is true, *ne c'est pas?*"

"I have only said that it is undignified." Eduardo lifted his chin high, the picture of dignity—apart from the braids in his mane and the small child bouncing up and down on his back.

"So do you have a motor that might suit this?" Maggiormente asked.

Delon nodded. "I have a small motor that once ran a water pump at the linen factory near here. It wore out from constant use, but I have been restoring it."

Maggiormente rubbed his hands together. "That sounds ideal. How much?"

Delon sighed. "That is a very good question. There is the work I have put into it and the new parts it required, but there is also a very important question to ask you."

The alchemist raised an eyebrow, afraid what new question he would have to face next. Obtaining a motor had been far more difficult than he had anticipated. He was unaccustomed to answering so many questions about his work. "What is it monsieur?"

Delon looked him up and down before he asked with a grim expression, "You swear you are not an anarchist?"

Maggiormente clapped his hands together. He did not mind the question, although it seemed his countrymen were unfairly maligned with this charge. "Monsieur, I swear on the life of my mother and all the she holds holy that I am not an anarchist."

Delon looked at Fabien, who nodded. "You cannot be too careful, monsieur. There are many strange ideas in the world at present."

"Indeed," the alchemist agreed, though he had no idea to what the mechanic might be referring. When it came to politics, the alchemist was a bit like a child. His opinions tended toward fairness, respect and above all freedom for alchemical experimentation.

"As long as you are not an anarchist planning to create chaos with your explosions, I am willing to sell this motor to you," Delon said. He clapped the alchemist on the shoulder. "I would not want to have such a thing on my conscience."

"Nor I."

Fabien nodded agreement. "I have known Maggiormente for some weeks now and I can say he and Eduardo are most agreeable and only dangerous by accident."

Eduardo snorted. "I am dangerous on purpose."

The alchemist frowned at his familiar. "Yes, on purpose, but not often."

"And not to most people," Fabien agreed.

Eduardo raised his head a little higher. "I am selective."

"Indeed." Maggiormente was eager to change the subject before Eduardo began boasting of his exploits. The lion's inflated sense of his own dangerousness could fool less observant people. "This motor will offer a great chance to develop—"

"I once killed a duke," Eduardo began.

"Not a duke," the alchemist corrected.

"What is it he was then? Something like a duke."

"He was an alderman."

Eduardo sniffed.

"And he didn't die. He was rather frightened though." Brigitte crowed from the lion's back and bounced up and down as if delighted with the thought of startling a minor official.

"The pigeons did not survive."

"That is true. So, monsieur, the price?" Maggiormente and Delon haggled amiably for a bit and at last agreed on a mutually satisfying amount and exchanged francs for the motor.

"Well, what will you attach it to?" Delon asked as the alchemist tucked the motor under his arm.

Maggiormente stared. "Attach it to?"

"Yes, to test it you'll need to attach it to something."

"But I do not need to propel anything, just to see how the motor works."

"And what? Hold it in your hand while you fire it up?" Delon and Fabien both laughed, as much at

Maggiormente's puzzled expression as at his failure to see the issues at hand. "Monsieur, the motor will get very hot as it works."

"Ah," the alchemist said, enlightened.

"You could attach it to Mme. Gabor," Eduardo suggested. This provoked even more laughter, but Maggiormente did not join in.

"You are only making things worse, Eduardo." He frowned.

Delon disappeared into the depths of the garage once more and returned with a short wooden plank. "Let's see if we can attach the motor to this. It will offer some stability."

The mechanic and the alchemist bent over the plank and in a few minutes the motor had been secured to the wood.

"*Eccellente!* Now we shall go try it out."

Delon shook his hand. "Now, no explosions, monsieur."

"I shall endeavour," Maggiormente said with grave solemnity. "I think we are nearly there. To perfection!"

"Would you like to stop for some cake?" Fabien asked as they walked back toward the house.

"Yes," Eduardo said, provoking excited squeals from Brigitte. The truth of the matter was that the Venetian lion generally always found himself ready to stop for cake, whether any was on offer or not.

Brigitte simply enjoyed anything that involved Eduardo—and she likewise found the idea of cake exciting despite being the child of a baker. One might expect that familiarity would breed contempt, but clearly that had not happened to this girl.

"I don't think we should," Maggiormente said with a frown. With the motor acquired all his thoughts leaped ahead to the use he could make of it. "There is so much to be done."

"But cakes, " Eduardo argued. "We need cakes."

"You ate this morning," the alchemist scolded him. "Don't be greedy."

"Oh come now, it is afternoon already," Fabien said, throwing his weight behind the clear majority. "A little sustenance before you return to your labours cannot be bad, eh?"

The alchemist chafed at the delay. However, he was not without some sympathy for his friend and his familiar. "I suppose a little cake and some coffee would not be a bad thing."

His acquiescence inspired cheers from the other three who immediately dragged him through the door of the bakery. The inviting interior welcomed them. The heat from the oven created a good portion of the warmth, but it wasn't the only source.

"There you are!" Madame Fabien gave her husband a look of mock severity. "I had begun to wonder if you had run off with the *boulangereuse*."

Fabien leaned across the counter to greet his wife with an enthusiastic kiss. "I thought better of it. I knew I couldn't last five minutes without you."

The alchemist looked away, embarrassed as he always did at these public displays of affection between a man and his wife. It was one thing between men. That was natural. *I will never get used to Paris*, he thought, shaking his head.

"*Maman, maman!*" Brigitte ran around the counter to hug her mother's legs tightly. "I rode on Eduardo's back and we flew all around the city."

"All around the city?" Adèle Fabien raised an eyebrow at her daughter. "I am wondering if that is in fact true at all."

"It is not," Eduardo said, peering at the selection of baked goods with quite focused attention. When it came to cakes, Eduardo exhibited a rather unexpected earnestness.

It is true that cakes are a very serious matter.

"Brigitte, you are exaggerating again." Her mother shook her head and tousled the girl's hair. "You mustn't exaggerate so much."

Brigitte folded her arms and frowned. "I imagined it."

"Exactly, *ma cherie.*"

"If I imagined it, it could be real."

"There is some logic to that," Maggiormente said.

The others stared at him. Fabien laughed. Adèle said, "Is there, monsieur? I must admit I cannot see the logic."

"Can I have that cake?" Eduardo said, pointing at one covered in pink icing.

Adèle moved over with her knife poised. "You want a piece of this one?"

"Piece?" The lion blinked.

The baker laughed and brought the plate out for him.

"The logic," Maggiorment continued, noticing that no one had listened to his comment, "is the same one that animates my work."

"I am an alchemist?" Brigitte looked up with delighted surprise, flakes of her *pain au chocolat* scattered across her frock.

Maggiormente chuckled. "You are like an alchemist to be."

Brigitte considered this. "I am pleased. How am I so? I do not make things explode."

"One need not explode things," Maggiormente said, accepting a croissant from Adèle. "It is like the master wrote, 'What is now proved was once only *imagined.*' That is the true alchemy."

"This seems like philosophy," Fabien said frowning.

"Perhaps a little," Maggiormente admitted.

"That calls for wine!" Fabien and Eduardo cheered.

"Wine?" Maggiormente rubbed his beard.

"We cannot discuss philosophy without wine," Fabien said. His shrugged as if were impossible to debate the point.

"Ah, but there's this motor to consider." Maggiormente said, patting the motor which sat on the table before him.

Eduardo looked up from his plate, a smear of chocolate across his muzzle. "There will be time enough for the motor later. A little contemplation and discussion first will put you in the correct frame of mind to delve into its mysteries."

"And more cake!" Brigitte crowed.

"I do not think we need more cake," the alchemist said frowning at his familiar. Eduardo licked the plate, which no longer contained evidence of the cake that had been served upon it. Plenty of chocolate crumbs and pink icing remained on the lion's face. "I think we may safely say that the cake has been eaten."

Eduardo looked up. "There's no more cake?"

"There is no more cake for you." Maggiormente wagged a finger at the lion, who growled and shook his mane.

"I am full anyway," Eduardo said, sitting down on his haunches to begin grooming himself. He folded his wings demurely as he started licking his paw.

"Never mind, *mes amis*," Fabien said, returning with a bottle of red wine already unstoppered. "We have other matters to discuss."

"Oh, Alain, let the poor man get to his work!" Adèle tutted, as she picked up Eduardo's plate.

"Nooo!" Brigitte threw her arms around the lion's neck, starling him once again. "Don't make them leave!"

"*Ma petite*," her mother scolded, "Monsieur Maggiormente and Eduardo have important work to do. You cannot keep them from their endeavours."

"We're not in that much of a hurry," Eduardo admitted, struggling ever so gently to free himself from Brigitte's grip.

"You cannot go yet" Fabien said, grabbing a few glasses. "I have already opened the wine. We must drink." He began pouring out the wine and handing glasses out. His wife shook her head at him, but accepted the offered stem.

The alchemist took the wine but hesitated before sitting at the table with his friends. Maggiormente found himself impatient to get to work at the compound that he would test inside the motor, but there was also a doubt niggling at the back of his mind.

There is something I have forgotten.

But what could it be?

"Tell us more, Maggiormente," Fabien said after sipping his wine and nodding approval. "What's this business about airships?"

The alchemist clapped his hands together with delight. "The procedure may be a bit complicated…"

"Give us the highlights," Adèle urged, lifting Brigitte up on to her lap.

"I am the most important part of the process," Eduardo said. Without a chair to sit on, he decided to rest his chin on the edge of the table and pout. "Essential."

Maggiormente laughed. "Indeed, my friend, you are."

"He never does anything but eat," Brigitte said, looking severely at the pouting lion. "He eats everything."

"That's not all I do," Eduardo said with a noisy huff of breath. "I inspire."

"It's true," the alchemist affirmed.

"Does he help with the alchemy?" Fabien's brow furrowed. "Can he carry beakers?"

"No, nothing like that."

"I *might* be able to carry beakers," Eduardo muttered, returning to grooming his whiskers with one paw, licking the chocolate cake crumbs from it.

Adèle laughed. "I would not want to see him try to carry glassware." Brigitte leaned over from her lap to pat the lion's head. Apart from the ruffling of his wings, he did not seem to mind the continued attention.

"I would not expect it of him. The compounds can be rather powerful smelling and it would hurt his sensitive nose to have to inhale them too closely. So, that is not how he usually helps." Maggiormente paused.

At times explaining his work to mundane people was too much trouble to be bothered with. However he had already become rather fond of the baker's family and accustomed to being surrounded by a large family—even if most of the time they were all engaged in their own pursuits—Maggiormente found not at all taxing to explain things to them, though always a little difficult to explain it in their language.

"Eduardo's help," the alchemist continued after a little thought, "comes from the ineffable."

"Where is that?" Fabien asked. "Near Napoli?"

"No, no," Maggiormente laughed. "From beyond our ken."

"Ken? I don't know him," the baker said, frowning as his wife chuckled.

"*Mon cher*, he means that Eduardo connects him to the ether, to the great beyond." She smiled down at Eduardo. "Is that not true, *mon petit?*"

The lion drew himself up to his full height and flapped his wings lightly. "Precisely. I am a mystic connection."

Both he and the alchemist seemed taken aback when Fabien laughed at this. "Ah, monsieur, you do not believe in these fairy stories, do you? I am a rationalist."

Maggiormente raised his hands in a helpless gesture. "What is irrational about the ineffable?"

Fabien chortled. "My friend, the very concept is irrational. Give me what I can taste, touch and see."

"That's a very limited outlook," the alchemist said, tutting.

"Limited!"

"*D'accord.* The master has shown the way once again. He says this vegetable world is but a mere shadow of the real and eternal one."

"Ah, but monsieur, there is no world beyond this one." The baker held aloft his glass of wine. "This is real." He took a sip. "The taste on my tongue, the kiss of the grape—that is tangible."

Maggiormente warmed to his topic. "That, *mon ami*, is certainly true, but only part of the story. You taste the sun and the hillsides, too. The rain of spring and the winds of the summer bring their flavours to the grape."

"Indeed, monsieur," Adèle said, elbowing her spouse. "It cannot be denied."

The alchemist held his wine glass up to the light. "All that is here and so much more. The seedling that became the vine. The earth that caressed its roots. The men and women who tended the rows. The air that they all breathed in and out, night and day."

Fabien waved his hand as if to dismiss the words. "But these are every bit as real as the wine in my glass." He swirled the red liquid before him.

Adèle shook her head. "You are so limited in these opinions my dear."

"I was not raised to see fairies at the bottom of the garden like you," the baker said, laying a hand on top of his wife's. There was no rancor in their disagreement.

"More's the pity," she said, laughing too, as this was an old topic between them.

"I believe in fairies," Brigitte said as she bounced up and down in her chair.

Her father laughed. "You are allowed your fancies, my little treasure. For now anyway."

"And when she is older…?"

The baker sighed. "We all have to face reality."

It was Maggiormente's turn to tut. "Reality! Over-rated. Incomplete."

"But our only certainty." Fabien took a sip as if to punctuate his point.

The alchemist pointed at his Venetian lion. "And before we came to Paris, what might you have said about the 'reality' of a Venetian lion?"

Eduardo ruffled his wings. "I am very real."

"That is not my point," Maggiormente soothed.

"And having seen a Venetian lion," Fabien said a little

tartly, "I know him to be genuine. Unusual, perhaps, but genuine."

"But would you have imagined such a thing?"

Fabien shrugged. "Does it matter? I believe in what I see."

"You do now, but would you have before?"

"Perhaps not."

"So what you believe now, you might have doubted before." Maggiormente shook his finger at his friend. "This is what it means to trust in the ineffable."

"Ah, monsieur," Fabien said, shaking his head with amusement. "You have twisted me around to your dreamy point of view. But how do such musings result in a fuel source for your motor? I must admit to having my doubts."

Maggiormente laughed. "These dreamy thoughts as you have called them are precisely the location from which my fuel source has come."

Fabien shook his head. "Dreams!"

"Indeed—everything that exists now was once imagined, as the master wrote."

Adèle asked, "Who is this master you speak of? Your teacher?"

The alchemist held his wine glass aloft. "Mr William Blake of England. A poet, an artist, a visionary."

The baker poured out more wine for them all. "I have not heard of him."

Maggiormente struck his chest with an open hand. "That is the true tragedy!" He sighed with regret while Eduardo lay down on the bakery floor. The lion knew this could take a while so he rested his head on his paws and folded his wings neatly across his back.

"It's a sad and painful story. Genius seldom finds its reward in its own time."

"This is true," Fabien admitted.

"Especially if one is a woman," Adèle added.

Her husband grabbed her hand and kissed it. "You are

magnificent. I know your genius. You make every day a wonder."

"*Je t'aime, mon cher.*"

The alchemist looked at the two of them with bemusement. This affection between married people was quite extraordinary. "The master, Mr William Blake, conceived of entire worlds then he wrote and drew them. He saw angels in his garden and created pictures of exquisite beauty that also explained his visions."

"He is your role model."

"Yes, in so many ways."

"An alchemist," Adèle suggested.

"Only with thought," Maggiormente said, "and words and images. Not in the classical sense of alchemy, but the magic he wrote with just letters, lines and spaces—ah! Such magic."

"A poet, that is a good thing." Fabien nodded as he sipped his wine.

"A poet and so much more," Maggiormente held his wine aloft and squinted into a distance he could only see. "'To see the world in a grain of sand, and to see heaven in a wild flower, hold infinity in the palm of your hands, and eternity in an hour.' That is the gift he gives us: to know the magic of vision of what has not yet been."

"But such imaginings can fall into idleness, too."

The alchemist waved away his friend's words. "Blake spoke not in idleness and fancy, but in deadly seriousness about our gifts." He gestured around the bakery.

"To have the ability to make such glorious pastries and breads and to deny the world your work, that the master would scorn. To avoid the work one was born to carry out—to make, to create!—this too he would disparage. As he wrote so long ago, 'I must create a system or be enslaved by another man's; I will not reason and compare: my business is to create.' And his business it was, too, to share the voices of the angels beyond comprehension, though he died alone, penniless and forgotten."

"Angels, bah!" Fabien said. "More irrationality."

"I think angels are pretty," Brigitte said. "They have wings like Eduardo."

Her father laughed. "Eduardo, to be sure, is no angel!"

Maggiormente leaned forward. "Where does genius come from? When it comes, it does not seem to come from within. To call this source god or angels, does it matter? Angels to some, demons to others, we might say, for genius does not always fit itself to human values."

"What is wrong with saying it comes from our own little heads?" Fabien tapped the table with his forefinger. "We conjure with our brains, not angels."

"Our brains are filled by the wisdom of the ages, by those who came before, by those who know so much more. When an idea comes, it comes as a gift from the whole of your life and all those before it."

"But from my own brain."

Maggiormente threw his hands up. "There are those who believe they owe no one. And those who know they owe everyone."

"But I give you credit for your discoveries," Fabien said, raising his glass to the alchemist.

"You are kind, my friend," Magggiormente said, "but I give credit to the masters who have taught me so much and lighted my path—and even you my friend, who force me to articulate the truths I know."

The alchemist lifted his glass and drained it. "And now I must return to my work." He set the glass down on the table then rubbed his hands together. "Eduardo, are you ready?"

"I have finished my cake," Eduardo said, flapping his wings lightly as he stretched his front legs out at a seemingly impossible length. Brigitte cooed and tousled his mane. The lion ignored her.

"*Mon ami!*" Fabien cried. "We were just getting into a very good discussion here."

Adèle kissed the top of her husband's head. "Your

work is done for the day, *mon amour*, but Monsieur Maggiormente has his duties ahead yet."

"Such a pity!"

Maggiormente clapped his friend on the shoulder. "Tomorrow is another day. We shall renew our argument."

"Discussion! A much better word, my friend." The two embraced and then the alchemist and his lion headed back out into the late afternoon light, the motor tucked under Maggiormente's arm.

"I hope Mme. Gabor is not around," the alchemist said. "I don't want her asking questions just now."

Eduardo coughed. "I don't think she will bother you at present."

Maggiormente looked down at his familiar. "What more did you do?"

"I?" The lion looked at him with exaggerated innocence. "I did nothing."

Maggiormente frowned, but did not press the matter. They returned to their *maison* and heard not a peep from the concierge as they climbed the stair to their flat on the top floor. Eduardo sneezed as they entered the workroom.

"Remnants of the failure," the alchemist said with regret.

"Mistakes are necessary; how can you find success if you do not eliminate the alternate avenues?" The lion sneezed again. "In the future I hope we can avoid this particular mistake, however."

"That matrix has been discarded," Maggiormente said as he set the motor on the work table. "How to affix this motor so it will not slide around awkwardly?"

"Lash it down," Eduardo suggested, walking over to the window and looking for pigeons.

"I think perhaps nails," Maggiormente said with a frown. He rooted around for some nails amongst the rubbish on the sideboard while Eduardo made himself comfortable on the rug near the window.

In a few minutes the motor board had been made fast

to the table. A master carpenter would likely have exclaimed at the expedition but hardly careful application of nails, but for the alchemist's purpose, the attachment would do well enough.

He stared at the little motor. After some careful scrutiny, Maggiormente affixed a funnel to the input of the wee engine. Then he stood back to examine it carefully.

"How many funnels do you have?" Eduardo asked sleepily.

The alchemist looked at him. "Three."

The Venetian lion put his head down on his paws. "That should be enough."

Maggiormente raised an eyebrow but Eduardo appeared to have fallen asleep. He stepped over to the other end of the work table to consult his notes. After a moment, he decided upon the formula to try and set to work. From the smoking coals in the fireplace, he lit the oil lamp under a mixture of pale green liquid.

By the time the liquid boiled, Maggiormente had an array of substances lined up to add to the base. He measured carefully and introduced each one in turn. The beaker roiled and bubbled. Sparks rose from the surface and dissipated in the air.

When the liquid had changed from green to gold, the alchemist lifted the concoction off the heat with tongs. He allowed it to cool for a few minutes. The gold colour grew richer. With infinite care, he poured the mixture into the funnel.

Nothing happened.

"You need a spark," Eduardo reminded him, his voice sleepy.

Maggiormente clapped his palm to his forehead. "Of course!" He went back to the fire where the coals still glowed and grabbed one with the tongs. Grabbing a spatula, the alchemist used the implement to knock some sparks from the glowing ember. After a few taps, sparks flew and all at once ignition began.

The golden liquid coursed through the motor and it began to turn as the sparks ignited the fluid. The pistons turned. The whirr of the engine filled the room. Even Eduardo lifted his head to watch the mechanical piece rotate as it shook the table beneath it.

All at once there was an explosion. Flames shot upward as the funnel flew up to the ceiling and shattered. As the pistons slowed Maggiormente nodded approvingly and said, "An excellent start."

7 VORTEX

"Pirates?"

"Surely not." Helen frowned. "Why on earth do you connect airships with pirates?"

The publican put down the glass he was cleaning and pointed an accusing finger at her. "There were that one not six months gone by. Landed here, ran up a lot of bills, stole a gentleman's daughter and, I heard, a wealth of jewels as well."

Helen attempted to hide her skepticism.

"What sort of 'jewels' did he supposedly steal?"

It was the publican's turn to look doubtful. "Why do you want to know?"

"If you're worried that I will be trying to steal the jewels," Helen said with more than a touch of venom, "I would point out that these valuables have supposedly already been stolen. I was not under the impression that the crown jewels were kept in the vicinity. There would be very little for any thief to steal in the way of jewels."

He looked as if he were mulling this proposition over. At last the publican decided it would be safe enough to relate more of the story to this potential pirate.

"I suppose that's true enough, but I don't want to think

you're some kind of buttoner after me wealth."

"I'm an airship captain," Helen said drawing herself up to full height with more than a pinch of her father's temper. "I am not here to 'hoist' anything but my airship."

"You'd be nibbed in a trice if you were to try," the publican said, laying a finger aside his nose and nodding.

"Would I? It doesn't seem to have been the case with that pirate."

His face fell with dismay. "We learned from that misfortune."

Helen closed her eyes and sighed. "I am not a pirate. I do not intend to steal anything. My father and I are on our way to France with my pilot, Signor Romano."

"Over the ocean?" Another gentleman entered the conversation. From his attire Helen guessed him to be a coach driver. There had been three outside the inn when they arrived, walking from where the airship had been tethered.

"Yes, over the ocean."

"I knew a father and daughter pair of toolers, some said they were gypsies. Preyed upon folks all the way from Canterbury to London." The publican nodded sagely. "They were finally caught and topped proper. My brother saw them swing."

"I am not a gypsy or a 'tooler' whatever that may be." Helen felt exasperation taking hold of her.

"But the ocean's a very long way," the driver said, tutting at her. "Surely your little balloon cannot make it so far."

"Yes, of course it can. And it's not a balloon, it's an airship."

"I'm not saying you are a tooler, but you have to leave me the right to be suspicious. I have a family and a business to protect."

I understand that," Helen said, feeling her nostrils flare as she exhaled too forcefully, "But why suspect me?"

"I'd bet fair money it wouldn't make it," the coachman

said with an irritating air of smugness.

"You will lose that bet," Helen said with a savage pleasure. "We have flown down from Yorkshire today."

"Yorkshire?" the publican said, shaking his head. "I think that's where that gypsy pair came from. Somewhere up north it were."

Helen closed her eyes. *Why bother with this?* Her father would be getting impatient and joining the argument. And *that* would be something worth avoiding. "If you want to bring the food over to our table when you have a chance, we'll gladly pay you in advance if that will set your mind at ease, sir."

"Oh, I didn't mean to cast aspersions, miss," the publican said waving his tea towel in his hand. "It just doesn't pay to be too gullible hereabouts."

"I'd lay some money on that," the driver said.

"How much?" Helen asked.

"A guinea."

"Done." She shook the man's hand and returned to the table where her father sat. He appeared amused by her stormy expression but wisely waited to allow her to speak first.

"Southerners!" she exclaimed at last.

Helen's father cocked an eyebrow at her with an air of amusement. "Are you fighting with the natives already? I thought that was going to be my position in the crew."

"I can't believe that people are so hostile to technological innovation!" Helen threw herself down in the chair with a huff of indignation.

"People don't like change."

"They treat strangers with suspicion."

Her father laughed quite loudly. "People don't like strangers."

Helen shot an angry look at her father. "I am always interested in strangers unless they appear to be obviously shifty."

"So, they thought you looked shifty."

She snorted with contempt. "They accused me of being a pirate or a gypsy."

Her father leaned back in his chair with a wide grin. "Both admirable groups of people, far more trustworthy than inn keepers or coach drivers on the whole."

Helen stared at her father. "What?"

His face grew more serious. "If you're going to get cheated in this life, my girl, you will find it is most often the people who look quite respectable and entirely normal. Like bankers. They're the worst."

Helen sighed. "It shakes my faith in human nature."

"Good."

"Papa!"

He laughed again, but his face remained serious. "My dearest child, you have had a singular upbringing amongst good people, educated beyond the means of most young ladies—"

"For which I am very grateful, Papa." Helen laid her hand upon his and squeezed it.

"Yes, but you must realise that you have a rather different position in the world than most girls of your age."

"Women, father," Helen corrected him. "I am a woman. Not a girl."

Her father looked at her with narrowed eyes. "Nevertheless, you have a distinct advantage over other *females* of your years and over many people in this country in general."

"And what is that?"

He threw his hands wide. "You have been further than the next village. You have read of great cities and philosophers and thinkers. You've read the newspapers."

"Yes, but don't most people?"

"No, they do not." He shook his head. "Especially young ladies who are still taught to be nice and be useful and keep their pretty little heads out of important matters like science and technology."

Helen laughed. "Oh, Papa! You are a bluestocking."

Much to her surprise, her father looked somewhat abashed at this pronouncement. "It was your mother's doing." His face softened as it always did when he spoke of his wife. "She has always been abominably curious about all manner of strange things, and you know it is not in my power to deny her anything."

Helen smiled. "I am grateful to you both that you gave me *most* of the same advantages you gave to Fairfax and Edmund. To be able to pursue my dreams! It is quite exhilarating, Papa."

Her father looked grumpy but she could tell he was pleased. "If only your brothers had done as much with their advantages."

"Oh, Fairfax has done well," Helen said grudgingly.

"I suppose well enough for that sort of thing. But it would have been better if he had a little more gumption!"

"Edmund has gumption." Helen said with a snort of laughter.

Her father's expression darkened immediately. "Gumption is not what I'd call it. Devil-may-care rakehell, confounded damnable cheek!"

"Papa!"

"Well, it's no less than the truth."

Helen shrugged. "At least he hasn't turned to piracy."

"So far," her father muttered.

"Have we any idea where Edmund is?" Helen looked at her father, who seemed to be quieter than usual.

He did not answer immediately, and she was on the verge of prompting him again, when he said, "Your brother's whereabouts remain uncertain."

Helen tutted. "Have the lawyers not located him?"

Her father sighed. "Where's our food?"

"Don't change the subject."

"Our subject was food when we came in here."

"Yes, but it has moved on while we waited."

Her father sighed dramatically. "I don't necessarily want to speak about your brother."

"Yes, but the last *I* heard he was still missing after being sent down. Has he been located? I think it is rather important information to know."

"He could become a pirate. That would at least show some gumption."

"Papa," Helen said with definite severity. "What do you know?"

"Well, it's not piracy."

"So——? What is it?"

"They're not certain." Her father frowned and his countenance took on the appearance of clouds. "The last the lawyers knew, he was booking passage for Katmandu."

"Katmandu!"

"Well, maybe it was only Köln…"

Helen stared at her father with narrowed eyes. "You are not being very helpful."

"He is somewhere in Europe, I think. But I do not know."

"Well, that's better than hearing that he is in Katmandu."

"For you, perhaps."

"Indeed. I am glad to hear my brother hasn't gone all the way to Tibet in a fit of pique for he is no adventurer, prepared for wild climates."

"It would appear that he is seemingly prepared for very little," her father said with a sniff. "He's a university student. Not a bold adventurer, however much he may want to imagine himself to be one. He is simply a failure."

"Papa," Helen said with a decided shake of her head, "Someone who does not live up to expectations is not a failure. He—or she—is simply finding another avenue of work."

"I don't think that applies here."

"Why not?"

Her father expelled a rather long breath. "Because your

brother has had all the necessary advantages of auspicious birth and parental largesse that should allow one to succeed in life and yet he has not."

"Papa!" Helen said with animation.

"Well, it's true. Your brother has had all the advantages and failed to put them to much of any use."

"At least he's not a pirate, as you suggested before..."

"Miss, sir, your viands." A waiter suddenly appeared at Helen's elbow.

"Yes, of course. Put it here." She indicated the table. The waiter put the large weight of sandwiches and nibbles on the table. Her father turned toward the food with a zealous interest.

"This looks like an adequate feast." He rubbed his hands together with glee.

"We need to take some of it back to Signor Romano, too," Helen reminded her father. He tended to consider the Italian out of sight and out of mind.

"Oh, pshaw. That Italian doesn't need much in the way of food."

"Papa! He needs as much food as you do. More in all likelihood."

"More!"

"Yes, he has a job to do, unlike you!"

"What sort of cheese is this?" Helen's father regarded the yellowish wedge with suspicion.

"Local specialty," Helen said. "I'm sure it's delicious, try it."

The bread looked delicious indeed, and the cured ham could equal their own Mr. Hitchcock's usual efforts. The wine left something to be desired, but they would surely have better offerings once they got to France.

Or so Helen attempted to persuade her father.

"I suspect I may begin to wish myself in Katmandu," her father said grumpily as they gathered up the leftovers to take to Signor Romano.

"You've been fine so far, everything's been fine,"

Helen said before hastily adding, "Except of course for the murmuration. But that's unlikely to occur again, especially out over the sea."

He grumbled on as they left the inn. Tuppence croaked a greeting to them as they stepped once more outside.

"No, it will probably be some kind of leviathan that attacks us next." He had his stick today. Helen noticed that he had not much used it on the way to the inn but now that they were returning to the ship her father leaned more pronouncedly upon it.

"Papa, there is no such thing."

"Can you be certain? There are more things in heaven and earth...""

Helen laughed. "Mother would be most amused by your citing Shakespeare to me."

"You make it sound as if I were some kind of uneducated boor," her father growled as he limped along. "I have read a few books, you know."

"I realise that, Papa. I'm just surprised, that's all. And I think it would amuse Mother." she noticed he limped less as his annoyance grew. "I suppose you had some education after all, beyond riding to the hounds and growling at servants."

Her father muttered some words that she was probably just as happy not to have heard. "My father did send me off to university where I may not have distinguished myself as much as some but I did master holding a pen in my foot for the occasional scribble."

Helen laughed. "You should have studied more of nautical skills, then you would be better prepared for our journey. While we ride the winds rather than the waves, many of the skills are the same."

Her father snorted. He had begun to outpace her. "I have been on plenty of ships and maintain a fine pair of sea legs. The idea!" He gave a sharp bark of laughter. "I have sailed across half this known world, my girl. You have never been on a storm in the middle of the Atlantic, waves as high as the York Minster's towers, winds set to throw the strongest sailor overboard."

"True enough, Papa," Helen said, watching the fire burn in his features. "But the air will not give you the opportunity of surviving that the waves offer."

Ahead the ship waited. Romano waved. Helen imagined he was likely famished and found herself glad that she had hustled her father along quickly from the inn.

"I do not plan to fall out of the ship like some novice," her father said with scorn.

"Things do not always happen according to plan," Helen said, "But I have confidence you will be up to the challenge, Papa. I couldn't ask for a finer sailor."

"France," he rumbled with embarrassed pride. "If only it were somewhere other than France."

"Grazie," Sr. Romano said, clasping his hands together with delight as they approached the airship. He fell upon the cheese and meats with good appetite while Helen and her father checked the slightly rearranged ballast of the gondola.

Tuppence hopped along the rail of the ship, offering a commentary as they worked.

"What are those?" Her father asked with dismay as she unrolled some canvas.

Helen looked up at him. "These are to keep out the rain."

Rochester looked up. "There's not a cloud in the sky."

"At the moment."

He laughed. "You'd hardly know it was England. What makes you think there'll be rain?"

"When we get out over the channel the odds of some squalls increase significantly."

"This is true," Romano added as he downed the last of the wine. "Over water the wind and the rain can be unpredictable, *signore*."

"Wonderful."

Helen gave everything a last look over. Tuppence flew

up to her shoulder and made a few clicks in her ear. "All looks well, eh Tuppence?"

"If the bird approves," her father said dryly, "then I suppose we're ready."

"Papa," Helen scolded. "You should be confident of my raven's acumen by now."

"Are we ready?"

Helen looked from Romano to her father, then grinned. "We are!"

The motor whirred into action again and the practiced crew set about their tasks to get the ship aloft once more. The trickiest time was take off, but they were soon lifting up over the green fields toward the channel.

"*Bonne chance, mes amis!*" Helen called out as she kept her eye on the motor. "Next stop France."

"Or Davy Jones' locker," her father muttered, looking down at the grey waves below them.

"Look, Papa—the white cliffs!" Helen pointed back toward the land they were swiftly leaving behind. The cliffs shone in the midday light with an almost uncanny brightness. There was something stirring about the sight.

She turned back to look over the bow and found a sight even more stirring. The English Channel stretched out before them, the water sparkling in the sunshine.

"Do you suppose we will see some fish?" Her father looked uncharacteristically nervous. He appeared to be staring off into the distance rather than below them.

"I think we could see some large schools of fish," Helen said as she gazed into the depths. The shadow of the ship undulated over the surface.

"Whales?" Her father continued to maintain a view of the uncertain distance.

"I'm not sure about that. I suspect they're further north. Probably Scotland and the Orkneys."

Her father laughed. "The day I see a whale sailing up the Tay, I'll eat my hat."

"I hope you like tweed."

Romano called out. "See over there!"

Their gazes turned to where he pointed. Helen's father swayed a little bit as he drew his gaze down to the water below. Though he looked a trifle green, he seemed to be holding up well for the most part. So far.

"I don't quite—what is that?"

"Are those fish?" Her father asked, wrinkling his brow and shading his eyes against the sun.

"They're too large to be fish, I think."

"*Sono focene*," Romano said, smiling happily.

Helen tried to remember her vocabulary lessons but nothing sprang to mind. She stared at the large shapes as they burst from the waves and then she knew.

"Porpoises! Of course."

"Of course?" Her father asked.

"Wouldn't go anywhere without one." She laughed.

Her father groaned at that. "We can still see the cliffs," he remarked, looking back from whence they had come with something of a wistful look upon his ravaged face.

"We have a long way to go yet," Helen reassured him.

"How far it is?" her father asked, looking a little forlorn.

"Not so far really," Helen said, attempting to make her voice sound as calm as possible.

"How far is 'not so far' then, my dear?"

"About one hundred and fifty miles."

"Ah."

"So, much less than the distance from Yorkshire to London—about half, indeed."

"Is that so?" He looked very casual. "It's not as if I were nervous or anything."

Helen smiled. "Of course not, Papa. I simply figured you would be interested in calculating the distances."

"That's true—and the fuel usage. After all, isn't that what your alchemist fellow is all about after all?"

"Indeed, Papa. I hope to be able to use up less space with a new fuel that will likewise be safer to transport, so we don't end up like the Lintons."

"So all those," her father pointed to the barrels at the back of the gondola, "could be lessened?"

"Indeed," Helen nodded. Tuppence added a croak or two to punctuate the point, walking back and forth along the rim of the gondola. "With luck, Signor Maggiormente will be able to provide a fuel that takes no more space than a small snuff box."

Her father cocked an eyebrow at her. "As small as that?"

"You doubt it?"

He laughed. "I do."

"Science, father. Science."

"I see, we are to believe miracles of science that have been denied to us in philosophy?"

"Nothing of the kind," Helen said, wrapping her cloak a little more warmly around her. "It is the business of science to improve upon our lives." She was particularly happy with the use of the word 'business' however, as she knew it pleased her father's northern heart. "Science at heart is just paying close attention to the world around us. Which is the same thing philosophers do, I suppose."

He rubbed his chin with thoughtfulness. "So you expect to find a commercial use for this scientific discovery eventually?"

"Of course, Papa."

"Oh, it's 'Papa' now, not 'father'?"

Helen snorted. "Yes, Papa. That's the whole point of these advances. To spread them far and wide and make life so much better for many people. This is the modern world! So many exciting things happening—new advances every day!"

Her father sniffed.

"You doubt me?"

He laughed. "The new world is a frightening place that offers a cold simulacrum of reality."

"Papa, I don't even know what you mean by that."

He walked back and forth across the gondola and then hazarded a look down. He looked up just as suddenly. "What I mean, my dear," he paused and ruminated a bit. "What I mean, ahem." He paused.

"What, Papa?"

"I'm not sure." He turned away quickly.

"Papa, the new world is full of challenges as well as opportunities."

"I know."

"So, you can take your time sorting out which you, er—"

Her father flushed angrily. "I am not some child that needs to be spared the scary boogeyman, my dear."

"Then I won't. But there is so much to be done, and I need to you to be my partner in this, Papa. There's a whole new world opening out before us and I hope to know that you are going to be an essential part of the enterprise!" She smiled at him, for the first time feeling as if she were truly grown up. Her pride was much tempered by humbleness: it was daunting.

"Pressure dropping, Signorina Captain!" Romano called out from the front of the ship.

"What the devil does that mean?" Helen's father asked, trying vainly to look nonchalant. "Is the airship deflating?"

"No, the weather, Papa." Helen stepped across the gondola to look over Romano's shoulders at the instruments.

"Not quickly," Romano added, "But steadily."

"Perhaps we are in for some rain."

"Nothing worse, though?" her father asked casually.

"We shall see," Helen said, looking about for Tuppence. She whistled and heard an answering croak from the raven. The bird flew down to the edge of the gondola and flapped her wings briskly as water drops flew off them.

Her father wiped his sleeve with exaggerated motions. "I take it things are looking wet out there."

Helen smiled and reached out to pat the raven's head. "It could just be condensation, but I suspect we may be in for a bit of a wet time."

Her father squinted out across the horizon. The white cliffs were impossible to see in the greyness; indeed it was increasingly difficult to see the division between sea and sky as they merged in the darkening day.

"It looks more cloudy."

"Clouds don't always mean rain."

"But certainly it's more likely."

"I'm really more concerned about the wind, Papa. It could make for a more interesting journey. A little dampness won't have much effect."

"It will on my joints," he father muttered.

"Tuppence, how does it look up there?"

The raven croaked and then emitted a serious of clicks and other sounds that Helen alone could interpret. She looked concerned, as her father muttered, but did not speak until the bird had delivered her message.

"So," he asked with a note of impatience, doubtless to mask his concern about the perilousness of the weather, "Are we in for some dirty weather or will it be all right?"

"Not to worry, *signore*," Romano reassured him. "Should the weather become more turgid we will still be all right."

"Turgid?" Rochester stared at him as if he were mad.

Romano paused. "Ah, the word escapes me. Perhaps another."

"According to Tuppence, the rain will definitely pick up, but the wind ought not be too strong," Helen said, "which will be a mercy for our stomachs if nothing else."

The waters below them already exhibited signs of the impending swirl. Helen could see the white caps on the waves. *Funny that the wind seems to be coming from the south as well as the west.*

The day darkened as they spoke. The clouds appeared to be thickening, too.

"What's that line from Shakespeare," her father muttered.

"You're going to have to give me more than that," Helen laughed. "There are a lot of lines in the whole treasure trove of his works."

"Oh, it's one of the history plays, I think," he continued, staring out into the gloom. "All the clouds that lowered upon our house in the deep bosom of the ocean buried."

Helen smiled. Her father surprised her in so many ways. "Richard III: *Now is the winter of our discontent made glorious summer by this sun of York*, and then all the clouds. Well spotted, Papa. Your tutor would be proud."

"Tutor," he grumbled, though she could tell he was pleased. "I might better have studied nautical lore so I would know as much as your bird."

"Tuppence has not only her own knowledge but the inherited wisdom of her entire species."

"Has she?" Her father looked at the bird with something like respect. "Can we tap into such a thing?"

"There are some who say so, in fact—"

"*Signorina*, I think we need to take a closer look at this."

"What is it, Romano?" Helen said following where he pointed. "Oh my! I've never seen that before!"

Helen and Signor Romano both leaned over the side of the gondola to concentrate on the water below them. Helen's father, however, reluctant to move so close to the edge—and even more reluctant to lean over it and look down—made noises of annoyance.

"Well, what is it? What are you looking at?"

Helen looked up. "We're not at all sure, Papa."

"Is it more whales?"

"They weren't whales, Papa." Helen frowned down at the waters, which made her father bristle with curiosity though he stubbornly stayed put.

"I know, I know," he blustered ineffectively. "Dolphins or porpoises or some such. Well, what are they now?

Lobsters doing a quadrille?"

"It's the water, *signore*," Romano interjected. He appeared to be as puzzled as Helen. "There's a large dark spot that seems to be growing."

Rochester heaved himself to his feet. He leaned on his stick a little and tried to see over the edge without approaching it in any way. This maneuver proved to be less successful than required. Tuppence croaked at him as if in admonishment.

"I'll be damned if I'm to be hectored by a raven," he muttered to no one in particular and make his way stiffly to the edge of the gondola. While he may have gripped the rail with rather white knuckles, he did lean over and peer down into the darkening sea.

Below the airship, almost like a shadow, a dark pool formed within the turbulent waters of the channel. It seemed rather wide, but it was impossible to tell immediately if it were changing.

"I think it's getting larger," Helen suggested.

"I do not think so," Romano said, but he frowned as if unsure. "Perhaps."

"Can't you even agree on that?" Helen's father asked irritably. "Is it any larger than when you first noticed it?"

"It's hard to tell, Papa."

"Is it our shadow maybe?" He grimaced. "All right, that was a fairly stupid suggestion, wasn't it?"

"Not one of your better ideas, Papa." Helen smiled but her face showed strain.

"Look, it's changing," Romano said, drawing their attention back to the water.

Helen and her father leaned back over the side of the ship. The dark patch of water had definitely begun to move, keeping pace with their flight.

Another shape formed on top of it. This one was lighter, floating like a disc on top of the water.

And twirling.

"I should be taking notes," Helen said at last as they

watched, mesmerized by the swirling shapes on the water.

"What can you possibly say?"

"Well," she said, gesturing out toward the water. "I can describe what I see. The circles in the water, moving."

"Moving faster."

They all stared.

"Look, it's rising up." Helen's father pointed. Sure enough the white-capped waves on the turning white disk began to lift up like peaks of whipped icing on a cream cake. The hypnotic swirl surely had sped up as they watched it, as well as rising. It was most peculiar.

"Certainly a remarkable occurrence," Helen said, feeling an unaccustomed sense of awe. "Should we be thinking of evasive moves if necessary?"

Romano looked up. "Evasive? Do you think so?"

"I'm just saying perhaps we should be prepared. This is not a phenomenon we have experienced before. It may remain solely on the surface of the water. It may be an indication of something else."

"It could be a whale," her father suggested, then flushing at her quick exasperation, "A school of whales maybe." He coughed and steadied himself against the rail. All at once he looked very tired.

"I don't think it is, Papa, but I have no idea what it is. Surely we can come up with a likely candidate from our memory of novels or newspapers…"

"Look!" Romano pointed up to the clouds.

Helen looked up into the clouds where the Italian pilot pointed. Her eyes grew large. "I've not seen one of those before."

Romano shook his head. "I have not seen one so large."

"What the blasted flatch are you two on about!" Helen's father demanded. He seemed determined to look everywhere but in the direction they stared.

"Papa, look there. It's descending from the cloud." Helen nodded toward the heavens, captivated by the sight of this strange albeit natural phenomenon.

"We call it *getto d'acqua*," Romano said. "You see them from time to time on the Mediterranean. Quite extraordinary."

"Are they dangerous?" Helen asked, sneaking a look at her father who had yet to turn and take in the strange formation snaking down from the clouds. Half wind, half water, the spout sought to join the dark clouds with the turgid waters.

Romano shrugged. "Not usually. They form, they dissipate, poof."

"I suppose they're usually far from land," Helen suggested, thinking about the possibilities of evasive movements. One disadvantage with an airship is that it took a while to change directions. You couldn't wheel and turn as on a horse. *Something to think about later,* Helen made a mental note to consider speeding the process of turning.

"They are more plentiful at the warmest times of the year," Romano noted. "I have only seen them from a distance. Or so small they appeared to be dissolving almost as quickly as they formed."

"What's the longest you've seen one last?"

The pilot considered this for a moment. "Minutes, surely no more."

Helen's father appeared vastly comforted by this news. "What's all this nonsense?" he blustered like his usual self. He even turned his head ever so slightly to take a look at the phenomenon.

"Bloody hell!" He goggled at the long cylindrical sweep from the clouds. The funnel had lengthened, nearly touching the dark waters below where the disk-like shape whirled darkly.

"Have you ever seen a water spout, Papa?" Helen asked, though she suspected his surprise was indication he had not.

"Not for many a long year," he said with a weariness

that seemed to have nothing to do with the sight before them.

His words surprised Helen. "Where did you see a water spout?"

He remained silent for a time and Helen had begun to think he would not answer, but he sighed as he watched the snaking shape in the distance. It swayed like a dancer held between sea and sky. "When I was in the West Indies," her father said at last, "I saw a few of them. They were generally larger and formed much more quickly."

"I have heard they are plentiful there," Romano said. "And hurricanes, too."

"You were in the West Indies, Papa?"

"Hurricanes were much worse," Helen's father said, his eyes upon the water spout, but his thoughts seemed very far away. "They cause real devastation across the land, ripping trees out at their roots and knocking down houses. Tropical regions are full of all kinds of horrible pestilences."

"When were you in the West Indies?"

Her father laughed but the sound lacked mirth. "Long before you were born, child. Long before I met your mother even." His face took on a darkness much more menacing than the dark clouds overhead.

"How exciting!" Helen said. "I would love to visit the West Indies."

"No, you wouldn't," her father said a little too sharply. "Horrid place. Hot, humid—it does terrible things to your brain. Saps your will. Makes you stupid. Drives you mad." He rubbed his eyes as if the view fatigued him. "Excessive heat was not mean to be borne."

Helen wondered, not for the first time, what tragedies lay in the distant days of her father's life. They all knew the story of the fire that scarred him so and how it had called their mother back to his side by some power they both regarded as almost mystic, but secrets abounded. There was such a Byronic air about his distant past that she often took it to be more jaunty and rakish than terrible, but the haggard look on his face now spoke of horror and tumult.

"See how the water dances," the pilot remarked, his voice full of wonder.

"I'm just glad it's dancing a good distance away," Helen's father murmured. Sure enough, it seemed to be moving away from the airship. They all watched in silence, eyes riveted to the strange sight.

"I must write of this in my journal," Helen said firmly.

Helen's father barked with laughter. "A dangerous weather development occurs and your only thought is, 'I must write this in my journal'? You are your mother's daughter indeed."

"I find that a great compliment, Papa."

"As you should." He continued to gaze at the water spout, but Helen thought his face looked much softer now, as if the dark clouds that sat upon his brow—like those that hung upon the other son of York's—had been buried in the deep bosom of the ocean for now.

The water spout, which had growing bigger and darker, suddenly seemed to be growing whiter and more transparent. As it curled down from the clouds the middle part grew whispy and the two halves parted. For some reason, Helen's mind jumped to the image of Michaelangelo's fresco of the creation, the hand of Adam and his creator meeting in the middle, though here the two limbs drew apart.

"And there it goes," Romano said, his comments punctuated by a squawk from Tuppence. The tail of the spout appeared to be absorbed into the grey clouds above it.

Helen sighed, unwilling to admit that she had found the phenomenon worrisome, more for her father's sake than her own. She could swim after all. And while the channel was very wide, it might be possible for a human to swim it. Or at least half of it, which is about how much they would have to do.

"Flotation devices," she muttered under her breath, and went at once to her journal, or as she thought of it to herself, captain's log of the journey. *For over-water travel, consider having some kind of Kisby Ring or cork device aboard.* She had heard of a lifeboat captain who had designed some kind of cork vest that could be worn, but Helen had neither seen one nor a drawing of one, so found herself imagining a waistcoat covered with bottle stoppers, which was surely wrong.

There were so many new inventions. This was truly an age of discovery! Helen burned to be seen as part of the age, to make her mark and be part of history.

Surely this present journey was a step in the right direction. Her face flushed with excitement. If the alchemist came through for her on that new miracle fuel— the art of air travel would be revolutionized!

"*Signorina!*"

Helen broke away from her thoughts of the future. "What is it, Romano?"

The pilot pointed toward the dark clouds gathered on the southern horizon. Helen found herself somewhat alarmed to see a sudden explosion of lighting strikes from their increasingly black depths.

"Perhaps we should steer a bit further north," she counseled Romano.

"Are we going to end up in Belgium?" her father asked as Tuppence began to croak somewhat urgently.

"Don't go on about Belgium, Papa," Helen scolded, consulting the map on the stand. "It's a lovely country."

"You've never had their stew," he muttered mysteriously.

"How can a stew be bad?"

"It's made with ale instead of wine," her father said as if the point could not be argued. "And they serve a most wretched dish made of eel with some kind of green sauce."

Helen blanched. "That does sound revolting, but I have had Belgian waffles with chocolate and they are sublime, so I can't imagine that all their food is like the eel dish. After all, there's not much of British cooking you could put in competition with it, is there?"

"Your mother's stew is superb."

"Indeed," Helen said, "but I understood her to use a Belgian recipe."

Her father stared at her in dismay.

"*Signorina*," Romano broke in again, "*la bufera*, she gets stronger."

"From which direction come the prevailing winds?"

Romano consulted his dials and meters. "South southeast."

"Let's chart a course another 15 degrees northward."

"Can we outrun the storm?" Her father asked, his face beginning to show a little shade of green like the Flemish dish.

"We shall endeavour," Helen said as Tuppence hopped over to land on her shoulder. "The storm looks fierce, but the winds don't seem too bad. The lighting is a little tricky but we ought to be fine." *Tuppence, help me keep watch*, she telegraphed to the bird.

Her father sat himself down once more, looking a little gloomy. "I bet it's sunny in Yorkshire."

"Doubtless," Helen agreed cheerfully. Across the channel to the south the lighting strikes flashed, their electric dance growing bolder. It was glorious.

8 THE SAMURAI

"Watch where you're going, *imbécile*!"

Signor Maggiormente jumped aside as the men threw down several large timbers. The clatter of the boards echoed loudly despite the considerable noise all around them. Eduardo drew himself up to his full stature, huffing audibly. His wings waved majestically in the hot afternoon air.

The fearsome effect, however, suffered some reduction due to the bright red fez the Venetian lion wore at a jaunty angle. Also he underestimated the nonchalance of builders.

"What are they building?" he asked the alchemist.

"This is the Exposition, Eduardo," Maggiormente tutted to his familiar. "The reason we came to Paris."

"It's a house?" The lion raised an eyebrow and took another look at the wooden frame erected before them. He sneezed. A lot of dust had been stirred up by the workers.

"It's not a house," the alchemist said, raising his hands to the sky. "It's an enormous undertaking!"

The lion remained unconvinced. "Many houses?"

Maggiormente sighed. "Come, look at this."

They walked over to another building that was more

fully built. There was a kind of wooden archway before the building proper, which had a couple of levels and both had roofs that looked like funny hats with up-turned brims.

"What is that?" Eduardo said, curling his tail around his feet as he gazed up at the sight. His expression suggested that he was not in favour of such structures.

"There will be the Chinese and Japanese exhibits. They have come from half way around the world to be here."

"It looks like the house is wearing a hat." Eduardo twitched his whiskers and wondered when they were going to eat something.

"That is the style of houses in the Orient," the alchemist said, admiring the novelty of the shape and humming without realizing he had started to do so.

"Why?"

Maggiormente, lost in admiration for the building while stroking his beard, didn't seem to hear the question at first. He had already begun to think about the Exposition and perhaps he might meet the Emperor of Japan—why not! The crowds were sure to be enormous and mix at random. He could say, 'I am Maggiormente, the alchemist. This is my new compound that fuels airships and perhaps trains and who knows, any kind of engine. Would you like to commission one for yourself?' Perhaps, perhaps. "Eh? What did you say?"

"Why?" Eduardo repeated. His stomach growled. He had begun to get cranky. It always happened when he got hungry. This wasn't even cake hungry. This was meat hungry. Perhaps a pigeon might land within reach just now, though the sky remained disappointingly empty.

"Why what?"

"Why is that the style there in the ornament?"

The alchemist laughed heartily. "You mishear, my friend."

"Mishear what?" The lion found his temper fraying.

"Not ornament, Orient." Maggiormente tried to stifle his urge to laugh. The lion hated to be laughed at and could show his temper in a variety of ways.

"What is Orient?"

"The east."

The lion frowned and narrowed his eyes at the alchemist. "I thought the east was Slovenia."

I am a long way from home, contemplating what I would say to a Japanese emperor, but here I am explaining geography to a Venetian lion. Maggiormente took a deep breath. "Slovenia is the land to the east of Italy. Japan and China lie much much further to the east than Slovenia."

"How much further?"

Maggiormente sighed. His ambitious musings had evaporated. "I don't know precisely."

"Further than Milan to Paris?"

"Much further," the alchemist assured him.

"We could not get there in a day?"

"It would take many many days to get there even if we took a train. Or an airship," he added as an afterthought.

"Do they have good food?" Eduardo asked hopefully.

"Do your thoughts ever leave the region of your stomach?" The alchemist smiled at his familiar's words, though his eyes remained on the building before them. He loved its exotic curls.

"If my belly is empty, what else matters?" The lion sniffed the air. This exposition did not appear to include food, so he could not see the point of it.

"Your view on life is simple but your logic unassailable," Maggiormente said with a sigh. He longed to have his discovery known and celebrated, but he also knew it would be good to be able to demonstrate its success on more than just the wee motor on his work table.

But would the airship woman get there in time? The alchemist scratched his beard as he looked to the sky. He had hoped for a letter or some sign of her arrival. Time had begun to grow short.

"Will there be cakes?" Eduardo said, insistently shouldering Maggiormente as the latter stood lost in thought.

"Yes, surely she will arrive," the alchemist muttered.

"What are you talking about?" The lion sighed. He found it so difficult to keep the alchemist focused on the important things in life. It had been at least an hour since he had had anything to eat.

Much too long!

Eduardo looked around. There didn't seem to be any cafés or patisseries around. Just workers and planks and buildings of funny shapes. There were a few trees, but the noise had doubtless frightened all the birds away so he would not be able to catch one too easily.

"We should go back to civilization," the lion urged.

Maggiormente laughed. "The lion tells me we should 'go back to civilisation'! Am I wrong to find this amusing?"

Eduardo huffed. His favourite sound of displeasure. "I only say so because I am always getting shouted at when I act naturally."

"Ah, this is true, *mio amico*." Maggiormente, however, felt the urge to idle a bit longer and take in the preparations for the great event. Everywhere there was noise and scurrying activity. His heart swelled with anticipation. There are few states more pleasurable than that of anticipation.

"*Voglio torta*," the lion reminded him. His thoughts were on the possibility of pie as well as cake, but cake seemed to be the simpler to ask for as he could not recall the words always in the French tongue and found it easier to simply ask for everything, or at least ask for what he could see. The thought of the cake he had eaten before at the wonderful bakery run by Adèle made his mouth water and he drooled just a bit. This made his belly rumble.

"Can you not hear how hungry I am?" the lion whinged, bumping the alchemist yet again with his head, ever mindful of his fez.

"Yes, yes," Maggiormente said absently. "What?"

"Food!" Eduardo roared.

Now, the alchemist thought little of this roar, having heard it many times and knowing that there was very little chance of much danger from his lazy familiar—provided of course that one were not a pigeon. He loathed the little creatures and delighted in eating them, even though he said the Paris pigeons had no flavour compared to Roman ones.

Others were not as sanguine about the alarming sound.

Unaccustomed to lions roaring in the middle of Paris, the workmen raised a hubbub at once, threw down their tools and called for their foreman. Gathering around the man, they demanded a solution at once.

"*Déraisonnable!*" cried one.

"*Ridicule!*" cried another.

They brandished their fists and complained about unfair labour practices that included wild animals roaming about at leisure. The general outcry alarmed Maggiormente, although Eduardo refused to take any notice of it nor admit that it had anything to do with him.

"Perhaps we should go," the alchemist said, reluctant to leave the sights but aware that they were becoming unpopular with the workmen.

"Then we can get some cake," Eduardo said, single-minded as always.

"Let us stop them!" One of the men cried, picking up his hammer. The others rallied around, shouting and brandishing tools.

The alchemist was nonplussed. He had not been the object of a mob before.

"Put down your tools!" A voice cried with unquestioning authority. Everyone looked around and saw nothing. All at once a flash of light exploded and a huge cloud of smoke surrounded Maggiormente and Eduardo, hiding them from sight.

"This way," a voice hissed as an arm grabbed Maggiormente's and drew him away from the angry workmen and their tools. He stumbled through the smoke and hoped that Eduardo followed behind him.

"In here!"

The alchemist couldn't be sure who it was that led them from the scene—and presumably caused the effusion of smoke. As the air cleared around them he saw a surprising figure in robes of bright colours flying before him.

"Eduardo, are you there?" He cocked his head to listen even as he hurried forward.

"I can't see anything," the lion grumbled but his voice came from near by. His words were followed by a sneeze.

"Just along here and we'll be safe," their new friend beckoned on.

Maggiormente realised they had gone into the Japanese exhibit's buildings he had been admiring. With wonder he looked around him, but from the inside the buildings did not look so very different. He squashed his initial sense of disappointment in hopes of new discoveries.

The first was their rescuer. Clad in colourful silk clothing and a tall conical headdress, she made quite a striking if diminutive figure. The alchemist smiled at her. "Hello, I am Maggiormente the Alchemist."

"I am Myojo the Magician." She released a small brightly coloured bird from her sleeve, which flew up to the ceiling and perched on a paper lantern.

"Is that to eat?" Eduardo sat down and contemplated the little bird who began to sing a sprightly tune.

"This is Eduardo. He seldom thinks of anything that is not food. You must not eat her bird, my friend. It may be her familiar." The alchemist did not want to pry but his curiosity had been aroused. Was a magician the same thing in Japan as it was in Italy? Or was she only a conjurer of tricks? In England, according to his airship captain, magicians were almost always considered to be mountebanks.

"Oh, you must not eat my little friend," Myojo held out her hand and the tiny bird flew over to perch on her finger. It continued to sing a lively air, the waterfall of notes falling trippingly through the air. "This is Seito," the magician said, smiling at her little friend.

"Hello, Seito," Maggiormente said, looking curiously at the little bird. It had bluish-black legs and a long black beak, and around its red eyes a black mask, but its other feathers ranged from tawny yellow to almost green and then blue as if it were clad in gems. He had never seen anything quite like it. Its lively song cheered him immensely. "What a lovely little creature!"

"Your friend here is rather impressive as well," the magician said with admiration. "He is no mere lion, is he? Although I have not seen lions except in books, he appears to be a different creature altogether."

Eduardo drew himself up to his full height and stretched his wings out, the better to show them off. Of course he tried to make it appear as if he were merely stretching, but as one could tell within moments of meeting him, the lion had quite a high opinion of his own beauty. "I am a Venetian lion. We are quite rare. In fact I do not know that there are any other in the entire world. Or at least Europe."

"He is so modest," Maggiormente said with a laugh.

"There must have been *some* other Venetian lions," Myojo said with a roguish smile.

Eduardo frowned. "I don't know. Perhaps I am unique."

"Did you not have parents?"

Eduardo pondered this. "I am fairly certain that I did."

"Then there must have been others at least then, yes? Unless your parents were an African lion and a chicken perhaps."

Maggiormente howled. Eduardo looked confused. "I am not certain. I was very small then. I am afraid I do not remember." His wings drooped a little as he considered his parentage, a vague memory to the lion who had lived with the alchemist since he was very young.

"We have rather magnificent chickens in Japan. I am certain you would not find them at all disgraceful as relatives. The emperor himself has a special chicken of which he is quite fond."

"Really?" Eduardo began to rethink his impression of chickens. Heretofore he had considered them to be unusually tasty pigeons.

"Yes," the magician said, trying to cover a smile. "It is quite delicious."

Maggiormente laughed until the tears rolled down his cheek while Eduardo stared at him, flaring his nostrils. More than anything, he loathed anyone to laugh at him. "I am not a chicken."

"No, you rascal, you are not," Maggiormente said at last, wiping the tears from his eyes. "And I hope things never get bad enough that we have to try to eat you!"

Eduardo stared. "There must be laws against such a thing!"

Maggiormente and Myojo both laughed. "Unless lions have joined the legal profession, I suspect there may not be," the alchemist added.

The creature looked deeply affronted. "Will no one protect the Venetian lions?"

Eduardo looked so appalled and forlorn that the alchemist took pity on him. "My dear one, you know that I shall always protect you."

This seemed to mollify his familiar somewhat. "I am grateful for that."

"Yet you were ready to eat Seito," Myojo said with mock seriousness as the bird continued to trill away on her hand.

Eduardo cocked his head. "Forgive my ignorance. I thought all birds were for eating. Perhaps if I am descended from chickens I should reconsider this practice."

The alchemist tried to hide his amusement with a cough. Yet his familiar looked so grave that he got his mirth under control quickly. "A wise decision. One must always be thoughtful about what one eats."

Myojo nodded her agreement. "So much depends upon our choices. There are many unintended repercussions to any action."

"Are you and Seito part of the exhibition here?" Maggiormente asked in order to change the subject away from food. And because he was dying to know more about the magician.

"We are indeed. The emperor had many petition him for admission to the exhibit. I was one of the fortunate few, although I must attribute most of my luck to Seito."

The little bird hopped along her arm then settled on the magician's shoulder.

"Do you do tricks?" Eduardo asked, staring at the bird with a new level of respect.

"We do illusions," Myojo said, removing her pointed hat. Seito hopped onto her head and she replaced the hat. From within it, the trilling song of the bird continued until it suddenly cut short. She removed the hat to show no Seito.

Suddenly the bird's song began anew from the rafters. The three of them looked up to see Seito perched high in the unfinished building. Seito took wing and flew down in lazy circles until once more she sat upon the magician's shoulder.

Maggiormente clapped his hands approvingly, but Myojo waved it away. "A mere trifle. We have much more impressive work to do."

"How so?"

"Our illusions are not just magic tricks, but stories that we tell. We have a stage and props and other things to create the illusion of a living tale. The emperor seemed most fascinated by the tale I call 'Child's Play' which tells of the friendship between a poor girl and boy."

"A happy tale?" Eduardo curled his tail around his feet, ready to hear a story now.

Myojo shook her head. "A tale to break the heart. Happy stories are all very well to cheer us for a moment, but sad stories live in the memory longer."

"I suppose that's true," Maggiormente said, rubbing his beard thoughtfully.

"We know how to cope with happiness, indeed nothing could be easier," Myojo said, pulling a red silk kerchief from her sleeve, "But we all seek ways to learn how to bear our unhappiness."

"I don't like to be unhappy," Eduardo said with a big frown.

"No one does." Maggiormente said, patting his familiar on the head. "But we are all unhappy at times, however rich or powerful. No one escapes sadness completely."

Myojo nodded. "The emperor himself had tears in his eyes at my performance. He rules Japan, the greatest nation in the world, yet he too knows unhappiness."

"Are you from an imperial family yourself?" The alchemist could no longer repress his curiosity completely and the young woman seemed entirely at ease with the conversation so he didn't really feel as if he were prying.

Myojo laughed. "Not at all. My given name is Higuchi Ichiyō. The Higuchi family comes from samurai lineage, however."

"What is a samurai?" Eduardo interrupted.

"Great warriors," Maggiormente said, "isn't that correct?"

The young magician nodded. "Men of power and action, who held to a code of warfare that promoted honour and courage."

"It sounds very grand," Maggiormente said, imagining the armoured warriors on the fields of war.

Myojo nodded but offered a wry smile. "They are magnificent, until they die leaving a wife and children behind friendless and impoverished." The sadness on her face left no doubt that the story she told was her own.

"Is this one of the stories you present in your

performance?" Maggiormente asked, unable to hide his curiosity about the show any longer. He had begun to think that the magician was very different from an alchemist, but no less fascinating for all that.

"It is not usually part of the grand story," Myojo said, "But it is a worthy story of its kind."

"Tell us," Eduardo demanded in his simple way.

"Tut," the alchemist hushed him. "Would you ask me to perform alchemical workings at the drop of a hat?" He shook his head.

"*I* would," Eduardo said, flapping his wings with a careless air.

"You would," Maggiormente agreed. His lion was a greedy thing, for food and for entertainment.

Myojo laughed. "If I perform for you, I shall ask the same in return. Fair?" Seito trilled a little tune to highlight the offer.

Maggiormente clapped his hands. "You want to see me work up an elixir?" He found himself giddy at the thought of an audience. Most people only complained about his work, its smells and the occasional explosion.

"I don't know anything about alchemy. I don't believe we have such a thing in Japan—or else it was not part of my learning. Perhaps it is a specialised art."

"Likely true," Maggiormente said, thinking about the implications. "Perhaps after Paris we should go to Japan."

"You would be welcome," Myojo said. "And you, Eduardo. What can you do?"

"I can eat pigeons," Eduardo said.

Myojo laughed. "My cat Jiji back home can do that. What can only an extraordinary lion like you do?"

Eduardo paused. "I can flap my wings."

"And?"

Eduardo looked confused. "I need do more? I am a Venetian lion."

"But what does that mean?"

Eduardo sat down, adjusted his fez and pondered this

for a moment. "I help the alchemical reactions."

"How?" Myojo found herself torn between amusement and fascination.

Eduardo appealed to Maggiormente. "How do I work?"

Maggiormente laid a hand on his familiar's shoulders. "Your presence brings a special *frisson* to the process, like an extra sun in the sky."

Eduardo nodded. "That seems suitable. I am pleased."

Myojo laughed. "I cannot wait to see you shine. But first, let me see. I shall use this as my stage. We can move these planks over here for you to sit on. You shall be my royal audience."

"I don't mind sitting on the floor," Eduardo said, wrapping his tail around his legs.

"I prefer to sit a little higher," Maggiormente said, piling up the broken planks into a precarious sort of seat. He settled on it gingerly and then nodded to Myojo.

The magician turned away and bowed her head, the tall pointed cap nodding with her. Seito took wing once more and began to trill a brief tune that had an air of pathos and discordant sorrow.

Myojo turned back to her small audience and her face looked different, almost like a mask, so bereft of emotion it had become. Her hands, however, became animated and Maggiormente found his eyes drawn there. The movements of her nimble hands began to sketch in a landscape. Green hills appeared in the air, then a village upon the hill and people within it.

Magic! The alchemist found himself delighted with the unexpected pleasure of the spell. The scene grew more distinct. He could see the sun rising on the day.

"Delightful!" he whispered to Eduardo.

"Shhhh," the lion said leaning toward the impromptu stage. "She's telling a story."

Maggiormente grinned and turned back to the scene. Myojo's exquisitely controlled athleticism had a beauty of its own. The magic she created was truly graceful.

"Here our story begins," she said her hand making a circle around a house with a cherry tree before it. "Here, a brave samurai lives with his wife and children. The wars are done, but something else has threatened the land."

Myojo's hands spread wide to highlight the scene she had created. Maggiormente and Eduardo followed her expressive gestures as they sketched in the scene, the hills and the little house and the trees hanging wispy in the air.

"The brave samurai thought that he could hang up his sword and live as a peaceful farmer in the house with the cherry tree. His young wife honoured him with two children, a girl and a boy, and he looked forward to watching them grow up in the quiet green hills.

"But the emperor sent a messenger who called him forth from his home. Bitter to his heart this demand; he hated to leave the serenity of his house and family. His wife reminded him of his honour due to the emperor."

Here Myojo changed her gesticulations and the samurai and his wife came to life. Insubstantial shapes yet distinct in the afternoon light. Another trill from Seito shifted the mood and the colours of the panorama. The alchemist found himself amazed.

"She told him, 'We are but small people to the great emperor, so we must do as he bids. I ask only one thing of you.'" Myojo gave the woman a sad mien but incredible beauty.

"'If you meet any small creature in distress, I beg you think of me and offer it a kindness. Though the rich and mighty command us, it is by how we treat the least of creatures that the gods will judge us. Promise me.' The wife took his hand in hers and implored him.

"There are those who say she had the sight, but others say it was only her good heart that prompted her to speak to him so. This is the way of legends that have been told over the ages."

"True, true, most fairly true," Maggiormente agreed,

nodding his head sagely.

"Hush," Eduardo growled. "Don't interrupt the story."

The alchemist felt chastened and clamped a hand over his mouth to reassure the lion. Myojo only smiled.

"The samurai promised his wife he would take her counsel and carry her wisdom in his heart. Then he donned his armour, sharpened his blade, kissed his children goodbye and said his sad farewell to his beloved.

"He mounted his charger, Dawn's Light, and rode to the imperial palace. Everywhere the glories of the spring saluted him and he felt a wistful sense of loss that he would not watch the season unfold at the side of his beloved wife while his children played on the hills around their home.

"Thus ever is the life of those whom providence has given less power. The emperor's fantastic palace greeted him with its familiar pomp and richness, but the samurai could only think with sorrow of the warm hearth he had left behind.

Myojo waved her hands with delicate movements, though they were bolder than before. In the air the mighty palace of the emperor emerged. The colours dazzled, the heights met the sky. Maggiormente remembered to keep his thoughts to himself, but he could not help the sighs of pleasure that slipped from his mouth.

"The samurai had been happy in his modest home with the love of his family surrounding him. Here the emperor sat amongst the greatest of riches—many of which had been won in the countless battles the samurai had been engaged in over the years. Yet the emperor was not happy."

Seito chirped a more subdued tune, one that caught a sudden spark of melancholy. Eduardo felt it at once, though he was puzzled by the sudden descent of darkness when his eyes were so delighted by the tableau.

Myojo continued the tale, highlighting the emperor in his palace, sitting on his red cushions, surrounded by golden wealth. "The gloom of the emperor infected those around him. There could be no laughter while the emperor sighed.

"Thus it is for the rich and mighty. They can command multitudes, but they cannot always command their own hearts.

"The samurai left his charger, Dawn's Light, at the stables and sought admittance to the emperor's chamber. There his fellow soldiers all shook their heads and declared the matter hopeless. The emperor's advisors all clucked their tongues. Hopeless, they repeated, it was all so hopeless.

"The samurai looked askance but no one offered an explanation. He stepped up to steps below the emperor himself and laid his sword on the floor before him.

"'Mighty emperor,' he said with all humility, 'I offer my sword to you again. I have served you with all the power in my bones. If there is anything I can do for you, you have only to command me and I will fly to fight you enemies, though they run to the deepest cave or flee across the oceans or ride across the great deserts.' With that he bowed low, pressing his forehead to the floor.

"But the emperor only sighed. His sorrow seemed too great to be spoken. The samurai considered the pain in the emperor's voice. How to unlock the silence of his suffering? He remembered his wife's wise advice when his daughter would not speak of her pain although she was in tears. His wife begged him to take her on his lap so she might whisper her secret in his ear.

"The samurai arose and spoke to the advisors. 'Let me speak to the emperor alone!'"

"Will he tell us the secret?" Maggiormente whispered.

Eduardo remained captivated. "Don't speak," he said as if to do so might break the spell. His tail lashed behind him but he never looked away from the wisps of scenery that Myojo's hands painted. The proud samurai and his elegant emperor floated in the air like water paintings brought to life.

"The advisors were loath to grant the samurai a private audience. After all, such a thing had never been granted to any of them."

Seito whistled a few impatient trills that caught the officiousness of the advisors perfectly, matching the illusions the young magician sketched in the air.

"But the emperor's sorrow oppressed them all and at last they gave way to the samurai's request. One by one they withdrew, the final advisor looking wistfully on. Although the samurai had fought bravely in the emperor's army for a decade, it seemed unnatural to leave the emperor alone with anyone at all."

Seito's song changed to a sorrowful refrain. Maggiormente felt his heart swell with sadness for the lonely emperor and his burden.

"The samurai spoke in gentle tones. 'Can you not share your sorrow with me, your old friend?' He bowed forward again, his forehead on the wooden floor and the room so quiet that he could hear the wind rustling the apple blossoms outside the emperor's palace."

The alchemist and his lion leaned forward. Now that the story concentrated on the two figures, Myojo cast their images larger. They could see plainly the sorrow on the emperor's face and the tender sympathy on that of the samurai.

He is a fine fellow, Maggiormente thought, nodding to himself.

I bet the emperor needs to eat a chicken, Eduardo felt certain. Hunger was the primary cause of sorrow in his experience.

"The samurai waited patiently, listening to the song of the wind in the cherry trees. He thought of the wind whispering his love to his wife and children and sent a kiss along its path.

"He had nearly forgotten what he awaited when at last the emperor spoke. 'I have been tortured by a dream for many nights now,' he said, his face betraying the cost of those sleepless evenings. 'A strange dream awakes me. A young woman of such matchless beauty that I can hardly breathe in her presence—she seeks me out.' He sighed.

"The samurai smiled. 'There are many who would pay great sums to have such dreams at night, my emperor.'

"Yet the emperor only shook his head. 'Her beauty bewitches, but a terrible sorrow weighs upon her heart and causes mine to ache.' He put his head in his hands and wept bitter tears of sympathy."

Seito's song now took on the character of dropping tears and real teardrops sprang into the eyes of Maggiormente and Eduardo as they beheld the swelling scene before them.

"Oh, that she and he should suffer so!" Maggiormente said with passion. Eduardo laid his paw upon the alchemist's arm, sharing his heartache for the emperor and his dream.

"The samurai allowed his own tears to flow, too, but determined that he would not stop there. 'Tell me her sorrow, emperor. Surely we can come to her aid.' The samurai longed to restore his emperor to calm peaceful contentment.

"'I do not know her sorrow,' the emperor confessed. 'I know she has been imprisoned, but when she seems about to speak a shadow falls over her, she quails, and silence overtakes her.' He shook his head sadly.

"The samurai thought about this. 'Where is she imprisoned? Can you tell?'

"The emperor rubbed his chin. 'I know she is in a cave in the foot of the Green Snake Mountain. I cannot tell how I know that, but even as I say it, I know it to be true. Something powerful binds her there, for when I think of sending my army to rescue her, the words catch in my throat and I am mute.' He sighed and his sorrow appeared deeper than ever.

"What can they do?" Maggiormente muttered.

"Shhh," Eduardo hissed. "The samurai will find a way."

"This is true," Myojo assured him, a little smile slipping out as she moved to take up another position. "For the samurai was fearless, proud, and loyal. No obstacle could keep him from protecting his emperor.

"At last he said, 'Let me seek her, my emperor.' The emperor could not speak his thanks but the joy on his face was enough to light a thousand lanterns. He could only nod his assent, tears flowing down his cheeks once more, but they were tears of joyful relief this time.

"He clapped his hands and his advisors returned at once, looking harried and even more so curious. 'My faithful samurai must undertake a long journey,' he told them his voice strong with command once more. 'Give him whatever he needs and help him on his way. He must be denied nothing!' The emperor clasped his friend with delight and the samurai loaded food and offerings onto Dawn's Light, then mounted his horse once more and rode toward the Green Snake Mountain."

Myojo showed no signs of fatigue as she continued to weave the story before them. Although she called the magic she created 'illusions' Maggiormente saw the resemblance in her work to what the painters he knew did. Her palette was broad even if her colours remained ethereal.

And Seito! The bird seemed to bring the vibrant paintings to life, animating them somehow with the simple trills of sound. It was alchemy of a most extraordinary kind. He felt a joy that was nearly inexpressible.

The power of magic!

Somehow the artistry of another renewed his own well of inspiration and the alchemist very nearly wished to leap up and go to his work table right then. Suddenly his mind filled with possibilities. He longed to show the emperor of Japan his work, for surely the man who recognized the genius of Myojo and Seito would understand his work as well.

But first there was the tale. Even hungry Eduardo

remained captivated, his rapt attention evident in the tense lines of his body and the way his tail whipped gently back and forth.

"Even loaded with extra supplies, Dawn's Light galloped swiftly across the land toward the Green Snake Mountain. The samurai could see it far in the distance, but he did not let the distance discourage him. The miles disappeared while he conjured happy thoughts of his loving wife and his happy children. Although far from them, he carried their voices in his head and imagined what they might be doing all day while he was gone.

"At midday he stopped to water his horse and let him crop some grass. The mountain remained a long way off, but he was not disheartened."

Seito made the sounds of a little waterfall and a stream. Eduardo looked at Maggiormente. "I am almost afraid I might get wet from the song."

"Shhh," the alchemist said, but nodded his head. The effect was uncanny.

"The samurai lay down to take a brief nap, but he heard a whimpering sound. Glancing around the clearing he noticed a small brown rabbit tangled fast in some vines. Probably it had been pursued by a hawk or fox until it ended up in its present situation."

Myojo cast the picture of the little frightened rabbit, her poor foot tangled fast in the grip of the green vine.

"She's trembling," Eduardo said, not even thinking of eating her.

"The samurai at first thought, 'It is the way of nature, the weak must suffer and die while the strong survive.' But then his wife's pleading words came to his mind. 'If you meet any small creature in distress, I beg you think of me and offer it a kindness.' The samurai bowed his head, acknowledging his wife's words as a command.

"He stepped over toward the small creature, who cowered before him. She well knew that humans hunted her and had only a moment to send farewell thoughts to her kits in their burrow."

Seito, who had been singing a dirge-like melody as the rabbit's little heart hammered with alarm, suddenly burst into a happy trill.

"The samurai gently extricated the rabbit from the twist of the wild vines and set her gently on the grass with a small bow. The rabbit could not believe her luck and looked up with awe at the samurai. Then she too bent and bowed to show her gratitude to the samurai before leaping off into the woods.

"Watching her go, the samurai's heart lifted and he felt the connection with his wife warm him across the many miles, and he could almost hear his children's laughter. He thought of the sorrow of the emperor and prayed again to his ancestors that he might be able to find the mysterious woman who haunted his emperor's dreams."

Seito's song managed to capture the melancholy and the hope that spun through the samurai's thoughts. The green of the clearing and the blue of the water filled the air between Myojo's hands.

"When they had both rested a time and refreshed themselves, the samurai remounted Dawn's Light and rode into the west toward the mountain. As he rode he did not mutter or worry, but observed the simple beauties of the land. The people working in the fields, the streams that fed the rice paddys, the hills and woods. The emperor's land was one filled with extraordinary beauty.

"In the evening, he slept with quiet gratitude, knowing he did his best every day.

"The journey went on for several days. The samurai did not worry, did not get impatient or disheartened, but went patiently on, adjusting his thoughts to the rhythm of Dawn's Light's hooves as they rode along."

Seito made a clicking sort of song that sounded very like horse hooves. Maggiormente clapped his hands with delight.

"On the seventh day, the samurai arrived at the foot of

the Green Snake Mountain. At the bottom of the mountain, at the foot of the path upward, there lay a small temple. He dismounted and entered the temple, which seemed to be empty—then he heard a voice."

"Who was it?" Maggiormente asked, but Eduardo shushed him with one huge paw. Myojo did not seem to notice the interruption. Seito sang a simple piper's tune.

"The samurai turned. The voice that beckoned him came from a tiny old woman, who walked with a bent back. Her abundant white hair piled on top of her head, knotted elaborately and held in place with a pair of ebony chopsticks.

"'You are not safe here,' she warned him. Her voice was gentle and even, but the concern in its tone was plain. 'The demon of Green Snake Mountain has driven everyone from this place except me. I am only allowed to remain to care for the temple.'

"'I have come seeking a beautiful woman who has visited the emperor in his dreams. He believes her to be held captive in the mountain,' the samurai declared.

"The woman blanched at his words," Myojo said, her hands flying up to protect herself as she had become the old woman. "'Do not speak of this! It is forbidden.' She looked over her shoulder as if someone might be watching her."

Seito suddenly fell silent. The alchemist and his lion felt a strange thrill of fear and looked worriedly around them, as if they had entered the temple with the samurai.

"However much the samurai pressed, the woman refused to speak of the matter, but it gave him hope that he was in the right place. The caretaker's distress moved him, but he knew he must try to find the mystery.

"At last the old woman realised he would not be thwarted. 'I can tell you nothing,' she repeated with a deep bow, 'but if you wish for enlightenment, leave an offering at the altar in the inner chamber. Flowers are best. And don't forget to light the incense.'

"Then she disappeared and he was left with the memory of her sad smile. The samurai squared his shoulders and turned toward the interior of the temple and found the inner chamber. The statue of a beautiful goddess drew his eye to the main altar. The great Amaterasu looked as beautiful as a summer morning and his heart lifted despite the dark mysteries of this place."

Seito began to sing a song of powerful joy that made Maggiormente and his lion sigh with happy peacefulness. Myojo's words and hands made the entire scene so vivid. They felt as if they were in the temple looking over the samurai's shoulder as he lit the incense. Then he stepped outside and gathered some blossoms from the flowers that surrounded the temple and brought them inside.

"The samurai spoke as he spread the flower petals before the goddess," Myojo continued. "'Great Amaterasu, I ask for your help and guidance that I may please my emperor and find this woman he seeks, who seems to be in so much trouble. Her I must aid. I ask you this for my emperor, for this imprisoned woman and for my wife and children whose love fills my heart always.' He bowed low before the altar, his breast full of hope and affection.

"When he arose, the samurai gasped. The flower petals danced on the air, swirling like autumn leaves. A sprightly tinkling music filled the temple and even the light of the air seemed alive."

Seito's jaunty tune made the alchemist wish to jump up and dance, yet he did not want to break the spell of the story. Eduardo seemed to sense the feeling, too, and he lashed his tail about him to show the excitement.

Myojo continued, "The samurai felt certain this was a sign of the goddess' favour, so he bowed low again to show his gratitude, then stepped lively to where Dawn's Light awaited, leaped into the saddle and headed to the path that led up the mountain.

"His horse climbed higher and higher and he began to feel as if all would be well, when suddenly a horrifying shriek filled the air. Dawn's Light shied with fear and it was all the samurai could do to remain on his back. He hopped down and held the reins as he did his best to soothe his mount.

"The samurai looked around in wonder but at first he could see nothing. He looped Dawn's Light's reins over a branch and continued up the path on foot. It had become rather steep but he was making good progress.

"As he crested another rise, the samurai saw a dark cave. Perhaps the woman was held captive inside there. In his eagerness he picked up speed again, though he also drew his sword, for the terrible cry had unsettled him.

"He had come within some hundred paces of the cave, where he could see a blue light flickering, when with a roar an enormous demon leapt onto the path before him. It had many arms each with a sword and many heads, all roaring the same terrible sound."

Seito managed to make an admirably terrible sound from her tiny throat that awed the alchemist and Eduardo. Surely the demon's voice resounded a thousand times more, but for a wee bird, the feat amazed.

"The samurai took up a fighting stance and challenged the demon. They both cried aloud, a warrior's yell, then the battle began. The samurai had been trained by great masters and had survived many battles. His sword flashed and parried. The mountainside rang with the clash of weapons. At first the samurai felt a sense of satisfaction as he was able to both protect himself from any blows and deprived the demon of several arms and even a couple of heads. But then he noticed a terrible thing.

"They grew back; each head that fell and rolled away was at once replaced by another horribly grimacing one and each new arm that dropped and became a snake immediately gave rise to another."

"How terrible!" Eduardo said with a sense of awe.

"How awful!" Maggiormente echoed, his heart going out to the brave samurai.

Myojo smiled grimly, yet continued with her tale. Seito had fallen silent for a moment as if she too were giving rapt attention to the adventures. "The samurai fought throughout the long day. The battle raged back and forth before the cave, however nothing really changed.

"The samurai continued to remove the heads and arms of the demon, but the demon always grew them back faster than a blossom falling to the ground. When at last the sun began to set, the samurai had to admit his defeat. The combatants bowed to one another as tradition dictated.

"'I shall face you again tomorrow, my friend', the demon said with an evil laugh, then turned and disappeared into Green Snake Mountain. The samurai walked back down the slope until he found Dawn's Light. While he took care of his horse, the samurai reflected on the uselessness of the battle with the demon. He was prepared to fight the demon again, just as fruitlessly the next day, yet he wondered if greater wisdom might lie beyond his military habits.

"After he had watered his horse and found it a little space on the mountain to graze, the samurai built a fire to cook his food, all the while pondering his problem. He barely tasted the soup and rice while he chewed, his thoughts worrying at the problem like a dog with a bone.

"Yet he could see no solution."

"If only he knew magic," the alchemist broke in. "There would be so many things he could do. Explode the ground in front of the demon or dazzle him with something that looked like gold for a few hours or make him sleepy with just the right concoction..." Maggiormente stroked his beard, thinking about the breadth of ideas he had that could help him face down a demon should the opportunity arise.

"Shhhhh," his lion said, "He's a samurai not an alchemist."

Myojo indulged the interruption and waited until they

seemed to settle before continuing on with the story. All at once the green mountain rose up again as her skillful hands painted the scene. "The samurai slept beside the fire, his gaze upon the stars in the heavens above him.

"'My wife sees these stars tonight,' he thought as he looked up. 'I send my love to her by starlight.' He could almost swear he heard her respond in kind. It made it easier for him to fall asleep, although his mind remained troubled with the problem of the demon. Nonetheless, knowing his wife waited for his return made him feel he could never really be alone."

Maggiormente sighed, but Eduardo raised a paw to his mouth to hush him and he did not express his own longings.

"In the morning the samurai saw to Dawn's Lights needs first, then returned to the small stream he had found the day before and went to perform his customary ablutions."

Seito trilled the sounds of a little brook. The alchemist and his lion wondered anew at the amazing little bird's incredible ability.

"He gave his thoughts over to silence for a moment as he had been taught long ago, clearing his mind. The samurai remembered the words of his master, that the true warrior has won the battle before he picks up his weapon, or he will never win at all.

"But then he sighed. The demon could not be defeated by conventional means. 'If I cannot defeat the demon, how will I rescue the woman within the mountain?' he wondered aloud.

"Just then on the other side of the wee brook a small brown rabbit appeared. The samurai expected that it would run once it realised he was there. He must have been awfully quiet for the rabbit to approach so near.

"Yet it simply stood there watching him for a moment, its tiny nose twitching. The samurai stared back, curious but puzzled. After a moment, the rabbit seemed to nod at him, then it turned and started away. Then it did a very odd thing.

"It looked over its shoulder as if waiting for the samurai. It hopped a few more steps, then looked back again. There could be no mistaking it. The rabbit waited for him."

"The samurai took up his sword and slowly stepped across the stream, worried that he might frighten the rabbit after all, but she only hopped further along, though never very quickly, and always looking back to make sure the samurai continued to follow her trail."

"The rabbit is magic," Eduardo said decidedly. "Like me." Maggiormente took the opportunity to shush him, but the lion already stared expectantly at the illusionist.

Myojo smiled. "The rabbit led the samurai along the mountain side until they came to a rather large boulder. She went around it and for a moment disappeared from sight. The samurai stepped around the border and saw a crevasse in the rock. He leaned into it. The air was cool and swift-moving.

"And in the distance, he could see a glimmer of blue light."

"The samurai peered into the darkness. There could be no doubt about it. The blue light flickered far away down in the depths of the cave."

"What was it?" Maggiormente could not stop himself from asking.

For once, Eduardo did not shush him, but also blurted out, "I think I know! I am almost sure of it." His tail whipped around to show his excitement.

Myojo smiled and her hands halted. "Are you sure?"

Her audience found themselves at once chastened. "Perhaps we should wait to see," the alchemist muttered. He did not want the magic to end, that was for sure—not a moment before it had to do so. His lion nodded his assent. "Let the story continue."

Myojo grinned in triumph. Seito whirred a little sound

that might have sounded suspiciously smug, too, but no one thought any the worse of her. Indeed it had been well earned.

"The samurai began the slow trek down the cave entrance. The way had great peril as the rock surface varied much and many loose stones threatened to roll across his path and block the way.

"Carefully he trod down the path and the flicker of blue light grew stronger. He could see a shape in the light. His heart leapt up because he became certain that the shape was a woman's.

"The samurai did not know whether the demon could sense his presence, thus he moved with care, but he thanked the rabbit who had shown him the way. How kind the little creature had been! He thanked his wife, too—it was her wise example that had guided him so far."

Seito's song managed to capture the enclosed space of the cave and the hope that had sprung again in the samurai's heart. The trill raised the hair's on Maggiormente's neck and he thrilled again to the excitement of the adventure.

"The samurai came around the last turn and saw there the woman of almost unearthly beauty. Her face offered a grimace of fear and pain but it could not diminish her beauty, which took light from something deep inside her. The samurai looked to the chains that held her. This was old magic, indeed."

Seito's song picked up a theme of melancholy and awe. The samurai became vivid in the sweep of Myojo's hands. So too did the beautiful woman cowering against the cave wall, chained by an unearthly evil. The demon had done this.

"The samurai bowed low before the woman. 'I have come on behalf of the emperor, who wishes you to be rescued.'

"The woman recovered herself enough to acknowledge

his obeisance, but shook her head sorrowfully. 'The demon who enslaved me here set his seal upon these chains.' She rattled them in vain. 'No human hand can free me from these bonds.' Her tears flowed anew at the pronouncement of her terrible fate.

"The samurai would not accept the truth of this and sought at once to attack the chains. His sword clanged against the rock and the chains, but could do nothing to release her, setting off a shower of sparks but making no mark even upon the links. He was at a loss.

"Just then a small sound behind him made him turn. There he saw the young rabbit doe once again. She had been joined by all her family, the little kits crowding around her. They were frightened by the presence of the humans, but they were also excited to be there. At once they set to nibbling at the chains. The samurai stared. Surely they could not have any effect on the heavy iron chains!

"The chains however were not forged from iron, but made of old magic. The rabbits made quick work of the links, chewing away at the bonds until they fell from the arms of the woman who cried again, this time with relief and delight. She picked up the rabbits one by one and kissed them each on the forehead.

"This is why to this day you will find the mark of the goddess on the forehead of exceptional rabbits, for goddess she was, sister of Amaterasu, and her seal was that of good luck and abundance.

"The samurai took her hand and they left the same way he had made his uncertain journey into the mountain. The rabbits followed behind them and skipped into the green meadow behind them, turning somersaults of delight.

"The samurai begged the woman to take a seat upon Dawn's Light, preparing to lead her back to the emperor's palace. But the woman only laughed at his offer. The samurai was distressed. Having been able to free her from the torment of the demon, it seemed an unutterable sorrow not to be able to bring her to his emperor."

"Oh, that is wrong!" Eduardo blurted out.

"Shhh," the alchemist threatened.

Myojo smiled broadly. "The woman said to the samurai, 'Mount your horse, good man. I shall fly by your side until we return to the palace of the emperor and all will be well with us. All abundance shall come to your land and your people.'

"The samurai felt such gladness in his heart at her words that he could not speak."

Maggiormente brushed away a tear, no less enraptured in the tale now that he could feel its end drawing near. Like the samurai he found a gladness filling his heart that made it feel as if it were bursting.

Eduardo did not even notice the hunger growing his belly, which may have been an occurrence without precedence. It had to be the combination of Seito's music and Myojo's storytelling magic.

She smiled with increased pleasure, knowing her audience had become as fully immersed in the samurai's exploits as she always did. Seito made a sort of clip-clop sound that mirrored the echo of horse hooves as much as possible and the journey of the goddess and her brave rescuer seemed so very real.

"In no time the samurai and the goddess reached the emperor's magnificent palace. The crowds of people busy at their work stopped and froze like painted images as they glimpsed the incredible beauty of the goddess.

"It was not merely her matchless face or her glorious robes—untouched by her cruel captivity—but the glorious loving kindness that radiated from her like a second sun. For some it was too much to experience and they turned away abashed. Small children ran toward her, laughing. Their parents thought to step in and restrain them, yet there was something in her countenance that let them know the children were welcome.

"Without a command, many people knelt, tears falling

from their eyes not in sadness, rather in a happiness that had the lightness of summer mornings when their hearts would sing with the pure joy of existence and all things seemed possible."

Seito outdid herself with a song so redolent of those delights that Eduardo whined with happy longing and the alchemist wept unashamed, a huge smile across his face. "Yes," he whispered to no one in particular. "Yes."

"When the travelers arrived at the emperor's palace the guards parted like rushes before a boat. The samurai strode into the hall buoyed by joy and the goddess deigned to walk upon the earth once more, modestly following behind the brave man.

"With the scent of cherry blossoms filling his senses, the samurai stepped into the emperor's hall and said, 'My liege, I bring you a wondrous miracle.' Then he bowed low and waited for the goddess to pass him, but she paused by his side and bad him rise and walk with her before the emperor."

Maggiormente was ready to swear that the delicate scent of cherry blossoms had filled the room. Even his lion sniffed the air, uncertain whether to believe in his nose or his ears.

"The emperor arose and swooned at the beauty of the goddess," Myojo continued, her arms sketching the scene in the air, "falling to his knees before her. All he could say was, 'My dream, my dream.'

"'I am real,' the goddess reassured him, 'and in real peril from a demon until this brave samurai released me. I am forever grateful to him.'

"The emperor felt a stab of disappointment that he had not been the one to rescue her. For a moment he hated the faithful samurai, but he gained control of his emotions in the next moment. 'Glorious goddess,' he said unable to hide the effort it took to say this, 'if you wish to reward your rescuer I will be grateful. I shall offer him whatever reward he desires.'

"The goddess, too, agreed. 'Let him have whatever he desires!'

"They both turned to regard the samurai whose heart leapt up at this declaration, but who could not bring himself immediately to declare his deepest desire. 'I serve the emperor and you, my lady. It was his dream that sent me to you. It was the rabbits who saved you by destroying the demon's chains. I did nothing.'

"Both the emperor and the goddess tutted at his modest declaration. 'Is there no boon you would ask of a goddess?' the emperor asked, fearing the answer.

"The samurai hesitated, but the two of them looked at him with such expectation that he at last relented. 'My heart's fondest wish is to return home to my wife and children to live happily as long as the seasons turn and I draw breath.'

"The emperor's own soul rejoiced and he insisted the samurai take great wealth with him. The goddess kissed his forehead and left the same mark of grace that the rabbits shared. And the samurai went home where his wife smiled at the kiss of the goddess on his forehead and his children laughed and played and there was not a happier family in the whole of Japan."

Myojo bowed low and Seito whistled a cheery tune while the alchemist applauded wildly with joy and tears and his lion ran crazy circles around them all, flapping his wings noisily.

"A fine tale! A grand tale! Well worth an emperor!"

"Let's eat cake," added Eduardo. "We know just the place."

"Indeed we do," Maggiormente said, wringing Myojo's hand with great feeling. "Come along to our friends' café and they will hear what a wonder you bring us. I cannot wait for the Exposition to begin!"

And away they all went.

9 INSPIRATION

"Set it down in the field there!" Helen pointed below them, where a reasonably wide expanse of green met the eye.

"Aye, aye, *signorina*," Romano called as he pulled the levers, a slightly worried expression on his brow. Some of it was due to the concentration it took to maneuver the airship down safely.

But not all of it.

Helen glanced over at her father. He seemed completely occupied in a battle of wills with Tuppence, who kept hopping over toward him, threatening to take a bite of his bread and cheese. Her father remained just as determined to keep the tasty treat to himself and to taunt the raven with his eating.

It was just as well.

Helen returned her gaze to the engine assembly. There was no doubt it was too hot and had been running rather too long a while. A part of her mind became engaged with working out a more efficient way of cooling the magnetic heart of the dynamo.

The other parts of her mind tried not to worry too much about the distance there was yet between the airship and a safe spot on the ground.

"Are we going down?" Helen's father asked abruptly.

Helen drew in a deep breath and let it out slowly. "Yes, Papa. We're landing down there."

He got up a little stiffly and tossed the last piece of cheese to the raven, who caught it mid-air and did a little dance of rejoicing to show she was pleased. "Is this Paris? This doesn't look like Paris." He looked over the side with a little more ease than he had shown when they first set off.

He's getting to be quite the airship sailor, Helen thought with satisfaction. *However he would not want to know that we're in some spot of bother at the moment.*

"Papa, we're landing outside Paris instead." *Keep it simple, Helen.*

"But the Bois de Boulogne—you said it was perfect." A hint of suspicion crept into his voice.

"I reconsidered the matter," Helen muttered as she watched Romano shift the gears again to counter the surprisingly strong headwinds that had dogged them since the crossing. *First it was the water spout and then the winds. We've really put her through her paces!*

"We're not crashing again, are we?"

"Papa! We didn't crash."

"We did once, *signorina*," Romano corrected her.

"That was ages ago," Helen said with a slight twinge of annoyance. "We've made so many improvements since then."

"So—not crashing?" her father persisted.

"Of course not," Helen said, seeing the ground near enough to fear little in the way of danger even if they should fall a little too precipitously to the ground. "I just wanted to take a precaution. After all, this is the first substantial trip for the ship. I don't want to take any risks."

"Like crashing?"

"Papa!"

"Isn't that why it's so bloody hot right now?"

Rochester mopped his brow as he gave the engine assembly a baleful look.

"Yes, enough to make me decide to stop rather than press on. I don't want any harm to come to the ship."

He laughed. "The ship! What about your father and your pilot?"

"I am not concerned," Romano shouted over his shoulder as he slowed the airship's descent a little more. There were few people below them, but they were now looking up at the ship, some waving in a friendly way.

"Perhaps you should be," Helen's father muttered, but took to watching the people in the green expanse below them. "My hell-bent-for-progress daughter seems ready to use us as ballast on her way to the future, *signore*."

Romano laughed and the airship set down on the grass with hardly a bump, and Helen allowed herself a sigh of relief. The heat from the engine continued to come off it in waves. It would take a while until it would be cool enough to the touch. Then she could examine it closely for damage, but despite the heat, everything appeared to remain in tip-top condition.

"Where do you suppose we are?" Helen's father asked.

"If I've kept track of things well, we should be near Poissy."

"How is your geography?" Helen's father said with a chuckle.

She ignored this. A number of people had begun to gather around the airship, curious and ready to explore. It took no time at all to discover from the crowd that they were indeed near Poissy. "A not very lengthy carriage ride away from Paris," she said to her father with satisfaction. "The briefest journey in our ship."

It was his turn to ignore what she said. "Who are all this hobbledehoy?"

"Papa, they're just curious."

"You don't suppose they'll do it any harm?" He scowled at a pair of young men who were tapping at the sides of the gondola as if to assess the carpentry.

Helen smiled. *He's feeling protective of my ship now!* It seemed to be a good sign that in the course of the journey so far his attitude toward the ship had gone from one of slight revulsion and mistrust to this rather more solicitous attitude. "I don't think they will harm it. She's a stoutly constructed craft after all."

"Does she have a name?"

The two of them turned to see a stout middle-aged woman regarding the two of them with frank interest. "*Pardonnez-moi*, I didn't mean to interrupt your conversation, but we are all fairly bursting with curiosity here. Your landing is quite the event in our quiet little town."

Helen smiled. "I can imagine it is. It was not part of our original plan, but we thought this might make a safer landing place than in the city proper."

The woman leaned her elbows on the edge of the gondola, watching the two young men now in intense conversation with Romano about his instruments. "Quite right, too. Life is more genteel out here. You would likely be mobbed in the city."

"You don't have guillotines anymore, do you?"

"Papa!"

The woman burst out laughing. "Only in the museums, *monsieur*. We are not as barbarous a land as you English like to think of us. We haven't beheaded a monarch in years."

"Well, I'm no aristocrat anyway," Helen's father said, crossing his arms as if he were feeling pugnacious, though the smile kept trying to break out on his face. "A plain man of the north, Yorkshire born. Doubtless I could hold my own with any revolutionary."

"We came to the practice a little later than you English," the woman continued, throwing her head back at an angle as if challenged, though her grin was broad. "You got your regicide out of the way early. We worked up to it, trying other methods of redress first."

Helen could tell her father was enjoying this immensely, even as he harrumphed. "You should have left us ruling things and you would never have come to such a pass. We could have kept the peace."

The woman shook her head regretfully. "Ah, but what of the wine and the sauces? Oh no, *monsieur*. English sauces? The price would be too great!" Her laughter rang out even as other people crowded around the ship.

Helen's father stuck out his hand to the woman. "Edward Rochester. *Enchanté, madame.*" She allowed him to enclose her hand in his and he bent somewhat stiffly to kiss it politely.

"I am Madame Mathilde Belcoeur. I occasionally write for *Le Figaro*, so I must persuade you to allow me to press you for further details about your journey and your delightful craft."

"*Avec plaisir*," Helen said, taking the woman's hand in turn. "*Je suis* Helen Rochester, sometimes known as my father's trial. Though you seem to be as ready to plague him as if we were already family."

Belcoeur laughed. "My husband says it is my greatest failing, but he relies on it too as he finds himself grateful for the extra income my writing brings us."

Helen hopped out of the gondola with her father's assistance. Tuppence flew down from the top of the ship, croaking with excitement at the murmuring crowds. A little girl pointed at the raven, beseeching her mother for one just like it.

"This is our navigator and weathercock," Helen said, stroking the bird's head as its lively eyes regarded the reporter as if assessing her character.

"How do you do?" Belcoeur said gravely to the raven, who croaked softly as if in hello.

She and Helen both turned to see her father heft himself out of the gondola with a fair bit of awkwardness. The older woman's face revealed concern, but Helen leaned toward her to whisper, "He doesn't like when I make a fuss over him. He's actually doing much better than when we set out."

"Air travel good for the constitution," Belcoeur said, as if setting the thought in her mind. "I'm sure our readers will want to know that. So, you never answered—"

"What's that?"

"Does the ship have a name?"

Helen laughed, blushing slightly. 'I must admit that I had not even worried about a name for the ship. I've been so busy with the design and refinements."

"It must have a name," her father said with immediate decision.

"I suppose so," Helen agreed, but found herself reluctant to jump into the topic. The idea loomed all at once with significance. How did one name a ship after all? What was the right way to go about it?

"A woman's name is often the basis," Mme. Belcoeur added, looking eagerly from one to the other. "Sometimes a goddess. Though there are many that represent a quality as well: endurance or dignity."

"*Liberté, egalité*—" Helen's father harrumphed.

"You're enjoying your joke," Helen said, pretending to be unamused. *Well, what do we call her?* Tuppence muttered a few indistinct clicks in her ear. Helen stared at her. The sound usually meant the raven saw her mother.

"Well, we don't have to start with the name," Belcoeur said, pulling out a small book and a pencil. Clearly the journalist had begun to work. "How long have you been working on this craft?" She looked pointedly at Helen.

"Forever."

"Papa!" Helen scolded. "It's been about two years from the planning to the first flight. We've had a variety of experiences with the craft—"

"She means crashes," Rochester muttered to Belcoeur who raised her eyebrows high.

"Surely not!" She looked very like Helen's mother in that moment, sensible concern uppermost.

"We only had one outright crash and that was not too bad," Helen hastened to add. "Very little damage."

"Signor Romano may disagree on that," her father added, goading her mercilessly. "It was his noggin that bore the brunt of it."

"He's perfectly fine. One cannot break new ground—"

"Without breaking a few necks?"

"Papa!" Helen frowned at her father, fists on her hips. "Mme. Belcoeur won't know that you're joking. He is exaggerating madly."

"I don't know about 'madly'," her father continued unruffled. "The doctor seemed to find it a fairly serious injury. He was laid up for a time."

"But recovered completely, as one does from routine injuries." Helen huffed with irritation. Her father could always wind her up like a mechanical toy.

"Did you study for a long time the field of mechanics or, how do you say, aeromechanicals?" Mme. Belcoeur tried to change the subject tactfully, which Helen appreciated. She noticed, too, that much of the small crowd had left off examination of the craft to gather around the interviewing. It was a most unusual feeling to have so many people paying attention to what she said.

"I made a study of ballooning in general and also studied nautical sciences and shipbuilding as well as the naturalists' writings on birds." Helen found herself somewhat intimidated by the watchful eyes of the curiosity seekers. She had never spoken to more than a handful of people, usually members of her own family. Yet there was something exhilarating in the power of a crowd, too. No doubt about that.

"Did you go to the university?"

"Alas, no. It was deemed more important for my brothers to attend, so I was left to my own devices, although my mother did a great deal to support my learning with the necessary expenditures."

"I helped, too," her father cut in. Helen guessed that he

had begun to see himself painted into an unflattering light.

"I suppose," Helen said feeling a little enjoyment in the sting of revenge for his earlier teasing. "Although mother did *far* more to assist me in my endeavours."

"I have always had the greatest confidence in my daughter's abilities," her father said to Mme. Belcoeur with a firm tone.

The woman seemed greatly amused at the struggle between father and daughter. "Were you afraid your daughter might sail off into the sky never to return?"

A few people in the crowd chuckled at this, which made her father's face grow a little bit pink. "I admire my daughter's pioneering spirit and fine mind. I have always had the utmost faith in her abilities."

Helen smiled at her father. "I suppose thwarting one's father is a time-honoured motivation. But I am grateful I always had my mother's support. She has always inspired me."

Mme. Belcoeur was about to ask another question, but Helen broke in. "That's what we'll call it! Jane's Inspiration!" She turned to her father. "It works so well, doesn't it? It's just the thing. It's what's behind it all. That's it, I know it!"

Her father appeared to mull it over for a moment, then gave a curt nod before breaking into a wide grin. "That will be a lucky name for sure."

Helen clapped her hands together in delight. "I shall have to get someone to paint it on the hull as they do for sailing ships."

"Get an Englishman," her father muttered.

Helen ignored him. "Mme. Belcoeur, I am so grateful to you for sparking that idea." She began to wring the woman's hand with vigour.

"I am glad to have been of some small help. Could I ask a boon in return? That I get an exclusive interview with the voyagers? Perhaps over a meal? M. Belcoeur and I would be happy to share dinner with you."

Helen found the prospect delightful. "If we can send some food to Signor Romano, we can leave him here in charge of the ship."

"We could leave at once. My carriage is nearby."

She conferred with Signor Romano, who had already been introduced with enthusiasm to a family of Milanese folk who were visiting Paris and who had already planned a sort of meal *al fresco* with the pilot. He waved Helen and her father off cheerily, already deep in conversation with his new friends. Helen found herself envying the open-hearted Italians, who delighted in finding their fellows in any land.

Helen suggested to Tuppence that she ride on top of the carriage. The bird looked the driver up and down with care, then hopped up top and sauntered back and forth as if to ascertain its solidity. The three of them got inside, Helen's father gallantly helping the ladies then climbing up himself. Helen was pleased to see that he managed the steps without discernable stiffness in his leg.

She would write her mother that night and say what a success the trip had been so far—and of course tell her the name of the ship. It felt as if a piece of the craft she had not known to be missing had been found.

Arriving at the Belcoeur villa in a short while, Helen's father raised an eyebrow as he examined the façade of the dainty building. "Can you smell the money?" he whispered to his daughter as he helped her out of the carriage after their hostess.

"Papa!" she hissed.

He paid her no attention, but made an exaggerated bow to Mme. Belcoeur. "I see we are traveling in rare circles, *madame*."

Mme. Belcoeur laughed. "I was a shopgirl who married well, monsieur. I do not stand on ceremony. I have learned to play the elegant hostess for my husband, but I have kept my own independent spirit." She threw her head back with a laugh and it was easy to see the saucy young woman who could draw any man's eye.

"I'm a Yorkshireman. We're not impressed with much and we don't go for a lot of folderol either." Helen's father stood a little taller, unable to quite look both proud and humble at the same time, he decided on proud.

"We shall get along famously then," Mme. Belcoeur said decidedly. "*Halo*, Maurice," she said to the servant who opened the door with a bow. "Is *monsiuer* expected home anytime soon?"

"No, *madame*. Henri said the master would be in the office all afternoon."

"Oh, that will not do. Send one of the boys to the office to say we have guests for supper—and I have an exclusive for the paper." Mme. Belcoeur looked quite like the cat with the cream. Clearly the lady was accustomed to ruling.

Helen could not imagine so much excitement surrounding herself, but as Tuppence landed on her shoulder she thought about the eager crowd around the ship and began to reconsider.

"Would your bird be comfortable inside?" her hostess asked. "If not, there is a fine garden behind the house. If it stays this comfortable, we shall take tea there."

What a thoughtful woman! "Did you hear that Tuppence? Would you like to fly over to the garden behind this house?" The bird took wing at once, ready to explore.

"How marvelous to know the language of birds!" Mme. Belcoeur showed them the way through the foyer and into the corridor past a rather lovely small library, which Helen's father regarded with interest.

"Well, I wouldn't say the language of birds so much as the conversations of *one* bird," Helen said shrugging. "I have had Tuppence around me since I was young. We understand one another uncommonly well."

"Uncannily well," Helen's father growled as they stepped through the glass doors opened by another pair of servants and into a rather ornate and somewhat fussy garden.

"Papa," Helen said out of habit, then sat at the little metal table as Tuppence flew down to her shoulder.

"Now I shall have to ask you about this vicious rivalry of which I have heard," Mme. Belcoeur said with evident interest.

"Rivalry?!"

Helen looked over at Mme. Belcoeur with surprise. "Rivalry? With whom?"

"Why the other English airship, *naturalment*," the woman said, jotting down a few words in her tiny notebook.

"Other English ship? Here? In Paris?" Helen was nonplussed.

"We saw no one," her father added. "Did they fly here too?"

Mme. Belcoeur shook her head. "They are assembling the craft near the Exposition grounds and they say they will challenge you to a race."

"Challenge us!" Helen felt her competitive instinct rise to the bait. "We are ready for any challenge. More so when we have our new fuel in place."

"New fuel?" Mme. Belcoeur had a nose for finding a story and it was quivering just then. Admittedly it made her look just a bit like a large hare, but no less becoming for all that.

Helen waved away the questioning. "First tell me more about this challenge we have been issued. It has not been issued to me directly."

"Is that true? They seemed to know you quite well."

"They?" Helen's eyes narrowed sharply. Tuppence hopped off her shoulder and bounded off the table to land on a small pear tree. She made a rather incongruous figure. Although she looked at the single tiny pear on it with interest, the raven did not try to eat it.

"Yes," the *journaliste* looked through the pages of the small notebook until she located the information she sought. "A pair of brothers, I see. Their name is—"

"Linton," Helen said grimly.

"Those horrid young men?" her father said with amused interest. "Didn't their ship burn up in a terrible fire the last time they were foolish enough to cross your path?"

"Papa! *Madame* will think that I had something to do with their ship being destroyed—but surely it was destroyed, *ne c'est pas?*" She turned to the older woman who was consulting her notes.

"I can only guess," she said reading carefully, a finger guiding her along the tiny pages and the miniscule script. "They have a brand new craft that they are building in a large meadow not far from the Exposition site."

"Did they say what kind of motor they are using?"

"Motor?" Mme. pursed her lips as she squinted down the page. "I cannot be certain. I asked them about heights and airspeed—I hadn't really thought about the motor, I'm afraid."

"Ha!" Helen said and Tuppence seemed to echo her sentiments with a clacking series of sounds.

"Is it important?"

Helen's father laughed. "Only if you want to avoid explosions."

"Explosions?!" Mme. Belcoeur's eyes brightened considerably. "How dreadful! Tell me everything." She found a blank spot in her notebook and looked up expectantly.

"Ask the Lintons about the last time they faced my superior craft," Helen said with a little toss of her head. "They will doubtless make excuses for the poor work and cry for luck or happenstance, but their conception was poor from the design to the crafting."

"How is that so?"

"Ignorance," Helen said, nearly spitting the word. "Add a healthy disregard of the nature of physics and simple gravity and you have a recipe for disaster. The essence of a superb aircraft is a delicate combination of great power and efficiency."

"Hence your new fuel?"

"And my more thoughtful—and may I say, elegant—design." Helen felt a righteous fury fuel her limbs. It was not just foolishness to ignore mistakes, it was madness not to try to learn. "You cannot overload the engine with needless resistance."

"You need an aerodynamic design." Her father nodded his head sagely. Never mind that he had only recently learned the term.

"You need to study the flight of birds and the design of their bodies. Look," Helen held out her arm for Tuppence, who immediately flew over to perch upon it, making a few friendly sounds to her companion.

"Just watch out for the beak," her father muttered.

"Papa, don't be silly. Look at this raven. Now there's elegance!"

Tuppence clearly enjoyed being the center of attention as she balanced on Helen's arm. She stretched out her wings to show off the elegance under inspection, as if she did indeed understand Helen's words.

Even Helen could not say for sure how much the bird understood her, or she of it. Most of the time she never thought about it, but only found that the bird anticipated most of her directions before she even attempted to convey them. And it did at times seem as if she understood the creature itself, though often her needs were straightforward.

Ravens were clever birds; all corvids were, Helen knew. But Tuppence was particularly so. And yes, elegant too!

"You see," Helen said, lifting the raven's outstretched wing with the back of her hand. "Many of a bird's bones are hollow to preserve their lightness."

"Oh, that is quite amazing!" Mme. Belcoeur dutifully scribbled the information down in her little notebook. "Hollow!"

"But they are also strong. Birds have fewer bones than mammals because their bones are fused together in sections."

"Mammals?"

"Furry animals," Helen's father offered, who seemed proud to be able to supply some interesting information himself.

"Ah, yes, I see."

Helen reached down to pick up a slice of cucumber from the plates which had appeared as if by magic on the table, placed by the Belcoeurs' silently speedy servants, and held it out to Tuppence. The raven leaned forward to examine the treat and with a twist of her wrist, Helen flicked the cuke into the air.

Tuppence lifted off into the air, caught the slice mid-air and swallowed it down. She hung in the air a moment, then descended back to her mistress' arm.

"The muscles, too, are key," Helen said, smoothing down the feathers on the raven's head as she clicked and croaked back contentedly. "Amazing power and strength. Because birds have to flap in order to stay aloft, they need that strength."

"You have a motor instead," Mme. Belcoeur said, shaking her head to show she understood. "So, that is like the muscle."

Helen smiled. "In sense that's just right. It's what provides the lift. Though we don't have wings to power, we have lift from the engine inside the ship. But the motor does need power."

"And fuel." Helen's father stroked his chin. "Which is the conundrum: more powerful motors tend to need more fuel, which in turn weighs down the ship."

"Exactly!" Helen had warmed to her topic. "So a real breakthrough in the process—both in efficiency and speed—will have to come in the area of fuel."

"Please, let us sit and eat while we talk," Mme. Belcoeur said as she encouraged them to take their places around the table.

Helen threw a piece of cheese into the air, delighting in the raven's playful pursuit of the treasure. "A new fuel that requires less space in the gondola, less danger as far as explosion and greater speeds from its power—well, I shall be proud to be part of such an advancement in the new world of air travel."

"Do you really think it can grow beyond a hobby for, shall we say—" Mme. Belcoeur paused, "the more adventurous types?"

Rochester barked with laughter. "Do I look like the adventurous type?"

Helen smiled at her father. "Whether you wish to do so, you have become an adventurer, Papa. Be proud of the designation."

"My daughter is the brave one," her father said with evident gruffness, trying to cover his embarrassment. "I'm only along to chaperone her. Can't trust a young woman to go gallivanting on her own."

"We shall have to develop entirely new social protocols for air travel," Mme. Belcoeur said, surreptitiously making notes for an accompanying essay on the proper etiquette of air travel for young persons. *The French would always be forward thinking in matters of cultural delicacy*, she told herself, although she found much to admire in the somewhat feral young Englishwoman.

"These are not things I worry about," Helen said, aiming another piece of cheese up to where Tuppence sat on the limb of a pear tree. "I am far too busy seeing what is possible. And the sky, as they say, is the limit." She smiled to herself, proud to have an inspiring quotation for the journalist.

"I'd think instead that the ground was rather the harsh limit," her father opined, his mirth barely contained.

"Papa," she scolded. Mme. Becoeur only laughed.

"We have to fix our dreams on the farthest possible horizon," Helen said with sudden seriousness as she warmed to her topic. "It is only when we go further than we expect to go that we make breakthroughs."

"Advances that seem revolutionary today become essential to daily life tomorrow," Mme. Belcoeur said as she scribbled hastily, trying to capture her thoughts before they slipped away.

"Like the steam engine," Helen agreed.

"I find it hard to imagine that people will flit about in the air like birds," her father said with a harsh bark of laughter. "Just picture that! Madness."

"Papa, don't be too sure." Helen took small roll from the basket Mme. Belcoeur handed to her and used it as if to emphasise her point. "Once people imagined the railroad to be an evil invasion into the countryside—now it has become an essential part of transport and a delight for many."

"Delight might be putting it strongly."

"Don't be too sure, Papa." Helen smiled to herself and blew on her soup. "I suspect in fifty years there will be airships a-plenty across Europe. Why someday they may be able to cross the oceans!"

"I suspect they would have to be enormous." Her father frowned, as if contemplating a gigantic airship gave him pause. "Imagine their shadows. They might well blot out the sun!"

"Papa, you're being silly now. The sky is a big place."

"There is something to consider in his…exaggeration," Mme. Belcoeur said. She noticed Helen's expression of annoyance, but charged on in measured tones. "Just as there is the signal man and the conductor and so forth, must there not be officials for the airships, too?"

Helen considered this. "Once there is sufficient travel in the sky, we must begin to develop protocols and habits, so that we do not have accidents when airships meet in the sky. Perhaps some kind of international set of agreements."

"Doubtless some kind of government commission."

Her father harrumphed over his soup, which he had finished all too quickly. He did not want to go so far as to admit he had not tasted such an outstanding dish since his last visit to Paris many years before as that might reflect badly upon his dear lady, but he did find it distracting. "They will want to get their hooks into the process and get their unfair share."

"Alas, that must be true. Such is the life of the bureaucrat," Mme. Belcoeur said with a sigh.

"That sounds like my cue to enter," a new voice called from the doorway. A stout Frenchman stepped out into the garden patio with a broad smile and an open face. Helen liked him immediately and her father did not at once regard him with a scowl. "I am Hercule Belcoeur. I hope my wife has been entertaining you with all due courtesy." He leaned down to kiss her head.

"*Mon cher!*"

"*Ma cherie!*"

The English folks found their easy affection somewhat difficult to experience; nor could they comfortably look at one another. Rochester chose to stare off into the vague distance as if mesmerized by something remarkable and Helen gestured to her raven.

The moment of tenderness over, Belcoeur shook Helen and her father's hands gravely as he could manage, though a touch of merriment remained. "I hope my wife is getting a good story from you. I love when the newspapers pay her a lot of money!"

If the visitors were undone by the unbridled affection of the pair before, talk of money made them squirm yet further.

"Ah," said Helen.

Her father harrumphed something unintelligible.

M. Belcoeur, as if realizing his *faux pas* changed the subject with alacrity. "I can tell you all of Paris will be looking forward to the contest between the airships. You are bound to draw quite a crowd!"

"Contest?" Helen and her father exchanged looks of surprise—and in the latter's case, alarm.

"Is it not true that there is a challenge to come? Surely I have it right." He looked inquiringly at his wife.

"Oh, yes, that is what I heard, too."

"You mean us and the Lintons?" Helen said, her face becoming grim.

"Smart money will be on my daughter," Rochester said. "I have no doubt they will regret once again that they dared to go up against our ship!"

"*Our* ship," Helen said with a grin. "I like that."

"I only hope," her father said with a very grave expression, "that you will not force me to be part of some wild acrobatics. I think it would be a very undignified way to die."

Mme. Belcoeur gasped. "Is it really as dangerous as that?"

"Worse. In a racing situation I imagine all reasonable caution is flung to the winds in the heat of competition."

"*Madame,* you should know better by now than to listen to my father's exaggerations." Helen laughed. "We don't even know what sort of a race we have been challenged to yet."

"Oh, but I do have the information here. Let me see. Didon! Go fetch my portfolio from my desk." Mme. Belcoeur turned back to regard her guests with a look of animation. "I have the interview from the newspaper in which the brothers make their bold claims of success."

"Ha!"

She grinned at the young woman. "That is why I was ready for your arrival. Of course my natural sympathies are with you, *ma cherie*. We pioneering women have to stick together. Ah!"

Her maid returned with the portfolio and in a trice Mme. was able to extract the folded page of newsprint. "Yes, here it is." She handed the paper over to Helen who frowned in anticipation of what she would read.

Scanning the page where the interview appeared, she snorted with derision. "'Celebrated airship captains'! They give themselves such airs. Captains! Who awarded these commissions I wonder?"

"Perhaps they have been indulged by minor royalty," her father suggested, distracted by the extraordinary perfume of the fish dish placed before him by the serving staff. He couldn't quite recall the name of the herb that flavoured the sole, but it caused him to experience an enchantingly elusive tug from memory.

"I have known the rulers of small duchies to hand out commissions like bon bons," M. Belcoeur said, waving his hand for emphasis. "Of little value except to those who seek rewards they have not actually earned."

"Most men, then," Rochester said with a snort of laughter.

"You are a cynic, *monsieur*."

"I have observed the ways of men frankly and without romantic notions," Helen's father said before taking a bite of the sole. It was superb: flaky and delicately suffused with the herb. It galled him that he could not recall the name of the herb. If his wife were here, she could ask.

He didn't think it proper for an Englishman to show too much interest in cooking, especially in a French household.

"I certainly wouldn't put it past the Lintons," Helen said. "Look here, they do challenge us." She held the paper out toward her father.

"I'm eating. Read it to me, please." His gruffness belied the pleasure the food gave him. The herb's name might remain elusive but he recalled a café in Montmartre—something Russian, wasn't it?—that made a superb sole with just this flavour. Perhaps a little more butter, though.

"Knowing a rival ship to be on its way from England, the captains—ooh, that term again!—the captains plan to show the superiority of their design by racing the challengers—challengers!" Helen's face showed her animation with red blush on her high cheekbones.

"They don't know the full story," Mme. Belcoeur tutted, trying to defend her fellow journalist. "The men and their ship are yet a novelty."

"Get on with the story." Helen's father urged.

"I suppose so," Helen said, still fuming. "Let's see…by racing the challengers from Paris to Orleans and back again during the Exposition. The Lintons will reveal their all-new airship to attendees. The challenger crew may be expected to arrive this week. Challenger!"

"It is perhaps a little *malencontreux*," Mme. Belcoeur said as diplomatically as possible.

Helen handed the newspaper page back to her with a nod, not trusting herself to speak. Tuppence, ever vigilant of her moods, came to rest on her shoulder and offered some soothing sounds in her ear.

"It's a great deal *malencontreux*," Helen said at last, her face surprisingly grim. "But actions speak louder than words. I will show the Lintons."

"And we will have your words in my interview," Mme. Belcoeur hastened to add. "You will have your say, too."

"Good," Helen said. Tuppence added a few croaks for emphasis.

Helen slapped her hand on the table. It wasn't enough to make the cutlery jump, but it was decisive. "You can tell your readers that I will triumph yet again against these upstarts."

Mme. Belcoeur sought her pencil eagerly and began noting words in the little notebook she had kept near her.

"I assure you that we are not the least bit intimidated by the challenge of the Lintons' new ship. After defeating their last ship easily—due to its fundamental design flaws—we have continued to streamline our own craft."

"Streamline?" Mme. Belcoeur frowned. "I am unfamiliar with the term."

"It is a rather new coinage," Helen said, nodding her head with some excitement. "It's become the preferred terminology amongst airship crafters to denote the form which facilitates smooth navigation."

"New infernal machines," muttered her father, having finished the very last bite of the sole and feeling slightly bored, "and new infernal terminology."

"This new modern world," M. Belcoeur said with wonder, shaking his head and reaching for more bread. "So many things to learn."

"Well, then you may enjoy the fact that the next revolution will come via a time-honoured and traditional art."

Mme. Becoeur's eyes lit up. "Is this the alchemist of which you spoke?"

"Indeed!"

"How exciting!"

"Far be it from me to throw cold water on the subject," Rochester lied, "But we have yet to meet this man and he could be some sort of mountebank for all we know."

"Papa!"

If Mme. Belcoeur's eyes lit up before they were positively incandescent now. "Controversy sells a lot of papers."

"*Ma cherie*," her husband scolded. "It is not the thing."

"It is!"

"Signor Maggiormente is a respected alchemist," Helen said somewhat stiffly, her disapproval at the paternal mischief quite clear. *Why does he invariably do this! Why do I let it irritate me so?* She did her best to get her annoyance under control. It would not do to have her work doubted nor her potential breakthrough diminished—

—even if it remained only theoretical at this point.

"If you can use the two terms together," her father added to goad her.

Helen decided to ignore him.

"The new fuel that Maggiormente has developed," she said carefully, using the past perfect to convey the completion of the work she anticipated, "will allow us to travel farther with less weight and undoubtedly faster as well. For too long we have relied on the simple old fuels for combustion."

"Like coal," Mme. Belcoeur suggested, unable to name another type of fuel.

"And whale oil," Rochester remembered with surprise. "Those fools!"

Helen nodded. "Both heavy and the latter, inclined toward fire. Our magnetic dynamo offers the safety of not needing those kinds of fuels, but there are limitations on our power. Maggiormente's fuel will allow us to use combustion and steam, but without the loss of light weight and safety."

"What is this mysterious fuel?" Mme. Belcoeur's hand froze, poised for the revelation.

"Oh, we cannot reveal that information, *madame*!" Helen said, gravely shaking her head. "That will be revealed at the Exposition, of course."

"With great fanfare, whistles and bells," her father added, playing along. Helen shot him a quick look and wondered just what he imagined.

"My readers will be so excited!"

The meal was a delight for all, but as the day wore on Helen became more concerned about the ship. It was all right for Signor Romano, he would doubtless take good care of it, but Helen felt as she expected a mother might feel with a child.

The nurse had a job to do, but the mother had another.

"Oh, you don't mean to leave us!" Mme. Belcoeur could not believe her ears. "*Mon cher*, convince them this is madness!"

M. Belcoeur, however, smiled and shook his head. "*Ma petite gribouilleuse*, would you keep a mother from her wee baby? No, no—we cannot keep Mademoiselle from her *aérostat*…er, *ballon*?" He shrugged, uncertain what term to use.

Mme. Belcoeur sighed. "But you will give me a

complete exclusive series on the airship and the contest, no?"

Helen smiled. "With pleasure, madame! I wish my triumph to be recorded vividly for posterity."

Tuppence, perched on her shoulder, added a few croaks for emphasis. Every one laughed at the bird's effusiveness.

M. Belcoeur and Helen's father shook hands much more warmly than might have been expected a few hours earlier, given the latter's view of Frenchmen. But he was more than willing to admit of quality when he met it. Fair dues he was willing to pay.

The carriage returned them to the park where Signor Romano continued to celebrate with his fellow Italians. They welcomed the returning Englishwoman and her father, but the two of them made their apologies as they were determined to turn in early.

"That Italian," her father said as he rolled out a quilt and some bedding," will be up until dawn drinking and singing with his fellows."

"And what of it?" Helen said, feeding Tuppence a few more handfuls of grain. "He has done yeoman's work so far on the journey. Much more than you or I."

Her father's familiar bark of laughter rang out. "I'm sure I have done as much as he."

Helen snorted. "If you call vomiting and grousing and blustering 'doing much' then I suppose so."

"I have not vomited!"

Even in the deepening gloom, Helen could tell how red his face had become at her teasing. It was so simple. "Well, you have harrumphed and groused and blustered."

"Only in the name of doing things right by you. On your own, do you think you would have had such an easy passage?" He continued to mutter although Helen could only hear the occasional ejaculation of "Grouse! Bluster!" as he smoothed his bedding.

"I suppose I have to be fair, Papa. You have proved of

admirable worth on the journey and I am glad you are here."

Helen could only guess his face remained red—although for a different reason—as he muttered, "You'd not want to have to do without me."

Helen let Tuppence go, watching the bird disappear into the gloom. Where she went, Helen had no idea, but the bird always returned to her refreshed and eager. They each needed their own lives, but it could not be clearer that the raven enjoyed their partnership as much as she.

"Papa, do you suppose we will be able to beat the Lintons?" Because the gloom had become too dark to see well through, Helen let her moment of doubt escape. At times like this, it was helpful to hear that one hadn't lost the plot.

"Damnation!"

Helen sat up and tried to make out her father's face in the growing darkness. "Papa?"

"If you can't be bothered to know your own superiority, I am not going to be troubled to spell it out!" He harrumphed in a most startling way that made Helen smile to herself and lie back down. "The very idea! As if you were not born to make fools of those ninnies!"

Helen grimaced. "I know, Papa. I just worry sometimes. I don't know—"

"Stop worrying and get some rest. What would your mother say?"

Helen laughed. "She'd say, 'Have you got nice clean handkerchiefs? Do your best and have nothing with which to reproach yourself.' I wish she were here."

"So do I," her father said in a voice of such gentleness that Helen felt chastened for her selfish fears.

"She is here, she is always with us, wherever we go." Helen felt tears on her cheek as she pronounced these words, but she knew them to be absolutely true.

"Get some sleep," her father said gruffly. "Those bloody Lintons are probably sleeping in a swank hotel.

More fool them!" In the darkness, they both smiled
unseen.

10 ARRIVAL

"Signor Maggiormente! Signor Maggiormente!" The voice of Mme. Gabor echoed up the stairwell, evidently full of some kind of excitement.

Eduardo growled low, but did not lift his head from his paws where it rested.

The alchemist had not heard his name called anyway, as he was currently occupied with the latest of a series of tests on the new fuel. Inspired by the nearness of the Exposition's start, Maggiormente had finally dreamed himself a solution.

Literally: after pacing their flat for days on end, unhappy with his lack of progress and unable to come up with an alternative avenue of investigation, one night he stayed up until dawn, his rhythmic tread doubtless wearing on the nerves of the folks below him, but no one complained.

That fact doubtless had something to do with his familiar who had managed to intimidate even their garrulous concierge into a somewhat respectful silence most of the time.

Falling into a fitful slumber at dawn, the alchemist awoke late in the morning with a cry of triumph. He leapt

219

from his shabby bed to run to the workroom that sprawled across what might have been the kitchen and dining room in another tenant's existence and set to work.

An hour later—maybe less—he had a solution.

Solution—again, literally. He had a formula, that is; a liquid that needed to be proofed and tested by fire. He had confidence, too, that it was the right one. Before he could do the necessary tests, Maggiormente double-checked his notes, then asked a sleepy Eduardo to sniff the elixir.

"What am I smelling for?" the bemused lion asked.

"Does it smell all right?" Maggiormente asked with evident eagerness, his hair standing up in at least a dozen different directions. "Does it smell incendiary?"

Eduardo sighed. "Most of your concoctions smell incendiary."

The alchemist waved his hands with annoyance. "Yes, but no! This must be the *ne plus ultra*! It is both incendiary yet less volatile." He waved it about as if to demonstrate its safety.

Eduardo was less than convinced. "Don't slosh it around like that. You are likely to get some on my fur and I do not wish to be ignited."

Chastened, Maggiormente held the vial out slowly toward his familiar's snout. "Just give it a quick assessment."

Eduardo inhaled, slightly at first and then with more interest. "It's clearly incendiary…but it's not as acrid as your usual fuels are."

"But incendiary—that's good."

The lion inhaled again, a thoughtful look on his face. "Is there cinnamon in there?"

Maggiormente laughed and nodded his head. His beard bobbed up and down. "Just a pinch! I thought it would improve the scent as it burned away. A *nuance*, as they say. A little sprezzatura in the mix."

"I wouldn't mention it to the pilot. They might see it as frivolous." Eduardo sniffed. "As your fuels have gone, this is the least objectionable in smell. Does it actually work?" He gave the alchemist a close look. One who knew him well might characterise it as surprise or perhaps even pleasure. It was easy to forget that the lion encouraged the alchemist to his best work. "Let us test it."

They proceeded to fire up the small engine the two had purchased with the baker's help. The fuel worked satisfactorily in the engine, producing a reasonable speed and a light cloud of brown smoke that smelled rather faintly of cinnamon.

"Good," Eduardo pronounced it after a serious bit of thought. One wouldn't say it pained him to applaud his alchemist, but it had been so long since the Italian had produced something that did not precipitously explode that the lion could be forgiven for his surprise.

"Good yes," Maggiormente agreed. "But it could be better!"

"You mean—?"

"Yes, time to distill the mixture. And perhaps add cardamom!" Maggiormente had set to work at once, but distilling was a slow process. He paced around for some time before setting to work making more of the fuel simply to occupy his time. His attention no longer required, Eduardo went back to sleep.

The elixir was nearly ready when they were interrupted by the concierge's shouts. "*Signore, signore*! Do you not hear me?"

"What?" Maggiormente said absently as he raised the distilled elixir aloft, admiring its golden tone in the window's light as he walked over to open the door.

"Monsieur," Mme. Gabor said somewhat snippily. "I have been trying to tell you."

"Tell me what?" Maggiormente looked at the woman whose heavy kohled eyes regarded him with impatience. "What is it?"

"Your airship. She is here!" With that she thrust a newspaper before the alchemist and pointed to the column of print. "Look!"

Maggiormente shook his head. "No, no, you mistake, Madame. It is not the right one." *But there were more airships and they, too, might need fuel.* It was something to keep in mind.

"We read the papers yesterday, interviewing the brothers. In fact they sound rather horrible," Eduardo agreed. "Something in their tone struck me as wrong."

"The interview made them seem conceited and ignorant," the alchemist said, shaking his head. "A dangerous combination."

"No, no, you are mistaken, monsieur," the concierge insisted. "Not those two gentleman. A lady. A lady airship captain. See?"

She tapped the story in the newspaper for emphasis. The alchemist leaned over, blenching somewhat at the sudden wave of perfume that wafted off the woman. Madame Gabor's daily toilet had a curiously strong effect.

It made his eyes water some days. He could only imagine how it offended Eduardo's sensitive nose.

Maggiormente did his best to ignore the overpowering stench and concentrated on the newspaper while he breathed through his mouth. The pilot was indeed the one he had been expecting, the *signorina* from England.

He was pleased to see she had an Italian pilot even if he was Milanese. Of course he did not know the man but it seemed a good omen. The alchemist had met English men before (though no English women) and he found them a puzzle to communicate with. They were not on the whole inclined to be direct which led to much confusion.

"She sounds intelligent and direct. I am pleased."

"That would be a relief," Eduardo said, stretching elaborately before padding over to look at the newspaper, too. "Do you suppose she is one of those manly sort of women?"

"I do not like mannish women," Mme. Gabor said with a sniff.

"You do not much like other women at all," the alchemist said absently, stroking his beard. "I find that peculiar." He was thinking of the Japanese magician Myojo. He had nearly forgotten about her in the mad scramble to perfect the fuel. Surely she would want to know about his success. She was enjoying rambling the city, telling tales with her bird.

Mme. Gabor huffed. "I don't know what you mean." She clearly did not wish to admit the truth of his observation but one need only make her acquaintance for a day or two to see that she saw other women as potential competition. It made for a lonely life, as she saw men only as acquisitions.

Eduardo, who had crept up to the alchemist's side, shifted his weight to the other side and brushed against her. Mme. Gabor very nearly hopped away to avoid the lion. No one knew what Eduardo had said or done to make her so nervous around him, but there was a great deal of curiosity about it—except from Maggiormente, who was grateful she no longer hovered over them, but never thought to ask why.

"We should go find the airship and make ourselves acquainted," Eduardo said with a decisive nod.

Maggiormente considered this. "Why—yes! Of course we should do so. I can show her the fuel! We can try it on the ship."

"If she is planning to race the other ship, we will know just how successful the fuel is, too."

"Oh yes, there is something about a race," the alchemist said absently, already thinking of how much fuel to take and what sort of quantities would be needed for a journey. "I wonder how far the race is?"

Eduardo leaned over the paper, causing Mme. Gabor to lean away. "Paris to Orleans and back again."

"What is that in miles?"

"I haven't the slightest notion," Eduardo said, almost affronted by the assumption that he would have knowledge of such things.

"Madame?"

The concierge blinked. "How far? Ah, *signore*, it's…ah…very far. Maybe as much as a hundred miles."

"*Caspita!*" Maggiormente shook his head. "I suppose I could try calculating."

Eduardo yawned. "Calculating based on this tiny motor? I do not think that wise."

"Then we must go find the airship. Where did the newspaper say they were?"

"Poissy, *monsieur*," the concierge said. "They are not even in Paris."

"How far is Poissy?"

The poor woman coloured up and made a sound of exasperation. "I did not expect to be quizzed about distances and locations today! I will find you a map, if you insist." She tromped off down the stair with agitation.

"We shall have to wait a bit longer," Eduardo said as he returned to the best spot for sunbeams, curling his tail about his feet. The gesture indicated his decisiveness. He did not intend to move.

The alchemist looked nonplussed. "What do you mean?"

"The balloon object. It is not even in Paris. We shall have to bide our time a bit longer, you see?" The twitch of his whiskers indicated displeasure.

"Oh, it can't be that far," Maggiormente rubbed his beard and leaned over his work table, getting a little too close to the flame of his candle. As he reached for the vial of sulphur the fire singed his beard and a plume of smoke curled up. "It's in a Paris paper, *ne c'est pas?*"

Eduardo exhaled noisily. "The newspaper tells us of the pope in Rome. Does that mean we are a carriage ride away from the Vatican?"

The alchemist considered this, patting absently at his smoky beard. "You may be right."

"I am always right." Eduardo lay down with a rather

smug expression on his face, which he covered almost immediately with his tail. Fluffing his wings up, he draped them over his sides as if for warmth although the morning was already bright and shining.

"You are often right," Maggiormente conceded, "but that does not mean that Poissy is far. And if she is in the newspaper today, perhaps she has already come to Paris today if the city was not far."

The lion disdained to answer.

There were footsteps on the stairs. Eduardo lifted his head because he heard a second set of steps with the lighter tread of the concierge. "Gustave!"

The alchemist turned around with a big grin. "Gustave!" He and the poet embraced at once, slapping each other on the back with gusto. "My friend it has been too long."

"Ages, my friend. How have you been?"

"He was knocking downstairs," Mme. Gabor said, slightly nettled.

"I was just coming by to tell you the good news," Gustave said. His face flushed pink with excitement.

"Do you know how far it is to Poissy?" the alchemist asked him, wringing his hand urgently.

"What?"

"Poissy? Is it very far?"

The poet looked abashed. He glanced at Eduardo, who remained sitting erect watching the reunion. "Far?"

"I think it is rather far," Mme. Gabor said tentatively, afraid that the answer would be the wrong one. However, she feared more giving hope where there may not be much.

"Oh, not so far," Gustave said, casting his mind back to the memory of a visit to a distant relative when he was a child. "I think it is a day's ride in a carriage with four good horses. Don't you think, Mme. Gabor?" He turned to appeal to her but she look askance.

"I couldn't say, really. Now I must go or the dinner will burn." The concierge beat a hasty retreat down the stairs, leaving the poet and the alchemist looking puzzled and Eduardo looking rather smug.

"Twenty miles?" Maggiormente suggested.

"Surely no more. Do you need to get there? I could arrange a carriage." Gustave was all smiles. If the alchemist had spared a thought for anything but alchemy and airships, he would have been struck by the change in his friend who had been so low for so long, mourning his mystery love. The last time he saw him the poet was still seeking his goddess of the fiery hair, the artist he had fallen in love with from afar—then insulted her drawing before he had a chance to express his admiration for her.

"Do you not think," Eduardo broke in, "that if a horse and carriage can travel there in a day that the airship is here in Paris today?"

The two of them looked at him, then back at each other. "Seems likely, does it not?" Gustave said.

"If so, perhaps she is already at the Exposition grounds." The alchemist tugged at his beard with excitement. To think he might be able to try out his new formula! "We should go!"

"Now?" Gustave frowned.

"Yes, yes. At once. Eduardo, get your hat!" The alchemist grabbed for the formula, then considered what might be the safest way to transport the fuel. Surely the glass bottle was fragile. What better to use?

"But I have news to share!" Gustave wrung the hat he grasped in his hands. "I am getting married!"

The alchemist gaped. "Married?"

"Married?" Mme. Gabor made an unexpected reappearance, drawn back by the sudden news.

Even Eduardo looked surprised. "To whom?" he demanded with a raised eyebrow. When it came to eyebrows, none could match the Venetian lion for expressiveness.

"My beloved, of course!" The poet glowed with delight now that his news had been imparted. "I came to ask you to be part of the wedding party."

"The party? You want us to wear funny hats, eh?" Maggiormente laughed and clapped his hands together with vigour.

"Funny hats?" Eduardo frowned. He did not like the sound of that.

"No, no, you misunderstand." Gustave looked to Mme. Gabor for assistance.

"He wants you to take part in the ceremony, *monsieur alchemiste*. Although it is traditional to have some celebration afterward."

"No hats?"

"I shall wear my fez," Eduardo said with a slight growl.

"No funny hats required," Gustave said, looking anxiously between the alchemist and his lion. "The fez would be most elegant."

Eduardo lay back down, mollified for the moment. "You will have cake?"

The poet was nonplussed. "Cake?"

"I believe it to be customary." The lion looked out the window as if he were somewhat embarrassed by the man's ignorance on the topic.

"I like cake," the alchemist said, scratching his beard, trying to remember what it was he had been about to look for only a moment ago.

"When is the wedding, monsieur?" Mme. Gabor asked, trying to bring some order to the chaos. "And where?"

Gustave looked relieved to have a question he was prepared to answer. "Saturday at the little chapel."

"And this is your cousine Pauline?" The alchemist patted his pockets, certain there was something he had been about to do. Patting his pockets seldom resulted in actually finding an object, but he found the process useful nonetheless. It often served as a trigger to memory.

Gustave stared at him. "I don't have a cousine

Pauline."

"Then you are not going to marry her?" Maggiormente frowned. "She will be disappointed."

"What?" The poet blinked.

"What is your beloved's name?" Mme. Gabor asked gently.

The relief on Gustave's face shone brightly. "Beatrice! She is an artist herself and she has the most amazing, and lovely to paint, cascades of red hair—and her eyes! Did I mention her eyes? Like deep forest glades the green—"

"I'm sure monsieur Maggiormente looks forward to meeting her."

The alchemist nodded absently. "Yes, I look forward to meeting Pauline."

"Beatrice!"

"She has a sister?"

It proved fortunate at that moment that a very strange thing happened to distract them in the middle of this misunderstanding, which one fears could have gone on indefinitely.

What happened was that everything grew dark. Eduardo moved with his always fluid grace to look out the window as he was the first to realise the darkness meant something important and not simply a passing cloud. The alchemist continued to pat his pockets and mutter and the poet uprooted his already disheveled hair.

"Look," the lion said from the window, squinting up at the sky. "It's an airship."

The other three rushed to the window. The ship had cast its shadow right over their building and the sound of its motor echoed between the roofs.

"The airship!" The alchemist smiled broadly. It was wonderful to see at last the very thing that had occupied so much of his thoughts. It was not much like the drawings he had been sent so long ago, but far more wondrous and elegant.

And he would make it go faster and further than

before!

"I would never get up in that monstrosity," Mme. Gabor said with a shudder.

"*Incroyable!* It is not natural."

"Is a house natural, *madame*? Your clothes? A table?"

"My house does not fly, monsieur!" With that Mme. Gabor turned and left once more. She could be forgiven for desiring a rather large glass of wine at that moment for the alchemist never failed to frustrate her and today he had done so particularly egregiously.

The alchemist, the poet and the Venetian lion all stared with varying degrees of awe and wonder as the airship passed overhead. As the shadow passed away they noticed that others were also hanging out their windows to look up to the sky. The hubbub of excited speech filled the air.

"I want to go up in it," Maggiormente said with decision. After all this time of fussing with formulas and explosions, it had never occurred to him that he might take a journey in the ship.

"Do you think that wise?" Gustave frowned. "I am with Mme. Gabor on this question: it just is not natural."

"How high does it go?" Eduardo asked with a speculative look.

If the alchemist had been paying attention, he might have worried about that look, but his thoughts—so recently occupied in searching for some item he had already forgotten—now turned to the future journey in the airship, which he already could picture in his mind. "How high?"

"Yes, how high can it go?" Eduardo thought perhaps he could catch pigeons up there with greater facility, luring the foolish birds near and then swiping them from the sky.

"I don't really know." The alchemist rubbed his beard under his chin. "How high would you say it is now?"

"A furlong?" The poet suggested.

"Oh, not so much, surely."

"How long is furlong?" Eduardo asked. As usual,

human measurements were useless abstractions of no practical application.

"It is less than a fathom—or is it more?" The alchemist had his eyes on the ship yet, though he attempted to focus on the question. His interest quickly slipped away and back to imagining his flight. *I could fly to Rome in a trice!* He sighed for artichokes.

"I think a fathom is much less than a furlong," the poet said, "although they do alliterate."

Eduardo chuffed with annoyance. "Is it higher than birds go?"

The alchemist paid attention to him then. "Birds? No, I think not. Eduardo, you are not planning some mischief, are you?"

"*Moi?*" The lion did his best to look as innocent as a kitten. It was not a successful masquerade.

"I do not trust you as far as I can throw you, *mio piccolo gatto*," Maggiormente said with admirable seriousness. "And I cannot throw you very far at all."

"I would not jump out of the ship onto unsuspecting people," Eduardo said with a hurt air, curling his tail around his feet. "I am not evil."

The alchemist smothered a smile. It might be amusing at that to see the look on people's faces as a lion leapt from the skies—but no. He should not even encourage such a thing.

"Heavens," Gustave said with a horrified look. "What new terrors will come from the skies if we have airships full of great beasts soaring through it?"

"Oh, I don't think that will be a serious problem," Maggiormente said. "After all how many lions and tigers can there be in France?"

This proposition seemed to alarm the poet even more. "I somehow thought there was only this one," he said pointing at Eduardo.

"There is only one Venetian lion in Paris," Eduardo agreed. "But other creatures—"

"What about the zoo?"

"And the circuses," Eduardo added.

"I hear there is a nobleman with a huge menagerie of African beasts in Angoulême," the alchemist said. "They walk the walls of the city."

The poet staggered back. It had never occurred to him that such dangers lurked in the City of Lights. He fought a sudden urge to run to the countryside. But he could not be seen to quail before his lady love! Although he might as well suggest a honeymoon in his aunt's country home in Nohant, far from the dangers of the city. "Such wilderness!"

Eduardo thought it might be wise to change the subject. "Should we not try to pursue the airship? Likely they are heading to the Exposition grounds, eh?"

Maggiormente nodded. "Undoubtedly, yes. Let us go. I will take my fuel…" He looked about him for a suitable container, feeling a strange sense of *déjà vu*.

"We can arrange that later," the lion said with impatience. "Perhaps they cannot use it yet anyway. Let us meet and say hello and get to know this captain. We must be certain it is who we expect it to be."

"Ah, yes. It could be yet another ship!" Maggiormente clapped his hands together. "Let's go!"

The three ran down the stairs and into the avenue. Other people ran along the street, too, pointing above and talking with excited gestures about the airship flying above them. Children ran, laughing with delight as they tried to keep pace with the ship.

It had made considerable progress. Maggiormente tried to do a quick calculation to determine its speed, but he found it a challenge to keep running and calculate the speed at the same time, so he gave up and kept pace with the others.

"It's going very fast," he said to Gustave as the poet loped along. He only nodded in return, clearly unaccustomed to such strenuous exercise.

"I could go faster," Eduardo called. Indeed the lion ran with its wings outstretched as if they might provide additional speed or lift—in fact, as if he might take off into the sky himself.

Of course, it would have been impossible, but he did not mind allowing other people to *think* it might be possible. The people on their street generally gave him a wide berth anyway. To see him fly might more than many of them could have borne.

"But it does seem to be heading toward the Exposition," Gustave managed to wheeze out. "Perhaps we will catch them up there."

The alchemist nodded his agreement, but did not slack his pace at all, even as the poet began to lag behind them.

A knot of people stood before the his friend the baker's café, chatting with animation. Maggiormente waved to his friends but kept running as before. After a moment's reflection, his friend Alain, the baker, took to his heels as well, shouting a hasty farewell to his wife and daughter.

"Are you going to meet the airship?" He called to the alchemist as he paced by his side.

Maggiormente nodded and the two of them lengthened their strides to try to catch up with Eduardo. Behind them Gustave had slowed his steps and turned back to flop down in a chair outside the bakery to commiserate with Adèle.

Around them the crowd shifted. As some people stopped running and simply stared up into the sky at the retreating ship, other joined the throngs pursuing it, seemingly as much interested in the excitement of their fellow Parisians as the vehicle itself.

Maggiormente could see a large black bird circling the ship, which made him worry somewhat, though certainly the people aboard must be prepared to have problems with birds. It must be one of the many new problems flight would bring.

How the world will change!

They all ran on for some time. At last Maggiormente pulled up, calling to Alain that he needed to catch his breath.

"I am not tired," Eduardo said, crouching as if to spring on a passerby, which of course made the other people take a wider path around the lion. As they were far from their own neighbourhood, the Venetian lion had become much more of an object of interest. In fact several people started following him—although not too closely—to see where the lion might be going.

While Eduardo had not been doing anything in particular that might alarm gentle persons, one could not overlook the intimidating sight that a running lion offers to those unaccustomed to such a vision on the streets of a modern city.

It did, however, mean that the citizens quickly cleared a path before him.

Now that they had paused in their pell-mell flight, a murmuring crowd began to gather around the three of them. Alain, quick to notice the mutterings, urged Maggiormente on again. They had to push their way through the rapidly forming ring of spectators, but the baker had no trouble being abrupt with those who gaped at his friends.

"I had forgotten how far the Exposition grounds are," Maggiormente said as he picked up the pace once more.

"Is that where it will land?"

"I assume so," the alchemist said, frowning as he realised the only way to test this assumption was to keep running and hope for the best.

"Well, I needed to work up an appetite!" Alain grinned.

"Alessandro! Alain! Eduardo!"

The three of them stopped and turned to see who called out. At first it was impossible to peer through the crowds lining the streets but suddenly they saw Gustave, waving from an elevated position.

"What on earth…?"

Gustave's vigorous gesticulations drew them across the crowded avenue, where the three of them now saw that he sat atop a carriage, wedged behind another one delivering barrels of ale to the taverna on the corner.

"Transportation," the poet shouted as he continued to beckon. "We will get there much faster in a vehicle."

The alchemist clapped his hands together with delight. He had run much further that day than he had for many years and it was not something he wished to extend further. However much he desired to catch up with the airship, he hoped to have some breath left to speak when they arrived.

"I can run much further," Eduardo said, his tail whipping about him with some displeasure. He did not get enough chances to run as it was. People were always cautioning him away from pelting down the streets as he found natural. Maggiormente explained muskets to him but he was certain there would be few of them in a place like Montmartre. Surely he could dodge such crude instruments anyway.

"Will we be able to get through the avenue with such a carriage?" Alain asked, always the practical one.

Maggiormente paused in his attempt to clamber up onto the carriage with the poet. "Do you think there is too much in the way of congestion?"

The driver made a gesture of disdain. "I can get you where you need to be, messieurs. Tell me where and we will make haste. Your friend has paid me well."

"I may need to borrow a few francs the end of the week," Gustave muttered to Maggiormente as he settled down next to him on the seat. The alchemist nodded. It was no matter. That's what friends were for.

Alain hopped up on the carriage as well. "Are you coming, Eduardo—or will you brave the streets on foot?"

"All four of them," the lion answered coolly. It was clear he took it as a challenge now. The horses pulling the carriage clattered their hooves, anxious to put some space between themselves and the large cat whose scent alarmed them greatly.

"Allons-y!" the driver called with a laugh. The alchemist thought there was something he recognized in that laugh, but he could not put his finger on it and at once the carriage jolted them back and the horses lunged forward into the mêlée of the Montmartre streets.

Inside the three passengers found themselves on top of each other as the carriage bounced along. Eduardo ran through the crowds along the avenue as people jumped aside once they realised he was not a large dog and had no lead. Occasionally he slowed to allow the carriage to catch up, but it never managed to draw ahead of him, despite the nervousness of the horses yoked to the front.

Down the streets the strange procession hurtled, the lion on his feet, the carriage a clatter of wheels and hooves on the cobblestones. They dodged around other carriages, a wide variety of pedestrians crossing to and fro, and at one point a most unexpected sedan chair held aloft on the shoulders of liveried footmen. What person this relic from the previous century carried it was impossible to determine, for nothing appeared between the drapery but a lorgnette clasped in a jewel-encrusted hand.

As they moved out of Montmartre and the roads widened, the congestion became much less and the carriage made much better time, rolling along at a good clip with the driver swearing much less. Eduardo found the pace easy to maintain even though the variety of smells enchanted his nose with new delights.

The tents and the pavilions of the Exposition loomed in the distance and once more the airship could be seen above the place, making a graceful arc above the area as if searching for a place to set down.

"The ship, *mes amis*!" Eduardo called, his tongue lolling with the effort of the long gallop through town. Despite his protestations he had acclimated to the leisurely life with the alchemist. The occasional leap after pigeons was not the same as running after game every day as the lions on the savannah did (or so the alchemist had shown him once in a painting).

The driver cracked his whip over the horses, who picked up their heels again to go even faster, weaving the carriage between other vehicles as they drew closer to the Exposition grounds.

"Look at the ship," Alain called out, pointing into the air. They could all see it now flying slowly lower as it prepared to land in an open area beyond the pavilions. A crowd began to form as people were drawn to the excitement and the carriage had to slow once more.

"Oh, this is no good," Gustave said with annoyance. "We must find a way to work through all these people more quickly."

"So near and yet so far!" the alchemist said with a sigh.

All at once a frightening roar rang out. The people drew back at once, many shoving aside those who did not move quickly enough.

Eduardo grinned. It was good to be a lion.

The driver did not hesitate more than a moment, then again called out, "Allons-y!" to urge the horses on. Their hooves' tattoo and the continuing roar of the lion added to the cacophony of the crowd. If the organizers had hoped for a triumphantly memorable start to the Exposition, they were certainly getting it!

Eduardo continued to roar when the crowd ahead did not part quickly enough. He leapt up to make sure they were still heading in the right direction. Alain did his best to call out nautical directions, but the baker did not seem to realise that the lion did not have the same points of reference.

"Just point," the alchemist said at last, worried that they would not get to the airship in time. What it was they needed to be in time for, he could not have said. But somehow rushing through the streets of Paris in a carriage,

236

following a Venetian lion and pursuing an amazing airship gave him a sense of urgency that quite overtook any more sensible thoughts.

What is this Englishwoman going to be like? The alchemist had not really pondered the question much in the many months since he had agreed to work on the fuel in time for the Exposition. This may seem a bit odd. Most people would be deeply consumed with curiosity about such an important connection. Maggiormente was not most people and it did not take his winged lion to demonstrate that quite plainly. The alchemist was quite happy occupied with his studies and experiments most of the time. He regarded anything but a good meal and a drink with a friend as an interruption to his life's work.

He had great reserves of curiosity but they were mostly engaged with how to create new substances or how to control the reactions of known substances so that volatile eruptions could be kept to a minimum or at least found useful. His concierge, Mme. Gabor, would doubtless disparage his abilities on the controlling of eruptive substances.

The alchemist squinted toward the ship, which looked even more magnificent as they drew closer. The oblong elegance of the body—was it called a body? Perhaps like a ship he should call it the hull. Maggiormente tugged at his beard, lost in thought as the carriage bounced along behind the lion. Would there be a whole new vocabulary for airships as opposed to the watery ones? It seemed inefficient. The gondolas of Venice were his only real experience with ships and that was not much to go on, he realised. Perhaps Eduardo would know more.

The lion roared again, distracting the alchemist from his thoughts about his partner in air travel. The throngs of people parted before the beast, some turning to gape at the strange creature, others only hoping to return on their pell-mell flight toward the object of curiosity.

As the carriage bounced along, the driver seemed to

lose none of his enthusiasm. A strange light gleamed in his eye as if he had been in search of adventure all this time and had not found enough of it on the cobblestones of Montmartre. Maggiormente had learned not to be too surprised by the unusual people he had met in that *arrondissement*, but it made him curious all the same to know more about this man.

"Who is our driver?" he turned to ask Gustave.

The poet looked at him, nonplussed. "Who?"

"Yes."

The two stared at each for a moment, equally confused. The driver turned around and called over his shoulder, "What do we do when we reach the ship, messieurs? Get a little perspective, eh?"

"What?" Gustave and Maggiormente said in befuddled unison.

"We're meeting the airship," Alain broke in. "Monsieur Maggiormente here is a famous alchemist. He is making a special fuel for the ship."

"Is that so?" The driver grinned. "I don't know about all this modern technology. It may put my horses out of work."

Alain clapped him on the back. "Oh surely not, monsieur!"

"And what about me? Will I perhaps have to learn to drive an airship?"

"You never know," Gustave said with an edge of belligerence in his voice. "You might just find it exhilarating."

"It would have to be a living thing. It would not be the same without my horses, I fear." The driver laughed and reined the horses quickly over to the left to slip around a middle-aged banker who had fainted at the passage of the Venetian lion. His wife now fanned him with a copy of *Le Figaro*.

All of a sudden the crowd thinned out and there they were! The ship was coming down to earth and the people stood well back, as if they feared to get too close to the ship they had rushed to see.

Eduardo stood, his tail lashing around him as he gazed up at the ship, tongue lolling and eyes very bright indeed.

Such a hullabaloo!

All around them the crowd muttered its excitement—and a little bit of alarm, too, for those close to Eduardo were understandably concerned about the lion's very large teeth and the incongruity of his wings.

Most, however, had eyes only for the airship. While the idea of airships was no longer unknown as they filled the newspapers here and abroad, there was something breathtaking about this particular ship, an elegance that made it stand out even for those who had seen a ship or two before.

Maggiormente himself stared with excitement. Suddenly it was all real, the work he had been labouring over so many months. This magnificent ship would be the realisation of his efforts. He felt a sudden proprietary glow, as if he had already contributed to the flight.

The ship dropped slowly in height and the crowd could discern figures in the gondola. Many tried to shout and wave to the passengers, but they seemed quite preoccupied with duties at the moment.

"We must go meet them!" Maggiormente shook his friend's shoulder with decision.

The poet's head rolled on his neck from the unexpected grip. "Should we not wait here, out of the way?"

"Where's your sense of adventure, man?" Alain also clapped the poet on the back, eager to get going. "Pay the driver!"

They all hopped down from the carriage and waved a hearty goodbye to the driver, who reined his horses away back toward the city.

"Eduardo!" the alchemist called to his lion, who seemed completely enraptured by the craft.

"Look," Eduardo pointed with his paw. "There's a big bird flying around the ship." Sure enough a huge black bird circled the gondola and then perched on the rail around its edge.

"Don't get any ideas," the alchemist muttered to his familiar. "We must be friendly to our collaborators."

Eduardo looked insulted. "I do not eat everything I see."

"You would if you could," Maggiormente chortled.

A long rope ladder unfurled from the gondola. Ropes with anchors at their ends quickly followed suit.

"We should offer to help," Alain said, nudging the alchemist. They all trotted forward to see if they could lend a hand.

"Eduardo, you keep the crowds at bay," the alchemist called to his lion. He didn't so much worry about the people, who seemed quite willing to maintain a safe distance from the landing area, so much as about Eduardo. No good frightening the Englishwoman right from the start.

The lion took him at his word, sat facing the throng with a serious mien, his tail wrapping around him with dignity. Surely none would venture past him.

Alain and the poet grabbed the anchor ropes while the alchemist took hold of the rope ladder. A figure appeared at the top of the ladder. The voluminous skirts gave away the identity of the person:

It was the captain herself!

A thrill of excitement shot through Maggiormente. He hoped she would be as fascinating as her plans had been. He had not thought much about the woman as he worked on the formula, but now to suddenly see the partner he had worked for if not with, the anticipation of meeting a fellow experimenter in new technologies proved most thrilling.

He felt quite giddy.

The engines slowed to a halt and the ship floated gently

in the warm breeze. He could see his friends drawing out the guiding ropes as the Englishwoman made her way down the rope ladder with sure steps.

What was her name? All at once Maggiormente panicked. He tried to picture the letter with its sure black letters, but the name was not coming to mind. He cursed his poor memory and the preoccupations that always filled it. Madeleine? Genevieve? No, no. It was no good. He had only French names in his brain.

Her skirts were brown and her shoes thick, black walking shoes. All at once it came to the alchemist that it was not decorous of him to watch her descend from below and abashed he looked down at the ground, his cheeks reddening.

"Hello!" a confident voice called down to him. "Or should I say, *bonjour!*"

Maggiormente said, *"Buon giorno"* a little shyly and suddenly the woman had jumped down beside him. He looked down at last to see a pair of sparkling brown eyes.

"Buon giorno? Are you Signor Maggiormente? I am Helen Rochester!"

11 RARA AVIS

"*Signorina!*" The alchemist took the proffered hand and clasped it with enthusiasm. "Yes, yes, I am he. Maggiormente, at your service!" He seemed mesmerized by her face and forgot to let go of her hand until she pulled it very gently from his grip.

"How wonderful to meet at last," Helen said, untying the scarf which held the bonnet on her head. "We shall have so many things to talk about. But first we must bring the ship down safely."

"We have done our best to help," Maggiormente said, gesturing to his friends who waved to the ship's captain. "I hope we did all right."

"Indeed! It helped a great deal. Many hands make light work. It's usually very tricky landing with just the three of us."

"Three?"

"Signor Romano, my father and I. Four, I suppose, if you count Tuppence," Helen added as the raven flew down to perch on her shoulder.

The alchemist threw a glance over at his lion, but Eduardo continued to focus on intimidating the crowd, most of whom seemed quite willing to watch the little

242

drama from a distance. "That's a lovely bird."

"She's a wonder and so helpful to have along on the journey. All kinds of uses for a raven."

"No writing desk," the alchemist joked and then wished he hadn't. He stumbled over his words trying to introduce his friends as well. "Gustave, he is a poet and getting married this weekend. You must come! And this is Alain, the baker. His wife and he make the most excellent pies. Eduardo loves them especially."

Helen waved at the two men as they managed to pull the ship to its rest. "I must thank them properly when the ship is safely anchored. I will also ask you for recommendations for a hotel for my father and I. We were lucky enough to be accommodated last night by a new friend, a journalist. I don't think we will be staying at the places my father used to frequent."

"Why ever not?" said the man in question as he eased himself over the rail of the gondola. "I'm sure I could look up my old companions who would be ready to show us a proper tour."

"I'm not sure I want that kind of tour," Helen said with a sharp little smile.

Maggiormente had the feeling there was a lot he was missing in the conversation, but decided it would be best to leave it that way. "Signor Rochester, I presume?"

"Good heavens," the gentleman said, "Is all that beard on just one man?"

The alchemist's mouth fell open but he had no words. He patted his beard somewhat protectively. It had never occurred to him to consider the state of his beard, or its abundance—if anything, he had thought himself proud to have achieved a prodigious growth.

Perhaps they regarded beards differently in England.

"Papa!" Helen scolded. "Don't be so rude. My father is a terror, *signore*, and you have a most admirable beard."

Somewhat mollified, the alchemist stuck out his hand again to the other gentleman, whose impressive frame and odd scarring seemed to fit the barking voice a little too well, but the Roman was not one to refuse a challenge.

After a long hard look at the alchemist, Rochester deigned to take his hand and offered a grip every bit as firm as his own. "I still think your beard more befitting a wild man of the forest, but if my daughter is content, I won't grumble."

"I am pleased to meet you, sir," Maggiormente said with gravity and not a little trepidation. Yet seeing him eye to eye now, he noticed the twinkle akin to his daughter's gaze. Perhaps the bluster was just a front after all.

"Is that your lion over there?" Rochester said gruffly, squinting over at Eduardo.

"Oh yes, that is Eduardo. I should call him over—"

"Good heavens, he is a wild man! Look at that animal."

"Papa!"

"Eduardo, *per favore*," he called, hoping that the lion would not frighten the poor lady. While before he had thought only about the fuel and its success, the alchemist now had a very bewitching face that he wanted to please also.

The lion walked over slowly, stretching his wings out to their full size as he did so. Undoubtedly Eduardo would wish to have his fez as well when meeting someone for the first time, but alas, it could not always be so.

"This is Eduardo," he said with a mixture of pride and consternation.

"What a magnificent beast," Helen Rochester said, clapping her hands together.

Eduardo preened. He liked the English lady at once. She showed impeccable taste in admiring his magnificence. He stared up at her black bird. "Is that a raven?"

"Indeed, this is Tuppence," Helen said, looking up at her bird fondly. Tuppence croaked a hello to the lion, a mixture of bravado and humour.

"This bird is not for eating," the alchemist said nervously.

Eduardo apparently regarded his words as an insult and thus ignored them. He took the unusual step of bowing formally to the English lady and her raven. "At your service, *signorina, il corvo maggiore*" he said with due formality.

Maggiormente grinned with pride at his lion. Eduardo may be a lot of trouble at times, but he could be as regal as his breeding suggested. "Eduardo can be quite magnificent at times."

"Will we get to fly in your airship?" The lion asked with obvious longing.

The captain grinned. "I'd be delighted to take you for a ride. We shall have to try out the new fuel together."

"Good heavens," her father said, making a face. "Do you suppose Paris is ready for airborne lions?"

"Ready or not, Paris shall have one." Helen rubbed her hands together with evident pleasure. "Ah, here comes our pilot. You will be glad to meet a fellow countryman. Signor Romano, may I introduce the alchemist, Signor Maggiormente?"

The two clasped each other as if at last reunited brothers and within moments had determined an acquaintance in common back in Milan and shared a longing for fettuccine the absence of which was nigh unbearable in these supposedly civilized nations.

The English folks regarded them with a mild embarrassment, so busied themselves with admiring the lion.

"Can you fly with those wings?" Rochester demanded.

Eduardo waved his wings slightly and frowned. "I do not choose to fly."

Helen elbowed her father, who recovered himself quickly. "Quite right, too. That would be so vulgar. You shall be ferried aloft in our ship and cut quite the magnificent figure."

Eduardo was much pleased by this.

"Oh, look! Here are Gustave and Alain," the alchemist

cried, introducing them all around to much hand shaking and pleased-to-meet-yous.

"Let's go have a celebration at the bakery!" Alain invited them, slapping his friend on the back. "Pies for Eduardo! Cake for everyone else!"

"And some wine," Gustave added, for the poet's muse left him ever thirsty.

"But someone must keep watch on the airship," Romano said regretfully.

"Perhaps I should remain here with my pistols," Rochester said, relishing the thought of keeping the French crowds at bay.

"Papa, I hardly think pistols—" Helen broke off from her admonishments, hearing a raised voice nearby.

"Mademoiselle!" A formally dressed gentleman flanked by some *gendarmerie*. "Are you she? *Le capitaine* Rochester?"

"Indeed, I am. Are you M. Piéton? I am so pleased to find you in this crowd, or rather," she laughed, "to have you find me."

"Delighted, mademoiselle," the official said before bending to kiss her offered hand.

Maggiormente took an instant dislike to the man.

"I have a regiment to secure your ship. I imagine that you have many things to do upon your arrival, so we hope to take good care of your wonderful conveyance. If you will just sign here?" He brandished a rather formal letter of acceptance into the Exposition.

"Here, you'll note," Piéton said, pointing at the relevant paragraph, "We guarantee the safety of all and the protection of your property. Having already dealt with an airship, I knew the regiment would be useful."

"You are well prepared, monsieur," Helen said as she signed the form in the indicated place. "I am grateful to have the support of the Exposition. And yes, indeed, we have several errands to carry out and accommodations to arrange, and so forth."

"And wine to drink!" Gustave added.

"And cakes to eat!" Alain assured them.

"And pies," Eduardo growled, making M. Piéton sidle away suddenly with alarm.

"Don't worry," Maggiormente said with a waspish smile. "The lion comes with us."

With much kerfuffle and chaos the party made their way to the bakery, through a Paris that already reverberated with the news of the alliance. Alain and Adèle shooed out their remaining customers as their guests made themselves comfortable around the tables, except for Eduardo who was somewhat distracted by little Brigitte's squeals of delight as she hugged him with evident excitement.

"Eddie!" she repeated with gushing admiration. The lion tried to maintain his decorum in the midst of her wild embraces, but found it difficult as her little fingers dug into his mane.

Helen Rochester watched the two of them carefully, unable to completely feel at ease with the wee girl so near to such imposing teeth, but it was quickly apparent that the great beast had nothing but indulgence for his eager admirer.

"Would you credit it?" her father ventured to murmur in her ear. "What a risk they're taking with that creature."

"Nonsense," Helen said, feeling every confidence in her assessment. "I think Eduardo would be deeply offended at the suggestion that he would hurt such a tender young thing. I suspect beyond the occasional pigeon, no one need fear much from him despite the teeth and claws. He is far too elegant a creature." The latter words came out a bit louder than she planned, but that was all the better.

Eduardo looked up and she could swear that he swelled ever so slightly with pride at her recognition.

"So this is the famous airship captain?" Adèle smiled shyly and offered a glass of champagne to Helen and then her father. "We have heard so much about your expected arrival."

"Yes," her husband agreed, throwing an arm about her waist. "But I must say we did not expect such a handsome young woman to be she."

Helen's father raised a severe eyebrow. "What did you expect?"

Alain and Adèle laughed and exchanged a look. "I'm not entirely certain, monsieur," she said after flushing a little, "but perhaps someone as—shall we say—*unique* as our friend Maggiormente."

Helen laughed. "Is he?"

"What are you saying about me?" The alchemist heard the latter part and had no idea to what it was in reference, but he blushed anyway, feeling more than a little sensitive, which only made him feel more of an awkward giant among the petite French people and the reserved Englishwoman and her somewhat imposing father. "I hope nothing misleading!"

"No, no, nothing misleading," Alain patted his arm and refilled his glass. "We are only too delighted to meet the famous airship captain and to find her exquisite."

The alchemist tried to bow with something resembling precision and managed to spill some of the champagne on the floor before him. He almost used his boot to wipe up the wine, then decided that would look boorish and called for Eduardo. "Would you be so kind," he implored the lion, who gave him a baleful stare.

"Do I not get a bowl?" He looked indignant and the alchemist felt another flush of embarrassment fill his cheeks as his familiar regarded him with a haughty mien.

"Yes, yes, but you could be helpful here," he smiled at Mademoiselle Rochester and felt keenly how penetrating her gaze was, so like her father's although much more pleasant to look upon. *You silly fool, stop embarrassing yourself!*

"Does your lion enjoy wine?" She smiled up at him with a warm expression that made the alchemist feel like a volatile concoction over the flame. "How very extraordinary."

"I have been drinking wine since I was no more than a cub," Eduardo boasted, nodding with approval as the baker set a bowl before him and splashed some champagne into its depths.

"I hope this will not give Belial some ideas," Helen said with her father with a grin. "I don't think he would maintain the same composure as M. Eduardo here."

"I shudder to think," her father said over his glass, but he offered an almost unwilling smile, too, so there was no doubt he was greatly amused.

"But what of the challenge?" Alain broke in. "Will this happen at once?"

"Challenge?" Gustave looked up from his wine with something like alarm. "Is there to be a duel? Not on Saturday I hope. I am getting married."

"Not a duel, but a race—is that not so?" Maggiormente said looking over at the lovely captain, but looking away just as quickly as he swallowed, then took another mouthful of wine.

"Indeed, we have a challenge and I am determined that we shall win. We will have to give M. Maggiormente's new fuel a proper try, but even without it, I would be more than confident of our success."

Tuppence croaked from her perch on a chair near the counter.

"Quite right, my bird," Helen said, throwing a piece of cake into the air for the bird to catch. "We will sail ahead of them like the raven before the sparrow!"

They were all fast friends by the time the celebration at the bakery ended, the Rochesters promising to attend Gustave's bohemian wedding and everyone expressing their eagerness to watch the airship challenge.

"But first we shall have to find accommodations for *mademoiselle* and her entourage," Maggiormente said. "They must have a place to recover from their long journey."

"Shouldn't you consult your concierge? Are there not

rooms at your building?" Gustave asked.

Maggiormente frowned. "Are there?"

The poet laughed. "There is a sign in the window saying 'rooms to let' anyway. I interpreted it to mean that."

The alchemist opened and closed his mouth without a sound. "I had no idea. Perhaps that is why it has been so quiet," he said at last. "That would be ideal, no?"

"Would it?" Rochester raised an eyebrow at the alchemist and looked over at his daughter.

"How convenient," Helen said at once, clearly thinking about the efficiency of the situation. "Is it an amenable situation? Do you think your concierge would be willing to let the rooms to us for such a relatively short time?"

"I think we might persuade her," Eduardo said darkly, which made the alchemist frown.

"I'm sure we can ask her nicely," Maggiormente said at once.

Helen noticed the little exchange. "Do you think she might have some reason to say no?"

"I-I cannot say." Maggiormente shrugged.

Gustave laughed. "His concierge had thought to bat her lashes at him. But he only had eyes for his vials and beakers."

"She is a perfectly charming, er—" Maggiormente blushed.

"She was barking up the wrong tree, so to speak," the poet said with finality. Since his engagement he had come to believe himself to be an expert on affairs of the heart. This despite his near disastrous first encounter with the woman of his dreams.

But he had noticed that since they first beheld her his friend only had eyes for the English lady. Gustave was determined to make much of that if he could. Being happy in love, he assumed everyone else must be, too. Some might call it scheming: Gustave merely thought of it as helping a friend.

"Perhaps we should see if something can be arranged,"

Helen Rochester said, thinking about the unpleasant possibility of having to look further afield for rooms. "If not with your concierge, somewhere not too far. It would be convenient to be able to consult at leisure."

"Yes, yes," Maggiormente agreed at once, hopping to his feet and nearly upsetting the wine glass from which he had been drinking. "That would be most expeditious." He wasn't entirely certain where that word had welled up from and was not entirely certain that he had the English version and not the French, but the alchemist was intent on impressing the English captain with his ability to think as that was more or less supposed to be his strong point.

"Go," Alain said, waving the champagne bottle at him, "But come back and we will continue our celebrations!"

"Come, Papa," Helen said, wringing her father's attention away with some reluctance on his part. He was enjoying the atmosphere of jubilation much more than she would have expected.

They trooped over to their residence en masse— "Safety in numbers!" Adèle had cried—and hallooed for Mme. Gabor, who seemed nonplussed to be greeted by this small crowd at her door.

"Is this a revolution?" she asked, somewhat abashed. "I cannot lower the rent, monsieur!"

"No, no, calm yourself, *madame*," Maggiormente said with a soothing tone. "We have good news for you!"

"Do you?" Her face betrayed that she thought that highly unlikely.

"You have rooms to let, yes?"

"Ye-es."

"We have friends to let them!" He gestured behind him to indicate the airship captain and her father, but Mme. Gabor saw a huge crowd altogether and panicked.

"The rooms are the ones just below you. They are not suitable for such an...entourage."

"Oh, *madame*, it is only for me and my father," Helen reassured her, as Tuppence croaked agreement.

Mme. Gabor narrowed her eyes. She took an instant dislike to the English woman.

But she was a Frenchwoman and a concierge, so despite Mme. Gabor's misgivings it was soon settled that the Rochesters, *père et fille*, would lodge in the rooms while they attended the Exposition and Signor Romano would share the alchemist's rooms with him and Eduardo.

"I hope you are not alarmed by strange smells," Maggiormente said with great politeness to the pilot, who shrugged.

"There are always compromises to life," Romano said philosophically. "We shall have to seek out food from our homeland. If we can succeed that will make any inconvenience a trifle."

Maggiormente was reassured—and hungry. The artichokes of Rome haunted his dreams.

***

As they unpacked their belongings in the rooms below, Helen and her father argued. Something had shifted since their last argument. Helen found herself annoyed that her father had backtracked to an entirely different position. It was most provoking.

"I forbid it!" Her father harrumphed in a most peremptory way.

It had no effect on his daughter, as usual. "You cannot forbid me, Papa. I am going to accept this challenge. I thought you were eager for me to do so."

He made an irritated sound that ranged somewhere between a sigh and an oath. "I have since checked my enthusiasm with thoughts of what your mother would say if I were to return to England without her daughter."

Helen laughed. "Mama would never turn you away for any cause. I have known that since childhood." She marveled again at the depth of feeling between her parents and felt a stab of emotion, wishing her mother could have joined them, then feeling another strange emotion that had pricked her heart for the first time that day, a speculative sort of interest in the alchemist that was beyond mere curiosity.

However, she was in no mood to countenance that thought. Perhaps after the business of the challenge and the Exposition was over, her thoughts might be free for idle speculation. Until then, she must stay focused.

Her father's words suggested the worst woe. "Nonetheless, I would have to rough out the rest of my declining years in some horrid hotel in Montmartre like a dissolute mountebank." Warming to the topic, he brushed Tuppence aside from where she perched on the wardrobe in order to put away his shirts. He was missing the attentions of his valet particularly that night, which put him additionally out of sorts for it was the kind of thing that he considered beneath him while also taking it for granted.

He hardly wanted to think of himself as some kind of cosseted houseplant, fit only for the tender greenhouse, but he had become accustomed to the comforts of his home and the quiet grace of his wife. While he was loath to admit it, he was homesick—particularly so because he sensed there was an additional problem about to surface that he felt not the slightest competency to deal with. This wretched alchemist! Perhaps it would have been better if he were the madman Rochester presumed to call him.

Thus his mood darkened as he did his best to conceal such thoughts from himself as well as his daughter. Both did their best to hide the truth behind busy fussing, which only served to irritate each one even more.

The following day they were both cranky and out of sorts, but the early knock on their door turned out to be Adèle with some freshly baked rolls and creamy butter and jam. "I thought you would have no breakfast and I knew you would need some."

"Oh, how very kind!" Helen clapped her hands with glee, hoping that her father's mood would likewise improve as hers did at the sight of a friendly face and the golden bread.

A strange sound that was not quite a knock echoed from the door. Helen opened it to find Eduardo.

"Is there anything you require, *signorina*?" he asked while craning his neck toward the table where the rolls lay. His flaring nostrils were a bit of a giveaway. Helen tried not to smile too openly.

"Will you join us for some breakfast, if you have not had any yet?" Helen offered, waving him in.

Eduardo bowed. "I have had only one, er, bite," he said looking up at Tuppence with a strange expression of what seemed very close to embarrassment.

Helen leaned in close to him. "If you have been snacking on pigeons, do not worry about upsetting my bird. She considers them to hardly be the same species. Is that not right, my girl?"

Tuppence flew down and gave a series of croaks and clicks that expressed her opinion quite eloquently even to those who could not understand her language. The two of them began to chatter together as comfortably as old friends as they shared a roll Helen offered them.

"It is quite remarkable," Adèle said, shaking her head. "I would never have believed Eddie befriending a bird of any kind."

"She is a *rara avis* indeed." Helen smiled. There was another knock at the door and she turned to open it and found the alchemist and the pilot.

"We have come to ask if you need—" Maggiormente looked nonplussed to see that not only had Eduardo got there first but that his plans to bring breakfast had been superseded. "Ah, I see you have some lovely breakfast already."

"Adèle has been most kind to anticipate our needs," Helen said, but noticing the alchemist's crestfallen look she added, "Although I would not say no to some tea or coffee if we could get it."

"Ah!" Maggiormente's face brightened at once. "I have

254

just the thing!" He turned at once and bounded away and up the stairs, leaving them all a bit surprised.

The alchemist returned in a trice, bearing small cups that seemed absurdly so in his big hands. The rough digits were more accustomed to searing chemicals, hot beakers and oil lamps. But he carried the cups with great care and delicacy that even Eduardo noticed.

The lion looked at the alchemist, then looked over at the airship captain. She was a handsome woman with an intelligent face. Her smile for the alchemist was warm and genuine. Her raven, he noticed, was also looking curiously at her face and then regarding the alchemist with a searching look.

The two creatures then looked at one another, blinking for a moment. The raven made a sound that was very near a chuckle. The lion smiled. Many might have mistaken the expression for some kind of indication of hunger—the more timid might indeed have shook with a bit of fear—but a smile it was and a sort of shared moment with the bird as they both realised what was in the air.

Fortunately their human counterparts were completely oblivious to it all.

"What's this?" Helen said looking at the little cup with a big smile.

"Pressed *caffè*, my own invention." He handed around the tiny cups with great care not to spill a drop of the dark liquid.

Adèle inhaled the aroma with satisfaction. "What have you created, *mon cher alchimiste*?"

Maggiormente drew in a deep breath as if he would launch into a lengthy explanation, then held up a hand. "Taste first. If you like, I explain. If not, eh. No matter." He nodded to see if everyone agreed.

The others shrugged at one another and tasted the concoction, Helen with great zeal, Adèle only after inhaling the aroma deeply with relish and Rochester with a good deal of apparent suspicion, though one could be forgiven for thinking it mostly sham.

"Wow, that has quite a kick," Helen said, eyes wide.

"This needs cake," Adèle said, nodding sagely. Eduardo muttered his agreement but Tuppence chided him with a series of clicks. The lion sat back on his haunches with an amused look at the raven. He would have to find something to tease the bird about, that much was clear.

"This is like some kind of liquid coal, surely," Rochester said with a slight cough. "I think men might be sent off to their deaths quite happily fueled on nothing more than this."

The alchemist frowned at his words, uncertain how to interpret them. "You fear it would kill people? I assure you it is quite safe. Whenever I remember to make it, I am always quite chipper afterward. It is a stimulant to be sure, but harmless, certainly."

"You might warn people of weaker constitutions," Rochester muttered.

"Oh," Maggiormente reached for the gentleman's cup. "I did not realise you were in a delicate situation!"

"I didn't say *I was*," Helen's father said, snatching the cup away from his grasp while his daughter hooted with laughter.

"My father is only teasing," Helen said. "I think he finds it too difficult to say he is impressed with this delicious alchemy. It is *is* alchemy, isn't it?"

"Well," Maggiormente said, still a little nervous, "an accidental sort of alchemy. I was working on a refining process and distracted, I put in coffee instead of gypsum as I intended. But the results smelled very good, so we tried it and *voilà*! A new treat."

"I didn't much care for it." Eduardo said. "I prefer milk in the morning."

"I should think milk would make a good addition," Helen said, nodding. "A little less…stimulating. Although I must say, it is certainly an eye-opener."

"We could sell this in the café," Adèle said. "You

should discuss it with Alain. I know he would be very interested. Parisians do like their coffee and this *caffé presseau*—did you call it?—would appeal to real connoisseurs."

"Well, perhaps when I am finished with my work on the airship fuel," the alchemist said, for once focused on priorities, although delighted with the reception his little experiment achieved, especially the warm glow it brought to Mademoiselle Rochester's countenance.

He blushed and tried to disguise the fact by making a sudden lunge for a croissant. It would have worked, too, had not Helen decided that she would also get a croissant to distract herself from thinking about how charming this alchemist was in contrast to his rather dry and rambling letters, which while they got around to the topic of fuels eventually, did not suggest there was much else about the man to prove of any interest.

So it was a pleasant surprise to find him so very interesting.

Odd, true; unconventional, yes. But also quite distinctly charming. Helen smiled. "I am very much looking forward to trying the fuel. I expect it to be every bit the same success," she said as they both drew back their hands.

After their hands collided, Maggiormente handed the croissant to Helen with a small bow. Without warning, raised voices echoed up from the floor below. The alchemist and the airship captain remained oblivious to the sounds, but Tuppence cocked her head with clear attention. She let out a series of coughing sounds.

Helen did notice that. "What did you say, Tuppence?"

The bird repeated the sounds again with patient precision.

Helen gaped at her. "Surely not. You've got to be mistaken why he's supposed to be..." Then she checked herself. They hadn't actually been sure about his location.

"What the devil is that bird croaking about now?" Her father wouldn't have wanted to admit to it but the alchemist's coffee had quite perked up his mood, which he of course took pains to cover with extra helpings of gruffness.

"She's heard…a familiar voice," Helen said, setting down her drink and walking to the door.

Before she could get to it, however, a loud knocking came and a peremptory voice demanded, "Where are the Rochesters?"

Helen gave a little gasp of surprise and threw the door open to reveal a handsome young man and the very aggrieved face of Mme. Gabor who had clearly done her best to halt the persuasive interloper.

"Neddy!" Helen threw her arms around the young man and gave him a quick kiss on the cheek and the two danced around together.

It was hard to say who looked more ready to explode: Helen's father or Maggiormente, for both looked at the young man with something approaching murderous intent. The alchemist recovered first, realizing that he had little reason to make any claim on the lady's affections, but if he had looked in a mirror the expression of woebegone disappointment would not have been missed.

Rochester, on the other hand, felt his anger expand ever further the longer the two embraced happily, oblivious to his mood. "The prodigal returns," he said at last when the two finally stepped apart.

"Oh, Papa!" Helen admonished with a laugh.

"Hello, Papa," the young man said.

Maggiormente looked from the older man to the younger. The family resemblance was strong, including the haughty eyes and the strong nose. If he had missed it before it was only due to the fog of his unexpected emotional reaction. His grin reappeared at once.

"'Hello, Papa,'" Rochester mimicked his son. "Is that all you've got to say to me?"

"*Bonjour?*"

Helen ignored her father and led the young man over

to her friend. "Signor Maggiormente, please let me introduce you to my brother, Edmund."

The alchemist grabbed the young man's hand and shook it with great enthusiasm. His grin stretched so broadly that one might be forgiven for worrying that the top of his head might just pop off. "Your brother! How wonderful. Wonderful indeed. So pleased to meet you."

"And you, sir, as well," Edmund said, doing his best to extricate his hand from the mighty grip.

"We didn't know you were in Paris, Neddy." Helen grinned happily.

"I was waylaid on the way to Köln," Edmund said laughing with a little nervousness. He had not yet met his father's eye.

"I hope it was not a band of roving gamblers," his father said, "Or I'd suspect they would have taken off with the rest of your money."

"Papa, I haven't lost all my money. In fact, I think I've been rather frugal so far."

"Debauching doesn't come cheap even in Paris," his father growled. He was seething for something of a fight, it was apparent to everyone in the room. Only Helen knew how far back the sparring went, but the other could sense the explosion that was building.

"Papa, I don't know why you insist on painting me in such an unflattering light," Edmund said with decided calmness. "I have had far less experience with that kind of life than you think. Far less than you, so I hear."

If he thought to put off the rising anger of the *pater familias* that was not the right tack to take. If anything, it made the older man bristle with even more. "You insolent pup!"

"Papa," Helen soothed. "Let's not lose our temper."

"You can do as you like my girl. I shall lose my temper whenever the situation requires it and this situation certainly does."

"You won't say that when I tell you my news,"

Edmund said with a look of considerable smugness.

"News? What sort of news?" Helen seemed to be the only one eager to hear what her brother had to say. The alchemist had begun to drift off in preoccupying thoughts, Adèle, piled up the used plates, Eduardo and Tuppence carried on a conversation of their own device, while her father searched for words to adequately express his disapproval of his youngest spawn.

"Those reprehensible Lintons," Edmund said with vehemence, "They mean to challenge you to a race."

"Yes, I know that," Helen said, waving away his words. "All of Paris knows that."

Edmund looked crestfallen. "Do they?"

She tried to ameliorate his disappointment, a role typical of the peace-maker middle child. "How did you hear?"

"I was, er, playing cards with some English fellows and they happened to mention it. You remember Toby Stephens whom I was at school with? He knows them."

"Ah yes, the very tall one, with the Scottish mother?"

"Yes, that's the one. Well, he said they had challenged you and that they were rather more than confident of winning."

"They haven't a chance!" Helen brandished the heel of her croissant as if it were torch.

"Ah, but you misunderstand me." Edmund shook his head sorrowfully. "They intended to make is sure that they would win."

"How?" Their father cut in with his anger reaching near apoplectic levels. "Do you mean to say they'll use sabotage?"

Edmund raised his hands as if warding off an attack. "I don't know for certain. Toby just said that they had planned to win by any means necessary and he didn't think they'd stop at much."

"The devils!" Helen practically spat the words.

Her anger got the alchemist's attention again and he

sprang to attention, hoping to be of some use. "Do you think the ship is safe? Shall we not go make certain of it?"

"Yes, let's." Helen called to Tuppence and prepared to leave.

"You can't go unchaperoned," her father protested.

"Neddy, you can come along, yes?" Helen paused no more than a moment to get his hasty agreement, threw a wrap around her shoulders against the early morning chill, grabbed a parasol for the afternoon sun and headed for the door with the alchemist, the lion, the raven and her brother in tow.

"How are you going to get there?" her father asked from his chair when they were piling out the door.

"We can run," Eduardo said to the alchemist, who frowned as he considered this.

"It's not so very far," Helen said with a toss of her head. "We'll manage."

Her father threw himself to his feet. "Don't be foolish. Find a handsom and we'll all squeeze in—or around—it."

"Thank you, Papa," Helen said with a quick kiss on his cheek.

It took some doing but the entire menagerie of folk stuffed themselves in or around a hansom cab. The driver drew a very definite line against the inclusion of winged lions, but Eduardo was happy to run along beside and sometimes ahead of the cab, particularly once he recalled that doing so tended to limit the traffic in front of them, a not inconsiderable advantage on the busy streets of Paris.

Upon reaching the field where the ship was anchored, Helen felt a surge of happiness and pride as she saw the fine machine awaiting. "Do you know what we called it, Ned?"

Her brother stared at the machine somewhat nonplussed. "You made this, Hel? What a wonder you are."

"I had a lot of help, but it's my design and I've been tinkering with it as we've gone along. She's quite amazing.

Wait until you fly in her."

They pulled up as near as the cabbie cared to go. Many people still milled around the area, excitedly talking about the airship and the soon-to-be-opening Exposition. The air was charged with excitement.

M. Piéton waved from the base of the ladder where he waited with his men, which made Helen a lot more confident of the ship's safety. Tuppence quickly flew to the top in order to overlook the ship from the best angle, calling off her observations. All was well onboard the ship.

"Neddy, I'd like to invite you to take a ride on *Jane's Inspiration*." She grinned with pride.

"Is it safe?" Helen's brother asked with surprising timidity.

"Callow youth," her father sniffed with a superior air. Forgotten were his own misgivings and complaints about traveling in the craft. "You'll never find a more gentle conveyance."

Helen smiled, amused at her father's change of heart. "Quite right. You'll find it far superior to the bumpy ride a carriage or even a curricle offers. It's like sailing but on air."

"Are we going to go very high up?" Despite his best attempts to look sanguine, Edmund had taken on the faintest shade of green at the thought of taking to the clouds.

"We needn't," Helen said with a laugh. "I wouldn't want to give you a moment's distress, little brother."

Her brother cringed with annoyance, but he found it impossible to dispel his nerves entirely.

The alchemist, on the other hand, could hardly contain his excitement. At last to be experiencing the airship that this wonderful woman had designed—and for which he had begun working on the fuel. Now that he had seen the ship, the fuel was no longer just an interesting intellectual puzzle, it was an exciting reality that promised the chance of great success and very public acclaim. To see the ship reaching its greatest potential was now his wish.

And of course in large part because it was *her* ship.

Signor Romano climbed up first to get the engine started while Helen briefed the new crew on their forthcoming ride. "Remember not to all crowd onto one side of the gondola—it can make the ship run awkwardly if you throw off the balance markedly. It's not *dangerous*," Helen added quickly, noticing her brother's nervous mien, "but it's better for the ship's speed and mechanicals if it stays on a more or less even keel."

"No fire, either," Her father inserted unhelpfully. "Most dangerous."

"Papa!"

"Just offering my experience to the boy."

"I'm not a boy, Papa." Edmund drew himself up to his full height, which was very nearly the same as his father's.

Before the conversation could get more heated, the alchemist broke in. "It is alright for Eduardo to come along, isn't it?"

Edmund looked askance at the lion. "He's not dangerous, is he?" He had barely noticed Eduardo at first, perhaps mistaking him for a very large dog, the sort his father was inordinately fond of. Having a good look at him now, the young man seemed somewhat shocked to discover himself in the company of a lion. His thoughts were written across his wide brow: *Bad enough to be taking off in some sort of jury rigged balloon; to do so with a wild animal, surely the height of foolhardiness!*

"Not to people he knows," his father said coolly, "but I would suggest you avoid making any sudden moves. You're not carrying any food on your person, are you?"

"Papa!" Helen scolded her father.

"My lion is a most civilized creature," Maggiormente assured Edmund with all seriousness. "He would never harm anyone to whom he has been introduced. Come, Eduardo, say hello."

The lion, who had made a show of great offense at

being described as a dangerous animal (although he was secretly pleased to be thought frightening), seemed reluctant to properly greet the young man, but allowed himself to be cajoled into a solemn exchange of pleasantries. "How do you do?"

"He talks!" Edmund said in surprise, immediately captivated. "What a capital sort of lion. I am most impressed and pleased to meet you, sir!"

Helen smiled as she saw the lion preen at this praise. Her brother had more than his allotment of charm and it certainly came in handy at times. The lion bowed gravely and the delight on the alchemist's face glowed like a second sun.

"Excellent," Helen said clapping her hands together. "All aboard."

The made their way up the ladder and onto the waiting ship. While Tuppence called from above, Helen arranged her crew about the gondola to maintain a balance and, she hoped, some safety for the novice passengers. While she, Romano and her father had become well used to air travel, she knew the novelty would take some getting used to for the others. Tuppence approved of the placements and thought the ship well balanced. It was difficult to tell how much slower the ship would go with a larger payload, but Helen was eager to find out.

There were so many things to discover!

"Are you all ready now?" She looked around the gondola. Her father made a show of looking as bored as he possibly could manage. The alchemist looked as excited as a schoolboy. Eduardo was all delicate elegance. And her brother did his best to cover up his nerves. He gave a curt nod.

"Let's go!"

12 THE LINTONS

Edgar Linton hammered the last nail into the box around the engine, then looked down at it with satisfaction. *That should secure things nicely.* He looked around for his brother.

Israel was busy tinkering with the controls on the board at the front of their ship. He had decided to recalibrate the wheel to allow them to make more precise turns. Although it was a challenge to make a huge airship turn like anything resembling 'quickly' they had vastly improved the maneuverability of the ship.

"Shall we give it another go?" Edgar shouted to his brother.

Israel did not at first appear to hear him, but at last stood up and put his hands to his back as he stretched out his aching muscles. The two of them were about the same height with similarly chestnut-coloured hair. But while Israel's eyes veered off into a mixture of bluish-brown, Edgar's were a clear amber, like an owl's. He always figured it make him look wiser than his brother, though he had never said such a thing to his twin.

Israel asked, "Do you think it's ready?"

"If it's not ready then we are already failures. That

Rochester woman is already here in Paris." Edgar scowled. "She fancies herself quite the captain since that day she was lucky enough to get the better of us."

"Luck it was," Israel agreed.

"Lightning might be an act of god, but it was not a reason to claim any kind of victory. Admittedly her ship is rather sleeker, but we have the real power. When it comes to speed, we will win in the long run."

Israel finished tinkering with the case below the wheel, closed it up and returned his tools to the oak box on the floor of the gondola. "So you don't think there's anything to the rumours of her using an alchemist?"

Edgar frowned. He hadn't thought his brother had heard the rumours. "I think it speaks to a level of ridiculous desperation. Imagine! What is this, the Dark Ages? Alchemist!"

"You know, the Middle Ages were not really all that dark an age—"

Edgar cut off his brother before he got up on that favourite hobby horse again. "Yes, yes, I know. It was far more enlightened a time than the Renaissance folk gave it credit for, but in comparison to this bright modern era, all stages of the past look dark. Surely under the glorious reign of Victoria we have reached an apex of modernity that all past eras must envy."

"I suppose most ages think that," Israel said, his tone suggesting this thought had just occurred to him and offered a further complication to his usual fanaticism on the subject.

Edgar was not amused. "There has never been a time like now. We have technology at our fingertips that previous eras would have looked on as witchcraft or magic. We can traverse the globe in shorter and shorter times with more people moving to new lands and taking up the riches they find there. Air travel will usher in a new era of peace and prosperity, the like of which this world has never known."

"Although judging by previous technological advances—the printing press, for example—the mechanical advances end up being exploited by those who would make a quick penny for often nefarious means." Israel frowned down at the control panel.

Edgar had no patience for his brother's philosophising. "Don't be an ass."

Israel shrugged. "How long after Gutenberg's bible did people print more salacious stories?"

"We are not here to talk of salacious stories." Edgar huffed with irritation. "We are making the world a better place."

"Well, yes, that's what Gutenberg assumed, too. But the printing press works just as well for smut as for books of the bible."

"There is no way that air travel could be used for improper activities." Israel tried not to shout but his patience was severely tried as usual by his brother's mental meanderings.

"Oh, I don't know," Israel mused. "If the gondola were large enough…"

"Can we get back to the issue at hand?"

"Which is?"

"Our pending race against the Rochester ship." With an effort Edgar calmed his hair and spirits. "She must accept our challenge now that it's been splashed across the broadsheets of Paris. To do otherwise would be to admit defeat—and the superiority of our ship."

"And if she bests us?"

Edgar smiled. "Not a chance. After all the improvements we made? She will be lucky to spot us with binoculars once we get up a head of steam."

"As long as she hasn't really got some fancy new fuel invented by this alchemist of hers," Israel said helpfully.

Edgar made a sound of annoyance. "There is no alchemy!"

Israel shrugged. His brother's failure to accept the

reality of alchemy was not his problem. "If you say so. But I think we might consider employing a...chemist of some sort."

"Nonsense!" Edgar sniffed with finality. "It's quite patently a mechanical issue. The better engine makes the better flight. Fuel is just that: what makes the engine go."

"But if the engine runs more efficiently—"

"It cannot physically go faster than its top speed." Edgar was all out of patience. "Here. Take this." He handed over the tools for the case. "We shall challenge her and win."

"Messrs. Linton! *Messieurs*!"

"What is it, *garçon*?"

The young man arrived breathless, resting his hands on the gondola's edge for a moment. "Your rival, she is in the air with a party."

"How large a party?"

He shrugged uncertainly. "Half a dozen at least, so I hear from my brother. I think enough to maybe slow her down."

"Well, that's hardly sporting," Israel said.

"We're not racing them officially, we just want to put on a good show." Edgar sniffed. "The superiority of our ship will be obvious enough. She may turn tail and flee back to England without a race and we can spend our precious fuel in other ways—and make far more of a splash."

"Does that include our making commissions?"

"Indeed," Edgar said with satisfaction. "We will doubtless be the engineers of an entire army by the time we go back to England."

Israel frowned. "You don't mean to give our technology away to the French."

The young messenger frowned, too. "You are not giving away the technology, surely."

Edgar looked down at him with all the scorn of a superior being that he could muster. "We do not give away anything. A gentleman may share his bounty, but not with his enemy."

"*Monsieur!*" The young man's mouth gaped. "We are not enemies."

"I suppose M. Napoleon was a bit before your time, but rest assured, the English do not forget."

"But Napoleon was a hero, *vraiment?*" The young man was completely confused. He looked from one brother to the other. The value of the general was surely universal.

Edgar smiled and there was more than a portion of the reptile in it. "You would do well to investigate the end of the little general's career, courtesy of a man name of Wellington, the Iron Duke, proving once and for all the superior fighting know-how of the British."

"I suppose, " the young man said, though his doubtful tone suggested the Englishmen were entirely mistaken about the facts.

"Where is the airship?" Israel asked, trying to steer into more diplomatic waters.

"On the west side of the Pavilions. Although they are in the air now, I am not certain which direction they may be going. But I knew you would want the news as soon as possible, so boom boom, I am here."

"You did right," Israel assured him.

"We must get aloft at once," Edgar decided. "Prepare to fire up the engine and cast off." The flurry of activity this inspired made it seem like there were more than two brothers on the gondola.

The young messenger wondered if he was still wanted or if he should attend to his other duties, but he quailed before the peremptory Englishman. "Do you require anything further, *monsieur?*" he asked at last with considerable trepidation. His mother had warned him about the madness of the men of that nation, but he had thought only of the money the position offered.

He was secretly a painter, but he did not wish to have his mother know this as she had hopes of his becoming a banker. She thought all Englishmen to be bankers of some sort, so had pushed him forward for the position due to his good grasp of their language.

All in all, he rather hoped they would win their race and return to their homeland very soon.

"Could you perhaps obtain some food for us?" Israel had his mind on practical matters even if his brother eschewed them. They would always need a nibble of something.

In the meantime, the brothers meant to be aloft as soon as humanly possible. They swiftly put away the toolbox and made ready to fire up the engine. Israel still flinched a bit whenever the engine began to belch out smoke, but they had had many safe flights since the disastrous fire back in Yorkshire, so his brother could not understand it and simply grumbled under his breath.

"Keep a watch on our things," Edgar said needlessly to the French crew on the ground assigned to keep an eye on the brothers' site. The two of them began to guide the ship aloft as the engine chugged away. Though their first interest had always been in speed, Israel had insisted on a little more attention being paid to safety.

But Edgar remained certain that they had the faster ship and he was eager to show it off to all and sundry.

"I can see them over there," his brother shouted, pointing off in the distance.

Sure enough, the Rochester ship made a small shape in the sky, hovering over the open area where the Exposition was being laid out. Edgar's eyes narrowed as he got his target in sight.

"You're not planning any, ah, mischief, are you?" Israel asked, his face betraying his uncertainty about his brother's habits.

"Don't be ridiculous. We shall simply show off the superior qualities of our ship and expose the shortcomings of the Rochester ship. It should be the work of a few minutes," he laughed.

"I seem to recall you saying almost the same thing the last time we faced them," his brother reminded him.

Edgar waved away his words with a hand. "Don't even bring that up. There is no comparison to the new and improved ship we have now. And that was almost entirely due to the unfortunate weather conditions that day, dear brother." He had heard the complaints almost daily since then and Edgar had long ago run out of patience for his brother's doubts.

"True, that's true," Israel admitted although he could not keep his gaze from shifting to the sky. He knew the sun was shining but he worried that the sudden appearance of storm clouds could not always be predicted with precision.

"Stop looking up at the clouds then!"

Israel at least looked embarrassed. A fine co-captain he made, he scolded himself. "I just glanced up—"

"Well, don't. We need to focus on the competition."

"I thought this wasn't the competition?"

"Well, it's not, but if we succeed so well as I think we will, it will make the competition moot. And us famous."

"Do you think so?" Israel frowned.

"If there is a newspaperman anywhere around, it will be so. And our names will be splashed across the evening papers so everyone here will know our success. And soon after the London papers will pick up the story, too."

Israel frowned. "I don't know that I want fame particularly."

"It doesn't matter," his brother said with exasperation. "I can handle the press. You can handle the business side of things."

"Do you think we will get business commitments from newspapers?"

Edgar exhaled with noisy impatience. "Not from the newspapers, because of the newspaper stories." He kept his gaze on the distant ship, watching it grow larger.

"Because of the papers? How?"

Really, his brother could be surprisingly dense at times. One wondered how they could be related, let alone twins. "People will see the stories and know that we have a new and superior method of transportation. The avenues of use should be nearly limitless: commerce could range from any sort of goods—and people! And what about war? Think of the strategic uses."

"Not sure I want to think about these ships being employed in war. I wouldn't want to be hovering over cannons and gunfire."

"Well, *you* won't have to do so," Edgar said, smiling like a rather crafty sort of predator as he began to be able to make out the shapes of the people on board the Rochester ship. He squinted—it looked like they actually had some kind of animal aboard. How extraordinary!

"I suppose. Will we have a reputation like Napoleon's then?"

Edgar tore his gaze away from the other ship. "Napoleon? How on earth are we like Napoleon?"

"Our fame will be mixed," Israel said, his voice low and ominous.

"Piffle," Edgar said with a snort.

The ship forged on ahead and the Lintons approached the Rochester airship slowly but surely. Of course they were not as heavily laden as their opponent's craft was, but there was more to it than that.

Or so Edgar was convinced. They had the superior ship and now that they had addressed that minor design flaw, they would be able to demonstrate that fact with ease. It was simply a matter of scientific knowledge in service of the advancement of industry and commerce.

Certainly the fact that those advances came at the expense of putting the lovely nose of Miss Helen Rochester out of joint did not exactly disappoint him either. He admitted it was gratifying. It's not as if he had actually asked for her hand. Considering the madness of her father—oh, all right, not necessarily *madness* as he had known the true illness ran rather distantly in his own mother's family blood, as the story went—it was unlikely that the strange girl would be getting too many offers for her hand. After all, Miss Rochester was decidedly unfeminine for one thing. For another, there was that rather frightening father of hers. And for a third thing, she was not the most encouraging of young women to talk to.

So why extend such an honour? There was the genial appearance of her face. Though like her mother she was no beauty, there was a certain something about her visage that could inspire a man to daring. The family fortune, managed expertly by her brother, had only grown over time and though the bulk would remain with the name, surely a handsome amount would entail to the daughter.

That she would add to his airship expertise certainly had been a count in her favour. Perhaps she resented that? Edgar frowned. It was the first time the thought had occurred to him.

Women were so mysterious! They would take offense where none was intended. If he had been ham-handed in his testing of the matrimonial waters, she should have considered his lack of skill charming and a compliment to her attraction. After all he had not frittered away his time pledging to other women as his brother had done in his empty-headed histrionics. Apparently the bare pledging of interest was no use to the fragile creatures.

Poetry? Must it come to that?

But he must admit to having failed when she waved away any attempt to proceed toward something resembling endearments and a protestation of his affections. Not that he had much of an idea how to prove any kind of affection.

He was really more of the cerebral sort, not made for the gentle wooing of lovers.

Edgar looked over at his brother. He certainly had no trouble in that regard—and look where it got him.

"We're gaining on them rather quickly," Israel said,

noticing his brother's gaze upon him and apparently feeling as if he ought to say something.

Edgar nodded. "This comes as no surprise, my brother."

"I know, I know." Israel frowned. "Are you planning to challenge them as we approach?"

"Challenge them?"

"Well, yes. It seems more sporting that way. They may not realize that we intend to race." He smiled at his brother then seemed to think better of the expression.

"Are you mad? Surely they are prepared for a race. We have made our intentions quite clear." Edgar sneered. *Let them try to make excuses this time!*

"Well, I don't know that publishing stories in the French newspapers is really enough to challenge them. After all, they may not have read the papers."

Edgar found that Israel's expression of reasonableness irritated even beyond his words. There were things a brother could do that annoyed one out of all countenance. "Why else are they out at this time?"

"Perhaps they are simply taking the air."

His brother's expression of oafish simplicity nearly made Edgar lose his composure altogether. "Taking the air? This isn't Hyde Park!"

"Or the Tuileries, I suppose," his brother agreed.

Edgar muttered an oath under his breath. "What I meant was that they were hardly likely to be 'taking the air' as you say—"

"Though they may be on a sort of pleasurable turn about the, er, sky," his brother continued with infuriating doggedness. "After all, I think they have a rather large group of people onboard. And it looks like some sort of large cat or other creature." He squinted at the other ship, trying to divine what or who was aboard it.

"Nonetheless—"

"Oh, I think I know what it is," Israel said with an excited air.

"What what is?"

"The animal aboard their ship. Do you remember the summer Papa sent us to Venice with the tutor?"

"Vaguely."

"Oh, you never remember anything really important," Israel chastised him. "Really you don't."

For the umpteenth time, Edgar considered the doubtless exquisite pleasure of fratricide.

"You must remember it," Israel tutted as his brother busied himself with checking the motor's operation. "We were staying in that lovely little pension that Mama had lodged at when she was on her grand tour."

"Of what possible interest could that be now?" His brother's irritation had only grown as they bickered. Edgar's only thought was for the competition—and destroying their competitor. Once he conquered Helen Rochester, he could bring her around to the idea of marrying him. That's what a woman needed after all: a man who took charge.

"Don't you see?" Israel persisted. "The lions!"

Edgar blinked at his brother. "There aren't any lions in Venice."

"Yes, there are!"

"You're thinking of pigeons." Edgar was pleased to see the engine running so smoothly and with relatively little heat—at least compared to the old motor. No danger of fire at all.

"No, no. Not actual lions—though there must be some..." Israel's voice trailed off as he considered the thought. "Or one, surely."

"What are you on about?" Edgar usually did his best to ignore his brother's meandering rambles through conversation. It was difficult to manage here. One of the major drawbacks to airship travel was the limited range of movement and conversational partners.

"The Venetian lions," Israel continued implacably. "Remember outside the Doge's Palace? What's the

275

place…? It will come to me…" He tapped his chin thoughtfully. "It's on the tip of my tongue. I'm thinking a disciple. Help me, Edgar."

"Help you what?"

"What's in front of the Doge's Palace?"

"Is this a riddle?" His brother's irritation reached a level that would be dangerous for the motor but could not cause a conflagration in the human machine. "I hate riddles. You know this."

"No, I'm just trying to remember. If it's a disciple, there's only twelve, right? So we could narrow it down…"

"Disciples? Do I care about disciples?" Despite himself Edgar found he was being inexorably drawn into his brother's aimless cogitations.

"Wait a moment. Not disciples. The other ones. What are the other ones?"

"Other what?" Edgar was annoyed to realize he was completely lost now. The one thing he had hoped to avoid was getting caught up in Israel's wandering thoughts. He should just turn away and focus on the ship as they had a race to run. But an idea struck him. He hated being twins. Alas, he knew how Israel's mind worked. "Evangelists? Do you mean the evangelists?"

Israel smacked his forehead with his palm. "Yes, precisely! Ah, you have done it again, my brother. The evangelists. Only four of them."

"Indeed, now can we get back to—"

"Matthew, Mark, John and er, what's his name? Do you remember?"

"Does it matter?" Edgar snorted. His hands itched to close around his brother's throat. Again.

"Lawrence?"

"Who cares?!"

"Well, I think it was Mark anyway." Israel nodded, slowly at first and then more rapidly. "Yes, I'm almost certain. Mark. St Mark."

"Well, if that's sorted now—"

"The square!"

Edgar stared. "What?"

"St Mark's Square!" Israel looked so very pleased with himself, it was difficult to hate him at the moment, but Edgar very nearly managed it.

"What about St Mark's Square?"

"The lion! The Venetian Lion. It's there. Don't you remember the wings?"

Edgar opened his mouth to scream at his brother, when all at once he remembered the statue in the square.

A winged lion.

"Oh yes, you must remember it," his brother went on heedless of any reply. "Napoleon brought it to Paris and then they took it back when he died or was exiled or something. Maybe that's why it's back now." He looked questioningly at his brother as if he might have the answer.

Edgar had only just arrived at the notion of the creature his brother spoke of. "Why it's back now?" he echoed, feeling utterly lost in the mind of his brother.

"Back in Paris," Israel added with an encouraging smile.

"Who is?"

"The lion."

"The winged lion?"

"Yes!" Israel practically clapped his hands together in delight to see they were of an accord.

Edgar squinted at him. "What lion?"

Israel looked at him with evident surprise, turned and pointed to the other airship with a kind of triumph. "That one!"

Edgar turned his head to look at the other airship. Now that they had come closer together he could see that his brother was right. As peculiar as it was to see an animal of that nature riding aloft in a ship, he could make out the wings on the large cat where it sat next to the horrid raven that woman always had with her.

Not to mention her rather intimidating father—who,

he saw, stood on the other side of the creature. Rochester had a penchant for large and rather intimidating animals. Edgar had chanced to be menaced on several occasions by the fearsome beast alleged to be a dog that resided upon their estate, one that would make the Cù Sìth tremble in fear.

Why did they have a lion in their gondola—

Especially one with wings?

"Do you suppose they have it for protection? Or as some kind of a threat?"

"Threat?" Israel frowned. "Who would threaten them up here?"

"We would." Edgar's expression became very grim indeed. If they wanted to play that kind of game, he would see what he could find in Paris. There were all manner of things one might acquire in the City of Lights if one knew where to look. He had no idea where one might go to search for monsters, but he was certain he could find out.

"Surely not," his brother said, breaking into Edgar's thoughts. "We didn't even know they would be about."

"We can't leave this challenge unmet. It is crucial not to leave a gap in weaponry."

Israel's brow furrowed. "Weaponry?"

Edgar sighed. "The lion. It must be some kind of weapon. They're using it to protect the ship, surely. We have to be prepared for any kind of retaliatory move."

"Isn't it retaliatory only if we attack them? We're not attacking them. Are we?" Israel's look of concern grew.

"Not unless we need to do so," Edgar admitted somewhat grudgingly. He had worked up a certain amount of steam toward self-righteous indignation and did not want to let go of it for a placid reasonableness quite so soon.

"We should keep everything reasonably amicable if we can," Israel said and it was evident from the chiding tone of his words that he did not approve of thoughts of weapons or retaliation. "Why not get closer and then we can make further plans instead of assumptions." He hid his face away so he would not have to look at his brother's scowl.

Edgar scowled anyway. "Yes, yes, all right." Nonetheless he nursed thoughts of the rather magnificent beast they might arrange to have join their menagerie. Perhaps a hippogriff might be impressive, though he wondered if that were simply a mythical creature. Then again, he had though winged lions to be only fancy, so who knew what might be obtainable in this foreign capital?

As he turned on the speed, it became apparent that the people in the other ship's gondola had noticed them and had also turned in their direction now. The two ships were coming together now and it was becoming easier to make out the folks on board.

However, apart from the lovely captain, the Italian pilot and the ever-intimidating Mr Rochester, none of the others seemed to be familiar. There was one, however, whose appearance gave Edgar a chill, though he could not say why. The man was tall, bearded and reasonably affable of expression, but he looked at Miss Rochester with such affection that Edgar felt stung by the wasp of jealousy.

"What?" Edgar had drifted off to his own dark thoughts and didn't hear what his brother was saying.

"We should hail them. I think they may be close enough for the horn now." Israel brandished that instrument aloft with an expression of delight. Having so few airships about, he had not yet had time to try it out. His face practically glowed with the excitement.

"Are you sure that's necessary?"

"We owe it to posterity to set up the norms of airship travel and interaction, modeled—as I have argued extensively—on the rules of the sea, although perhaps not slavishly so, water not actually mirroring the behaviour or dangers of water.'

"You can't drown in air," Edgar said dryly.

'True, but a man overboard is a serious issue and even

more dangerous in most cases." Israel nodded his head in that way that irritated his brother so, mostly because he was never aware of doing it. One nod was sufficient to convey the attitude of agreement, but Israel often went on nodding for minutes altogether, unconscious that he had continued to do so.

Edgar found it vexing. "Can you even be heard over both engines?"

"We shall have to find out." Israel turned to his task, taking in the wary expressions on the faces of the other airship's passengers. Wary with good reason, if one were to consider their last encounter and the rough challenge offered them in the newspapers.

Israel had considered his brother's brash flaunting of the challenge most unhelpful. "Why can't we combine our efforts and advance things that much faster?" he had asked for the umpteenth time.

"Because innovation doesn't have room for many names. We know Watt, we know Newton, we know Faraday. We do not know those who came after them."

"Or those who came before them but didn't manage to interest enough people to invest in their ideas." Israel started nodding again. "That happens a lot, I would imagine."

"Precisely. It shall not happen to us because we will make sure the name Linton sails much higher and longer than that of Rochester." Edgar smiled. He never looked his best when he did, as there was something rather chilling in the expression that it was difficult to identify. Perhaps it was his rather large teeth, perhaps it was only their feral shape. One would be hard put to define it, but few would not feel some misgivings at meeting such a smile in a dark wood.

"Halloo!" Israel had apparently decided not to worry too much about what his brother thought and instead concentrate on what the meeting of minds might bring. The happy look of anticipation lit his features, which while they were not markedly different from his brother's offered a much more welcoming visage altogether despite his rather sizable teeth.

He had just put the horn to his lips to halloo again when he saw Mr Rochester put a similar instrument up to his lips. It looked wider and less curving than the horn and Israel squinted to see if he could make out its construction. He could tell by the way the man hefted it that it was very light.

"Halloo!"

"Halloo!"

"Well, we can hear each other at what remains a reasonably considerable distance,' Israel said to his brother with evident satisfaction.

"Do you have anything else to say to them other than idiotic hallooing?" Edgar grumbled the words, uncharitably thinking little of his brother's contribution and bristling in advance at having to deal with Rochester.

After giving it a moment's thought, Israel called out, "Are you just taking the air?"

"Taking the air?" Rochester replied with what the brothers had no trouble realizing to be irritation. "We are demonstrating the fine qualities of our ship to a rather large contingency of observers."

He turned to say something to Helen, who seemed a little agitated with him, but then she often found herself so, as they well knew.

"Shall we challenge them to a race now?" Israel asked his brother.

"Don't be an ass. Look at them. Loaded down with extra people. It won't look good for us to beat them now." *Though it will make no difference with fewer people. We shall trounce them just the same!* "Ask if they want to discuss the match on the ground."

Israel turned and prepared to ask, but stopped and pointed. "Oh look, that's jolly. They've named their ship!"

Edgar looked over and made a face. This would never

do. It certainly raised the stakes and they would have to come up with a name swiftly. But what?

Edgar rummaged through his brain to try to locate a proper idea for a name of their ship. He thought Rochester's name entirely too luxuriant in nature and sought something more modern and forward looking. After all, this was the new age and the folderol of the past would be dismissed into the mists of time.

Forward looking? Hmmmm, he mused. *Could you call a ship that?* He glanced over at his brother, who still smiled vaguely toward the oncoming ship. Israel had no concept of the proper competitive spirit. He had never much excelled at sport, it must be said. Edgar always made sure he was captain, whatever the game might be. Someone had to lead. He wasn't willing for it to be anyone else.

Progress? It seemed a little too naked for a name. He didn't want anything too poetic—poetry was for watery ships. Airships needed serious and lucrative sort of titles. It should be forward leaning but not anything that suggested something radical. Bad enough they had to show it off in France. They certainly didn't want any of those sort of political shenanigans creeping into its image.

Israel waved to the other ship. Edgar quashed the sudden flare of temper that rose in his bosom. Never mind that now, he had to think fast.

Fast Progress? Forward Progress? He wasn't sure he liked them at all. Too close to *Pilgrim's Progress*, that loathsome book their tutor always made them read when he wanted an extra nap.

What about 'rise' or 'rising' in the name? Edgar considered the word. This naming business was tricky. Did all inventors pause at the edge of magnificence to ponder the name for their breakthrough?

Edge of Magnificence? Edgar frowned. He repeated it a few times in his head, listening to the balance of sounds. He decided against it on the grounds that it was both too old fashioned in construction and decidedly tentative in meaning. Best not to let anyone wonder about it. Sounding certain was clearly the way to go.

Progress Forward? Sure, it had the dread 'progress' in it, but Edgar found himself more pleased by the reversal of the terms. But maybe 'progress' wasn't the right word anyway. It was more about movement anyway.

If only I had my thesaurus!

The cheery Rochester ship drew close enough that he could see the passengers clearly now. Who was that wild bearded man? He finally recognised Helen's brother, the profligate Edmund who was doubtless here in Paris tearing his way through any inheritance he might have left or ever hope to get. Appalling young man! Edgar could not understand why Rochester would countenance that wild rake ambling anywhere near him. Doubtless he'd been run quite off his legs or was in some kind of scrape or another. The fact that their sister Charlotte had fallen madly (and hopelessly) in love with the reprobate doubtless did little to endear him to the rest of the Lintons. That was the problem with girls of an impressionable age. They were always falling in love with someone. If one could marry them off sooner there wouldn't be time for this love nonsense. Once they started pinning their hair up, it was a downward spiral into silliness and giggling. There was little chance to stop the forward momentum once it got going. Horrible, really.

Edgar paused in his ruminations, which admittedly had gone far afield of the subject matter in question. But something had tickled his fancy. What had it been? He rewound the last few thoughts to figure out what it had been.

Forward momentum.

It had the right sense of movement, but had a pleasing Latinate construction as well. Edgar pictured it written in an elegant script on the side of the ship. Then he erased that image from his brain and tried it again with a bold typeface.

That suited it much better. He gave a small nod, satisfied with himself.

"Israel, I have a brilliant idea."

His brother turned back to him, smiling vaguely. "What's that?"

"I have a name for our craft! I think you'll agree it is superb and captures the spirit of the times as well as the audacity of our work."

"Yorkshire."

Edgar blinked. "What?"

"We should call it 'Yorkshire' in honour of the place of our birth."

I shall kill him one day. Edgar sputtered a little as he said, "We certainly shall *not* call it that. No, I have a much more magnificent name altogether." He smiled seraphically.

"So what are we going to call it?" Israel looked complacently at his brother. Apparently he had no concerns about the name and took the dismissal of his suggestion with serene equanimity, which was just as well because there was no possibility that Edgar would have considered his brother's suggestions anyway, even if the only one so far had *not* been idiotic. Someone had to be the brains of every institution. Edgar had known it was he since the two of them were in short pants. His brother never seemed to mind.

The other ship was calling out to them again, but Edgar left his brother to the more social aspects of the travel, as usual. At least he was good for something. He rolled the name around in his head a little more to make sure that it was right. And he knew now: block letters with gold finishing at the edges: *Forward Momentum.*

Edgar's smile grew broad and a little sinister once more. Then he shook his head. "What?"

"They want to know if we want to land somewhere and enjoy a luncheon together." Israel smiled blandly at him, certain that he would agree. Who would not?

"I suppose we must be sociable," Edgar said with

evident reluctance, though he stopped short of sneering.

His brother chose to take this as a positive step. "Shall we return where we began or go back to the fields where they took off?"

"Does it matter?"

"Well, as a matter of convenience so we all end up in the same place—"

"Beyond that, is it relevant?" Edgar sighed. "I am indifferent."

Israel raised the horn once more to his lips. "Wherever you like!" he cried and Edgar felt a grimace of revulsion pass across his face as he hated the idea of conceding anything to another. He strode across the gondola and took the horn from his brother.

"We shall follow you so we do not get too far ahead." He smiled grimly, satisfied with his quick thinking. "Loaded down as you are."

He could hear no response, but saw Helen Rochester and her father confer, then wave them on, setting their calling horn down. Apparently they had nothing to add to that, either. *Check, my dear Miss Rochester.*

"I don't suppose we have anything to add to a luncheon," Israel mused aloud.

"Add to a luncheon?" Edgar frowned. "What are you on about?"

"It would be good if we have some of mother's hot cross buns." Israel had a far away look in his eyes, as if he were recalling the taste of this lost childhood treat.

Madness, Edgar shook his head. "It's not even the season for hot cross buns and unlike Miss Rochester I don't think it necessary to drag members of the family along on our triumphant journey."

"Except each other," Israel pointed out.

"Well, obviously that, but only because I can't run the ship on my own."

Israel's face fell. "You'd go without me?"

Edgar exhaled with blind impatience. "Would you not

go alone if you could?"

"No, never. It would not be at all fun on my own."
Israel seemed wounded by the suggestion.

"I see."

"You wouldn't want to go without me, not really—
would you, Edgar?"

"I suppose not."

Israel was cheered at once. "We need to maintain our
forward momentum! And as we go on—"

"That's it, by the way."

"That's what?"

"The name!"

"As we go on?"

"Forward Momentum!"

"Oh," Israel said thoughtfully. "That's rather good."

13 PERSPECTIVES

"That was awkward." Helen sighed as she threw herself down into a chair. Her cheeks were pink with lingering embarrassment from the stilted conversations over the meal. Lunch had never been such an ordeal at any time in her memory—even including the worst days of the wrangling between Mrs Hitchcock and Fairfax when the latter decided to tell her how she should be cooking the meat for their meals. Only the most delicate negotiations on behalf of their mother were able to restore equanimity to the family table, though their housekeeper continued to give the eldest son baleful glances until he took himself off for a long visit with a chum.

Helen's father on the other hand, positively glowed. "Awkward? Nonsense! A fine meal, a fine one." He also threw himself down into a chair but it was with considerable pleasure—and force. Adèle looked on with some concern.

They had returned to the bakery after their adventures, perhaps unsurprisingly, a magnanimous Alain beckoning them all to the comfortable shop to repair the mood of some and maintain the high spirits of Rochester *père* and Eduardo, who paid no attention to the human conversation and busied himself with devouring as much of the luncheon as he might. Now he looked forward to a little wine and then a nap. Surely the alchemist could not need him any further.

The alchemist in question was yet rather agitated, both for reasons he well knew, some he could almost admit and a few he had not yet realised. Specifically, he was excited about the demonstration of the fuel, he was eager to have success but—from long practice—prepared for failure and more tinkering. Yet he was even more eager to prove himself to Miss Rochester, for far from some British matron with an umbrella and a small dog (why, oh why had he pictured that? Maggiormente could not really say. Perhaps it was a painting he remembered.) she was a most fascinating young woman.

Of course Miss Rochester's father made that need to succeed even more important and quite possibly even more nerve-wracking. The alchemist was unaffected by the idea of failure in general. One could not succeed without a good deal of defeat first; if a thing were to be worth doing, it must be not simply a success, but a triumph. Triumph did not come without error and mistakes. The immortal da Vinci said it best: *Life is simple. You try many things, most fail.*

And what else did he say? Maggiormente frowned. When you do succeed, others quickly copy it. Maggiormente saw the Lintons in this light. He felt scorn but something more—a kind of pity. Until he thought on his lady and their attempts to imitate her and then he felt a fury of righteous anger on her behalf even though it was more or less the same process. He could be sanguine about his own developments being appropriated by others, but he could not be about hers.

She was sublime!

"Are we to have some wine, I heard it rumoured." Helen attempted to hush her father but the baker only laughed and brought forth a couple of bottles of his favourite red and the two men began to pour it out for the gathered group.

Maggiormente frowned as he took his glass. Her father was a puzzle and a bit intimidating, he didn't mind thinking at all, though he would be loath to admit it to the man himself. The alchemist had an unaccustomed knot in his chest as he suppressed his natural desire to argue forthrightly with the man when he tutted at his daughter. He held back and he was unable to say precisely why.

Certainly part of it was that he had only just met the man and it seemed impolite to be so direct with English people. They were notoriously rule-bound and he did not wish to get off on the wrong foot by shouting at them as he would a fellow of his land. Those people seemed so easily offended. The pilot, Romano, said as much during lunch.

And he was *her* father after all. He did not wish to distress his, ah—patroness?

Maggiormente felt a flush of something acutely similar to embarrassment rise up the back of his neck. Why did his thoughts about her flutter like some bird in the air? Mme. Gabor certainly made him uncomfortable many times, but it was nothing like this. He was conscious of not offending his landlady but he desired only to have her stop her foolish attentions upon him.

He had no desire to have Miss Rochester stop anything. Her every word conveyed sense and intelligence. None had ever given rise to any sense of annoyance in him, in fact quite the reverse and he longed for the others to retire or go away or anything but to leave him the opportunity to sit with her and talk of—of what?

Motors? Fuel?

Maggiormente flushed with annoyance at himself. What was wrong with him anyway? He sounded as foolish as Gustave with his poetry.

"And you wonder why that is?" Eduardo said in a surprisingly soft voice as he looked up from his bowl of wine.

The alchemist looked down at his familiar and saw a strange expression on the lion's face that made him fidget even more uncomfortably.

"I don't know what you mean," Maggiormente mumbled more to his wine than to Eduardo, but he was spared the need to respond to his familiar's penetrating question by the incredulous voice of Helen's brother.

"You can't be seriously contemplating racing this ship with an entirely new fuel this Friday!" He shook his head. "It's madness."

Helen laughed. "I find it amusing that my rakehell brother has become all solicitous of my health and safety."

Edmund flushed. "I am no rakehell."

"That's not what your tutor said," his father commented in a rather waspish tone.

"He was a low man of ill-repute himself who accused me of worse things than he'd ever done." Edmund seldom showed the temper he had inherited from his father, but the latter had been needling him since his arrival and his patience was wearing thin.

"A likely story," his father harrumphed.

"He wished to remain in your good graces. Because you were willing to believe everything bad of me and everything good of him, he found it easy to manage you."

"Manage me!"

"Papa! Ned! Please." Helen stood up, hands on her hips, eye flashing. "I have had enough out of both of you. Sit down, be polite and do not spoil the afternoon for our friends." She sat down once more and lifted her glass. "Can someone propose a toast?"

Maggiormente found himself inexplicably tongue-tied as he sought through his brain for words sufficiently powerful to honour the lady.

Adèle beat him to the punch. "To our intrepid airship *capitaine*!"

Everyone cheered and drank, though Helen waved away their praise. Instead she held her glass aloft once more. "To our fine ship, *Jane's Inspiration*, and the new fuel the *Signore* has promised me!"

"Victory shall be ours!" Signor Romano cheered on his fellow countryman.

Maggiormente could feel the sweat break out on his brow. He usually worked in isolation, meandering through problems and musing on possibilities. Suddenly here was a pressure in a way he had never experienced before.

Not only must the result of his work be public, but so very much depended upon the red wheels turning in his mind, blending substances into a fabulous fuel that would prove efficient and powerful. He *thought* the formula would prove sound.

What if it didn't?

"Stop worrying so much. Your hair will fall out."

Maggiormente looked down at his Venetian lion. "What?"

"It's a well known fact: excessive worry makes the hair fall out." Eduardo slurped more wine from the bowl on the floor and looked up expectantly. "Also, insufficient wine leaves a lion grumpy," he added stretching his neck to see where the nearest wine bottle could be found.

The alchemist reached for a bottle on the table and splashed a little more into the lion's bowl. "You ought not have much. It's much too rich for your digestion."

Eduardo ignored him and lapped at the red liquid. He had done his part, it seemed, by ignoring little Brigitte's attempt to tidy his hair into plaits. A more rambunctious beast might have been expected to devour the child. Never mind that the lion found the look flattering and the attention well-deserved. "I am serious and entirely truthful, you know," he said to the alchemist as he licked drops of wine from his whiskers.

"I know."

"So don't be so anxious. The fuel will work and all will be well."

"I hope you are right," Maggiormente said. "But I fear

the trial tomorrow."

"That's why it's a trial." Eduardo bent his muzzle to the bowl once more, savouring the taste of the wine after all the riches of the luncheon. "If it doesn't work, you fix it. You always do."

"Do I?"

"Eventually."

The alchemist winced. "I am not certain that 'eventually' will be enough in this case. I must prove myself to the esteemed Miss Rochester. I must not fail her."

Eduardo regarded him with an expression that seemed mischievously amused. "I have every faith in our success. I just hope England is not as cold as I have heard."

"Eh?" Maggiormente stared at his lion.

The lion kept his head down in the bowl as he licked the last of the wine with a decadent luxuriousness. Eduardo would sleep very soon whether he wanted to do so or not, though he well knew the risk of falling asleep in the bakery with young Brigitte at hand. He did not mind a certain amount of plaiting but he would draw the line at ribbons. Well, if he were still awake he would.

The alchemist watched the eyelids droop on his familiar as he gradually lost the battle with sleep. It distracted him from thoughts he found less comfortable, but when the little girl went in for the kill, so to speak, he gave up trying as there was less entertainment to be had from watching the child weave ribbons of various colours into the plaits on the lion's mane. Although he would be amused again later when Eduardo would demand their removal once he saw them.

"Is it not true, *signore?*"

Maggiormente looked up, startled. "*Scusi?*" His face blushed pink with embarrassment once more.

"You have every confidence that the compound will offer greater power without the bulk of traditional fuel, is that not the case?" Miss Rochester smiled with encouragement. It was a delightful expression upon her handsome face.

The thought flustered the alchemist further. "Yes, yes, that is the plan, that is rather—the thing is I am trying to say, the fuel is—*voglio dire*—" He stumbled over his words and found it difficult to recover himself again.

"It is lighter than kerosene, is it not?"

"Oh, most definitely. And oil of the whale? Some people use that, am I not right?" Maggiormente worried that he had got hold of the wrong end of the stick again. Was it whale oil or was he mixing things up again? It wasn't like good old alchemy with its clear qualities and predictable results. Well, except when you struck off in a new direction to try new combinations. Then things were a little less predictable but a lot more fun. Until you need results that is, Maggiormente paused to think.

"And much lighter than coal. Imagine," Helen said turning back to her brother and father. "Imagine trying to bring enough coal to fuel an airship for even a short journey. You would have to fill the gondola!"

"Ridiculous," her father harrumphed. "Besides you'd end up looking like a Welsh miner. Which would be rather more ridiculous."

Helen beamed. Her father's good humour seemed to fire her own confidence. Maggiormente could tell the young woman had much of her father's temper as far as courage and determination went, though she seemed rather more tractable in general than her hot-headed father. He rather reminded Maggiormente of his fiery uncle who had terrified him as a small child and who could yet prove a challenging man in debate over dinner, when they chanced to meet. His appreciation for the man had only grown over the intervening years.

He wondered what her mother was like. He gathered that the ship had been named in her honour. The alchemist remembered Eduardo's implication about visiting England and felt a surge of excitement mixed with abashed embarrassment. *I must not let my mind skip ahead. First, the fuel!*

"My fuel shall prove economical, dependable, aromatic and precise." Maggiormente paused. "That is not the word, is it? How should I say—compact? Is that better?"

"Compact is good. Light also, or am I mistaken? It takes up little space but also weighs very little," Miss Rochester said with a most encouraging smile. "Both considerations are important in an airship."

"I endeavour to meet your every expectation, *signorina*. I have worked long and hard to make it so." Maggiormente could feel the sheen of sweat on his brow for which he blamed the red wine and went to surreptitiously push the glass a bit further from himself to avoid drinking more, but he managed to upset the glass instead, pouring a good portion of it onto the table before he could spring up and right the glass, which managed to spill a good portion back toward him as well—all of which left him more flustered than before.

Miss Rochester ignored his fumblings and only smiled with warmth. "I am most delighted, *signore*. I expect it will all be wonderful."

"Just don't let him pour the wine," Mr Rochester muttered, greatly amused at the Italian's anxious movements.

"You're not going to be flying in the ship during the race, are you, monsieur?" Edmund asked the alchemist. Clearly he thought the man would make a poor passenger for the trip.

"I shall be delighted to ride along for the trial, but I imagine the race should have no extra passengers," Maggiormente said with an attempt to restore his dignity.

The next day the alchemist awoke with a song already bursting from his lips. He took extra care with his morning ablutions, a fact which did not escape Eduardo. "You are very cheery this morning. And clean. Except for that bit on the back of your neck."

Maggiormente frowned and tried to look at the back of his neck in the mirror without success. "Where?"

The lion did his best to direct the alchemist's hand to the correct spot. When they were both more or less satisfied with the results, the endeavor was declared a success and the water used to nourish the small herb garden Eduardo had nurtured in the east window.

"My basil has grown very fast." He sniffed the plants with pleasure.

"I hope you did not eat all the mint." Maggiormente leaned over the collection of pots on the window sill. "I should like some tea made from that."

"I do not eat everything all at once."

The alchemist laughed. "Not always, perhaps."

They went downstairs and knocked gently on the door. Eduardo glanced up at the alchemist and frowned. "Stop patting your hair. It is fine."

"Ought I to have trimmed my beard? You don't think it's too unruly?"

"You never used to worry about the state of your beard. I recall you setting it on fire many a time before without noticing the effect," he teased.

"I do not wish Mlle. Rochester to think I am some kind of madman," Maggiormente hissed quietly.

The door opened to reveal the woman's brother who, rather than greet them, turned and called back to her, "Your madman monk is here."

"I am no monk," the alchemist said, nonplussed by this unexpected appellation.

"Good thing to focus on," Eduardo said, weaving between the alchemist's legs to enter the room, nostrils sniffing the air with anticipation.

"*Signore*! Eduardo!" Helen Rochester beamed. "We have croissants."

What a cheery face to welcome one first thing in the morning, Maggiormente thought. *I would wish to start every morning with such a smile.* A blush adorned his cheeks for he felt the heat of it rise and, at a loss for words, he said nothing, but took the offered croissant on a plate and smiled back at the captain.

"Would you like some butter for that?" Helen handed him the butter dish and Maggiormente took it with a beatific smile and a nod. This perplexed the hostess, but she sat back down in her chair at the table and after a moment, the alchemist followed suit.

"Are you going to eat that?" Eduardo said with a little rumble of hunger.

"Oh, pardon me, my friend!" The alchemist put the plate down on the floor for the lion to eat it, but the creature only stared balefully at him. "What?"

"No butter?"

"Ah, yes." The alchemist, flustered, picked the plate up again and slathered some of the creamy butter over the flaky pastry and returned it to the floor, where a grateful Eduardo devoured it swiftly but delicately. The alchemist turned back to face his hostess and smiled.

"Perhaps a croissant for yourself now?" She urged him.

"Oh yes, that would be delightful," he murmured and took the offered plate rather mechanically, adding a croissant and buttering it negligently. He took a bite and chewed it with pleasure though the sensation came mostly from the feast of his eyes.

Helen squirmed a little under the observation and her brother snorted with suppressed laughter, but she frowned at him and he went back to eating his own breakfast. "I'm looking forward to the experimental flight today. Have you brought the fuel with you or do you plan to fetch it afterward?"

Maggiormente paused, mid-chew. "Oh, I have it with me now!" he said excitedly, spraying a few flaky crumbs onto his beard. He rummaged in his pockets while the airship captain looked on with curiosity.

At last he found what he was looking for in the jumble of items and pulled them out. "I did not know which would be more practical," he said holding a small paper-wrapped cube and a small glass bottle with a stopper tied down firmly.

"But they're the same fuel?"

"Indeed. My own invention. And so fragrant!"

Helen stared in surprise. "They are so tiny! How long will they fuel the engine for?" In her excitement she hardly noticed how mangled her grammar had become.

Maggiormente laughed and spread his hands wide. "I am not certain. I had to guess so much about your ship, its size and weight and wind resistance—"

"There are a lot of factors," Helen admitted. It had become second nature to her to calculate additional factors, but she had every specification of the craft at her fingertips. "I guess it didn't occur to me that you might need to know some of that information as well."

He waved away her protestations. "We learn by experimenting. That is the system."

"You're not experimenting on my daughter," said Helen's father as he came into the room. He looked like he had slept ill, or perhaps he was simply not very happy about any of this business.

"I meant only the aircraft," Maggiormente said, feeling a little flustered and patting at his beard, aware that some flakes from the croissant had become entangled in its tendrils. "There is no harm to come, I am certain."

"Didn't I just hear your lion say you set fire to your beard?" Rochester looked at the alchemist with an expression of amazement.

Maggiormente's heart pounded a bit faster. He wanted to impress this man with his expertise and his acumen but it was proving to be rather difficult—even if he did almost believe the man was doing his best to conceal a smile behind his rough words. "You have very good hearing, *signore*. That was unrelated to our chemical works."

"It was breakfast however," Eduardo muttered before downing the last of his croissant. "Not usually considered to be a dangerous meal."

"Are there dangerous meals?" The idea seemed to charm Rochester.

"With him, yes," Eduardo said in all seriousness.

"That is hardly fair," the alchemist argued. "You frighten far more people than I ever have and yet you give this gentleman the impression that I am some kind of wandering pyromaniac."

"Are you a wandering pyromaniac?" There could be no doubt of his smile now.

"I am not wandering nor am I any more inclined to loosing the salamander than anyone else." Maggiormente frowned. "I blame the artists."

"Oh yes," Eduardo said. "It was they who started the fire."

"There was a fire?" Helen's brows drew together as she tried to follow the devolving conversation. Her expression balanced between amusement and puzzlement.

"We only investigated after it was already out," Maggiormente hastened to explain. "The artists were experimenting with colour. For a time I tried some of their oil in possible compounds but it didn't really work out."

"What is in the fuel?" the captain asked, eager to return the conversation to something more solid.

The alchemist smiled. "Ah, that is a different question, but one I cannot yet answer. I want to be sure it works—and that it does not need further adjustment—before I should reveal the formula."

"It's not, erm, explosive?" It seemed to cost her an effort to ask the question, but surely it was better coming from her than from her brusque father. "I mean in its...resting state."

"No," Maggiormente said, making a waving motion with his hands. "There is no chance of that. If anything, it may be too little—ah, what is the word?" He stroked his beard thinking for a moment or two. "Conflagratory?"

Helen Rochester looked somewhat nonplussed. "I'm

not sure—you mean, it's possibly less explosive or incendiary than you would like?"

"Incendiary," he repeated, allowing the word to roll around in his mouth and thoughts for a moment. It was surely the right word. "Yes, that is precise. I want it to burn but at a slower rate. To last but to nonetheless exude powerful output."

"I think we should just try it out and stand well back," the ship captain's father said with a bark of laughter.

"No, no, it is quite safe. I think it will propel the ship well and there is no danger." Maggiormente said.

"Or very little," Eduardo said cautiously.

"Well, why not chuck a bit into the fireplace and we'll see it burn." Edmund offered from the other end of the table.

"Oh no," the alchemist said quickly. "Unless you want the fireplace to move next door!"

"Next door!" Edmund looked at his sister. "I think you're making a huge mistake. Papa, you have to put a stop to this."

"I assure you, *signore*—"

"I cannot listen to this madman."

"Ned! You're being ridiculous." Helen had been ready to laugh off her brother's nervousness, but she had become increasingly wound up by his peremptory tone. "This is no business of yours anyhow."

"I must protest. You should be protected from charlatans and your own foolishness."

"*Signore*! I am not inclined to anger, but you insult me." Maggiormente felt his cheeks grow warm, though he checked Eduardo's growl with a gentle hand on his familiar's head.

"I am furious! You have no right to speak, you are insulting my friend, to say nothing of your treatment of me. I am no infant, I need no protector, I am a free human being with an independent will, not a bird in a cage or ensnared in a net." Helen's face glowed with her fury. Her voice remained low but her hands clenched tightly.

"Your mother would be proud of you, my dear," Helen's father said softly, laying a hand on her shoulder not to control but to soothe her temper. "And she would be most appalled at you, Edmund. You have been too long among the French with their disregard of women."

"But Papa—!"

"Yorkshire women—and I suspect also those in the rest of the islands—are not inclined to be treated as dressmaker's models, good only for wearing fripperies." He squeezed his daughter's shoulder and tried to clear his throat which had seemed to thicken as he spoke. "If you had seen your sister pilot this ship through rain and clouds, and murmurations of starlings—and water spouts and whatnot, you would be more than content to leave the business of air travel in her capable hands."

"I was only trying to say—"

"If you would be wise, my son, you should be quiet. That is, if you wish to stay. Otherwise put your hat on and leave at once."

"Thank you, Papa," Helen said with a crackle of fire in her eyes. Maggiormente felt his heart sing a little louder to catch a glimpse of those eyes. As if she could rise no higher in his esteem! How exquisite she was. As if the salamander lived in her heart. And her father, while often intimidating, showed his true colours. Such a family— apart from her brother. Perhaps he had been too long away from home. He needed their good influence. What must her mother be like? The alchemist was prepared to adore her immediately.

"Signor Maggiormente, shall we go try out your fuel?"

"With pleasure, *signorina*!"

They located a cab in a trice and headed back toward the grounds where the airship awaited them. Though it was early, a crowd had gathered around the craft and watched eagerly to see the approach of the captain and her crew.

"Are you flying?"

"Will you take passengers? I can pay handsomely, mademoiselle!"

"Can you see heaven from the air?"

Helen smiled at the crowd but shook her head gently to discourage the imprecations. Signor Romano had been chatting with M. Piéton's men, who had been keeping a close watch on the airship during the night, and welcomed the captain's return. "We voyage on new fuel today, *signorina?*"

"Indeed we do, *signore.* Keep your fingers crossed that it is everything we hope."

Maggiormente grinned and shook the hand of his fellow countryman. "I hope it goes well for us, if not I go right back to the drawing board and improve."

Helen looked at him with an odd smile. "I'm glad you say 'us' now, *signore.*"

Maggiormente bowed slightly to her. "I am very pleased to be part of your crew, *signorina.* Eduardo is, too, *ne c'est pas, mon ami?*"

Eduardo nodded. "I have not worn my fez today, not because I have doubts, but because it does not seem especially aerodynamic."

"It would be a shame to lose such an elegant hat," said Helen's father, who seemed to have become rather fond of the lion now that he had gotten over his nervousness about the very large teeth. One might suspect that it was the beast in him who recognised a kindred.

"Perhaps we can get you a helmet like mine," Helen said.

"Or give him yours as you never wear it," her father scolded.

"Let us take the ship aloft with the dynamo," Signor Romano suggested as the crew settled themselves. "That way we will be away from crowds when we try the alternative."

"Just in case—" Helen said, nodding agreement.

"Better safe than sorry," her father agreed, looking just a bit pale at the thought.

"I am certain it will be fine," Maggiormente said hastily. "It may not be as powerful as you would like, but I do not think it will cause any harm."

"We shall see," Helen said with a careless air. "I can't wait to find out."

The ship rose into the air with its usual smoothness. Maggiormente was not certain that he would ever get accustomed to the sensation, but it was easier than the first time and he was filled with excitement and anticipation.

The crowd below them watched in wonder, waving furiously. The alchemist waved back. He felt as if someone ought to do so and no one else seemed inclined. Eduardo was busy scanning the sky for birds.

The ground below them passed away. The many strange constructions of the Exposition grew smaller as the ship nosed its way through the sky. Maggiormente felt his nerves calm. There was something wonderful about this sensation of flying, as if the cares remained below.

How different the perspective of a bird!

"And yet there are none to be seen," Eduardo complained somewhat grumpily.

"You would not want to be leaping out to catch them," the alchemist said, shaking his head. "It would be most dangerous."

"We could put you in a harness to hang below the gondola," Helen's father told the lion. "That way you could catch birds as they passed."

Eduardo considered the plan, not realizing that the man was joshing him. His brow furrowed as he thought about the details. "Do you not think it would impede my wingspan?"

"Surely we could work around them."

"I cannot bear to have my wings impeded." Eduardo frowned.

"Perhaps it will not work." Rochester shrugged, letting

the joke go with a chuckle. "We must concentrate our attentions elsewhere. Are you indeed fond of hunting birds?"

"I am. I excel at the sport."

The alchemist shook his head, abandoning the argument. Eduardo's conquests mostly relied on pigeons being lazy and unwatchful, foolishly perching on an open window, expecting nothing more dangerous to face them than a housecat.

No one expected a Venetian lion in a Paris flat, least of all a pigeon.

The last of the city sprawled before them and only countryside lay ahead of them. "Shall we try the new fuel soon?" The alchemist rubbed his hands together eagerly.

"Why not?" Helen smiled up at him and the alchemist considered once more the beauty of that face, particularly when lit by a smile.

They went around to the rear, where the new combustion motor, sat atop the old dynamo's casing. Helen opened the wooden case with a twist of a knob on the door. Suddenly the sound of it grew much louder. Maggiormente leaned in to look at the engine that kept the ship aloft at this speed. It was far more complicated than he expected. His only real experience with motors was the small one he had purchased from the garage.

Helen turned the engine off and closed the casing door. The sudden quiet fell upon the craft. The gondola creaked around them as the airship began to slowly descend. Helen made a few adjustments to connect the new motor to the assembly. Noticing the alchemist's curiosity she said, "It's a Lenoir. And I think we're ready."

"Where does the fuel go?"

Helen reached over to twist off a lid made from some kind of rubber. Maggiormente looked inside the interior but it was too dark to see anything.

"There may be some liquid hydrocarbon in the reservoir. Can we burn the two fuels without effect?"

Helen looked a little concerned.

The alchemist considered the point. He had not really reckoned on the mixture of the compounds. He smelled the fuel and made a mental assessment. "I do not think there is anything dangerous in the compounds' mixture." He looked up at the captain and smiled. "But we ought not tell your father of this complication. He may not take the news well, I fear."

Helen laughed. "You're probably right."

"Let us try it and hope for the best." Maggiormente took the small bottle out of his pocket. "In the future we may want to adapt the engine for a lesser flow of fuel. To regulate its passage, you see."

"Indeed." Helen's eyes were bright as she watched him pour the liquid into the engine's reservoir. Her heart hammered in her chest. But she was not prepared for what happened when it began to run. Helen started the motor. As the flywheel turned, there was a bright shower of sparks. It was as if a jet of stars rose from the exhaust pipe.

"What's that?" she asked anxiously.

"Harmless!" Maggiormente said, raising his hands as if to ward off her protestations. "A little vanity that is all. I thought it would look nice if the engine would start off with a little *panache*. You use that word? I don't know the English for it. We use the French."

"Yes, panache." Helen smiled. "I never thought of a motor having anything of whimsy."

"It is perhaps foolish, but I thought it would make it an occasion." The alchemist smiled, feeling his face warm with a sense of uncertain embarrassment. It would not do to have her see him as silly. In truth he had completely forgotten about adding the sparks. A momentary inspiration, a bit of *sprezzatura*: it was his nature after all. Unprofessional, perhaps. He couldn't help that she made him feel just a bit giddy. In any case the motor seemed to be working well. And anyhow, she smiled.

"The flywheel's running smoothly," Helen noted, her

attention turned back to the motor once more. She held her hands over the motor for a moment. Maggiormente wondered what she could be doing—feeling vibrations perhaps? Maybe motors were as much mysterious as mechanical.

"Good so far," Helen said, nodding with approval.

"What is?" The alchemist asked a little hesitantly.

"The heat level. The engine is running faster but it does not seem to be generating the usual amount of friction heat. That's good."

"I am so glad!"

"How much of the bottle did you add to the engine?" Helen looked up at the alchemist and smiled again for no reason.

It threw him for a moment, admiring that lovely face. "How much?" He pulled out the bottle again to look for he had not really noted the amount. "About half, it seems."

"Which is les than half the amount of liquid hydrocarbon we have used in the past. Let's see how far it takes us. That way we can make the return journey on the remainder of the fuel. With luck it will prove a success. It's already a success in one regard."

Maggiormente nodded his head quickly. "It has not exploded."

Helen laughed. "I meant rather that it has a very pleasant scent in the exhaust. It certainly makes being in the proximity of the engine a lot more appealing. I find the usual fuel quite loathsome."

"I am so pleased." Maggiormente felt his heart batter his chest a little at this initial sign of success. He had been rather nervous when the sparks were brighter and more plentiful than he had expected, but this settled his nerves a little more.

"Are we going to explode?"

Helen and the alchemist looked up as her father strolled over, looking more nonchalant than usual. He seemed to be relaxing more as other novices were introduced to the ship like the alchemist and his familiar. Perhaps their nerves braced his own. Doubtless he felt quite the expert now.

"We are not going to explode and the engine appears to be running very well, barely warm. Perhaps we should have the *signore* work on a coolant for the engine as well. Is there something that would be better than just water alone?" Helen turned back to the alchemist, her mind racing again.

"It is likely. I should have to think about it, but doubtless there could be something that would improve the matter. To keep the engine cool? Yes, that is possible." Maggiormente nodded agreeably, but his mind could not concentrate just then. He looked over his shoulder where Eduardo and Tuppence seemed to be in an intimate conversation.

What could they possibly have to say to each other?

"Every little bit will help," Helen said with enthusiasm. "I hear there are some Germans here at the Exhibition who will be unveiling a new motor that is even more efficient than the Belgian's model."

"Efficient how?"

"It requires less fuel and there's something different about the mechanics of the piston. I'm not entirely certain, but it will be exciting to see. There are bound to be so many wonderful discoveries here."

"Indeed. I cannot wait to see the Exhibition open. Many wonders await us. How many people will be excited to see your craft. Especially once it wins the race."

"And win we shall," Helen said with an ill-concealed note of triumph.

"I take it the engine is running well then?" Helen's father harrumphed behind her interrupting the intense conversation going on between his daughter and the alchemist.

The latter continued to find himself a bit put off by the

abrupt arrivals and interjections of that gentleman. Surely the success of the motor should calm some of his concerns, if concerns they were. Perhaps he simply did not like Maggiormente, a thought the man had had recently discussed with his familiar.

"Perhaps he simply objects to all my country men?" the alchemist had said while contemplating the proper proportion of sulphur to add to the mixture. "I have heard the English consider themselves superior to all other peoples, even those in their own kingdom. They are particularly scandalous to the Scots."

"I think it more likely that he objects, like many a father does, to all the men who show an interest in his daughter. I have seen it happen time and again. That's why Beatrice's father disliked you."

Maggiormente had stood a time in thought, pulling at his beard but he could not conjure up the picture in his mind. "Beatrice?"

The Venetian lion sighed luxuriously. It was difficult to say whether he sighed with genuine exasperation at the alchemist's poor retention of details or simply because he had had a rather fine repast that evening on top of a bellyful of wine. "You must remember Beatrice!"

"Did she have blonde hair?"

"No, black."

The alchemist frowned. "Blue eyes?"

"Green. I think." People who did not make a habit of feeding him seldom remained long in Eduardo's memory, whereas those who gave him treats he could name, describe and probably regale with a list of the treats given.

"In Milan?"

"No, Rome. You must remember."

"I think perhaps—her father you say?"

Eduardo sighed again. There could be no doubting the impatience in that sound. "She married your friend Paolo. The vintner."

"Paolo! What a lovely man. Ah ha, Beatrice, yes. Of

course—the one with the sister." Maggiormente nodded quickly, certain at last.

Eduardo had no memory of any sister, but he decided to quit while he was more or less ahead. It wasn't the sister that had anything to do with the point in question. "She also had a father, one with a marked hostility to you."

"Did he?" Maggiormente frowned. "He seemed friendly enough."

"Even when he threatened to set fire to your beard?"

The alchemist laughed and shrugged. "I have set it on fire so many times myself, I thought nothing of it."

"But that is how he showed his displeasure," Eduardo explained patiently.

"Displeasure?"

"He thought you were wooing his daughter and he did not approve of alchemists," Eduardo wrapped around his legs, hoping the point had been made at last.

"But why! Alchemists are generally thoughtful men of a creative character."

The lion shook his head. "I am not suggesting anything else—a man's foolish prejudice is just that—but it was his mistaken belief that you and not Paolo had been the man who evinced interest in his daughter that made him furious."

"Ah, so mistaken identity."

"Yes, but the salient point was that some fathers object to *any* man showing interest in their daughters."

"But such is life!" Maggiormente had said, hands wide apart with expansive feeling as if to embrace all doubting fathers.

"Yes, but many do not accept the natural and fight against its path. Fathers are sometimes among this group. Particularly with regard to their daughters."

"This is doubtless true."

Eduardo blinked at his master and chuckled. "So this may be the case with Mr Rochester and his daughter."

Although the alchemist had expressed doubt when

Eduardo told him this, he had now begun to suspect that once again his familiar had the right theory to account for the situation. Of course, Mr Rochester suspected what the alchemist had only begun to understand himself—a most unexpected development.

Maggiormente turned his face to the wind and hoped that it would calm his brain. He was unaccustomed to thoughts along these lines. This was the province of the poets and the artists. Gustave, he would know what to do with such thoughts. But the alchemist found himself struggling. It would be best to let the wind blow them quite away.

But that wasn't going to happen.

"You're not ill are you?" Helen Rochester's voice carried a solicitous concern. Her face shone in the bright sunlight as if it could never be dark when she was about.

You are far gone indeed, Maggiormente.

He shook his head. "Are we going faster than before? I know the engine seems to be running soundly." He cocked his ear to ascertain it was true before continuing. Not that the alchemist doubted his fuel at all. "Can we measure speed?"

"Ah, you have reminded me." Helen ran to the wicker box where she stored a jumble of things most of the time. She pulled out a strange instrument that looked as if it might be designed to entertain a child. "My brother brought me this."

"What is it?"

"It's an anemometer. This is the very latest model by Mr Robinson. I had not thought of such a simple answer to figuring speed."

The alchemist frowned. "How have you figured out the speed before?"

"We estimated from measuring distances back in Yorkshire," Helen said, placing the instrument on the ledge of the gondola. "That's much harder to do here where I do not know the lay of the land. I can tell we're going faster, however."

"You know your ship well."

Helen flushed. "I have spent the better part of my days for the last year either aboard this ship or thinking about it."

"Do you dream of it as well?" Maggiormente asked, genuinely curious.

Helen laughed and blushed a little. "I do. Is it so strange?"

"It is perfectly natural," Maggiormente said, looking absently at Eduardo. 'When you do exciting work, it occupies your mind even when you are asleep. Particularly if you have a sticky problem that eludes an easy solution."

"I'm glad I'm not the only one," Helen said with another little laugh as she adjusted the dial on the anemometer. The dial sat near the base of the instrument which rose up like a needle or a plinth. She placed on top of it an assembly with four semi-circular cups set sideways to catch the wind at the end of crossed arms that looked like an X.

"So these cups catch the wind and spin around and you judge the speed from that?" The alchemist nodded. He approved of handsome instruments that worked efficiently. It was not always the case in the rather more experimental world of alchemy, so straightforward mechanicals were always a delight.

"Yes, precisely." Helen looked up and smiled as the cups began slowly to spin. "It's such a relief not to have to explain everything, *signore*. Especially to someone too impatient to listen to the explanation."

They both looked toward her father who begun some kind of argument with Tuppence who taunted him from the air. The man enjoyed a good tussle of wits, that was well evident. The alchemist found he rather liked the man, different as their natures were. From hints he had caught in conversation, he suspected the man to have survived much sorrow. *We all battle demons in our own style.*

"One has to understand obsession," Maggiormente said with sudden passion. "Not all do. Many are happy to ask nothing of life but a lack of sorrow. Others burn. It is difficult to explain to others when you burn to accomplish something that no one has done."

Helen looked up at him, her face suddenly serious. "Something no one has done…"

"It is true, is it not?" The alchemist could not quite contain the admiration he felt for this intrepid woman. She was surely sublime, to use the poet's word. Her spirit shone through her eyes and captivated him completely. *Maybe Gustave was right about that.*

"I suppose it is. When I think of discovery, I think of the great names we learn in history books. I cannot think that little me from Yorkshire is really doing something important." Helen laughed, looking as if she wished she had said nothing as she watched the cups circle around in their dance.

"Ridiculous!"

Helen looked surprised. "Am I?"

"Yes," Maggiormente said then saw how her face fell. "No, no, not you. I am stumbling in my words." He smacked his head with his hand. "*You* are not ridiculous. *Your work* is not ridiculous. It is ridiculous that you doubt yourself or think you are so little. Michaelangelo is the greatest, such a mind, such an artist, such a thinker. And yet he is just a man or was."

"I suppose…"

"Did Michaelangelo strut around thinking 'What a genius I am?' I don't know," the alchemist shrugged. "Perhaps he did. But I suspect that most of the time he just thought, 'How do I paint this? How do I carve this? Can a man fly?' And that is what we must do, too. Do our work. Ask our questions. Let the fire burn. Put our heads down over the problems, obsess about our dreams and keep working."

Her glowing smile suggested she agreed.

14 THE RACE

It was the day of the great race. Paris seemed to have taken the match to heart and the papers were full of the competition and speculation about its outcome. In every café and taverna, people declared for one ship or the other. *Les grands dirigeables* were on everyone's lips as the crowds swelled around the Exposition grounds. Images of the ships and their crew became desirable from market stalls and the broadsheet sellers in the streets. The City of Lights had a fever of anticipation.

Mathilde Belcoeur led the charge, delighting in her inside information since the craft's unexpected landing in Poissy. Helen could not resist Mme. Belcoeur's enthusiasm and anyway she had been so kind to them then, it would have been churlish to refuse to give her more background and a little about their plans. And the journalist certainly made no secret of her favouring *Jane's Inspiration* over the Linton's *Forward Momentum*. Naturally her competitors took up the Lintons' cause as a matter of course.

Despite the constant barrage of provocative questions, Helen always kept her remarks to simple expressions of good sportsmanship and eagerness for both ships to demonstrate the very best air travel had to offer of the newly mobile future. It seemed to be the best way to take the high road.

Not that her father agreed.

"We shall crush them in the competition!" Helen overheard him telling one journalist as she and Signor Romano tinkered with the steering assembly. He didn't even try to converse in French. "They'll wish their mother never met their father!" His fist raised in triumph as if he would strike the Lintons' ship out of the air with his own hand.

The journalists wrote it all down, doubtless adding their own embellishments as she had seen in the earlier editions. The popular press had very few compunctions about sticking to truthfulness when it came to making a good story. It was all quite vexing but there appeared to be very little she could do about it. Certainly stopping her father from his infernal boasting would not be not easy to accomplish. She could be grateful, at least, that they weren't dealing with the London papers.

Helen adjusted a nut with a spanner and considered the Lintons themselves. They were no shrinking violets. Their tone—well, Edgar's anyway—had been one of smug self-satisfaction. It was really most provoking, but something in her held back from entering the verbal fray. Her mother would doubtless counsel action rather than words and Helen found herself content with that. After all, the race was the thing.

"Should we have another test, *signorina*?" Romano broke into her thoughts as he stood up and stretched his back with a little groan.

"I don't think we need to do so," Helen said frowning at the press of people all around the ship. "And we could never conceal the flight from all these prying eyes."

Romano looked a little anxious. The pressure of the hoopla had an effect on him as well. "Are you confident in the fuel?"

Helen smiled. She could see Maggiormente and

Eduardo making their way through the crowd, people moving aside from the lion's mouth. "Yes, I have every confidence in our alchemist."

It was funny how her heart fluttered a little at the sight of the alchemist. *You're being very foolish*, Helen scolded. She found it impossible to say just what it was that affected her so. He was kindly, of course, and very sweet. His head was full of prodigious information about very obscure things which fascinated her a great deal. And he seemed to understand obsession in a way that made her feel...*comprehended*. Even her mother, who loved her dearly and supported her utterly, could not quite comprehend this zeal for flight that Helen had. That the alchemist did was a wonder in itself.

Other people might only see the strangeness of him with his beard and his lion and that distracted air of lostness, but Helen saw only the incredible and singular mind that worked so perfectly with an open and honest heart. He had a happy smile on his face even now. Helen knew he was just as excited about the race. They both had so much to gain if all went as well as they anticipated. *We shall win!* Helen's confidence surged as she waved to her friend. Her heart flew in anticipation of the ship's journey. "We're ready for the race. You made it in plenty of time."

Maggiormente's grin only broadened. He turned to say something to someone next to him and that's when Helen noticed the woman who walked beside him, on the opposite side from Eduardo. At first she had assumed the woman to be just another part of the crowd that milled around the ships with barely suppressed excitement.

But she stood out. She wore an unusual dress of bright colours and a fabric that softly enfolded her small form. The patterns and style looked like nothing Helen had seen in the short time in Paris and at once she became certain that the woman must come from a distant land.

It was only when Tuppence squawked behind her that she noticed the woman had a small bird perched on her shoulder. The bizarre little creature seemed to be crafted out of rare jewels, so striking were its colours, but it moved. It could be a very clever clockwork doll, Helen supposed. Then the bird took off and flew right up to Tuppence, bold as anything. Even Tuppence seemed taken aback by this unexpected development and clicked with consternation at the little thing. The two birds eyeballed each other, their heads moving around quickly back and forth as if to see everything in the other's plumed mystery.

Helen turned her attention back to Maggiormente's companion and could not help staring at the woman. She was small and delicate, her face very pale and her dark eyes and hair making the contrast sharper. Every limb expressed grace and her movement had the natural fluidity of a river. Helen felt absurdly conscious of her own large hands, covered with oil, rough from work and travel, and became keenly aware of how tall she was and not at all tiny—rangy as her father, if not quite as tall or with his blustery movements. Her mind jumped to an analogy that made her blush with annoyance: *like a Highland coo beside a sleek race horse.*

Words bottle-necked in her throat and all she could say was "Hello."

"A glorious day, is it not?" The alchemist rubbed his hands together as if he could not wait any longer. Indeed he appeared ready to explode with delight. "And look! I brought my dear friend, Myojo. She has come all the way to Paris from Japan. Such a delight." He laughed as if to make it clear just how delightful she was.

The woman looked up at Helen with a shy smile, although her expression mirrored the look of curiosity Helen knew to be on her own face. *What did she see?* Helen wondered, thinking she must look awfully strange to this beautiful woman who seemed to embody all that was perfect as she lowered her head in a bow of greeting.

"Pleased to meet you, Miss Rochester. I have heard so much about you from my friend. I am so grateful on his behalf."

Something in the way she said 'friend' made Helen's heart thump unnecessarily as she thought, *oh*. "I see you have an unusual bird, too, Miss Myojo."

The woman laughed and nodded. "Seito is much intrigued by your *karasu*. She usually only sees pigeons in this city."

"Pigeons are very common," Eduardo said as he squeezed between the two of them, clearly thinking he had not got enough attention in this conversation. "That is why I eat them." Everyone laughed. Eduardo couldn't tell whether to be pleased by their mirth, but he chose to think it was in his favour. "People should be grateful to me," he added, quite certain that was always true.

The two birds took the opportunity to tease the lion, flapping over and plucking at his wings with their beaks, as if they would get him to fly as well. Eduardo soon became irritated. "Stop that." The birds paid him no attention, enjoying their game while the humans focused on the flying craft.

"Is everything ready?" the alchemist asked, his expression eager.

Helen thought again what a lovely smile he had, how his kindness radiated through it. *Never mind, my girl, it appears his heart is taken.* "All ready. We await only the starter's gun."

Maggiormente frowned. "They shoot a gun to start the race? How very odd and so dangerous. What if someone were to get hurt?"

Helen smiled. "It's an expression. In horse races in Britain we use a pistol to start the contest. There is no bullet in the gun, so it is quite safe."

"Perhaps we need something else dramatic to start the race," the alchemist said, stroking his beard. "My friend Myojo could probably—Oh! I know what we could do. Fireworks!" He rubbed his hands together gleefully.

"Fireworks? That sounds much more dangerous."

"No, certainly not with Myojo's help. She is quite amazingly magical. A magician in fact. I don't even know how she does it," Maggiormente confessed.

"It is a secret knowledge," the woman said with a shy smile. "But not at all dangerous. We would keep it well away from the airships."

Helen got the impression that she meant to reassure her. Despite the kindness, however, she felt an irrational irritation with the woman. It wasn't entirely fair but then life seldom was. *I should be concentrating on the race anyway*, Helen scolded herself.

She could not stop the twinge of pain in her heart when the alchemist and the magician bent their heads together in animated conversation. She turned back to the engine, although there was nothing really to be done. Signor Romano was shining the brass panels, seemingly as a way to occupy his nervousness while waiting. His movements were too quick, too jerky.

"Here come the Lintons," her father shouted and Helen started, looking over her shoulder where a large team of horses drew an enormous flat wagon with the Lintons' ship balanced on it and another behind it with the envelope, which struck her as very odd. To reassemble their ship just before the big race? How dramatic and foolhardy. What potential problems might be introduced in a careless moment? But that was not her concern. They should have simply flown over to the field. Less dramatic, but surely more sensible. With the Lintons, however, Helen had learned that sense and sensibility did not always coincide. They clearly meant to make themselves the center of attention with a lot of shouting and ordering about of their band of hired hands.

This could take some time.

"Perhaps we should have a bite to eat, as we will have to wait some time for the Lintons to be ready." Helen frowned. She had no appetite, but it was better than staring gloomily at her competitors while they put on their show. "I think we have some cheese in the wicker basket."

"No, even better! Now we have the fireworks. That will draw the attention away," Maggiormente added with a laugh. Helen was surprised to see that the preparations had been made from the pouch Myojo had carried over her shoulder. It hardly seemed big enough to hold explosives. Perhaps they were very weak.

While most of the crowds had gathered around the Lintons' hasty activity, a few began to drift over to where the alchemist and the magician were busy preparing the impromptu display. The little bird Seito had returned to her shoulder and the raven Tuppence was bursting with curiosity to see what was being done. Eduardo, however, stood well back. Having heard the word 'explosions' he had no apparent desire to come any closer. Instead he sat near the ship in the guise of protector. It certainly worked to keep the curious at bay.

"*Mesdames et messieurs*! My ladies and gentlemen!" Myojo may have been a tiny lass, but her voice carried almost as if she had a megaphone. Perhaps this was part of her magic. "To celebrate the great airship race, a little display of light and magic."

She held a sort of canister in her hands and opened the lid with a flourish. From the cylinder arose a flowering of sparks and then a spray of what seemed to look like red flower petals shot up into the air. It was a gentle sort of fireworks, with very little in the way of fire and it proved a charming sight to the crowd who cheered and exclaimed their delight.

"*Coriandoli*!" Signor Romano said with a happy look, obviously recognizing the display. "They are little paper— paper disks from the silk worm cages. A Milanese favourite. We throw them at carnival."

"How ingenious." Helen smiled. "I can see they would be more genteel than traditional fireworks." And they had done the trick of bringing the audience back to their side of the field, doubtless annoying the Lintons. Myojo opened another canister, this time of blue paper disks. Helen watched more closely and saw that the sparks that preceded the *coriandoli* came from something up the magician's sleeve.

Magic and sleight of hand: it was all right for the crowd, but winning the race would take more than that. Helen patted the rail of the gondola. The fuel had worked so well in the test. She had every faith that they would triumph. Her affectionate spirit felt a tug yet to think that not all triumphs might be hers that day. However Helen's heart had learned long ago to occupy itself with meaningful activity to assuage any aches.

She turned back to the matters of the ship while the crowd oohed and ahhed over the display of colours and lights. Presumably the Lintons would be ready to race soon, so she wanted a chance to double check all the preparations. It was never a bad idea and today it was particularly important. The race to Orléans would demonstrate the superiority of her ship and her choice of fuel. "Or I'll eat my hat," Helen muttered to Tuppence. She saw M. Piéton approaching and stood up to greet him. "Monsieur, are we ready to begin?"

"*Oui, mademoiselle capitaine.* I just wish to be certain you are ready. *Les messieurs* assure me they are ready." The Lintons waved over from their ship, at least Israel did. Helen waved back tentatively. Now that the time was near, her heart began to beat a little faster.

"I am ready as well, monsieur." She put her helmet on (her father had insisted) and nodded to Signor Romano as he did the same. They both brought down their goggles as well.

Her father suddenly appeared. His face looked grave, but he smiled. "I shall not wish you luck. You don't need it. Triumph because you are the better man. Er, ship captain." He laughed and tried very hard to conceal his pride and embarrassment. Helen leaned over the gondola and gave him a kiss.

"Thank you, Papa. I shall make you proud." Tuppence gave him a few croaks to let him know that she would keep an eye on the captain and crew.

"All the best, *signorina* Helen." The alchemist appeared at her father's elbow. The two tall men made a strange pair, one stiffly English even in a Paris meadow, the other all rumpled curlicues of disjointed directions. There were a couple of the paper disks in his hair and one stuck to his beard. Yet Helen felt again the tug of comforting affection even as she mourned there being any other possibility for more between them. She knew herself to be a plain Englishwoman and no match for the exquisitely beautiful magician whose every movement seemed art itself.

"I hope to prove the success of your fuel. The airship field is small yet, but as it grows your miraculous fuel will be much in demand."

Maggiormente waved away the words, but it was not only for modesty. "Come back to us safely, that is all I ask. The rest is unimportant. Though I do hope you embarrass those men terribly with your success. They are not gentlemen, I think." He frowned with displeasure. Eduardo behind him nodded agreement, whipping his tail around in a temper.

Helen laughed. "I shall endeavor to do so. Triumph shall be ours."

The alchemist leaned forward and took her hands in his. "You are so wonderful to say so. Let it be so. If a success, perhaps—well, perhaps many things will be possible." The warmth of his smile proved infectious and Helen wondered again if she were simply mistaken in him. These Mediterranean types were so much more affectionate than she was accustomed to in Yorkshire. Perhaps it was only a friendly kindness, but her heart did not listen to sense and soared once more with hope. Only time would tell. For now, Helen did her best not to let her imagination run away with her. She would come down to earth soon enough.

"*Mesdames et messieurs*, ladies and gentlemen, *meine Damen und Herren!*" M. Piéton had a speaking trumpet to his lips as he tried to reach the crowd. "Welcome to the great airship race from the Exposition to Orléans *et retour*. The Exposition is proud to offer a glimpse of the future in our two ships as they race to bring new *technologie* to this eager audience. In Orléans officials await to greet them with large yellow flags which will wave when the ship must turn and voyage back to Paris. If you are of a sporting nature, perhaps your should wager a bottle of wine on the winner. We will toast them with champagne, *d'accord!*

"Captaines, are you ready for the race?" Helen nodded as Romano readied the system. She saw the Lintons salute to the official to show their compliance. To her surprise, M. Piéton pulled out a traditional starter's pistol and aimed it to the sky. After an agonizing moment, he fired and the race was begun!

Helen waved farewell as Romano started the engine. The sparks that issued forth from the motor caused some consternation in the crowd, except for Maggiormente who clapped his hands with delight while Helen's father looked on him with some disbelief. His look of panic changed to rueful amusement as the ship moved. Helen felt such excitement as the ship lifted into the air. *Jane's Inspiration* was afloat!

The Lintons' ship with its larger frame offered more noise and smoke as it attempted to make its name manifest. *Forward Momentum*'s motor roared into life and people quickly backed away from the path of the ship which soon moved forward but not with sufficient lift for such a situation. Many of the crowd became alarmed as it bore down upon them, but eventually it began to rise, too, at first only as high as their heads, but eventually growing higher bit by bit, though still well below Helen's ship which had risen effortlessly like a cloud. She smiled with satisfaction as the ship kept pace easily with the Lintons' own. It was a tremendous start.

Helen checked the compass to be certain they were heading in the right direction, though as they soon discovered, many volunteers lined the route with yellow flags that were easy to spot along the way. As they sailed out of Paris Helen could not stop grinning, particularly when she looked over at her competitors and saw their flurry of activity.

"Should be go faster, *signorina*?" Romano could not hide his eagerness.

"Not yet," Helen said, a mischievous grin on her lips. "It's all about the timing, *signore*."

They had an easy time following the yellow flags along the route. Here and there people had gathered to watch the famous race. Helen moved between the anemometer and Romano's array of instruments, but everything ran smoothly and efficiently. It was easy to imagine ships like this piloting around the world. No wonder people were excited. She could not quite believe that her little obsession had become the talk of Paris—and beyond, but the evidence was everywhere around her. She waved to the latest knot of well-wishers before returning to check the motor.

Not that it was necessary! The motor purred along with an almost musical precision. She held her hands over the engine, fingers spread. Such a difference in the level of heat produced by the alchemist's fuel! Helen could not stop marveling. Truth to tell, she would have been delighted in Signor Maggiormente even if his fuel had not been quite so remarkable. At least she thought so. It didn't really matter, she scolded herself. This fuel worked wonderfully, the engine stayed remarkably cool and yes, it smelled rather wonderful, too. Was that a bit of cardamom she caught a whiff of? Like a fresh bakery that scent was. What more could one ask? They would make a true revolution in air travel between her design and the alchemist's aromatically propulsive chemistry.

Why did she feel so wistful then?

Helen sighed. Of course it was because of that beautiful Japanese woman and her little bird of many colours. He didn't say there was any understanding between them, she reasoned, but surely any man would be drawn to a woman of that exquisite beauty and grace. Such elegance and skill! Those beautiful explosions of colour that she created. They were quite amazing.

"Face it, Tuppence," Helen muttered to her bird, who hopped along beside her on the gondola's frame. "We're just rough Yorkshire women. Too tough for mere mortal men." Tuppence clicked at her as if in admonishment, but it did not have much of an effect on Helen. She squared her shoulders. It wouldn't do to mope. After all, she had the finest airship anywhere (at least as far as she knew) and it was going to be gratifying to trump the Lintons in this race. As there was little else to do, she waved to another knot of people along the road with their yellow flags. It was cheering to see them.

Helen glanced over at the Lintons' ship. There was so much going on. They seemed to have a lot of folderol in motion. She frowned. What on earth could they be doing that needed so much work? Were they trying to do something more than simply reaching a higher speed? Once you had the proper lift, what was there to do but steer in the right direction? They really did engage in a lot of folderol. Helen was glad they couldn't see her smile. Wait until they saw what this fuel could *really* do.

The Linton brothers seemed to be running back and forth around their ship, moving things around. Oh wait, it seemed to be scuttles. Could it be they were actually using coal in their engine now? How ridiculous. How much extra weight it added, too. Helen shook her head. The men just had no original thinking at all. Coal was so old-fashioned. New transportation required new thinking about fuel. No wonder they had such a plume of black smoke behind them. *You might as well put balloons on a steam engine.*

The two ships must be approaching Orléans soon. They crazy activity of the two over there must surely suggest that as much as the increase in houses near the post road. The Lintons began slowly to gain speed as they shoveled coal into their motor at an ever more frantic pace. Helen saw Edgar glancing over his shoulder at an oblique angle, attempting to gauge their relative speeds as they approached the town.

"Now, *signorina*?" Romano could barely contain his eagerness. The glee shone through his expression and the excitement radiated out his eyes.

Helen shook her head, however. "No, *signore*. Not until we make the turn." She felt as eager as he, but it wouldn't do to tip their hand too early. It was plain that the Lintons had a great deal of confidence in their new engine despite the old fuel (had they not said it was a new fuel too? Perhaps a new and better type of coal—oh, the smallness of their hidebound imaginations). She could be patient a little while longer. When they turned back it would be easier to have their success without any risks of interference.

The Lintons were poor losers, as she knew all too well.

Already they were moving closer to the path of her own ship as well as ever so slowly moving out ahead of it. They wanted to be able to shout their triumph at her, she was quite certain. Little did they know who would be triumphant. Just then Helen saw the raised dais where the officials of the town stood to signal to the ships. There could be no mistake: such a crowd of formal wear contrasted oddly with the bright yellow flag that rose above them. It was hard to imagine the French cheering so enthusiastically for two ships piloted by people with whom they had gone to war not a generation before (and many generations in the more distant past) but there was no mistaking the delight people showed as the two ships approached the waiting audience. The cheers were audible over the engine and the joyful expressions lit all their faces.

The Lintons had already begun to turn their ship, so Helen nodded to Romano to do the same. As the big craft began to arc in the sky, the intrepid captain leaned over the edge of the gondola to wave to the people below. They cheered and returned the greeting, eager to outdo one another in the sport. Many were drinking champagne and looked quite excited that their town had been chosen for this revolutionary sport. Orléans had not had such prominence since the Middle Ages.

Helen grinned with pleasure. Whatever the outcome of the race, surely the future lay in the beckoning fair world of air travel. *Jane's Inspiration* and yes, the *Forward Momentum* would be talked about for some time to come and, she hoped, inspire others to dare air travel as well. Forget the ugly belch of the railroad with its track that marred the pleasant green land. Horses could be used for sport and leisure instead of hauling passengers and great burdens. And the world would open up to people everywhere, bringing on a new era of peace and prosperity as friendship across the miles would displace ignorance.

"Now, *signorina*?" Romano burst into her happy preoccupations with a wheedling call.

Helen laughed. "*Si, signore*. Now!"

As the pilot opened the throttle there was a barely discernable increase in the purring hum of the engine. Helen could hardly believe the difference from how it had once sounded. The noise of the Lintons' ship was audible over the machinations of her own, even as close as she sat. Her smile of satisfaction grew.

The speed of the ship also increased—and how!

Helen glanced over at her rivals to see twin expressions of surprise on their faces. Though the two ships had kept an even pace all the way to Orléans, the superiority of her ship grew more apparent every moment. Helen nearly clapped her hands with glee at the success of Signor Maggiormente's fuel. How he would delight to see it!

The Lintons, however, did not find anything to delight

them in this new development. They burst into a frenzy of activity—that is, after Edgar smacked his thunderstruck brother. The two of them began to run about the gondola of their ship, perhaps shoveling more fuel into the heavy combustion engine. At least as far as she could guess as they grew smaller and smaller in the distance.

Helen finally turned around to look forward, feeling a good deal of satisfaction in her ship, her crew and of course the alchemist. "Bravo, *signore*!" She sighed. In part it was a happy sigh, but there was a tinge of melancholy about it. Being a Yorkshire woman, however, she bustled her mind around and focused on the success that lay ahead.

"What is it, Tuppence?" Helen said as the bird flapped around her head making a series of strange clicks. For a moment she simply stared at the raven, her brow furrowed. Then a sense of urgency put mobility into her limbs, for she recognized the signs of distress that Tuppence meant to convey. She ran to the engine but all seemed well. It functioned smoothly, easily and there was very little heat from the workings. Tuppence landed on her shoulder and plucked at her collar. "What do you mean, my dear?"

The bird hopped into the air and flew away behind the ship. Helen leaned over the edge of the gondola but saw nothing below to alarm her. "I'm so sorry, Tuppence. I'm afraid I don't understand." It was frustrating for them both. Normally she had no trouble understanding the bird's meaning, but clearly there was something new they had not dealt with before.

All at once there was a terrible sound. Helen gasped. A huge column of fire shot up from the gondola of the Lintons' ship. Then a plume of black smoke rose up in its wake and began to spread through the air. Something had gone horribly awry!

"*Signore*! Turn the ship around." Helen shouted to her pilot who had heard the sound as well and stood gaping at the other ship. But as a well-trained pilot he quickly regained his composure and spun the wheel around to turn the ship, keeping up a stream of excited speech so swift that Helen could not catch one word in ten of his hasty Italian.

We are going even faster now, Helen thought. The pilot must have kept a little bit in reserve, just for show or for doubt or fear of going too fast. Now he threw caution to the winds because they could both see the way the terrible fire had spread through the ship. Could they make it in time to save the men?

Helen glanced around the land below the ship. They were a good bit too far up in the air to give any chance of leaping from the ship into the trees. They were few, scattered along the hedgeways, a good distance from the road they had been navigating by. But what else was there? Houses that were very small and rather more of a distance away—they could offer little in the way of sanctuary for the endangered crew.

"Are we going as fast as possible now, *signore*?" Helen shouted into the wind toward the pilot, hoping that he could hear. He nodded back to her, still keeping up a steady stream of curses, imprecations and prayers. She had not thought of the effects of wind on travel. Their pace had always been so genteel, the wind was not much of a factor. She would have to think of some way to protect the passengers. It would be a pity to lose the glorious view by enclosing the gondola! There must be some way around it. But glass was so heavy.

I must not get distracted!

Helen shook herself. There was time for such thoughts later. Even at top speed it would take them a few more minutes to reach the ship. What did she have that would be helpful? Helen gathered up the tools and ropes that there were at hand, while she made a mental note for what ought to be carried in all ships in the way of emergency materials to make certain that one could do what was possible to help the passengers of one's own ship but also to lend aid to another ship nearby. The problems of being a trailblazer could not always be readily anticipated, but Helen cursed herself for not carrying through on some of the recommendations she'd come up with after the last race with the Lintons. Good intentions mean nothing without action, as her mother often repeated.

"Careful now!" She shouted needlessly to Romano as they approached the other ship. He had already slacked the rapid pace and taken the ship down a little lower so they were almost even with the Lintons' damaged craft where a wild fire raged.

Was there anyone left alive?

Helen looked with alarm for Tuppence. The bird had flown close to the fire. Surely every fibre of its being would shrink from going so close to the conflagration. Her raven must know how serious an issue it was to try to save the two men. She wondered anew at the bird's intelligence—so remarkable.

Below them people were gathering, doubtless drawn by the fire. Some came running, others on horseback. They did not seem to want to come too close for fear of the flames, but nearness assure that the even when the ship fell to earth—as surely it must do eventually—they could control the burn and keep it from consuming any buildings. Helen breathed some quick words of gratitude that there were no homes or barns too nearby. How much more horrible that would be.

She could see the flames were spreading across the gondola toward the men though they seemed to be throwing buckets of sand and water at the source. It wasn't enough to stop the hungry fire, but it seemed to have been enough to slow it while her ship approached. Helen grabbed the rope ladder, ready to throw it across once she got their attention. The problem was, as she saw it, there was nowhere safe to attach it to so they could climb between the ships. That had seemed like the safest way to transfer them, but now it was looking ever more dangerous. Soon the envelope would begin to burn and then it would be too late.

"Can you hear me?" Helen called over to the men while they frantically ran back and forth across the blazing gondola. If they heard, they made no acknowledgement. "Bring us closer," she shouted to Signor Romano.

The pilot shook his head in disbelief. "My lady, we will catch fire too."

Helen held up the rope ladder. "We have to try to save them, *signore*. It's our duty."

Romano muttered a handful of words that were probably oaths of some kind or other, but he very carefully brought the ship closer to the flaming one, gingerly creeping closer. Helen was about to try shouting again when she saw Tuppence dart between the ropes of the gondola and pull at Israel's hair.

The two Linton brothers had been running, flailing their arms and shouting at each other for so long that it was not until then that either of them noticed the other airship. When Israel looked up, Helen waved and held up the rope ladder. He nodded at her and then ran to his brother, slapping him on the shoulder and pointing to the rescuers.

Tuppence flew up, croaking away loudly as if to urge them on. For a moment Helen feared that Edgar would refuse to comply, stubborn as he was. He threw a last bit of water onto the conflagration to no apparent change, then they both raced between the flames to the side of the gondola nearest *Jane's Inspiration*.

Helen tossed the rope ladder over to the brothers, leaning away from the intense heat of the fire. They missed the first throw but the second worked. Tuppence flew back to Helen's side as she hurried to fix the ladder tightly to her ship. Helen was fairly certain it would bear the weight of both of them at once, though she could not stop imagining the ladder falling away as the two men perished.

Best not to think too much at times like these.

"Ready?" The two of them nodded. Helen gave them a wave to show that it was all right and they stepped out into the edge of the gondola. Just then a horrible sound exploded as the fire shot up the sides of the envelope. Their efforts to contain the flames had not lasted long.

The two men swung low on the ladder as their momentum took them under the ship. Tuppence made another alarmed croak and flew down to see where they went. Helen bit her lip to keep from giving voice to all the fear she felt, though she was grateful to see the Romano had already begun to move the ship away from the fire.

The brothers swung back into sight and closer to their own ship before the pendulum-like swing took them out of sight under the ship again.

"Shall I go down to the ground, *signorina*?" The pilot looked worried but his hands on the controls were steady.

"Yes, that makes the most sense. Carefully so!"

The ship lowered gently as the blasts of hot air came toward them in waves. The *Forward Momentum* had been slowly descending, too, but now its blackened carcass fell to the green grass below, smoking and burning in equal measures. The crowds that had gathered kept well back, but as Helen watched a few hearty souls helped catch the two men as they approached the ground. Israel fell down into the grass, but Edgar sprang up and ran toward the wreckage.

A few people tried to hold him back for he seemed wild with anger. Helen could see him gesticulating as he shouted something incoherent. When the blackened frame of the ship collapsed and then settled into smoking wreckage, his shoulders drooped as if at last admitting defeat. Israel came up behind him and put an arm over his shoulder. The last few flames gave way to greasy black smoke.

The *Forward Momentum* was no more.

Helen sank back down against the edge of the gondola.

Tuppence flew up and perched beside her, croaking a mile a minute, as if to get in all her opinions on the Lintons' disaster. She reached out a hand to the bird and gently ruffled her feathers. The idea passed through her mind that she should offer the two brothers a ride back to Paris, but before she spoke Helen thought better of it. They would never wish to return in such ignominy. It was going to be bad enough to return to Yorkshire and know that they would have to live adjacent to the victor.

Victor. The word sounded good to Helen. She had earned it. Rising to her feet again, she told her pilot, "Shall we head back to Paris now?"

Signor Romano grinned back at her. "*Si, si, signorina.* We have some champagne awaiting us, I think."

"Let's see how fast *Jane's Inspiration* can go, *signore.* No holding back!"

Romano took her at her word and soon they were going faster than ever they had. Helen knew that the pilot had kept some power in reserve, afraid even now that some fault with the fuel would be discovered. The pleasant scent of the alchemist's concoction filled the gondola even as the increasing wind swept it away.

The glory of flying could not be equaled, Helen knew. "Is this how it feels?" she murmured to Tuppence, who faced the wind with eyes closed as if entertained by the novelty of flying without any effort for the first time. She had always been too impatient with the pace before to sit long in the gondola. A bird's approval was priceless.

Helen closed her own eyes, the better to feel the wind on her face. She knew her father was right and she should wear the protective goggles and helmet, but even as her eyes streamed tears from the bite of the wind, Helen did not wish for them. From the time when she had first seen the picture of an airship in the newspapers from London and imagined riding one aloft, this—this pure bliss—this is the way she imagined it would be. Just a girl with a dream, one people thought foolish—or deranged, or even ridiculous. A dream many men would shrink from pursuing, Helen knew.

I've done it. We've done it!

Was there a feeling more sublime than a dream realised? If there was, Helen didn't think her heart could bear it. Already her chest felt as if it would burst. She wanted to hug her father and even more, she wanted to clasp her mother in her arms. They would cry, she knew, but the tears would be a triumph, too. How grateful she was for a mother who did not simply hurry her off to the altar, one who always said that conventionality was not morality and that a woman had every right to be as free and as ambitious as a man.

Helen knew she could not do better than to sail the four winds in *Jane's Inspiration*, for she had sailed in her mother's love all her life. A great sob broke from her as tears of emotion joined those caused by the wild breezes. If she could, she would have them sail all the way to Yorkshire now so she could feel those loving arms around her once more.

But Paris lay ahead and she could see it now, and her father who had remained so intrepid throughout this journey deserved his part of her joy as well. How he would enjoy having the City of Lights at their feet too. For all his blustering and complaining, he had done so well and seemed even much stronger and happier than he had been before. His grumbling was more in the order of habit and he rose much more lively and walked even quicker than she could remember from years before. This journey had strengthened him and returned that vital spark which had dimmed through habit.

As the city came into sight ahead of them, Helen imagined the fun they would have, how her father would regale the French with harrowing tales of their journey across the channel—exaggerating slightly, of course, but only for dramatic effect. To think that she had been so chagrined that he would accompany her! But now Helen's gratitude knew no bounds. Her only sorrow was the tender look on his face as he wrote to her mother. They had not been parted so in many a year. Though he reveled in their adventures, his heart yearned for home like a pigeon for its roost.

So homeward they would go when the cheering was over. She felt a twinge for the alchemist. Signor Maggiormente had been such a delight. His mind worked in many ways opposite to hers but they always seemed to end up in accord. It was safe to say that she had never known another mind like his. She would always cherish the memory of their collaboration, and look forward to his latest discoveries. But clearly his heart yearned toward another and she must gracefully withdraw.

They could see the fields of the Exposition ahead. Such wonders there would be to see in the coming days, but Helen could find little in her heart to leap at the idea now. Her trophy had been won. Her miracles were discovered. Home tugged on her heart. It would be good to fly there.

As Signor Romano slowed the ship, Tuppence took off, winging her way down to her friends which made it easier for Helen to spot her father among the heaving masses. At once she waved and even aloft the sound of the crowd below reached them. They could tell how the race had ended even if they did not know the whole story yet. "We are the conquerors, *signore*!" Helen shouted to her pilot.

"We will have champagne and endless delights tonight, *signorina*." Food was always uppermost in his mind. The dazzle of Paris held less sway with him.

Helen hoped he felt the same pride in the ship that she did. "Signor, we have accomplished so much. I thank you for your work. You have been brave and true."

The pilot flushed with pleasure. "No less than you, *signorina*. I am honoured to serve. One day, we shall have entire fleets of ships to pilot."

Helen threw down the rope ladder, singed as it was

from the Lintons' fire and began her descent to the crowd. The cheers overwhelmed her. Tuppence flew in circles around her, doing her best to be heard over the crowd. Helen's father was the first to greet them as it was he who held the end of the ladder firmly.

"Welcome back, my clever girl. You have won." Heedless of the clamouring crowds around them, he clasped her tightly in his arms and kissed her cheek. "I am so very proud of you," he whispered, his voice choking a little with the emotion. Helen could not remember ever being happier.

When they finally let go of one another both their faces bore the tracks of happy tears, but they were quickly surrounded by well wishers, clapping them on their backs, thrusting gifts and bottles at them. Her brother Edmund clasped her hands in his and shouted his congratulations, while others tried to elbow him aside.

Suddenly a roar made the crowd quiet quickly and part at once. Helen turned to see Eduardo looking very peeved, his wings spread as wide as they could go and Tuppence perched between them like some black rider. It was in service of his master however, for the gentle alchemist grinned broadly, tears flowing without shame as he repeated, "You did it, *signorina miracolosa*. You have won. I knew you would!" He grabbed her hands and led her in a merry dance as the people clapped and cheered.

Suddenly the alchemist fell to his knees. Helen cried out, afraid he had been hurt. But he smiled through his tears. *"Per favore, bella signorina.* Tell me true. Have I a chance with you?"

"Of course," Helen said, confused and alarmed. "The fuel is superb. It worked a charm!"

"I can't believe I raised such an idiot for a child," Helen's father broke in with impatience. "The man wants to marry you, Helen!".

AFTERWORD

Reader, she married him. Oh, not right away—in fact it took a rather long time for the promised event to happen. The immediate effect of the somewhat confused proposal was a slow reverberation through the crowds surrounding them both until they were hoisted aloft while bottles of champagne popped open all around them. Let it not be said that anyone outdid the Parisians in their celebration of romance—even a modern airship one.

It was impossible for Helen to say anything—even to offer her assent—for the crowds were too boisterous for them to speak and they were carried to the very center of the Exhibition while the others in their party were lost behind them somewhere. Her father struggled on for a time then waved with a sort of impatient resignation. Her brother Edmund, much to her surprised eyes as she glanced over her shoulder, had turned away from the excited exodus, arm in arm with the magician Myojo. She did not see him until late that evening when he announced his latest scheme: a visit to the Emperor of Japan to discover new trading companies to bring teas and herbs to the west.

Only Eduardo the Venetian lion was able to keep pace

with them, assisted by the croaking of Tuppence, who seemed to tease and console him in equal measures as they made their way through the press of people. Signor Romano she had last seen in the arms of a great number of his country people. He did not return to Mme. Gabor's house for three days.

There were speeches from dignitaries at the pavilion, while her father fought to rejoin her and Signor Maggiormente beamed happily at the whole world. And when they finally returned elated and nearly exhausted to his flat, the whole neighbourhood seemed to have gathered there for a party that went on long into the night. Everyone seemed to delight in the successful flight and the pending nuptials—everyone except the concierge, that Mme. Gabor who continued to glare at Helen until the airship captain finally escaped to her room and slept until late the next morning.

Only then did she creep out the door without alerting her father's notice and knock on the alchemist's door. He greeted her with a face that was mostly clean save for a smudge of something that looked like verdigris and Helen felt such a overflowing fondness for that dear face and the man who bore it that she found herself unexpectedly speechless and only nodded when he offered her tea.

Then so very gently he took her hand and asked her once again, would she join their fates together as one, to ride the winds of change forever and she said "Yes, yes, a thousand times yes" and they kissed. The first of many kisses, it was tentative and unschooled yet so heartfelt that each had the sensation that their hearts skipped a beat and then begin anew in unison, as if they would always be so.

Helen finally understood the words her mother had spoken long ago when she tried to explain the nature of love to a girl who knew nothing outside a family's affectionate ties. "To be together is for us to be at once free as in solitude, as gay as in company." In all the years they had been together, her parents had disagreed many times over things trivial and weighty. They negotiated this or that option, but never had an unkind word had passed between them; perhaps more remarkably, never had her father's quick temper turned upon her mother.

In their adventurous journey she had seen the side of her father that must have been more prominent in his youth, when he was a young man casting about for excitement. He reveled in the excitement often. But she could feel his longing to be home, as if a string stretched from his heart to her mother's tugged ever at him. The pigeon would return to its roost and be happier for all its adventures. Adventures shine brighter in the recounting.

Signor Maggiormente made the journey too, as did Eduardo. The Venetian lion created a sensation everywhere they stopped, particularly after newspapers on both sides of the channel trumpeted the news that Manet and Morisot had painted dual portraits of the lion, which had also been unveiled at the Exposition. Helen's father tried to convince the creature that he could start his own circus and travel across Europe but Eduardo looked at the man as if he were mad—or worse, only teasing him. He became more relaxed as the acclaim increased and he would allow people to touch him as long as they bribed him with food especially cakes.

"Cakes are good," the lion would always announce when strangers gaped at him in surprise. "I like wine, too. And pigeons."

He was most pleased to hear that pigeon pie was plentiful and quite delightful in England, though the concept of countries irked him. Eduardo did not understand why people had such attachment to the arbitrary declaration of nationalities. Borders to him were incomprehensible. After all, he had an uncanny ability to understand almost any language spoken to him, so the concept of different nations seemed at best unimportant and mostly important only as an indication of what sort of food he might receive.

Tuppence seemed to think he was her very own pet. She teased him mercilessly, but protected him (quite unnecessarily) from every other creature that she imagined to show him hostility.

And what did Helen's mother think of this motley crew when they returned? If she was surprised or disappointed in Helen's choice of mate, it was certainly not evident for she treated the alchemist with grave dignity upon his arrival, welcoming him to their home and paying no attention to his many eccentricities and her husband's habit of disparaging his forgetful conversations and inability to complete a chess match without wandering off to admire volumes in the library.

Within days the lady had formed a much warmer attachment to him. Though distressed that the engaged couple wished to fly off to his homelands to announce their intentions to the alchemists' parents, friends and family, she agreed that it was the right thing to do. And though abashed that they next urged her to join them and her husband for the flight to Rome, Milan and Venice, she gave in when they all persuaded her that she could hardly refuse a flight in the airship named for her own good self.

"Are you pleased, mama?" Helen asked as they sat arm and arm before the fire as it died down, while her father and the alchemist argued over maps.

"Those we most love are happy, so your father and I are happy: and the more so, because you have both accomplished so much already, my child. A life of purpose is a happy life. When I think of all the fine minds neglected only because they were born women—," she shook her head. "May you inspire other women to great heights too. We have so many dreams to make real."

"Yes, mama, we do."

THE END

ABOUT THE AUTHOR

Kathryn 'Kit' Marlowe is a writer of historical fiction, often with a good bit of humour. There are those who say she's secretly an English professor who writes under other names (like K. A. Laity, Graham Wynd and C. Margery Kempe). You can find her on Facebook. Her lovely author portrait was created by the fabulous artist S. L. Johnson.

Marlowe is penning a series of medieval adventure novels, The Breton Lais. The first is **Knight of the White Hart**, which tells the story of Guigemar, a knight who fought valiantly with King Arthur and won tournaments with his fearless spirit, but when he shoots a white hart she curses him to suffer until he finds another who will suffer as much for him. A fast-paced narrative and plenty of thrills prove that in the Middles Ages 'romance' meant adventure. The next adventure is **Blood Moon** based on Marie de France's Bisclavret.

Kit's writing is both historical and comic, including the really very silly gothic novel **The Mangrove Legacy** and her madcap jazz age novella series The World of Constance and Collier, available from Tirgearr Publishing. Her short story "Black Ethel's Beast" takes place in the world of The Mangrove Legacy and can be found in the Fox Spirit Books anthology **Piracy**. Visit her Amazon page to read more and be sure to drop by her website for the latest serial: Kit-Marlowe.com

www.ingramcontent.com/pod-product-compliance
Lightning Source LLC
Chambersburg PA
CBHW031133260626
47153CB00021B/240